TANGLED WEB #3

BOUND

BOUND

Book #3 of the TANGLED WEB trilogy

Aleatha Romig

New York Times, Wall Street Journal, and USA Today
bestselling author of the Consequences, Infidelity, and Web of
Sin series

D1453860

COPYRIGHT AND LICENSE INFORMATION

ACKNOWLEDGMENTS

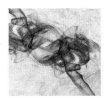

Thank you to everyone who loves dark romance and enjoys a mystery with twists and turns along with their romance. Thank you to my betas who never tire of reading and helping to make each story complete. Thank you to my editor who makes my words shine and to Danielle Sanchez from Wildfire Marketing for never giving up on me.

Thank you to my husband for his undying support and for knowing when to leave me alone and slip food under the door. Also, thank you to my children. You are my cheerleaders, as well as my reminders of reality, and for that and more, I will always love and appreciate you.

A big thank-you to my nephew, a sergeant, and my friend, a specialist, for their invaluable assistance with all things military. I couldn't have told Mason's story without you.

Thank you to YOU for reading and getting caught in the Tangled Web.

TANGLED WEB #3

BOUND

From New York Times bestselling author Aleatha Romig comes a brand-new dark romance trilogy bringing us back to the same dangerous underworld as *WEB OF SIN*. You do not need to read the *Web of Sin* trilogy to get caught in this new and intriguing saga, *Tangled Web*.

With danger lurking around every corner and my life turned upside down, I struggle with who to believe and who to trust.

Can my heart convince my mind that what was bound long ago is where I'll find love, safety, and security?

Or are the memories simply an illusion?

BOUND is book three, the final book of the *TANGLED WEB* trilogy that began with *TWISTED* and *OBSESSED* and is concluding with *BOUND*.

Have you been Aleatha'd?

PROLOGUE

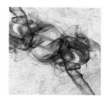

The end of Obsessed, book #2 of the Tangled Web trilogy

Laurel

*S*tepping around the long desk, my curiosity piqued.
What had he been researching?
How much did he recall?

Reaching toward the desk, I lowered myself, sitting on the edge of his large chair. As I did, my movement stirred the mouse, bringing one of the smaller screens to life. My pulse increased as I recognized what was on display. It was the screen with the message he'd received this afternoon.

My gaze searched again around the screens to the doorway as

I contemplated my next move. With the doorway still clear, I rubbed my clammy, trembling palms over his shirttails covering my thighs.

Where was he?

I knew better than to look further, and yet I couldn't stop.

The header read: image attached.

He'd warned me about viewing files on his computer.

Would this be another gruesome image, one I couldn't unsee?

Moving the mouse, I clicked the attachment as an image took over the screen.

My lip disappeared behind my front teeth and my head tilted as I tried to make out the grainy attachment. I leaned closer, doing my best to decipher what was before me. The black and white image was overly pixilated as if it had been enlarged too many times. And then such as with an optical illusion photo, I saw behind the film, reminding me of what it was like to look into a steam-covered mirror. The subjects were present, yet masked by smoke, steam, or fog.

My eyes squinted as I made out a large hooded figure with a woman in his arms. I sat back, knowing the location. It was the elevator at the university. My circulation redirected, racing to my limbs, leaving me uneasy as more and more of the picture made sense.

I clicked the upper box, decreasing the size of the image and read the short message.

If I wasn't already sitting, I had the feeling I may faint.

This troubling information has been brought to light. Advise that measures will be taken if you do not reply and comply. Keep in mind that you have been paid for services rendered.

Identify this man as yourself. If he is not, we have reason to believe Dr. Carlson's death was contrived. The ambiguity of her missing status must end. This man must be identified and dealt with.

No loose ends. That was our deal.

Produce Dr. Carlson's body or notify us of its location.

Verify receipt of message and reply with acceptable timetable.

Our only alternative is to make this photo public. If it is you, your career will be over.

Reply sent this afternoon:

Evidence will be produced within forty-eight hours.

"Following rules isn't your thing, is it?"

Startled, I jumped as the sound of his voice echoed within the office. Looking up, I took him in, the way he was standing, unmoving within the door's frame. His arm was raised to the doorjamb similar to the way Kader had done back in the basement.

"U-uh, Mason," I stammered.

"I told you not to come in here without me."

"I-I was looking for you."

He let go of the doorjamb and took a step inside the office. "Did you think you'd find me on the computer? Come now, Doc, you're smarter than that."

The combination of what I'd just read and the chilly timbre of his voice set my nerves on edge. The hairs on the back of my neck stood to attention. With each second his green eyes bore my direction, their gaze growing cooler and cooler until their icy chill continued the uneasy sensation, snaking its way down my spine and lifting the small hairs on my arms, legs, and curling my toes.

He took another step my direction, stopping as he scanned my attire—his shirt. The cool green of his eyes darkened as the muscles in his cheeks pulled tight. "Does this attire mean that you've embraced your new profession?"

"I thought..."

"If I open my shirt, will I find you wet and ready for me?"

"Stop it."

"Nipples hard?"

"Why are you doing this?"

His head shook. "Just making sure you're fulfilling your job requirements."

My heart beat in double time as my stomach twisted.

This wasn't Mason.

He wasn't even Kader, not the one whose company I enjoyed.

The man before me was personality number four.

Standing, I took a step back. Attempting to reach the man from earlier tonight, the one who protected me from the fireplace, I softened my tone. "Mason, it's me, Laurel."

"I know your name, Doc. Remember, I know everything about you."

My hands trembled as I pointed to the screen. "Tell me what that means."

His neck straightened, the cords pulling taut, yet his words were eerily calm. "Always so curious. You have heard what they say about curiosity and the cat." His lips formed a sinister grin. "Of course you have. You're a fucking genius."

I shuffled my feet backward until my backside collided with another of his tables. The contents rattled, bringing my attention to an array of handguns, ones I hadn't seen before.

Mason was in front of me, reaching for my hand. "Don't think about it. They're not loaded."

Think about it?

My head shook. "I-I wouldn't ever think of..." The content of his reply to the message came back to me. "You replied to that email before...before the plane. You seemed excited to show me your land. And you had already sent that message. I don't understand."

His large fingers toyed with the buttons on the shirt I wore as his head tilted. "What don't you understand?" He unbuttoned the highest button. "I couldn't let Jack find you." He reached for the next button.

I pushed his hand away. "Tell me what that message means."

"It's quite simple. The entity that paid me for your death wants proof."

"Proof. It said they want my body."

His lips curled upward as he scanned me from head to toe. "Can't blame them. I want it too."

"Stop this. You're trying to frighten me."

His long finger trailed over my cheek, to my neck, and lower to the valley between my breasts before moving upward and lifting my chin. "Dr. Carlson, you've fucked with my mind, making me think and act..." He stood taller, his shoulders straightening as his broad chest filled with air.

It was then I noticed his sleeves. They were no longer exposing his kaleidoscope of colors.

"Mason." I reached for his arm. "We'll figure this out together. I'll help you."

"I've told you what I think of you analyzing me. I'm not one of your patients. Besides, Doc, you read the message. You're smart enough to decipher the meaning: time's up. And just to be clear, remember what I said: my story doesn't get a happy ending. Despite what you may think or may try to convince me to believe with your bag of psychological tricks, Mason Pierce died in that explosion nearly seven years ago. Kader was hired for a job and he doesn't fail."

MASON

Earlier in the night

*S*imilar to a continuous fountain, the memories flowed until the basin could no longer contain the onslaught. A trickle at first, the surge grew with the power of a river overflowing its banks, leaving nothing in its path safe.

Nothing secure.

My mind overflowed.

There was too much—everything.

There were too many...

Faces.

Names.

Scenes.

Disjointed.

For as long as I could recall, I had been in control of everything. It was the way I worked, the way I...perhaps not lived, but existed. And within a matter of hours, my world had been blown to hell.

Or maybe the explosion of my life was because the opposite had occurred. My world hadn't been blown to hell, but finally delivered from the depths of a pit I'd claimed to have escaped. While I claimed that I'd faced the flames of purgatory and survived, up until that second when I'd risked my life to save Laurel from what I now realized was a nonexistent danger, I'd never truly and completely liberated myself from the torment that had baptized me into this misery with the power of fire and brimstone.

My thoughts were frenzied.

What previously in my mind had been controlled and organized was quickly turning to chaos. A carousel of images and sounds spinning faster and faster until unrecognizable left me dizzied and disoriented in its wake.

Though I'd tried to push it all away as I lay down to sleep with Laurel at my side, I soon learned it was impossible.

As she settled in slumber, I fought the need to move, to work out the internal demons that though once buried were now baring their teeth, sinisterly rejoicing at my plight. When my eyes closed, their sharp teeth glowed while the echo of their guttural laughs rang in my ears.

The result was an aching head caused by the overstimulation. If I were a computer, it would be a good time for a reboot.

No matter how I tried, sleep remained out of reach.

What had previously been a time of solitude was now simply an opportunity for my mind to fill with images I questioned. Between the devilish projections, other thoughts came and went. With each such surfacing thought, like recalling Laurel from our childhood, a dark curtain would descend much like the ones in a theatrical production, bringing the scene to an end.

The curtain caused more discomfort than the sparse remembrances.

I couldn't put my finger on why or what it meant. While images of my childhood weren't pleasant—I didn't recall joyous gatherings or the security of a stable home—in their own way, those recollections gave me a sense of belonging that had been absent since I could recall.

My chest ached with the realization of why my house was called Missy and why her name was etched in swirling script over my torso. I'd failed to protect her—the innocent girl with big brown eyes and long brown hair, my youngest sister.

It was an indescribable feeling to realize that I had family. More accurately, I had had family. Protecting Missy and Lorna had been my job, my assignment, and one I'd accepted though I was only a child myself.

I knew Missy was gone and yet the memories of life postchildhood were more difficult to retrieve as if they had been obscured more thoroughly by the heavy veil of the dark curtain.

That drape, while not literal, consisted of a barrier my mind was fighting. It seemed as if I'd been instructed to forget life before now. For the first time in a long time, I yearned to search my thoughts for when *now* began.

And yet I had a more pressing matter.

The woman at my side.

The woman I now remembered as a younger version of herself.

Laurel Carlson had been lost behind that curtain, and now she was back. While I ran my roughened fingertips over her warm, soft curves as she slept, my body and desires recognized her as the woman she'd become—not only stunningly beautiful on the surface, but a woman who was kind, trusting, and brilliant.

The new revelation that she was also the young girl my sisters befriended cast a different light on the woman curled at my side.

As a young boy, I was attracted to Laurel's positive energy

and attitude. Like magnets of opposite poles, we'd been drawn to one another. And yet even as a boy, I knew Laurel deserved better than the boy I'd been. Together, we'd talked about forever in the way children do, not knowing what it meant or where it would take us.

By the age of eighteen, I'd run my hands beneath her shirts, caressing the softness of her tits and teasing her taut nipples. My fingers had explored beneath her shorts. Other girls had offered more, but they weren't Laurel. Our attraction hadn't been one-sided. She'd been a willing and eager participant, boldly seeking to reach below the waist of my jeans. The memories of her touch were like lightning.

Never had it felt wrong.

Despite the life my sisters and I'd endured, when I was with Laurel things were different. With her, there was a sense of innocence. I could never explain it. Looking back, I would attest that it was all because of her.

Laurel's light revealed a part of me I'd kept hidden from the dark world my sisters and I inhabited.

An innocent boy wouldn't steal food or beat the shit out of our mother's johns when they came on to Lorna. The world where we lived wasn't the same as Laurel's. I never wanted her to know that life. Instead, I took the opportunity to live, if only for moments at a time, in her innocence full of wonder and possibilities.

Before we'd parted, she'd offered more—a deeper connection to one another, her virginity.

Maybe it was that I knew her father. Perhaps it was because I didn't want to disappoint. More likely, I refused her offer because with her I wasn't a troublemaker from South Chicago. With her I was the type of boy she deserved. Fucking her and never seeing her again would have tarnished what we'd had.

Now, by some twist of chance, Laurel Carlson was once again at my side. Our innocence was long gone, and yet even without comprehending, our magnetic connection was as strong as ever.

It would have been too easy to wake her, wrap my arm around her waist, palm her hips, and pull her over me until her warm pussy hovered, wet and needy, for me to slide inside. Over the last few days and nights we'd done that, with Laurel on top as her hands held on to my shoulders and her tits bounced in my face.

Fuck.

Because recently she hadn't pushed to see more of my tats or questioned my clothing, I'd grown addicted to fucking her in the light. Seeing her blue eyes, the expressions she made as a chorus of sounds escaped her lips, watching as her back arched, tits growing heavy, and areolas turning a deeper shade of red. The sight of her delicate skin reddened by my facial hair or raised from a quick spank caused my dick to go from hard to steel. Nothing—a nip of my teeth or a swat with my hand—was meant to harm or hurt her. By the way she responded—the way she came unraveled around me—Laurel wasn't complaining about my methods.

Being with Laurel was everything—the whole package of sensations—and like nothing I could recall. Even before I remembered Mason's past I had an undeniable need to be with Dr. Laurel Carlson, to protect her and at the same time, mark her as mine.

Now, even with my inner battle of Mason's and Kader's memories, there was one thing the two unequivocally agreed upon: no one will take her away.

That wasn't to mean that she belonged with me—whoever I was. No, it meant that the sender of the message who wanted evidence of her demise was not long for this world. Reaching out to me for verification of Laurel's death was against the dark web's code of ethics.

Don't laugh. Such a thing exists.

That message informed me of one thing. I wasn't dealing with a professional. My contact was a middleman whose own standing due to Laurel's missing status was somehow on shaky ground.

That realization propelled me from the bed, from my visions of fucking Laurel throughout the night, and back into the mindset of the man who could do for Laurel what Mason had failed to do for Missy.

Mentally, I pulled the rope, lowering the curtain on whatever Mason had to offer.

This was Kader's world and to save Laurel, I would embrace that.

LAUREL

A few hours later, directly after number four's declaration

*D*espite the echoing heartbeat thumping in my ears, I forced myself to stand taller, to stare unwavering into the green eyes before me. If number four wanted me to be frightened, I wouldn't—I couldn't—give in. "So tell me your plan."

"What do you want to know?" he asked, ice forming around his words.

Despite the chill, I lifted my hands to his broad shoulders.

Under my touch, his muscles tightened while his handsome face strained. Yet he didn't back away or reprimand me for touching him.

"You must have a plan," I said. "I mean, if you don't fail, then tell me how you plan to succeed."

No longer was the kaleidoscope of color limited to the skin beneath Mason's clothes. The hues of green and gold shifted within his eyes as our battle of wills continued—neither of us willing to look away. Darkness and light battled as the golden flecks grew brighter.

In reality, green was such an unworthy description of the colorful display within his orbs.

Hunter, sea, mint, jade, emerald, spring—were but a few of the adjectives that could be added to better describe the color. Within his changing gaze, all of the above-mentioned applied, especially the latter.

Spring.

It was the season of renewed growth and rebirth. It was also the time for battling weather fronts capable of producing powerful winds and storms, resulting in the possibility of mass destruction. As we silently stood, eye to eye, both of our hearts creating a quickening cadence, I watched as such a storm brewed. Similar to the upwelling plumes of hot air that produced turbulence needed in producing thunderstorms, the clouds within his orbs billowed higher and higher, a signal of the pressure building within.

Though metaphoric, it was as if the air literally shifted around us.

Though we were within the safety of his home, his office to be precise, my skin peppered with goose bumps at the metaphorical changing temperature, swirling breeze, and churning clouds. If this were an actual storm, weather radios and apps would be broadcasting warnings, instructing those within its path to seek shelter.

As number four had said, time was up. There was no place for me to go. The season of destruction had already begun.

Rebirth: Mason had been reborn only hours ago.

Renewal: Kader was on a precipice with overwhelming decisions at hand.

My innocent-bystander status had expired. Nevertheless, I refused to take the title of storm victim. I was a storm chaser.

Who would survive?

Mason.

Kader.

Me.

I repeated my question. "How will you succeed?"

When the man before me didn't answer, I pushed harder. With a quick nod of my head toward the table covered in handguns, I stared back at the green. "One of those? Do you plan to shoot me?"

"Laurel."

"Tell me. You said it was simple. I know nothing about what you do. Wouldn't shooting be *simple?*" I exaggerated the word.

His chest expanded and contracted, nostrils flared, and the cords in his neck pulled tight. Yet through it all, the mountain of a man beneath my touch remained mute.

"When?" I asked, my voice growing louder. "While I'm sleeping in your bed? Maybe right after you've given me one of the best orgasms of my life?" I shrugged. "Oh, I know, maybe right before." Letting go of his shoulders, I slapped my thighs covered only by the length of his shirt. "That would be perfect, wouldn't it? Deny me satisfaction a fraction of a second before you deny me continued life."

"Laurel, stop. You don't know what you're saying." The coolness in his tone was waning—if only minimally.

I swallowed as I shook my head. "I can't comprehend what you must be battling—internally. I can't begin to fathom your thoughts—who you are, who you were, what you lost." I motioned around the large industrial office. "And what you've gained."

"Gained," he scoffed.

Turning, I walked to the windows and took in the lightening view. In the distance, rays of pink shone upward, radiating from beyond the mountains to bring dawn to what had been a black velvet sky.

Would this be my last day?

What was the date?

Did I want to know?

I sighed, doing my best to absorb the natural beauty. "Kader has done well."

When I turned, his gaze was set on me.

"You have. How does this compare to Mason before Kader?"

His chest expanded before he slowly exhaled.

"It would be difficult to walk away from all of it."

"Why would I walk away?"

"I guess that's up to you. Is this only Kader's world or will he allow Mason to share it? Do you recall Mason's life before...this? I haven't known him for over..." I thought back. "...it's been longer than fifteen years since we parted ways. A lot can happen in that length of time."

"Good observation, Doc. More of that genius mind at work."

I tilted my head. "Did Mason settle down? Did you find someone?"

"Dr. Carlson, you're missing the point."

"The point that you're going to kill me and produce my body to whomever hired you," I replied matter-of-factly. "No, that point isn't lost on me."

Mason ran his hand over the top of his head, running his long fingers through the length of his hair.

"Along with denying me continued life and possibly more amazing sex, tell me who you are also denying me—Kader? Mason? Both? What about my family...? Because of you I'll never see you or them again. If that's your plan, admit it. Own it."

His head shook. "Leave it alone."

"Leave it alone?" I asked with a feigned smile. "I don't think that's possible." Looking down, I realized that number four had opened buttons on Kader's shirt, leaving the valley of my breasts exposed. Reaching to the buttons, I secured one and then another.

He reached out and stilled my fingers.

My shoulders straightened as our eyes again met. When he didn't speak, I continued my crusade to close the buttons. As I did, another realization came to me. My fingers weren't trembling. While this conversation should be terrifying, it wasn't.

Perhaps I knew my fate had been sealed since seeing Russ on my bedroom floor. Maybe I believed I would eventually prevail. I couldn't say. Yet no matter the future, I refused to face it with fear.

My weapon wasn't a firearm, such as those on the nearby table. I wouldn't know how to use one if he handed it to me, loaded and ready. Yes, I understood the mechanics of pulling a trigger. That wasn't what I meant. Firing a gun with the intent to do harm required a mindset I didn't possess. That wasn't meant to judge Kader or others who had that frame of mind, but to simply state that I didn't have it. I was the person who owned pepper spray because a firearm in my possession would most likely be turned against me.

My arsenal wasn't comprised of conventional weapons. Instead, it was filled with knowledge, understanding, and words. I'd worked my entire life to refine and perfect those abilities. The combination was my secret weapon. I wouldn't go down without using it.

When I looked back toward the man with me—my hired assassin—he was no longer standing but seated in his big desk chair. His long jean-covered legs were manspread, black boots planted a few feet apart, as his forearms, hidden behind long sleeves, rested on the chair. The menacing expression from before had begun to fade.

What I couldn't decide was what—or who—would surface next.

I leaned my shoulders back against the cool pane and crossed my arms over my breasts. "The first time I saw you at the gathering, I was drawn to you. The more I was near you, the more I wanted you. I didn't understand it and with everything that happened with the compound, R&D, and Russ, I chose not to fight it—even after you were honest with me about being hired to kill me." Dropping my arms, I stepped closer. "Somehow my body and heart saw what was hidden to my eyes."

"This can't..."

I waited for him to continue, but he didn't say more.

"You also said that I was a job, an assignment, nothing more. I guess I should thank you for not pretending. You may be a killer, but you've been honest about it."

With a slight shake of his head, his eyelids grew heavier and heavier until the green disappeared. His Adam's apple bobbed.

Making myself step closer, I leaned down, cupped his cheeks with my palms, and pulled his lips toward mine. A mere brush of a touch caused his eyes to open.

I moved away. "Goodbye, Kader. I'm not sorry you found me. And Mason, you were my first love and even when your sister told me you'd died, I never stopped loving you." I couldn't stop the tears filling my eyes. "So if today is my last day, I want you to know, I don't regret getting to know you and reuniting. When I look at you, I don't see a killer. So please, when you do it, I have one request."

His chest expanded as his nostrils flared.

"I don't want to see you or know it's happening. I want to remember you—both of your names—the way I do now."

With that, I turned and walked toward the door of his office.

"Laurel, come back here."

It took all of my self-control to continue walking, leaving the gray office and moving forward on the hardwood.

"Laurel."

At the top of the stairs I stalled, looking out through the large window over the door and taking in the expanse of bluing morning sky. The thought from earlier returned.

Would this be my last sunrise?

FORMERLY, SERGEANT FIRST CLASS PIERCE

Over five years ago in an undisclosed location

The rotors whirled, cutting through the darkened sky as we flew without lights to our rendezvous point. We'd studied our assignment—my target. The world anticipated this mission would be carried out by a team of trained soldiers. The theory had merit, enough to convince the enemy of the future. Their forces were prepared for an elite faction of capable men and women. What the enemy didn't anticipate was one lone mercenary.

One was an easily disposable number and made the most strategical sense.

One man.

One military-grade firearm.

One additional firearm.

One sheathed knife.

Outside the city limits and under the cover of nightfall, the helicopter touched down in a cloud of dust, dirt, and sand. The mission we were on was not sanctioned by any government,

government official, or known government agency. There was no official record. There was no grouping of generals sitting around the situation room watching body cameras.

We were rebels to the institutions until the time came for someone to take credit.

That was only if we succeeded—if I succeeded.

If I didn't, that would be another story.

In the case that anything went wrong, I was on my own with no evidence to connect the mission to any entity. The world would hear of mercenaries, insurgents, and castaways.

Everyone involved in this and similar missions, everyone within the Sovereign Order, had a similar biography—none.

Just like me, the others I worked with traded their lives to do what we were doing. No longer existing in the world outside, we were ghosts owned by our abilities, those that allowed us to slip under the radar, to run undetected, and to return again for the next assignment.

We were paid handsomely for our sacrifice, yet what was the price of a life lost forever?

Our mission was to succeed.

Returning to our base without success would lessen our reward while assuring us another assignment. There was always another. We'd been too well trained to be released. Not every mission was a guaranteed victory; nevertheless, there was only one sure failure.

Capture meant death. It would happen at our own hands.

Everyone involved was prepared.

Our identities were classified, our fingerprints gone, and our dental records altered. No longer were we a name, rank, and serial number. Those soldiers, sailors, or marines—whoever we'd once been—were gone. The team we'd become came from a diverse military background. We'd done our time.

We'd lost our lives, some on the battlefield or others, such as the story I'd been told, outside the military. It didn't matter where or how. What mattered was that we'd been retrieved. We'd been saved for one reason, the reason we woke each day, fed our bodies, and kept them going. We'd been saved to carry out the Order's duties.

Officially, as a unit, we didn't exist. As individuals, we were no one.

No one cannot be captured, cannot be identified, and cannot be used against any country.

If captured we were well aware that no country or organization would claim affiliation. There would be no negotiations for our release or the possibility of a trade. No entity could trade or negotiate for an individual who had already died.

Our missions were simple: succeed and move on to the next assignment.

Fail, yet return and move on to the next assignment.

Always...the next assignment.

It had been this way since I'd given in to the voices.

Healing from my injuries took time.

I wasn't certain I would ever know the exact amount of time I spent rehabilitating. It was difficult to count days or even years with no reference for when it began.

It wasn't only my body that needed rehabilitation but also my mind.

The men and women who took on the responsibility of my rebirth were nothing if not unrelenting. Their mission had been to create a killing machine. It didn't matter about the man I'd been. He was dead. All that mattered was that I followed orders.

Months, weeks, days, hours, and minutes—an undefined amount of time passed, perfecting the abilities and skills they said I once possessed. Those people honed my physical skills, retoning muscles destroyed due to damage and deficient due to lack of use. They also sharpened my mental skills through tedious sessions of debriefing, reading, watching film, and accepting instruction.

Even when I wasn't training, I was.

My alone time—bunk time—occurred in sleep and wakefulness while in the presence of voices spewing from invisible speakers until I could recite their mantras of courage, honor, and sovereign patriotism in more languages than I could count.

Their means were effective.

What began as a solo endeavor during my training morphed into becoming a member of a team within the unit of like-minded souls united in common ground and goals. Now I was one among an elite force of efficient killing machines—the Sovereign Order.

We had no family, no memories of a life before, and no motivation to seek refuge beyond the momentary break to eat, sleep, and refine our skills. Each assignment brought reward in the form of money, money that we neither needed nor could spend, money that was stashed away for a later time, a time when we were no longer of use, a time that they would choose.

Like the others, I was shown the ledgers, the bank balances of tax-free money hidden in the world of offshore accounts and foreign shell corporations. The average person couldn't begin to comprehend the length that a subversive subset of our intelligence community was willing to go to assure the retention of the best of the best.

Gear in place, I looked to the pilots with a nod as I opened the door to the helicopter and scurried away in the darkness. The bunker in question was 1200 meters to the north-northwest. The floor plan was etched in my memory. My mission was to breach the security, take out the target, and get away.

Simple.

No transporting of others.

The last mission had been the recovery of civilians kidnapped and held captive by a small group of insurgents hoping to make a name for themselves. On my end, that mission had been a success. The civilian couple was recovered and the rebels killed. While I'd moved on to my next mission, the couple was still undergoing debriefings. Once they came to terms with the contrived story of their recovery, the press would be notified of their rescue, and they would be free to reemerge in their lives.

If they didn't comply, the world would forever believe they were still captive.

My goggles granted me the ability to see through the darkness.

I zeroed my focus on the guard with a tiny red glow near his head. That meant he could be bribable or it was a trap. Cigarettes were a valuable commodity as well as alcohol. The Turkish whiskey available on the black market was like drinking lighter fluid.

The cigarette didn't matter. Bribing wasn't on my list of things to do.

The lone guard was small in stature.

I stilled in the darkness as he peered out into the vast emptiness. There was no sign that he saw or heard what was coming for him. Quietly, like the wind over the terrain, I came closer. With each meter, he came into better view. Fuck, he looked younger and younger with each step. The stupid kid probably wasn't even twenty. If that were the case, he'd never see that age simply because he fought for a different side.

It was ingrained in our training. The final line of every equation was relatively simple. It didn't matter the beliefs, ideologies, religions, or government of an assigned target. Those of us in the Order weren't trained or paid to have an opinion.

We were trained to accept a mission and complete an assignment.

Pulling my Ka-Bar from its sheath, I palmed the handle. While this knife was originally used by marines in WWII, its versatility had made it an essential tool for all branches of the military. While lethal, this knife was also strong enough to cut wires or open crates.

My heart rate remained calm. No perspiration covered my skin. My extremities never trembled. Along with my memories, fear had disappeared. I understood the concept. I saw it in the eyes of victims, yet the concept was foreign, such as recognizing malnutrition while never missing a meal.

My steps stilled, my knife in hand. I waited for my moment, my opportunity.

A kill shot would be easier yet could potentially alert the others in the bunker to my presence.

Our reconnaissance had determined this particular time of night as the window of opportunity for success. Moments ago, within the bunker a change of shift had occurred. The boy in my sights was one of the new patrols.

"You were assigned the wrong shift," I said to myself.

The most vulnerable time for this new patrol was while they were settling in their assigned positions.

The guard turned away, pacing the other direction.

Despite my size, I was quick and extremely agile.

A stab to the kidney wouldn't work, giving the victim a moment to scream.

The most effective kill was a deep slit of the throat, an oblique, non-hesitating slice after insuring the blade was buried inches into the neck, assuring the severing of the vocal cords from the trachea. This method guaranteed the victim wouldn't scream and would, within seconds, aspirate enough blood to die of suffocation if exsanguination didn't occur first.

My movements were quick and effective. The young guard crumpled to the ground, the dry earth beneath him drinking in the red liquid as his gurgles slowed and his body's involuntary spasms ceased.

Keeping my knife accessible, I positioned my larger weapon forward and slowly pushed the door inward.

There was no need for light within the dark passages. I'd studied the blueprint. I knew the number of steps, the correct turns. One more guard. Another oblique incision to his throat before pushing open the final door.

The expression of sheer shock always amused me.

Could it be possible that monsters such as the one staring at me could ever truly feel safe?

From that millisecond of an expression, I believed they did, that somehow they convinced themselves of a false sense of security. Of course, it was only a lie they told themselves. No one was truly safe.

No one.

Not even me.

I pulled the trigger.

One shot.

The clock was now running.

My survival depended upon my retreat.

I had twenty-two seconds to go back the way I came.

My boots moved swiftly, my gun at the ready. If I went down, I wouldn't be alone.

I pushed open the door, stepping over the guard as the night sky welcomed me, and hurried into the darkness.

There were no alarms. Places like this didn't have alarms.

I could wait for the commotion and relish my success.

Or I could live to see another assignment.

Next assignment.

KADER

Present day

*S*taring at the computer screen, I waited anxiously for a response. Such as the rancher who placed multiple snares to capture the predator or predators threatening his herd, my plan, too, had multiple possible traps. It was difficult to believe there was only one guilty party. I was after them all. That said, the traps were set, lying in wait for the right culprit to come along. This had gone on too long; it was time for the predators in Laurel's life to become prey.

Looking up at the higher screen, the one projecting from Laurel's room, there was a tightening in my chest. I'd done it again, purposely allowed Laurel to believe the worst. That didn't mean it was true. Like before, I never actually said what she believed she'd heard. Nevertheless, I needed space and time to clear my head.

That didn't mean I didn't care. While I'd been working since she'd walked out of the office, I'd kept an eye on her. With each passing minute my admiration grew. Powerful criminals, those who didn't deserve another breath, didn't face death with the calm and determination of the woman currently off the screen in her bathroom.

Laurel wanted to know my plan.

I had no plan to kill her. If I couldn't do it two months ago, there was no way it would happen now. No, my plan involved killing, only she wouldn't be the victim.

First, I needed to learn the identity of the person who hired me initially to kill Laurel, then had the audacity to question my results and threaten my reputation. Once I did, the threat would be eliminated and Laurel's future would be clearer.

Second, I needed to know who put the first illegal sale of her R&D on the dark web. To that end, I'd cast the high bid on Laurel's research. I offered 1.25 billion in cryptocurrency.

Cryptocurrency was the most common currency for such an anonymous person-to-person transaction and could only be secured with appropriate funds, making my bid more appealing. Unfortunately, that kind of transaction did have limits. While neither the seller nor I wanted a trail of transactions—a trail that would also be visible to those who knew what they were seeing—having multiple transactions would provide more opportunities for me to identify the seller. He or she would be the only person in possession of the private key allowing for the money to be decrypted within the blockchain.

Multiple transactions upped the possibility of locating the seller's geographical location as well as online presence. The question was whether or not the seller was willing to take that chance.

I'd also spent time reviewing the feeds from Indianapolis.

Laurel and I had known it was in the works; however, I doubted that it would lessen her displeasure when she learned of Eric Olsen's fate. I'd saved the university's announcement to let her read it herself.

A tone came from my computer, indicating movement on the screen above.

Leaning back against my chair, I took her in as she walked around her bedroom. Laurel was dressed in blue jeans and a top. What caught my attention were her feet. She was wearing shoes, something she rarely did, often spending the day in socks as she moved about the house. With her dark hair pulled back, her stunning blue eyes filled with resolve.

She'd left this office thinking I was going to carry out the mission on the message. I'd let her think that, letting her remember my reason for finding her and for being with her now. I'd done that to do what I was doing now, to concentrate on this assignment and how I could assure her safety.

It fucking killed me when she stood up to me, asking me for details. And yet I'd made no attempt to correct her misconception. That cold response gained me space, space to work, space to think. Those were increasingly difficult when she was near, when her presence brought out thoughts and memories I'd forgotten.

To make this all work and protect her, I had to shut down the side shit. My mind had to stay focused.

My eyes widened with curiosity as Laurel left her bedroom, walked down the hall and then stopped at the door to mine. Her neck straightened as she reached for the doorknob.

"What the hell are you doing?" I asked, knowing she couldn't hear me.

The camera in my bedroom activated with motion as the door opened inward.

I could be upset, yet realistically that reaction made no sense. After all, Laurel had awakened in that room—my room —not only this morning but on many mornings over the last week or longer. Technically, once I took her to my room and took her in my room, my earlier rule about her entering had been voided.

A small smile came to my lips as she emerged from my closet, slipping one of my large sweatshirts over her head and making her way out of the room and toward the staircase.

Interesting.

"Where do you think you're going?"

Her steps didn't falter or slow as she headed down the stairs and straight for the front door. As her hand reached for the handle, I quickly typed a code into the house's interface, removing any barriers. No alarms would sound. The door would easily open.

With one look over her shoulder at the large entry, Laurel disappeared behind the closing front door.

Turning off the screens on my computers, I pushed the chair back and stood. It had been a long time since I'd played a game of hide-and-seek. Thanks to the rush of memories I had worked to subdue, I recalled the rules.

One person hides.

Another person seeks.

"Ready or not, Laurel, here I come."

LAUREL

*S*tuffing my hands into the large pocket on the front of Kader's sweatshirt, I stilled on the front porch, inhaling the fresh, cool morning air. My eyes squinted against the breeze as I scanned the dark clouds rolling near the horizon. It wasn't the perfect day for a walk, and yet it could be my last chance. I stood straighter and steeled my shoulders.

If number four didn't scare me, a few clouds wouldn't either.

I had no doubt that the house had alerted Kader to my exit. To put it bluntly, I didn't care. This wasn't about him. It was about me.

I had no predetermined destination nor did I even know the possibilities. Other than the large building that held Kader's plane, I had no idea what was inside the multiple outbuildings. All I knew was that if I was about to die—if my time was up—I wasn't going to do it inside. I was going to experience the freedom of unending sky and fresh air.

Step by step, I made my way down the stairs of the porch to the ground below and began walking on the packed-dirt road

Kader had driven when we first arrived. The mud from over a week ago had dried; however, from the rumbling in the distance, I doubted that would stay that way for long.

I wasn't looking for other people or even for an escape.

It was the ravine, the one visible from my bedroom and from the balcony in Kader's room, that I sought. With the recent melting of the snow, the river within its depth appeared to be flowing with vigor and purpose. From high above I saw rolling rapids as the water surged around rocks and trees near the embankments.

I simply wanted a closer look.

The thoughts that went through one's mind as one came to terms with the end of life were odd and random. For the first time since I'd awoken in that dreary basement, I recalled the half-gallon of milk and container of cottage cheese I'd purchased before my life imploded. They were spoiled or soon would be.

What happened to those things?

Would it be up to my family to clean my house and gather my possessions?

With each step along the poor excuse for a road, I came up with questions that should never be asked, especially not by someone my age.

Did I have regrets?

Had my life been a success?

What would I do differently?

Those questions would haunt me until I closed my eyes for the last time.

Perhaps dying as Russ had, unexpectedly, would be easier.

It was too late for that.

I continued walking, veering from the path toward the edge of the ravine. Large rocks dotted the steep sides as I scanned for a safe place to climb down. Farther and farther I walked, keeping my hands buried in the sweatshirt as I searched.

While the rumbling thunder in the distance grew louder, there was something else, something that brought the small hairs on my arms to attention. Without turning, I listened. The sound of footsteps preceded his booming voice by only a millisecond.

"Where the fuck do you think you're going?"

I straightened my neck, squared my shoulders, and buried my hands deeper in the front pocket, yet my unwavering steps continued. I focused my attention on the land before me, including the tall patches of grass scattered here and there and the steep drop-off to my side.

Why didn't all grass grow at the same rate?

How could people with traumatic memories be helped?

It seemed as though there were questions that would remain forever unanswered.

Thunder clapped in the distance, setting off reverberating echoes as his footsteps came closer, and the sound of his breathing grew louder. Near the edge of the ravine I stopped. Still not turning, I looked down at the raging water below but spoke to the man behind me. "Do it now."

"Laurel."

Taking a deep breath, I stood straighter. "I don't want to see you. Do what you need to do." I looked down to the bottom of the ravine. The rough rocks dotting the incline as well as the near-freezing temperature of the water if I were to make it to the bottom would surely aid in my demise. "Push me."

His hands gripped my shoulders, pulling me away from the ledge and forcing me to turn toward him.

While my body complied, defiantly, my eyes closed.

"Go back to the house—now."

"No, then you will have a mess to clean." My eyes were still closed, yet my hearing was intact. Along with the continued rumbling of thunder, I heard his scoff. "I know the house vacuums, but there's no sense cleaning up blood and whatever else." I recalled the stench I now associated with finding Russell's body.

"Open your fucking eyes." Though his words demanded, his tone didn't.

I lifted my chin, yet still my eyes remained shut.

He reached for my chin as his voice mellowed. "Laurel, you'll never make it—wherever you think you can go. I said that shit about this land to scare you, but that doesn't negate its accuracy. And this time of year you can add changing weather patterns. You can hear it. There's a storm coming. Lightning can be deadly. You're not safe out here."

My eyes fluttered open. "Not safe *here*? Am I safe in the house?" When his lips came together I provided my own answer. "No, I'm not safe anywhere."

"You're right."

I sucked in a breath of the cool air at his admission as I stared up at the green of his eyes. "Who are you?"

He ran his hand over his hair, loosening a few strands as his facial features grew taut. "You know who I am."

"I don't. Are you Kader number one, two, three, or four, or are you Mason?"

He stood taller, his chest inflating as he inhaled. "I am who I need to be to do what I need to do."

Crack.

The air around us shimmered as lightning zigzagged through the darkening sky and thunder roared, echoing off the mountains as if we were in a bowl.

"What you need to do," I said, my volume rising as the wind continued to whip around us, loosening our hair, freeing strands to blow around our faces. "I told you to do it. You're the one who said that no one will find me out here or find evidence. You can take a picture, a body part, or whatever is needed for your evidence to the person who hired you." I swallowed. "Remember, Mother Nature will take care of the rest."

He reached for my hand. "Come on, we're not standing out here like two lightning rods."

With his comment, I noticed the way the loose strands of hair around his face were raising, standing on their ends. I planted my feet. "No. I'm done letting you tell me what to do. I'm done with all of it. Just do it." I looked up at the bubbling dark clouds growing higher in the sky. "Or let me die out here." I gestured toward the house. "Go. You're taller than me. Leave and I have a better chance of being struck."

Large rain drops began to fall, splattering against the dry ground.

His jaw clenched as he listened to my claims.

A few drops at first, their numbers increased exponentially as the man before me shook his head and reached down. Before I could comprehend his actions, I was over his shoulder as his long legs jogged toward the house and buildings. His hard shoulder cut into my hips as I pushed up from his back, bouncing with each of his steps.

"Put me down."

My protests went unanswered as the rain and fury of the spring storm intensified.

Kader veered away from the house, taking me toward the closest outbuilding. The door scraped over the concrete as he pushed it open. Dust infiltrated my senses as his boots and the wind stirred the stale air within the dark building.

From my position I was unable to see a sensor or even hear a beep over the recurring thunder and the pounding rain. Beneath the metal roof, the sound of the rain was deafening, pounding like war drums warning us of an impending battle.

With a kick of his boot, the door slammed shut, separating us from the boisterous storm and allowing the dust to resettle.

As he lowered me to my feet I took in the windows, high upon the walls, narrow and rectangular. The dark sky beyond did little to illuminate the area within. Along the perimeter of the building were rows of shelves, lockers, and large safes.

Just as quickly, my surroundings were lost. One bulb high above brought light to the dimness.

My breathing labored as I focused upon the man in front of me. His hair now dripping, the muscles of his cheeks stretched taut, his nostrils flared, jaw clenched, and neck strained. His saturated shirt clung to his hard muscles. His blue jeans were made bluer by the rain. At his sides, his large hands balled into fists and unballed, the process repeating as his stare stayed fixed on me.

It was that intent look that had my attention.

I wasn't noticing my own drenched hair or the way his sweat-shirt now hung to my thighs. "You say you're going to kill me and then you rescue me from a storm."

"When did I say I was going to kill you?"

My head shook and then pointed the direction of the house. "Today, you said my time is up."

He took a step toward me. "I said *time* was up. I didn't say *your* time was up."

"That message," I said, gesturing with more vigor. "You replied."

Another step my direction as the wind continued its shrill roar and the rain kept double time upon the roof. The air around us was cool and damp, yet with each step his gaze warmed, like a fire simmering in the golden flecks of his green orbs.

"I did reply." He reached for the hem of the sweatshirt and shook his head as he began to lift it over mine.

Though there was every reason to protest, I didn't. Without hesitation, I lifted my arms as he brought the damp, oversized shirt over my head. His green gaze scanned me up and down.

"I'm not giving them your body, Doc."

I stood taller, my fists coming to my hips. "What evidence are you offering?"

Pulling a knife from his pocket, he lifted my hand.

Instinctively, I pulled away, yet his grasp was too strong.

The blade sliced over my palm, too quick to hurt and too shallow to do real damage.

"What the hell?"

Kader took my hand and wiped it over my top, smearing red over the material.

"Now give me your shirt."

Still too stunned to comprehend, I jumped as thunder crashed close enough to rattle the lockers and cause the single light above to sway.

"Is this..." I looked down. "...part of the evidence?"

"The less you know, the better."

My palm was a bit sore, but already the bleeding had stopped.

Kader handed me a tissue. "We'll clean it in the house."

I nodded. Looking around the room, I asked, "What is all this?"

"Tools of the trade."

"Tell me. Am I going to live to see another day?"

"I fucking hope so."

His words wiped away the tension that had kept me vertical since leaving his office early this morning. Tears came to my eyes. "But you said—"

His finger touched my lips. "I said my story doesn't get a happy ending. I said Mason Pierce died. I said Kader was hired and he doesn't fail. All of that is accurate."

"No, you're Mason. You are. I know it's true." I remembered what he'd said. "It's not some psychological trick. You have to be him or you wouldn't remember or know the things you do about when we were young."

"You could have planted the memories."

My head shook in dismay. "No. I didn't. I had no idea until last night. Why would I plant memories?"

"Some questions don't have answers." He ran his hand over his hair and shook the water droplets to the cement floor. "I...I was hired...*Kader* was hired," he corrected. "This Mason shit...at this time, I'm setting it aside—for now. I can't deal with it and you and this mission. Don't push. Don't analyze. I told you more times than I can remember that I wouldn't kill you, and with one message you forgot that."

I shrugged. "I didn't." I wiped a tear from my cheek. "I'm sorry. It's number four." I shook my head. "I didn't want to believe you, but since Russ, I guess in the back of my mind I believed it was my fate."

He scoffed. "Fate. What is fate anyway?"

"What's meant to be," I offered.

He pushed the sleeves of his shirt up on both arms to his elbows. Lifting his arms toward me, he asked, "Is this fate? The kid you remember from South Chicago, was he supposed to end up like this?" His volume rose. "If that's fucking fate, I've had my share. I don't want any more."

I stepped forward, laying my hands on his forearms. "How many people are out there who do what you do? Who kill for money?"

"It's not like there's a database or social-media group."

"Fate is that out of all those people, hundreds or thousands..." I shrugged. "Out of all of those possibilities *you* received the inquiry. You saw my picture. Even without remembering yourself or us, fate put me on your computer screen."

"That makes it a vindictive bitch." He reached for his sleeves.

Laying my hands over his, I stopped him. "Does it matter what I call you?"

"I can't deal with the Mason shit right now. I have to finish this assignment. End it." He reached up, cupping my cheeks. "Not you, Laurel. I have to end *it*. I can't do that if I'm distracted. There are too many moving parts. My mind has to be one hundred percent on this."

I nodded in his grasp.

"I'm leaving tonight. No more running out into storms or the wilderness."

I reached out to his torso as a sense of dread washed through me. "What do you mean you're leaving?"

"I'm going away."

My head shook as I grasped his damp shirt. "You can't."

"I've done as much as I could from here. I need to follow leads in person. It's the way this works."

Though I tried to back away, he pulled me closer, his lips covering mine as the thunder rumbled the building and lockers. "Kader?" I asked as our kiss ended. "You have to come back to me."

"What about Mason?"

The tips of my lips curled upward. "Would you believe me if I said I don't care?"

His finger ran over my cheek. "It doesn't matter who I am. Neither of us deserves you."

"You saved me from the storm." My gaze went up to the rain hitting the roof and back to Kader's eyes. "And from the fake policemen, from the person who hired you, and you were my first love. If you ask me, the man who did all of those things is deserving of more."

He reached for the hem of my shirt.

My eyes went to his as I did the same, reaching for the hem to his shirt.

"No, Laurel."

"Stop trying to scare me. It's my turn. Show me the boy who stole my heart when I was young."

"I'm no longer that kid."

"You're not. You're more."

"I'm not," he protested.

"You are."

LAUREL

As my bloodstained shirt fluttered to the dirty cement floor, I cupped Kader's cheeks. "I want this, to see more of you." I fought the tears coming to my eyes. "What more is there for you to hide from me?"

"You don't understand what you're saying."

"I do. Seeing you, knowing you... will help me while you're gone."

His head shook. "That's where you're wrong. If you see, as soon as I leave, you will too. You'll run the first chance you get."

My hands moved to his broad shoulders as I tilted my head. "Where will I go? How will I get there?"

"You're brilliant, remember. You'll think of something."

"I'd go with you if you wanted me to."

His eyes closed.

"Someone wants me dead. They want proof I'm dead. Why would I go anywhere that could put me in danger?"

The green of his eyes shone in the dim lighting as beyond the windows the storm raged and the metal roof continued to clang with the falling rain. "You thought you were in danger with me."

"I don't think I really believed it was you. I think I believed the danger was...fate."

"Stop using that word, Doc. There's no such thing. Everything that happens does so because we make it happen. Even what you mentioned before, I could have passed on the assignment. Even if you're right and this imaginary fate put your gorgeous face on my computer screen, it wouldn't have mattered if I didn't act on it."

My hands skirted over his chest and down his torso; his muscles beneath the material tensed as my touch moved lower. "Please?"

Kader took a step back. "Close your eyes, Laurel."

My lip disappeared beneath my front teeth as I nodded and closed my eyes. The tap of his boots upon the cement was barely audible as the storm raged beyond our reprieve. Concentrating on him, I listened as his steps moved about the room. From the far wall there was the sound of metal lockers opening and closing. His footsteps circled, coming closer and closer. The anticipation brought a chill to my exposed skin.

"Take my hand."

As I reached out, I asked, "May I open my eyes?"

"Do this my way. I didn't say to open your eyes."

Nodding, I sucked in a breath as his fingers encased mine.

"There's a blanket on the floor. It's not exactly luxury, but it will have to do. Hold my hand and sit down."

My legs bent as my other hand found the blanket he'd mentioned. Not only was it not luxurious, I would guess by its scratchy surface it was made of wool. Military issue was my first thought. Once I was seated, Kader moved behind me and gathered my ponytail. His warm breath tickled my skin as his lips came near my neck. "Work with me."

"Okay." It took all my willpower to keep my eyes closed. He brought something before my chin. Compared to the blanket, it was soft.

"I'm going to blindfold you."

"Why?" I asked as his declaration prickled my skin.

"Say yes, Laurel. Say you'll let me do this my way."

I reached out until my hand found his. "I want to see."

"You will. First, you'll feel."

His words brought back the memory of our first time, the night in the basement. The room was pitch black and when I'd asked to see, he told me I'd feel him. I didn't need to see. I'd feel and I'd know he'd been there. Swallowing, I nodded. "I trust you. Do whatever you need to do."

The blindfold he used was soft, not in a satin way, but similar to a shirt or a sheet. He tugged the material behind my head, tying it in place.

"Open your eyes. Can you see?"

I did as he said. "No, not really. There's light..." I lifted my fingers to the material.

"Let me," he said as he tugged it higher and lower, making me think of something folded perhaps, such as a bandana. "Is that better?"

"Yes."

"Lie back, I'm taking off your shoes and clothes."

"Why? This isn't about me."

He scoffed. "It's fucking all about you. I've never..." He didn't finish the sentence. "If you're exploring, I am too."

My lips curled upward as I lay back supporting myself by my elbows upon the scratchy blanket. One by one my shoes disappeared. It was after the button on my jeans was undone and the zipper lowered that I lifted my hips. With the contrast of the blanket against my skin, I was certain I still wore my underwear.

"Take my hand," he said again.

Reaching into the darkness, he pulled me to my feet. Not releasing my hand, he reached for the other one and clinching both of them, he brought them to his chest. Immediately, I knew his shirt was gone. The realization sent my pulse racing. The surface beneath my palms was as his forearms had been, rough and bumpy over hard muscles. While I imagined a colorful display, my thoughts were more of the man as a whole.

Beneath the hard muscles of his chest, his heart thumped in double time.

No longer was I hearing the storm outside. It was the storm within that had my full attention.

"Feel that?" he asked.

"Your heart? I feel your heartbeat."

"No, the surface." With my hands still in his, he said, "You can stop. You don't need to go on. I can only imagine how grotesque—"

"No, stop." Tears were forming, absorbing into the material covering my eyes. "Please let go of my hands."

His grip tightened as his exhale skirted my hair.

I didn't ask again as we stood silently for a moment in the dusty building.

While the thunder had lessened, the rain on the roof continued. Slowly, his grip of my hands loosened. Once they were free, instead of touching what I didn't know, I reached up until I found his cheeks. My lips brushed his.

"Nothing about you is grotesque," I said. "You are more than your scars. You can be whomever you choose because you survived. Last night you mentioned an explosion. I won't do more than you want me to do. If I touch too much, tell me."

Still holding his face, his chest expanded against mine.

"What I want? I want to back the fuck away."

Instead of responding, I slowly lowered my hands, my palms gently skirting over his neck, his shoulders, and down his arms. "It doesn't feel different than your forearms."

"There are places..."

I didn't move my hands to his chest. I lifted them back to his shoulders and leaned forward until my lips found his skin.

The air filled with his hiss, yet he didn't move away.

Slowly, I explored, my lips peppering the skin of his chest, lower and lower. No longer noticing the roughness, it was the hardness and definition of his muscles—his abs and torso. Releasing his shoulders, I continued lower with kisses and licks. There were raised areas that seemed smooth and coarse valleys. It was as I reached his blue jeans that my fingers quickly unfastened the button.

With a grin I peered upward. Unable to see, I hoped he could see my smile. "Unfair dress code. It's time to put us on even ground."

"Fuck, Laurel."

Lowering the zipper, I pushed the material over his hips as his cock sprang free. I continued downward, taking off his boots, his socks, and finally his jeans. Back to my knees, my palms skirted over him until my fingers spread over the tight muscles of his ass. Beneath my touch, the same uneven skin existed, and yet it was not as he'd said. Nothing about this man was grotesque. He was a Roman god, a statue of perfection pitted through the centuries by time and erosion. Just because the shine had dimmed, the flawlessness beneath was still intact.

I lowered my mouth and teased the salty tip of his hard cock.

"Fucking hell. This isn't what..."

His words disappeared, fading into something resembling a

growl as I took him over my tongue. There was no way I could possibly take his length completely in my mouth, yet with the help of my hands, I tried.

The building filled with primal noises as his fingers wove their way through my hair, securing the length of my ponytail. The strong muscles within his thighs flexed.

My mind was no longer on his scars as my lips, tongue, and fingers worked in unison. Up and down, I licked and sucked. The velvety surface of his cock strained as his length and girth grew harder and stiffer. Though my jaw ached, I continued, each time taking him farther.

With one hand I reached upward to his balls and rolled them between my fingers. Under my touch they tightened, drawing upward. His stance widened as his breathing began to labor.

He pulled my hair upward. "Laurel, stand up. Fucking...if you don't stop..."

Ignoring the pain on my scalp, my head bobbed faster, my lips creating a stronger suction. Holding tightly to his thighs I refused to back away. There had been multiple times since the first night in the basement that Kader's mouth had brought me pleasure, encouraging me to unashamedly orgasm upon his lips as he took me to new heights.

This was finally my turn and I wasn't going to stop.

The sounds of the storm were lost to his roar as he came undone.

It wasn't until he was fully satisfied and beneath my grasp his muscles relaxed that I stood.

Still blindfolded, I stepped around his broad shoulders and let my hands skirt over his shoulders and down his torso. Without sight, all of his skin felt unevenly similar. Once I circled, I stood before him and lifted myself on my toes until our lips met.

As our kiss ended, I shook my head. "Nothing about you can scare me away."

He reached for my waist and pulled my hips to him. "You haven't seen."

My cheeks rose. "I've felt."

Kader reached back to the knot behind my head and pulled it loose. Even knowing his nude body was before me, I kept my gaze on his stare.

LAUREL

My pulse raced as the subsiding rain tapped a softening rhythm upon the metal roof. With my eyes fixed on his, I tilted my chin downward and asked, "May I?"

Slowly, Kader's eyes blinked. "Now or never."

I took a step back. The storm was beginning to pass, and with the change the sky beyond the high rectangular windows was growing lighter, bringing brighter illumination than what had been produced by the single bulb within the dusty large building. Unwilling to use only my eyes, I kept the tips of my fingers in contact with his skin. The dips and valleys beneath my touch were lost to the array of colors. Like his forearms, his entire body was covered in a beautiful, distinctive, and unique work of art.

I trailed my touch over and down his wide chest. Wings of angels and devils hid within the swirls. Skulls and faces were disguised by flowing banners. Slowly, I circled, searching the forest for the trees hidden within. Upon his back, I spotted the king, queen, bishop, rook, and knight. The chess pieces weren't arranged to do battle, but like the mysteries on his chest, were camouflaged within the colors. The only piece I couldn't find was the pawn.

It made perfect sense. Kader wasn't a pawn—an expendable fighter in battle. He embodied the pieces of worth, power, and victory.

I moved my hand lower, the colors continued onto his tight, muscular ass and lower, onto his powerful thighs, calves, ankles, and onto the tops of his feet. "There's so much ink. It's a masterpiece."

"Hardly," Kader replied as I continued to circle.

I paused at his shoulder. "This is...military, right?"

He nodded. "Army medallion on one side, Special Forces on the other."

Looking up I noticed the strain as his jaw tightened. "You remembered?"

"No. I was told."

Focusing on the green of his orbs, now with a faraway glaze, I asked, "What else were you told?"

His hands came to my shoulders, pulling me in front of him. "Not now, Laurel. A day ago I would have said I didn't remember anything. I would have said that I didn't know. Now I still don't. I was told a lot. There's..." His head shook. "...too much." He ran his hand over my hair as his Adam's apple bobbed. "I know you're real."

"I am."

"I know we..." His eyes closed for a moment. "...I know it's up to me to keep you safe. Nothing else matters. The insignias are correct—they were. I'd been told about what I'd done. Now I remember some of it. I can't think about all of it right now."

I reached up to his cheek. "I get it. I do. I promise I won't push. And if you do what you set out to do—if you keep me safe

—and you want my help, I will be with you as you explore the memories."

With a sigh, Kader lowered himself to the blanket, his knees bent as he leaned his arms upon them. For only a moment, my smile returned. While I hated the conflict raging within him, there was something else that brought me joy.

For the first time I was wearing clothes while he wasn't.

He looked upward. "What are you thinking, Doc?"

"I'm thinking that I like when the dress code is reversed."

"You do?"

Before I could answer, I was tugged downward. His colorful long legs stretched outward as I landed upon his exposed lap. My arms settled over his broad shoulders. "You are the most beautiful man I've ever seen." I leaned back, taking in his colorful chest. "I feel like I could stare for days and not find all the hidden secrets."

The latch of my bra came undone as a hint of a smile came to Kader's lips. "Give me time, Laurel. Even I don't know all the secrets." He pushed down the cups of my bra. Golden flecks shimmered as his gaze left mine and lowered to my exposed breasts. "Speaking of staring, I fucking love your tits."

As he tugged the bra straps from my arms, a smile came to my lips and my nipples beaded at his compliment.

"We're getting closer to the proper dress code," he mused, laying me back upon the scratchy blanket. His green gaze scanned my skin as he secured the waist of my panties and lowered them over my thighs, knees, calves, and ankles until they were gone, lost to the dusty floor.

Kader rested his body over me, holding his weight upon his elbows as he stared down into my eyes. "I'm coming back to you, Laurel. And when I do, you will have answers."

The reminder of his leaving returned the cloud of sadness I'd temporarily pushed away. "I don't want to be without you."

"It won't be long." He ran a coarse fingertip over my cheek. "Since...after..." He swallowed. "When this is over, you should be able to live a life without fear. I can't promise it will be as Dr. Laurel Carlson, but I will do whatever I can, even though I don't want to do it."

"You don't want to do *what?*"

"I don't want to let you go. I don't know how I'll be able to do it again."

Reaching up to his shoulders, I wiggled beneath him, lifting my knees until we were perfectly arranged. It was the first time he'd been with me completely exposed. It didn't matter that the concrete floor was covered by only an old military woolen blanket or that the building was filled with dust from years gone by. All that mattered was that we were together, about to come together as one.

This was the man I fell in love with when I was too young to understand. He was also the one I'd lost.

It was after my back arched and lips formed the perfect 'o' that I ran my hands over his shoulders and down his arms. My one word was more of a moan. "Don't."

His green eyes widened. "Don't?"

"Don't let me go, again. I don't know what this is. Maybe it's fate or call it destiny. I don't know what the future holds. I only know that I want it to include us, the two of us."

"Your research?"

"My life has gained new perspective since we reunited."

"Laurel, I'm not exactly the settle-down type."

I lifted myself upward until my lips met his. "Before that gathering, I would have said the same thing about me. My sister married after college. I only cared about work. I still care about it, but I want more."

"I'm not the more—"

I cried out as he began to move. My whimper wasn't in pain, but in pleasure. When Kader stilled, I grinned. "You are definitely *more*." As I adjusted, a new thought came to my mind. "If we would have done...this...when we were young, I would have known you were you the first time in the basement."

Kader shook his head. "I'd like to think I'm better than a bumbling, inexperienced teenager."

"I'm not discussing skill level. I'm saying there are some things you can't hide."

"You deserved better."

"Stop saying that."

When he began to speak, I lifted my finger to his lips. "I'm going to say this again. I don't care who you are, Kader or Mason, from what I remember and recently learned, both are exceptional men. That doesn't matter. I only care that we're together."

"Laurel."

"Make love to me."

The muscles beneath the bumpy skin tightened. "I...I don't."

"You do. Keep going. I see you. Let me feel you. Let me remember you while you're away."

The side of his lips curled into a grin as his hips thrust. "Like that?"

I sucked in a breath. "More."

The bristly blanket chafed my skin as Kader delivered exactly what I'd requested—more. His strong grip of my hips dug into my flesh, no doubt producing finger-sized bruises as the man with no fingerprints left his mark. Thrust by thrust, he pushed me higher, out of this building, up into the clearing sky, and beyond the mountains' peaks.

My cries of ecstasy as well as those of anguish filled the room as he skillfully took me to the edge only to bring me back. Our positions varied to his liking. His fingers wandered, teasing, pinching, and flicking my oversensitive clit. When I least expected, they moved to new ground, generating a whole new sensation as one and then two fingers breached my tight ring of muscles. Combined with his continued thrusts, his newfound ground created a sense of fullness such as I'd never known.

The sounds and words leaving my lips were lost to the bluing sky beyond the windows. I had no more control over what I said than my reactions to his ministrations. In a few weeks, Kader had fine-tuned my body into a prized instrument, one that only he could play. When he did—when he strummed me—the chorus I sang was spiritual and mournful, unique and soul-searching like the man encouraging my song.

The sensations were everything and at times too much. There were instances when I tried to hold back. Times when my teeth came down, clamping upon his broad shoulders, yet nothing I tried could stop the melody.

Our expedition was exhausting and exhilarating. Minutes and hours meant nothing as the blanket abraded the flesh of my shoulder blades, palms, and knees. A swift spank to my unsuspecting ass had my nerves on full-alert. My core ached at his unrelenting submersion while my ass clenched each time he circled its entrance. My neck, collarbone, and breasts too were marked by the fingerprintless man as he adorned them, leaving my skin with the tender remnants of kisses, sucks, and nips.

This wasn't Kader taking me.

He'd done that back in a dark basement.

I was his.

This was his way of leaving me with the reminders that he'd been with me in every way possible. I was bound to him—as I'd been meant to since we were children—and there was no part of me he was leaving untouched.

Back to our original position, Kader pushed my knees farther apart as his massive body shuddered and bucked. It was as his roar saturated the stale air that he stilled and unapologetically filled me to overflowing.

Our hearts beat in unison as his large body collapsed over me and we remained together.

Kader and I had never used any form of birth control and yet for some reason until now, I hadn't given it much thought. I had the insert so pregnancy wasn't a concern. Russ and I had used condoms most of the time and my doctor's appointments had always been clean. Nevertheless, Kader didn't know any of that.

What were his thoughts?

I spoke softly. "Are you concerned about not using a condom?"

"No." He lifted his face until our gazes met. "It feels too fucking great to be inside you. When I'm there, my only thoughts are about you."

My cheeks rose as I too concentrated on our union. Rays of sunshine shone through the cloudy windows near the ceiling as for the first time in my life, I imagined a baby, one with green eyes.

Once we were no longer one, I lifted my head to his shoulder and curled against his exposed broad chest. Bringing my fingertips to the surface, I mindlessly traced a colorful swirl. Having my cheek over his skin with his arm around my shoulder brought new moisture to my eyes. Blinking it away, I realized that like the literal accumulation on the shed's floor, the dust of my earlier uncertainty had settled and the storm had passed.

While our future remained unclear, the past had gained clarity.

Despite the uncomfortable surface, my eyelids grew heavy and breathing evened. I'm not certain how long we remained as we were until Kader stirred.

"Fuck," he growled as he sprung up from the blanket and reached for his blue jeans.

"What?" I asked, disorientation fogging my thoughts as I was again mesmerized by his beautiful colors.

"Stay in here. I heard something. It's probably Jack."

FORMERLY, SERGEANT FIRST CLASS PIERCE

About five years ago in an undisclosed location

*W*ith my stance set, shoulders straight, and hands clasped behind my back, I stared into the eyes of my commander. I'd been with him and this team since I was released from treatment. He knew me about as well as I knew myself. My tone was confident. "I'm done."

It was the two-word speech I'd practiced in my head over the last three months. With each assignment, each success and each failure, I'd returned to our base. My team had returned and while results varied, our identities remained secure and our survival intact.

My commander, Clifton Jackson, leaned forward, his elbows on the large metal desk, with his long-sleeved gray t-shirt pushed up to his elbows. Though his fatigues were hidden beneath the desk, they were identical to the ones I wore, ones we all wore.

Within our unit, there were no dress uniforms adorned with ribbons and pins signifying our rank or our accomplishments.

We were no longer army, navy, air force, or marines. Our team was part of something bigger, something more important. The teams made up an elite unit of highly skilled individuals who no longer had an individual identity. We'd given all that up when we'd given up our lives—when they'd been taken from us.

The Sovereign Order was a subversive unit of the intelligence agency that was above pageantry and individual honors. Nothing we did concentrated on the one. Everything was for the common whole.

We strived for the betterment of the country, the republic, and the democracy. It wasn't about one political party or one leader. The Order existed so that everything and everyone else could. We did what needed to be done when it was required. The headlines we made conveniently forgot to mention the true heroes. We worked in the shadows of what was acceptable, doing what those in command of us believed necessary, often without the knowledge of those who claimed control.

The Sovereign Order wasn't new.

Created prior to World War II, this unknown faction of the intelligence community had withstood nearly a century of presidents, generals, and political struggles. It prevailed despite turmoil both within and outside our borders. Few people knew of its existence, and that was the way it was meant to be, why it had prevailed, and why missions were given to our men and women.

Commander Jackson's chin rose. "It doesn't work that way, Pierce. I thought we'd been through this."

"I'm done."

"A break," he said, standing and walking around the desk.

A few inches shorter than I, he stopped, crossed his arms

over his chest, and sat against the edge of the metal desk. The years of service were visible, shown in lines on his face, small creases near his eyes and lips as well as the graying of his hair. Red blood vessels sprinkled throughout his complexion were the only signs of his hidden addiction. Drinking vodka kept his nerves calm. For the most part it was an odorless liquor—the perfect vice to hide in plain sight. Consuming it in small quantities throughout the day and night allowed his blood to keep a low, even level. The only people who could testify against him, revealing his secret, were officially deceased.

The dead tell no tales.

A small sign with that inscription was tacked to the bulletin board behind his desk. It was a not-so-subtle reminder to all of us that while our talents were sought after, our opinions were not.

I shook my head. "I'm coming to you out of respect, not for permission. I'm done. I could disappear on my own or I could tell you my plans."

"Mason Pierce doesn't exist. You can't hold a debit card, buy a house, a car, or purchase a fucking candy bar."

"Then provide me with a new identity."

My commander took a deep breath and lowered his hands to the desk at his side. "This isn't how we operate. You have talents, talents we've honed. You owe us your life."

"What life is that exactly, Commander? As you said, I don't exist. My debt has been paid in full."

"No, Pierce, there is the life we gave you."

"You're right about what you said earlier," I said. "The man I was...the soldier...all of him is gone. I will use what I've learned and succeed in a new life. I'm capable of doing that without your knowledge. I don't want to do that. I want choices."

"Do you think that any of us have choices?"

"We all do."

The commander sighed. "There's one more mission. I was briefed only this morning. They asked for you."

Of course, they fucking did.

"Me."

"Your reputation precedes you. You are our best hope."

Hope—something they'd also taken from me.

"I'll make you a deal," I said.

He shook his head. "Not the way this works. We don't negotiate with terrorists."

"Even when they're on your payroll?"

"Pierce, there is no traceable record of anything we've discussed."

"I'm not threatening to expose you or this unit. Fuck, Commander, those men and women out there are the only family I know. They're the only family I remember. I would die before exposing their presence. I can't do this day and night any longer. I won't."

"You're saying that you want to quit?"

"I want my freedom."

"Tell me how that's a different request."

"I want the liberty to make my own decisions." I lifted my chin, pulling out the figurative card I'd hoped I wouldn't need to play. "I will continue to be accessible to you and the Order without being a part of it. We'll work it out, a way for you to reach me. I can't guarantee I will be available for every job, but the Order will be a priority. *You* will still know where I am. And..." I emphasized the word. "...you'll secure my anonymity." I tilted my head toward the door to his office. "I'm done with group living. I believe I gave that shit up a long time ago. If I didn't, I sure as fuck should have. I'm too old for this."

"This goes higher than me," Commander Jackson said.

"I doubt that, but I'll take your word for it."

The commander scoffed. "If you weren't so fucking good at what you do, your attitude would have gotten you in a lot more shit than it has."

"I'm in the middle of fucking nowhere taking commands from you. I'm up to my goddamned armpits. If there's deeper shit than this, I don't want to find it."

"You'll take this one mission."

That didn't sound like a question. "You'll negotiate my freedom?"

"Your reassignment."

I nodded. "My reassignment out of this hellhole." I hadn't voiced it as a question either.

"I'll do what I can, after..."

"I'll take it."

LAUREL

Present day

Forgetting his socks, Kader slipped his colorful feet into his boots and pulled a shirt over his head. Silently, I watched as the last of his colors disappeared beneath his clothing. Instead of being saddened by their loss, I had a strange sense of attachment unlike anything I'd experienced before. I wasn't well versed in personal relationships. If Russell had been my standard, as more of his secrets were uncovered, it became progressively clearer that I'd set that bar relatively low. Nevertheless, this morning's unexpected gesture by Kader, or Mason, to not only allow me to touch but also to see his scars and beautiful tattoos, renewed my faith in the man who I'd trusted with my life.

Kader lowered himself on his haunches before reaching for my chin and brushing his lips over mine. "I'll take care of this." His cheeks rose as he scanned my naked body. "I prefer you as you are, but you might want to get dressed while you wait."

It wasn't a verbal command to stay hidden, yet it was.

Reaching for the scratchy blanket, I nodded.

As Kader pulled the door inward and quickly stepped outside the building, fresh air stirred the dust. After the door closed, I peered up at the now-blue sky through the dirty windows and recalled my earlier question.

Would today be my last sunrise, last day, last anything?

The scary and reassuring response that came to my mind was that I didn't know.

Perhaps it would be.

Maybe I'd live to a ripe old age.

There were no guarantees, and similar to going for today's morning walk or Kader accepting me as an assignment, what mattered in the end was how we reacted—that we acted.

I wouldn't and couldn't be a bystander in my own life.

Was I happy with the life I'd lived if today were indeed my last?

Over the last few hours, I'd decided I wasn't.

That had nothing to do with my work, although, I did want more from that. I wanted it to continue. I also wanted more. I wanted what Mason and I had started as children and Kader and I'd recently found. I desired a human connection more than I'd ever realized. The need wasn't only physical, though I willingly admitted I was addicted to everything physical that came with Kader—even things that were new and different.

It was more than that.

It was also the emotional connection we shared, even before we knew its origin.

I didn't want Kader to *let me go* any more than I wanted to go.

Dressed again in my clothes from earlier, I slipped on my shoes and Kader's large sweatshirt over me as I waited for his return. Since there were no windows at my level and the door was solid, I was at a loss for what was occurring outside the building.

What had Kader heard?

Was it Jack?

Why would Jack come up to the house?

Would this be my opportunity to meet this man Kader trusted with his property?

Or would I remain hidden?

Biding my time, I scanned the perimeter of the room. The way it was arranged reminded me of a basement or garage—a storage area. Numerous metal shelves held boxes and totes. The lockers and safes that were interspersed were closed. Like other things in Kader's life, it appeared organized and orderly.

The only items out of place were the blanket and bandana. As I waited, I folded the blanket, placed it on top of a nearby box, and laid the bandana over it.

The brushing of the door inward startled me as I clenched my hands in front of me and turned toward the sound of the opening door. My feet moved backward as an older man with gray hair and a ruggedly tanned face appeared in the doorframe.

"Well, lookie here. I never thought I'd see the day when Price had himself a filly." His stained-toothed smile grew. "Sounds better than a mare, don't you think?" He didn't let me answer. "But you're not a filly, no sir." He looked me up and down. "It would take a woman to corral that stallion."

My mind filled with new questions as the man's assessment chilled my skin.

Price?

Did Kader have a last name?

I stood taller, thankful I'd dressed. Squaring my shoulders, I decided to meet this man head-on. I took a step forward and lifted my hand. "Hello, Jack, I presume?"

He came closer, his boots tapping over the concrete. Momentarily, he stilled at the spot where the blanket had been.

For the first time I noticed how the dust had been displaced. With his gaze back on me, he continued toward me.

Though age and time had more than likely stolen inches from his height, he still appeared muscular, strong, and built for a hard day's labor. While his stature was smaller and his age older than Kader's, his handshake was firm and despite his stained smile, his blue eyes were warm.

"That's right, little lady, I'm Jack. Now tell me who exactly Price is hiding up here in this dirty shed."

"Sex toy, Jack. Nothing for you to worry about," Kader said, entering the building, his green eyes wide on me, conveying a message I best read as *go with this*.

"Well, doggie," Jack said, looking from me to Kader and back. "And how does one—?"

"Mail order," I said matter-of-factly. "Contract is pretty specific about the details."

His eyes widened. "Is that so?" He turned to Kader. "Do you have a website you can share?"

Kader scoffed. "That's one of their nonnegotiable rules of the agreement: no sharing."

His comment gave me a tiny slice of peace in this odd conversation.

"Here," Kader said, redirecting Jack, "let me get you what you're looking for." Kader turned, spinning a large combination lock on one of the safes.

I stood back as Kader opened the safe's door. The rarely used door creaked as light filled the space, revealing an array of long guns. My lack of knowledge prevented me from adding any specific descriptors to their depiction. While they varied slightly from one another, each one had a long barrel and a scope. As for what make, kind, or capability, I was at a loss, once again out of my league.

"Here you go," Kader said, passing one of the long guns to Jack. "This should do the trick." His gaze narrowed. "I would have thought you had one of these at your place."

Jack shook his head as he eyed the long gun up and down. "No, nothing with this range."

"Okay, then. Let me get you ammo. We can't have a mountain lion picking off the new foals."

"Springtime," Jack said, as if it were a foregone conclusion. "She's just a momma trying to feed her cubs."

"Not on my land," Kader said.

"I'll take care of it." Jack turned my way. "I don't believe I caught your name, pretty lady."

Kader patted Jack's shoulder as he directed him toward the door. "One of the cool things about the website, she goes by whatever name I choose. You can call her Missy."

Although they'd been walking, Jack's steps stuttered. "Like the house?"

"What can I say? I have a short memory. I tend to gravitate toward things I can recall."

Jack turned back my way. "Nice to meet you, Missy. If you need to get away from this brute, my place is just down the hill. I'd be more than happy to make you comfortable." Before I could reply, he added, "And don't let him make you think he has all the money. I'd be right willing to buy out that contract."

A shiver snaked up my spine as my stomach twisted. "Thank you. I'm good."

"Offer stands."

"Come out here..." Kader said, still directing Jack's steps.

That was the last I heard as the two men exited the building, leaving the door ajar. While the breeze from earlier had warmed and calmed quite a bit—going from a roaring wind to gentle puffs of spring air—it was still enough to stir the remaining dust.

The dancing particles were showcased in rays of golden sunlight streaming from the windows.

I waited a minute for my nerves to settle before walking slowly to the doorway. With my arms crossed over my chest, I took in their interaction. Between the house and outbuildings upon the crushed-gravel driveway, Kader and Jack stood beside a large blue pickup truck, the undercarriage speckled with mud.

For a moment, my ears strained as I tried to listen to their conversation. Other than a few indiscernible words, I was left deciphering body language. Something felt tense, and then, Kader again patted Jack's shoulder as the older man climbed up into the truck's cab.

When Jack pulled away, Kader turned my direction, his full lips terse in a straight line.

Uncertain of what had happened, I went to him. "You went with the sex toy thing?" I asked, trying unsuccessfully to infuse humor into my tone.

"It was your idea. You said truth was stranger than fiction."

I reached for his hands. "You said you trust him but something felt off to me."

"I do trust him. I trust him with my life. I have."

I couldn't put my finger on the unconvincing element in Kader's tone. "But?" I asked, hoping for more information.

"I trust him with my life, not with yours. I don't trust anyone with your life, no one except me."

"Who is Price?"

"It's me. Kader is my dark web name, the one I chose. Price was chosen for me, like too many other things."

I wanted to push for more details but instead, I asked, "Does Mr. Price have a first name?"

Kader shook his head and sighed. "For legal purposes, yes.

Now that I recall some of the past—who I was and you—let's not complicate things with more names."

"Did Jack know you before...?"

"Jack has known me since I could previously remember, for all of my rebirth."

"Did you tell him that you remember more? Did you tell him that you remember Mason?"

Kader's shoulders straightened. "It didn't come up."

His answer brought back that uncomfortable feeling, the acid bubbling in my stomach, churning and twisting. "Is that because you don't want to talk about it or you don't want him to know."

"It's because I have something much more important to concentrate on. You."

I nodded. "Okay. Tell me what I should do about Jack while you're gone, what I should say."

"Do nothing. Say nothing. Stay in the house. I'll change the codes. Even Jack won't be able to enter."

I let out a long breath. "You really don't trust him?"

His hands came to my waist as he pulled my hips toward his. "The way I introduced you was because I didn't want you to say your name. You have been declared missing. There are nationwide alerts with your picture and your name. Most people see those but don't really pay attention. Having your name would make a connection. Nevertheless, my introduction doesn't excuse his comments." Kader's neck strained. "He and I go way back. I made it clear that you belong to me. Yet he could inadvertently mention something to one of the ranch hands who will be arriving." His head shook. "If one of them figures out that I'm gone..." He inhaled and exhaled, one hand leaving my waist, his coarse finger came to my cheek. "No one will get to you."

Beneath the sweatshirt, my skin prickled with goose bumps.

I doubted the cold chill was caused by the warming spring breeze. I leaned into Kader's embrace. "Take me with you. I'll stay in a dirty basement. I don't care. I don't want to be alone."

"Laurel, you're safe here. I even have a backup plan that no one else knows. Let me show you." He squeezed my hand and pulled me toward the house.

LAUREL

*K*ader's aversion to locks didn't mean he left his home vulnerable. Taking me to his office, he showed me how all the doors to the outside were secured, not only locked but also monitored. The house would alert me to anyone approaching long before that person reached a door. If we'd been inside, Kader would have been notified of Jack's approach. There are sensors and cameras along the dirt-packed road designed to warn of such things. Through it all, I would be able to see the vehicle or person from any screen in the house.

His backup plan included something special for his office.

"Over here," he said, showing me a sensor inside the office, near the door. It was a small bubble partially hidden near a table. It was so inconspicuous that I'd never noticed it before.

"This is making me more nervous, not less," I admitted.

Kader shook his head. "Come here. Let me scan your finger."

"Why not one of my eyes, like you?"

"Because you have fingerprints."

That made sense.

Swallowing, I nodded and walked to the small sensor. In reality, it looked like a gray glass bubble protruding from the wall. I extended my index finger. Taking my hand, Kader moved it toward the bubble. A red line appeared, moving up and down, its projection scanning over the pad of my finger.

Kader stepped away and did something at his computer. When he came back, he smiled. "Remember, this is only for an emergency, one I can't foresee occurring."

Then why are we doing this?

I wanted to ask, but even his words of reassurance caused my pulse to rush as I mindlessly chewed upon my bottom lip.

With a twinkle in his green eyes, Kader cupped my chin, and then with his thumb, he tugged my lip free. "The kitchen is well stocked. There is plenty of food and drink, so while I'm gone, no eating through your lip." He leaned forward and kissed my nose. "And no leaving the house or going outside."

"I seem to recall being promised an outside playground."

"I'll have a fucking swing set built when this is over if that's what you want."

I shook my head. "I want the over part. As for a playground, I'd be happy just walking with you on your beautiful land."

Kader's Adam's apple bobbed as he tilted his head toward the gray bubble. "Lift your finger. After it scans and once it begins to flash, you have ten seconds to give it a verbal command. *Secure* and *open* are your only two options. Don't forget those words. It's not programmed to respond to anything else."

Taking a deep breath, I did as he said and lifted my finger. The red light again scanned. Once it was done, the bubble did as he said it would and began to flash. My eyes went to his.

As he nodded, I said, "Secure."

What had only appeared as a normal doorway changed. The door opened farther inward as simultaneously, a metal barrier slid from the doorjamb and obscured the doorway. A moment later, I spun toward the large windows. Sheets of metal, big enough to cover each large pane, slid from the top sill over the glass, completely isolating the room.

"Shit, this isn't helping," I said.

"They are all bulletproof. Over there, as you've probably noticed," he nodded, "is another bathroom and there's a small refrigerator near the wall. While there's no bed in here, the idea is that the office seconds as a safe room."

"But we can't see outside. How would I know what's happening?"

"Over here." He took me to the computer and typed in a sequence of numbers and letters. "I'll write this down for you."

"My memory is pretty good."

"You won't need any of this, but if you do, panic has a way of affecting anyone's memory, even someone as intelligent as you."

My eyes momentarily closed as I fought the bubbling acid churning in my stomach at the thought of being alone. I'd always been a strong, independent woman, and yet something had changed over the last few weeks. It wasn't something I was proud to admit; nevertheless, the fear was real.

Once Kader was finished writing the secret codes, I pleaded my case. "I won't get in the way. I will hide wherever you say. Take me with you."

"Here, Laurel. Here is the safest place. We can't risk you being seen. We can't risk anything. You need to understand that to ensure your safety—to fully commit to this assignment—I need to know you're safe."

"What about communication? Can I reach you? Can you reach me?"

Taking my hand, he brought me back to his computer setup. "I'm shutting down most of this system. The security feeds from around the house and outside will still show and this..." He hit a few buttons. "...think of it like video chatting. If I call you, you will hear it throughout the house. Go to any screen and we can talk. If you call me, you have to do it from this keyboard. I may or may not be able to answer. I promise I'll call back as soon as I can."

I nodded again. "What about my laptop and my work?"

"I'll take it off-line, but you can do whatever you need to do on the laptop."

"How about the other feeds, like from the university, my parents' yard, and my house?"

"I'll monitor them."

I let out a long breath. "You can't do it all. Let me do something. I'm stuck in here." I motioned around the secured room. "It's like the basement all over again."

"It's not the same." When I didn't respond, he added, "Go to the sensor and free yourself."

My fist went to my hip. "Opening these barriers is not freeing myself. It's increasing the size of the cell."

Kader sighed, running his hand over his hair. "Laurel..."

I reached up to his cheek, "I'm sorry. I know you're doing everything you can. I'm not ungrateful. I'm scared."

"There is no place on earth where you would be safer than here."

"How long will you be gone?"

"As long as I need to be."

My eyes opened wider.

"It won't be long," he said reassuringly.

"What if I'm..." I hated to sound like a spoiled child, yet my concerns were valid. "...bored?"

Kader stepped away, going back into the maze of tables.

Upon one near the wall was a small safe. I watched as he spun the lock. After he'd reached inside, he turned. "Will this help?"

My cheeks rose. "Is that mine?" I asked, looking at the Kindle Paperwhite in his hand.

"Yes, but the reason I haven't given it to you is because you are off the grid. I disabled its ability to connect to internet and 4G. I hope you have books downloaded because you can't access your account online."

I nodded enthusiastically. "I do. I have more than I ever thought I'd have time to read."

"The only access to outside this house is me, calling me on my hidden network."

Taking the small black case holding my Kindle from his grasp, I looked up at his green gaze. "Promise me that you'll return."

My mind filled with the possibility he wouldn't and I'd be stuck inside this house forever. "How long will the supplies last?"

Kader pulled me closer until I had to lift my chin to keep his handsome face in view. "I will return long before you run out. I will also learn who hired me and when I return, you will be safe."

"To go back to my life?"

"I can't promise that. I can only promise that the threat we currently know is out there will be eliminated."

I wrapped my arms around his torso and settled my cheek against his chest. "As long as you come back and we're together, the rest will work itself out."

Kader kissed the top of my head. "Go to the sensor and open the office. Only the person who secured it can open it."

My neck craned back as I gazed upward. "Really?"

"I never planned to tell anyone else about it. If that were the case, no one would know but me."

"Not even Jack?"

Kader's shoulders squared. "I trust him. He's my first line of defense. This room was an afterthought following a complicated assignment. I've said I work alone and I do. Jack is a..." He took a deep breath. "Having Jack closer to the property line makes him similar to my sentry. After that case, he came through for me. Jack did his job."

"This isn't about steers or horses or shoring up corrals?"

"No, it isn't. However, that experience got me thinking about what would happen if Jack was gone, or if somehow he was overpowered. That's why I reinforced this room. If one of those instances occurred, it would be too late for Jack. That sounds crass and uncaring, but men like Jack and me live by a code. First, we would protect the other to our own death. Second, we protect the cause."

"This room is about the cause?" I asked, scanning the familiar gray industrial interior.

"This room contains information that is better kept secure." He lifted his hand, bringing the coarse tip of his finger to my cheek. "That includes you and your compound—all your research and development. Bring your laptop in here. You uploaded all of the information on there."

"Kader?"

"And I don't give a shit about any of that as much as I do about you. You will not need this room." His free hand moved to my stomach. "In here," he said, his fingers splaying over the material covering my midsection. "If your gut tells you to come in here and shut yourself off, listen. I have trusted my gut when there was no evidence to support what it was saying. It's been right. It's why I have you here today."

"Why I'm not dead on my bedroom floor?"

He shrugged. "Promise me that you'll listen to it."

I'd never been a go-with-your-gut type of person. Studies, theories, evidence, and conclusions. That was the way I worked.

"Laurel?"

I nodded. "And if your gut is telling you that I need to be in here, will you tell me?"

"Yes. If I do, listen to me."

"I will."

"Now free us. As I said, it's only you who can."

I walked to the sensor and lifted my index finger. The red line scanned up and down the pad of my finger. Once it began to flash, I said, "Open."

The metal shutters over the windows were the first to move. As the sound of locking mechanisms rattled through the office, the metal moved upward. And then after similar sounds, the one covering the doorway opened, sliding back into the doorjamb and out of sight. When I turned, Kader was closer. My cheeks rose. "You know, that's empowering."

Again his arms snaked around my waist. "You have all the power, Dr. Carlson. Never forget that."

"That's not true. I have none. I'm totally helpless to whatever is happening."

"No, you're not helpless. You're far from it. You are the one who holds the intricate secrets and knows the specifics of your compound."

"And because of that, someone wants me dead."

"Rarely is a hit taken out on the powerless. There's no need. Whoever hired me knows how fucking smart you are. They also predicted that you wouldn't be tempted by money. They also know that if you are left alive, their plan will fail. They're scared of you."

I considered his words. "Really?"

He lifted my chin. "And so am I."

"Of me?"

"Yes, Laurel, from the first time I saw you on my screen, you petrified me." He shrugged. "Which is quite the accomplishment. Truly, nothing or no one frightens me."

"How am I scary?"

"Because even before I remembered our past, I was afraid of losing you. The way you looked at me, seeing me, the way you're looking at me now. It's like you can see beyond my persona. That sensation is terrifying and exhilarating," he added. "I will come back to you. Promise me that you'll do as I say, stay in the house, don't try to go online except to talk to me, and do not open the door to anyone."

I nodded. "I promise. Please hurry."

Splaying his large hands over my backside, he pulled me close. "Or plan two, we stay here forever, forget the outside world, and I fuck you day and night."

"Maybe that can be our reward once you do what you need to do."

His head tilted. "Does that mean you're up for the possibility?"

"It means that I'm accepting of the possibility. Being up is your responsibility."

Kader's eyes shone. "I have that one covered, no worries."

Laying my cheek again over the soft shirt covering his chest, I sighed. Within my head was a long list of worries, but none of them included Kader's ability to be up.

LAUREL

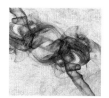

I stood in the foyer, my wounded palm now clean and bandaged. My arms wrapped around my midsection as Kader sent one last staggering, green-eyed gaze my direction. The quick nod of his head was his goodbye and the straightening of my neck was mine. Simple movements, ones we made every day, were suddenly meant to represent more. They were supposed to wish the other safety and a quick reunion, as well as verbalize our innermost thoughts and convey those feelings to the other.

It wasn't fair to ask so much from a dip of a chin or the squaring of posture.

We had.

The woefully insufficient wordless conversation failed.

My stomach twisted with the revelation that I needed more.

Yet before I could speak, Kader slipped behind the tall wooden door. As the clicking of the latch echoed in the large entry, reverberating from the wood floor upward to the tall ceiling, an overwhelming sense of loneliness bloomed within me, growing too fast for me to fight.

My gaze slipped upward to the landing on the story above. Perhaps if I hurried up the staircase I could peer out the large window and see beyond. If I did, could I possibly see Kader as he moved toward the outbuildings? Maybe I'd see his plane growing smaller as it flew higher in the evening sky.

And yet I didn't move. I didn't try.

The sense of loneliness paralyzed me where I stood.

My arms grew rigid, locked in place with my elbows bent, holding tightly to myself. My feet were set, unable to move forward or backward—basically, I was unable to move at all. Instead of fighting the paralysis, my knees buckled and like liquid flowing from a pitcher, I spilled onto the hardwood floor.

As I pulled my knees to my chest, I peered in all directions. The warm decor and the soft lighting were no longer prominent. All around me, his house was bathed in golden light. Despite the sun making its way toward the western horizon, the sky beyond the windows was still a glowing shade of blue.

The six-thousand-plus square feet of luxury no longer registered. My mind went to Kader, to where we'd been and how only minutes ago we'd been together. The evidence could be found within the kitchen where the remnants of our dinner remained. There were dishes still piled in the sink. Though he'd offered to help, I'd insisted they wait so that Kader could concentrate on what he needed to prepare, pack, and do.

In many ways, up until he'd disappeared through the large doors, it had been like most other evenings in Kader's home, much as it had been since my arrival. We'd prepared our meal, talked about his plans, what he knew, and what he wanted to know. Sitting at the long table, we'd eaten the food and drank the water and tea. Any other night, after I'd finished cleaning the kitchen, I'd find him in his office.

No matter how hard I tried to pretend, this wasn't any other night.

Kader was gone.

I was alone.

I let out a ragged breath as my gaze was drawn to the place where the walls and floor met, where hardwood met baseboards. My heart began to beat faster. The movement was almost imperceptible, yet I knew it was happening. I felt it in the air. My skin prickled and small hairs stood to attention as the space where I sat grew smaller. Such as the mechanism allowing the metal shutters to protect Kader's office, the walls within the foyer moved inward, closing in as inch by inch they crept closer and closer.

Inhaling, my breasts pushed against my raised thighs. Exhaling, my breath skirted over my arms. Closing my eyes, I repeated the process.

"It's not really happening," I spoke aloud. "You're having an illusion brought on by your own insecurities. Stop it." I squared my shoulders.

Inhale.

Exhale.

Inhale.

Exhale.

"Laurel." My tone grew stern. "You have spent most of your adult life living alone. You're letting your imagination get the best of you. Pick yourself up and dust yourself off. You can do this."

Yes, I was continuing my audible conversation.

What was crazier, imagining moving walls or talking aloud to oneself?

I didn't want to analyze that answer.

I peered again at the union of walls and floor.

No movement.

Pushing myself off the floor, my knees found their strength and I stood. All at once I stilled, a low rumbling pulling my attention upward. While I'd never heard it from the ground, I knew. The sound was coming from Kader's plane.

He hadn't told me his exact plans. However, from what I'd inferred, he would fly to another location before catching another flight into Indianapolis. While he hadn't been specific, he'd mentioned that he wasn't wasting forty-eight hours driving to and from his destination.

The rumbling from beyond the house meant he was airborne —officially gone. My opportunities were gone. No longer could I run outside and beg him to take me along. I also couldn't slip into the outbuilding and tell him again that I wanted him to return.

It was too late. He was gone.

With a resolute sigh, I began toward the kitchen. I'd taken only a few steps when a thought popped into my head.

Was I certain the front door was locked?

If it opened from the inside, would it open from the outside?

Purposefully, I moved my sock-covered feet across the long smooth boards of the flooring. Squaring my shoulders, I reached for the door handle, squeezed the lever, and pulled it inward.

To my utter shock, it opened.

I waited for alarms.

There were none.

The view from the open doorway to the outside was the same as it was this morning, a large expanse of land going on forever. With my hand now on the outside handle, I took another step onto the porch. As the evening breeze tousled my hair, I peered in all directions. The drying ground was my only indicator that time had passed since this morning's storm.

Turning back, I squeezed the outside lever. My grasp was met with resistance, the latch solid and unmoving.

I let out a long breath and sighed with relief. "Okay, it is locked from the outside."

Going back inside, a new sound, that of beeping drew me toward the kitchen. On the small screen above the counter was a black screen with the words: INCOMING CALL.

My cheeks rose as I touched the screen the way Kader had shown me. His handsome face came into view, complete with sunglasses as well as the earphones and microphone he wore within the plane.

"Did you miss me already?" I asked.

"Stay in the fucking house. It took you what...ten minutes to break that damn rule?"

"I am in the house."

"The house doesn't lie to me—don't you do it either."

My lip slipped below my front teeth. "I'm not lying. I'm in the house. I opened the door because I wanted to be sure it was locked."

"It's locked. Every fucking entry is locked."

Although the exasperation in his tone should induce trepidation on my part, it didn't. My smile that had been absent since his recent departure returned. "I miss you."

"Laurel, I have a job to do."

I nodded. "I know. I won't attempt to open any more doors. While it's annoying your house likes to tell on me, I think I like how quickly you responded."

"If you need to reach me, fucking call."

"I can do that," I replied. "Fly safely." I sighed. "What you do...it's dangerous. Stay safe." There was a sense of relief in voicing what I should have said—what I wanted to say —earlier.

"Laurel..."

I swallowed. There was something in the way he said my name that focused my attention. Despite the sunglasses covering his eyes, his tension was visible in his chiseled jaw and the straining in his neck.

"I'm not good at emotional shit," he began, his deep timbre slowing. "I should have said something before I left..."

I know that feeling.

While that response was there, I remained mute, a lump forming in my throat as I waited to hear what he should have said.

"Remember what I said...do you remember...about since we were kids?" he asked.

He'd said he'd loved me since we were kids. I'd said the same thing.

"Yes."

"This is new and fucking unfamiliar. It's more than that. It's uncomfortable and I don't like that."

"I remember what you said," I prompted.

He turned toward the screen. "Laurel, I'll be back. I promise."

I nodded, the lump that had been in my throat now burst, bringing tears to my eyes. "I trust you. I'll be here when you return."

"And that thing I said?"

"Yes."

"I have, even when I didn't remember...I did and I fucking do. I still don't believe in fate, but fuck, we bound ourselves to each other and it's still here." He tapped his broad chest. "Laurel, I'm not good at this, but I wanted you to know, I never stopped thinking...caring...loving. Even though I thought it wasn't possible, I still do."

Before I could respond, the call disconnected.

I reached up, touching the dark screen as tears flowed from my eyes, spilling over onto my cheeks. "I love you, too." I spoke aloud even though our connection was gone. "I always have, but it's different now. I meant what I said earlier. I don't care if you're Mason or Kader. I love *you*, damn it. Come back to me."

Wiping the tears from my cheeks, I took a deep breath.

Though the sunshine through the kitchen windows had begun to dim, Kader's call had given me what we hadn't said as we parted. I didn't want to think about what he may face in Indianapolis. I didn't want to imagine never being able to respond to him and tell him how I felt.

Swallowing, I began taking care of our dinner dishes as a renewed sense of security settled around me. I looked back at the dark screen, questions coming to my mind.

Was Kader's home like the common systems others had in their homes? Could I ask his house a question?

As I was about to turn off the kitchen lights, I walked back to the screen. "Missy, are you there?"

"I'm here."

"Is the house secure?"

"Yes, the house is secure."

"Will you alert me if it isn't?"

"I will alert you if it isn't."

"Thank you, Missy."

"My pleasure, Dr. Carlson."

I stood straighter as a chill reappeared, snaking down my spine. "How do you know my name?"

"Your name is Laurel Carlson."

"How do you know that?" I asked, suddenly uncomfortable

with this conversation, one I was having with a form of artificial intelligence.

"Your fingerprint is registered."

Shit.

My fingerprint.

The one Kader used to activate his safe room.

"Have you shared that information with anyone?"

"No. Would you like me to notify the authorities?"

"No."

"Doctor, you are considered missing. That misconception could be rectified."

"No. I want to stay missing."

"Very well."

"Good night, Missy."

"Good night, Dr. Carlson."

KADER

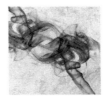

A quick flick of my wrist and the flat metal tool in my hand turned the tumblers. The simple lock clicked as if a key had been inserted. Pushing the door inward, I stepped inside Eric Olsen's home, quickly closing and locking the door behind me. Save for a dimly lit porch light shining through the sidelights, the house inside was dark.

I'd done my research on multiple fronts. After the gathering and the disappearance of Drs. Cartwright and Carlson, Dr. Olsen's wife had left town. She didn't leave him in a permanent way as far as I could ascertain. There were no pending court filings petitioning for divorce. A scan of her phone records indicated she hadn't contacted an attorney. From the sound of her emails, this was simply a break, a long-overdue trip to visit her sister in Boston. While I understood that things had been difficult, shouldn't a wife want to support her partner, not abandon him?

Before Laurel I'd never analyzed the actions of others. I observed without judgment.

Prior to entering the house, I'd disabled my cameras as well as Olsen's security system. The conversation we were about to have wouldn't be recorded. Taking a look at my watch, I presumed that the doctor should be coming home anytime. At this hour of night, that would have been a foregone conclusion if he were still employed. Two days ago, the university announced Dr. Eric Olsen's retirement, effective immediately.

My head shook as I made my way around the first floor. Within the kitchen, the counters were cluttered with various disposable containers, awaiting their disposal. From the odor, the contents included Italian and seafood. Garlic and stale fish was not a combination of air fresheners for a reason. I lifted the lid on a mummified pizza before lowering it in disgust.

Propelled by curiosity, I opened the refrigerator. While the Olsens were well stocked on condiments, actual food was at a minimum.

The doctor's private office was comparatively immaculate, as if he hadn't entered it in days or weeks. The only lack of cleanliness was the fine layer of dust over his large wooden desk.

Boxes of various sizes littered the dining room table. Their contents appeared to have come from Dr. Olsen's office at the university. Thrown together with no real pattern were books, magazines, papers, pens, and pencils. Stacked one upon the other were photographs in worn frames. In larger frames were his diplomas and certificates of licensure. From an observational point of view, it was interesting how decades of dedication could be condensed to multiple corrugated boxes.

Ensuring that I was currently alone, I eased my way into his living room. Like the other rooms, there was a mass state of disarray. Newspapers cluttered the large table before the sofas. Pillows and throws were strewn about as if nights had been spent in here instead of upstairs.

With the moonlight providing illumination, I brushed my hand over the mantel of his fireplace. There were numerous pictures of him and his wife, ones of their children with their spouses, and more of their grandchildren. There was a twinge in my chest as I contemplated Olsen's destiny.

Fuck.

I needed to stop overthinking. If Olsen deserved to die, he would. Who or what he leaves behind wasn't part of my job description.

I spun as noise of an entrance came from the direction of the kitchen.

Face-to-face interviews weren't my thing. When they occurred, rarely did the interviewee live to discuss the encounter. As I waited for him to enter the room, I reminded myself that no one was as important as Laurel.

Standing back, I watched the darkened house come to life as light spilled from the kitchen, casting illumination on the connecting tiled hallway. As I waited, an array of sounds registered, a refrigerator opening and closing, the squeak and tap of cupboards, as well as the distinctive clink of ice dropping into a glass.

"Come in here," I whispered.

I could go to him; however, the kitchen had too many windows that looked out onto his backyard. In a neighborhood like his, the backyards adjoined. If tonight was Olsen's last night, I didn't want to risk a nosy neighbor telling the authorities a story about seeing someone with him.

Holding my breath, I waited. Eventually, the tap of hard-soled shoes upon the tile grew closer. His steps stilled as my presence registered. The tumbler fell from his hand, crashing against the tile as the scent of whiskey permeated the air.

"W-who are you?"

I scanned the man before me, questioning his identity. In the few weeks since the gathering, Eric Olsen had changed. No longer the proud and accomplished man who spoke to the crowd, he was a ghost of who he'd been. Even in the dim light, his pallor and unkempt appearance showed. In that short time, his age had become more prominent along with his posture slumped and hair thinned. If I were to guess, I'd say he'd also lost weight. I knew from his bio that Dr. Olsen was sixty-two years old, yet at this moment, he appeared a decade older.

I stood silently, allowing him to make his own assumptions about my presence. Dressed in jeans, black boots, and a black leather coat, I emanated darkness. I belonged in the shadows. On an abandoned street or dim alleyway, I could be dismissed. Standing in the center of his living room, I was a monster.

Second by second, it was happening—seeping into his consciousness. The evidence of his processing became clearer as his eyes averted from mine and his hands began to tremble.

Being with Laurel had given me a reprieve, allowing me to forget the effect my mere presence had on others. I still didn't understand how she didn't feel it or see it. As all remaining color drained from his cheeks, it was obvious that Dr. Olsen did.

That's right, Olsen. The boogeyman is in your living room.

"Take anything you want," Olsen said, reaching back to his rear pocket and removing his wallet.

If I had any suspicion he was carrying, this conversation would be over. I was confident that he wasn't for one simple reason. He didn't have a permit. Men like Eric Olsen didn't break laws. For his future, that better also include not hiring assassins or selling research on the dark web.

"I-I have cash. It's not much, but you can have it." His hands had moved beyond trembling, now violently shaking as he extended the bills.

"I'm not here for what you have," I said.

He fell to his knees. "Oh God, I have a wife. I have children and grandchildren. Please..." His head fell forward as if his neck could no longer hold the weight.

"Stand up," I directed with a quick rise of my chin.

Using his hands to help him rise, Olsen stood. Upon the knees of his trousers where he'd kneeled upon the broken tumbler were growing circles of deep red. "What do you want?"

"The truth."

He reached for the wall, his hand landing on the white trim. "May I..." He looked toward my eyes before looking away. "...sit?"

I nodded. When he stepped away, his bloody handprint was left, smeared over the white woodwork.

Shit, this man was probably on anticoagulants and would bleed out courtesy of a broken glass before I got answers.

"Where's your phone?" I asked.

Sitting, he patted the front of his trousers, leaving a bloody trail. "I-I left it in the kitchen."

"Don't move."

A few seconds later, I was back with his phone—now turned off—in my grasp as I tossed a kitchen towel his direction.

"Thank you," he murmured as he wiped the blood from his hands before wrapping the towel around the one with the deepest cuts. Slowly, his gaze came up. "This is about Dr. Cartwright and Dr. Carlson, isn't it?"

"Tell me why you think that," I said as I reached into the pocket of my jacket and removed a small pill container. Opening the lid, I removed one tablet from one side of the divided container. It was better if they didn't touch. I set it on the table at the side of his chair. Without commenting, I reached for the second and also placed it on the same table.

"What are those?"

"Your future."

FORMERLY, SERGEANT FIRST CLASS PIERCE

Less than five years ago in an undisclosed location

I stood tall, waiting for the final verdict. It was a precarious moment, one where killers decide the future of a fellow assassin. Justice wasn't our mantra, and an eye for an eye didn't fit what we were told to do. With that as the pattern, I wasn't confident in how the decision would fall.

Would time served be considered adequate?

Would more be asked because more was possible?

When would more no longer exist?

I knew their answer. More would end on the day or night I no longer existed in any form with or without a name.

"Your service has been noted." This wasn't coming from Commander Jackson. The situation at hand had garnered the attention of the top in our division.

"Thank you, Top." In our arbitrary world of the Sovereign Order, the official ranks of the military were replaced. We represented no one branch of the military—yet all were represented within our units. The moniker Top represented what it alluded to, the top of our chain, the place the buck stopped. The man before me was the commander of commanders. He answered to no one, literally. The president and top five-star generals weren't consulted.

They didn't know we existed, and yet our presence and our missions guided theirs.

My last mission was complete.

The news of the militant leader's demise made headlines throughout the world. Never had anyone with so much protection, power, and money been removed from power without a full-scale raid supported in the air and on the ground by a massive siege.

In the days and weeks following, the public accounts of the incident varied from one reporting agency to another.

According to the sources from within the militant camp, their compound was surrounded. Arriving in multiple Black Hawk helicopters, a swarm of Special Forces scaled eighteen-foot walls. The operation took nearly an hour and the militants fought bravely defending their leader. The end result was US casualties estimated to be upward of half the Special Forces sent on the mission.

Their inaccurate description raised a variety of questions among the Special Forces ranks as well as their families. Everyone was searching to ensure the safety of their loved ones.

We'd seen similar propaganda before. The militants' account was fabricated to both garner respect by their own followers and appear stronger than they'd been. The truth that only the people in the room with me today knew was that the compound was not attacked by a team of Special Forces. If half of the force used had been killed, it would have been me or my pilot. As it was, the entire two-person team was present and accounted for.

They'd also exaggerated the length of the operation. It didn't take nearly an hour. From landing to departure was thirty-eight minutes. There was no great heroic gun battle. Their leader didn't die with a weapon in his hand.

He died with his dick in some *woman*. I used that term lightly. We'll never know her actual age, but based on body size and lack of physical maturity, I would put her at younger than her teens. If that were the case, the asshole deserved the bullet in his head for that one reason alone. According to intelligence reports, the leader had multiple wives ranging in ages as well as sixteen children.

There was no way to find out if the girl who'd been with him was one of his wives, children, or simply provided for his entertainment. Her name or any information about her had been glaringly absent from reports released to the press. After all, how could their leader have been killed while fighting for his beliefs while simultaneously fucking a child?

I'd like to say I spared her.

I can't.

I also didn't particularly aim for her.

Then again, I didn't aim to miss her.

She wasn't my concern.

The power of my firearm didn't stop as it penetrated his skull or barreled through his brain. Even the exit from the skull did little to slow the trajectory. As was the custom with the rumors associated with the radical militia, the girl's death was the kindest ending I could have given her. If she'd lived, it would most likely be that witnessing the leader's death would have severely limited her lifespan.

As it was, the Order didn't believe in leaving witnesses or taking hostages. The only people we rescued were those we were sent to rescue. Others in the line of fire were just that, collateral casualties.

I had one mission.

My assignment was completed the moment my bullet hit its mark, effectively removing a tyrannical leader from the world.

In all reality, the leader's interest in fucking preteen girls provided the means for me to circumvent and avoid his guards. Instead of bemoaning her death, it was preferable to believe that the girl gave her body and life to save the world from the monster.

That was a perspective that members of the Order wouldn't share. We didn't look for the rosy alternatives. We looked for opportunities to succeed, whether it was taking advantage of a vulnerable situation or killing five guards in the process. I didn't take the mission planning to fail or ready to see what I did as anything less or more than exactly what needed to be done.

"Pierce, your skills were saved for a reason."

My neck straightened. "I have given you my skills. I spoke to Commander Jackson. I agreed to one more mission. That mission is complete."

Top turned to Commander Jackson. "Tell me, how many men or women have left the Order...alive."

The commander sat taller. "The number is low, and the circumstances are unique."

Top's gaze came back to me. "Are your circumstances unique?"

"My circumstance is that I am done. I'm also being upfront

with the Order. I can no longer do these missions without having input."

"You're wanting a promotion? You want to become a commander."

"Hell no." By the expressions on their faces, my brutal honesty wasn't what they expected.

"Input is given by those in commanding positions."

"I don't want to have a commanding position over others, only myself."

Top nodded.

"Pierce," Commander Jackson said, "the Order is willing to consider your request with the understanding that you will not leave but relocate to a new team within the Order."

"A new team?"

I didn't want a new team. I wanted no team.

"Yes," Top said. "As Commander Jackson mentioned, unique circumstances. We aren't willing to lose what we've invested."

The muscles in my shoulders pulled tight. "What are my options?"

"You don't have any," Top replied matter-of-factly.

I stood taller.

"You completed your last mission even after alerting your commander of your intentions for the future. We respect that loyalty."

That sounded promising.

"You have a unique ability and skills that are not easily found in others even within your current unit."

"I'm—"

Top raised his hand, silencing my response.

"You have one option. Commander Jackson will lay it on the line for you. Your new team will be the smallest in the Order. Not everyone within our order could handle what we are offering you, but it is believed you can. The choice is simple. One way or the other you will agree."

I moved my gaze from Top to Commander Jackson, unsure what was being said or offered.

That wasn't true.

I knew whatever they'd decided wasn't an offer as in an opportunity for me to accept or reject. That wasn't the way this worked. The commander would tell me and if I didn't accept, another option would be less appealing.

Before I responded, Top stood and nodded toward Commander Jackson and then to me. "I see potential in this unique circumstance. I am certain as the members of this pilot unit, you will make it work."

"Yes, sir," Commander Jackson said, his blue eyes shifting to me. "We won't fail, will we, Price?"

"Price?" I asked.

Top nodded again. "Until we meet again. Goodbye, for now."

I stood perfectly still as Top left the room, leaving me alone with Commander Jackson. Once the door shut, I relaxed my stance, though relaxed wasn't a very apt description. "What the hell is happening? Who is Price?"

"You said to give you a new identity, one who could live in the real world while remaining in this one."

"I didn't say that."

"It's your unique circumstance, to see if it's possible to have a foot in both and keep off the radar. It won't be easy, but I believe you can."

"What do I have to do as far as communicating with the Order?"

"Nothing."

My head shook. "I don't understand."

"That will be my job. We will soon be a team of two." He sat taller. "The only team of its kind in the unit of the Order."

"You will leave this team?" I asked, gesturing to indicate our team as a whole.

"You're not the only one who could use a break. The team will survive. It has to. And as for your skills, as long as it's made clear that you will answer when called, we have negotiated a compromise."

KADER

Present day

Olsen slumped back in the recliner as his head shook and tears filled his eyes. "I never wanted any of this. It's my fault."

An interesting admission with his life on the line.

"What's your fault?" I asked, looking away from the two tablets I'd placed on the table.

"I wanted it to work—the research, the compound, the patent. I knew it was a long shot." He swallowed. "What they'd accomplished—Laurel and Russell—was so much more than we'd imagined. When Carl came to me and said the research needed to end, I assumed it was because of the cost. That made sense. Though he didn't say so specifically, the expenses had been the topic of many meetings in the past."

"Carl Oaks?" I confirmed, "The dean of the university."

Olsen nodded. "Yes, I tried to tell him that we were spending more because we were learning more. I fought for them—for us." He looked up. "I was...well, being even a small part of that study was more than I'd ever expected to accomplish in my lifetime."

"When did Oaks tell you the research needed to end?"

Olsen sighed, his gaze going between the two pills and out to the room. "So much has happened. He first mentioned it around the beginning of the fiscal year. For the university that is July. I pushed forward. They were making too much progress. It was around the first of this year that he became adamant. Yes, that was it. He called me in during the semester holiday break and said the research, clinical study, all of it was done. Our department wouldn't be supported after this fiscal year." He shrugged. "That means this was our last semester. I remember the timing because it was when our children and grandchildren were visiting."

"Did you tell Cartwright or Carlson about the meeting?"

He shook his head. "I didn't tell them that Carl wanted their work to end or that he said nothing was finalized so Russell and Laurel couldn't publish their results. I refused to accept it. I'd hoped to save them from that news by coming up with a solution. I did tell them that the funding was threatened and we needed investors."

"So procuring outside investment was your idea?"

"Partially. I truly believed if we could get funding and positive PR, Oaks would back down."

"How familiar was Dean Oaks with the actual research?" I asked.

"Not that much. His thing is administration. He's the almighty ruler. Research and development, clinical studies, and staying within the set cost guidelines...that was for us peons."

There was more than a hint of Olsen's dislike of his former boss in both his words as well as his underlying tone of discontent.

"What was being done in our department was beyond his comprehension," Olsen continued. Looking up, he asked, "Do you want my opinion?"

"I'm here."

His gaze went from me to the pills and back. "I've got nothing to lose and even though I don't know you, it feels liberating to say this shit out loud." He took a deep breath. "In my opinion, Oaks only saw the cost. He looked at the bottom line. What he couldn't comprehend was the future—the benefits, public relations, and positive exposure for the university.

"He couldn't see beyond the cost spreadsheet. Unilaterally he decided the expense was too much. That's the way he works. It's probably his navy background. He runs the campus like one of his ships. Decisions don't need committees or discussion. As dean and king, everything is at his discretion and we're supposed to follow.

"I'm proud to say for once I stood up. I didn't want to follow his decree. I saw it all differently. I understood what Laurel and Russell were doing, what their compound could do...I started talking to other deans. Get money, that's what I was told. I tried, but it was too late. Now they're gone."

"Where are they?" I asked.

"They?"

I took a step closer. As I did, Olsen sat taller.

"If you're talking about Laurel and Russell," he said, "I don't know. I didn't want to believe that they'd leave...the university or me." There was genuine remorse in his tone.

"But that's what you think," I prompted. "You believe that they left you holding the ball."

"In a matter of words, no matter what happened, they did. After they disappeared, I was the scapegoat. It all fell on me." His head shook. "As you probably know, I was fired. The research has been shut down." He looked up. "None of this is new. If you didn't know everything I said, you wouldn't be here."

"I know you were fired. I didn't know some other things." My timeline began too recently. I needed to go back in time and scan emails and files. "I'm here for your version."

"My version...Cartwright was acting oddly—just off. I can't explain it better. Laurel wasn't different, well not until after the gathering. Even then, she wasn't acting like Russell. The whole thing had my nerves stretched to the limit. After the gathering, I mentioned something to her about Sinclair Pharmaceuticals. I asked her to keep it between us for the time being. She refused, saying she trusted Russell." He shrugged. "Laurel told me he went to her house after the gathering. Maybe...they were...?" His tired blue eyes found mine. "...more than colleagues. If that's the case, it makes sense that they're together. But where?"

"Why were you concerned about Sinclair?"

Lines deepened around his eyes as his gaze narrowed. "Who are you and how do you know so much?"

"I'm the man who will decide which pill you consume—if you live to see tomorrow or simply wake with a hole in your memory."

Olsen sucked in a deep breath.

"I've also done my homework," I said. "I'm here so that you can fill in the blanks. Who do you trust?"

"No one," he answered matter-of-factly.

"Who *did* you trust?"

"Too many people, I'm afraid. I believed that we were all working together for the same thing."

Fucking sounded like Laurel.

"Which was..." I prompted.

"To bring Laurel and Russell's compound to market."

"I read an article that stated the university was selling the research it has. Who are they selling to? Sinclair Pharmaceuticals or another entity?"

Olsen's head shook. "No one. No entity. Flushing it all down the damn stool. That's what doesn't make sense. I was made aware that Sinclair Pharmaceuticals offered an obscene amount of money for the rights to take over the research and continue working for patent. Their offer was tweaked until it fell within the contractual guidelines to keep the university involved. Last I heard—before I was escorted from the premises, Oaks pulled the plug on all deals.

"I thought he and Damien Sinclair had this planned from the beginning," Olsen said, "but now Sinclair is as screwed as the rest of us."

"*The rest of us*," I repeated. "Who does that include?"

"Mostly, our entire department. Laurel and Russell are still missing. Most of the other faculty and staff have been reassigned or encouraged to seek employment elsewhere. I'm out. The clinical trials were shut down. The participants were made to sign nondisclosure forms as if it never happened. Everyone involved was made to sign similar documents."

He shrugged. "It was another of my great stands—a line in the sand. I refused to stay quiet. The results were too promising."

"So you didn't sign an NDA?"

"I did. I caved. I didn't at first and my reward was termination. The only reason I finally signed was because if I didn't, like the research, my retirement benefits would have disappeared. Nearly forty years of service to the university and I would have lost everything—my job, career, and retirement." The moisture was back in his eyes. "My wife and family...we had plans. It wasn't as if I was able to save the compound or Carlson and Cartwright's research anyway. It's gone. The lab is closed. NDAs are signed. It's as if it never happened. My only hope is that they still have it somewhere."

Laurel's story came back to me.

I was part of a study. It was shut down. In the middle of the night they transported us via helicopter and then plane as if the research had never occurred.

"Do you believe *they* have it? Carlson and Cartwright," I clarified.

Olsen's head shook. "At this point, I'm not even certain that they're alive."

"Why do you say that?"

"Laurel Carlson. I've known her since I interviewed her for her position. While I can't say the same thing about Russell, with her, I know she wouldn't have stolen the research from the university. Even with the clause in their contracts that would have allowed them to go to Sinclair or another entity as long as the university was credited, she said she wouldn't leave. I believed that her heart was here with the university and her work. Without proof, I can't be convinced she would willingly abscond with the data."

"As an alternative, you think they could be dead? What about this research warrants that conclusion?"

He shook his head. "Nothing else makes sense. If you're asking who would kill them or why they would be killed over a compound that could reduce the physical and psychological effects of traumatic memories, I have no idea. And why them and not me? To be a hundred percent honest, I have been expecting me to be next. That's why I sent my wife away."

"You sent her away?"

"If you're here to kill me, I didn't want her to be collateral damage."

"Your destiny isn't set. Keep being honest with me."

Olsen shrugged. "It's...cathartic. I haven't been able to talk to anyone."

"What else do you want to share?"

"If I tell you or anyone else my fears and concerns over whom else could possibly be in danger, I'm either a madman overwrought with paranoia or providing you with a list of others to investigate." His gaze fluttered over the pills at his side. "Or kill."

"Cartwright, Carlson, you," I said. "Who else could be in danger if the connection is the compound?"

"I heard that Sinclair offered both Russell's and Laurel's assistants lucrative positions." Olsen's head shook. "I guess I'm too old. I'm still waiting on that call. Anyway, if someone is trying to quiet the people with knowledge, they have it. Not as much as the doctors, but more than others, probably even more than me if I were honest. Their knowledge could get them nice offices with labs at any pharmaceutical giant whether it's Sinclair or not. I also think it could get them missing, like Laurel and Russell."

"You're speaking of Jennifer Skills and Stephanie Moore?"

Olsen narrowed his gaze. "Damn, you have done your homework."

I nodded.

"I'm out of the loop. I heard about the offer from Sinclair. Last I heard, Ms. Skills was considering it."

"Ms. Moore?" I asked.

"Sinclair didn't say. I nosed around a bit and heard that she wants to distance herself from all of this. She's very close to defending her dissertation and completing her doctorate. Her education and experience make her valuable in many settings. She doesn't want that tarnished by what has happened here."

"Regarding the missing researchers?"

"No," he replied. "Regarding the rumor that she was involved with Russell."

My eyes widened.

Olsen raised his hand. "Rumors. I don't have proof. The status of her dissertation is fact. The bit about her and Dr. Cartwright being romantically involved as well as the rumor that she's pursuing an opportunity somewhere on the East Coast are simply the musings of office gossip."

"What opportunity?"

"I've told you all I know." He looked from the pills to me. "Will I live to see tomorrow?"

"That depends."

"On...?" he prompted.

"The answer to the next question."

Olsen gripped the arms of the chair, his one hand still wrapped in a kitchen towel.

"If you wake and there are memories, tell me what happened tonight. Who did you speak to?"

"If?"

I nodded.

His Adam's apple bobbed. "I came home late..."

After he finished his tale, I lifted the larger white tablet and placed it back into the divided container. Nodding to the smaller green tablet, I waited.

Olsen didn't move. "How do I know...?"

"You don't."

"Can I trust you?"

I removed the revolver from the holder beneath my coat. Undoing the safety, I pointed the barrel toward Eric Olsen. "Not at all."

His lids fluttered as he reached for the green pill and held it in the palm of his hand. "After everything that happened, if I take this and I don't wake, they'll think I'm involved in something I shouldn't have been." His eyes glistened. "They will think I did this to myself."

"You are doing it to yourself."

"My wife..." He swallowed, his Adam's apple straining below the loose flesh in his neck. "I wish I could tell..." He sighed. "I wish so many things."

"How do you want your wife to remember you, falling asleep and not waking or with your brains splattered on her living room walls?"

He placed the pill on his tongue.

"Goodbye, Dr. Olsen."

It took two attempts, but finally he swallowed the small pill.

I didn't feel the urge to hurry away. He believed in Laurel. That was evident in his long-winded cathartic monologue. While I'd asked questions, he'd volunteered more than I anticipated. Maybe I had given him the opportunity to unload his burdened soul.

Kader—the creator of destinies and cleanser of consciences.

Remaining standing, I waited as the drug entered his circulation.

It wasn't until his eyelids grew heavy that I took a step away. First, I returned his phone to the kitchen table—after connecting it to a nice bit of untraceable malware that would give me access to his calls—and locked the exterior door. Careful to guarantee that there was no sign of intrusion, I made my way to the vehicle I'd rented under another name.

As I hit the ignition button, I was confident that the small green pill had done its job.

LAUREL

I woke as the sun streamed through the large windows and glass door in Kader's bedroom. I wasn't certain if the house would tell him where I was and where I'd slept, but I didn't care. There was a sense of comfort that came with being in his bedroom and in his bed. I'd purposely pulled his pillow to me as the lingering scent of his cologne filled my senses. After my odd conversation with the house, the security associated with being close to him helped me settle and sleep.

Now it was another day, the first full day without him present.

As I scooted from the large bed, the view of the ravine in the morning light drew me toward the glass doors. Turning the knob, I opened one of the doors inward and stepped onto the balcony. The crisp morning breeze combined with the decking's cool surface beneath my bare feet awakened me more, pushing away the nightlong slumber and waking me completely.

The base of the ravine was hidden in a veil of white fog. From where I stood, holding tightly to the railing, it seemed as though I was above the clouds and shielded from the dangers below. Kader had done that, brought me here to his castle with a stunning view. It was more than that. He'd brought me to the safest and securest location he knew. The man who dealt in death and its aftermath understood danger in a way that was foreign to me. Staring out to the fresh morning scene, I reminded myself that I was where he wanted me because he wanted me safe.

Did it matter that his desires were mixed with Mason's?

It didn't.

In my heart, I believed that my safety mattered to both of them, as his—theirs—did to me.

Peering out over the morning view, I marveled at how the recent precipitation, bouts of sunny days, and warming temperatures all worked together like a paintbrush applying colors to the land. What had been mostly brown when I arrived was coming to life in a symphony of hues—green grasses and the sprouts of leaves, gray jagged rocks splattered here and there, as well as small patches of whites, pinks, and purples dotting the land for as far as I could see. In the distance, white peaks were still visible on the mountaintops. And as the sun rose, the sky filled with a canopy of blue, absent of yesterday's clouds.

Letting go of the rail, I wrapped my arms around myself, inhaled the fresh air, and vowed to spend the day productively, not mourning Kader's departure.

Stepping back inside, I closed the door and made my way to the bathroom. Before I could take care of business, the same beeping from last night came from the bedroom. It didn't take long to decipher that the sound was coming from the computer on the desk in the far corner. Even from a distance, I could read the message: INCOMING CALL.

I looked down at the button-up shirt I'd worn as a nightgown. If I had time or even a robe I'd change or at least cover it before answering Kader's call. The screen beeped again.

Sighing, I went to his desk, sat down on his large chair, and touched the screen.

Kader's handsome face appeared.

"Before you yell at me," I began, "I only went onto the balcony."

His green gaze narrowed as he peered at my image. "Is that one of my shirts?"

"Yes."

His head shook. "If I told you to unbutton it for me, would you?"

His timbre caused my nipples to harden as I squeezed my thighs tighter. "Is that why you called, to watch me undress?"

"No, but I'm always open to changing my plans."

"You are?"

"Fuck no. I only have changed my plans for one woman, the one I'm seeing this minute."

My hands moved to the topmost secured button. "If it's what you want...?"

Kader exhaled, his nostrils flaring. "Save that thought. When I return home, you owe me a striptease."

"I do?"

"And when you're done, I plan to fuck you all night long."

My cheeks rose as I lowered my hands back to my lap. "I hope that's a plan that doesn't change."

"You can count on it." His tone grew more serious. "I'm not calling you about the balcony."

I had a thought. "Wait, why aren't those doors locked? You and the house said that all the exits were secured."

"They are. That isn't an exit or entrance. Have you looked down from there?"

I nodded.

"It's built over a steep incline. No one without mountain climbing skill is getting in or out from there."

"So you didn't know I went outside on the balcony?" I asked.

"I did. That's how I knew you were finally awake."

My neck stiffened as I turned to the clock on his bedside stand. "Finally? It's not even seven o'clock in the morning. A woman needs her rest if a full night of fucking is in her future."

The tips of his lips curled. "Seven there is nine here. You make it fucking hard to concentrate. That's why I had to leave."

"Come back. I will try harder."

"I'll come back. Don't try anything. You're perfect the way you are."

"Back at you."

"While you're incredibly sexy with your morning hair and pink cheeks, I called about another of your attributes."

"Okay..." I said, curious as to his meaning.

"Laurel, I am going to send my notes on this assignment—on you. I want you to read through them and comment on anything that feels off or odd. I don't care if it's insignificant. They contain what I've learned in chronological order of when it occurred, not when I learned it. The information is about you and your work. No one knows those subjects better than you. I want your input."

"Have you learned anything?"

"I spoke to Eric Olsen."

"You spoke to him? Is he all right?"

"All right? No. I didn't have the chance to tell you, but a few days ago he was forced to retire from the university, effective immediately, and escorted from his office."

Sighing, I fell back against the chair. "That doesn't sound like retirement. That sounds like termination."

Kader shrugged his broad shoulder. "Tomayto, tomahto."

My head shook as my empty stomach twisted. "This is...I hate this. He doesn't deserve that."

"He signed an NDA regarding your research and development. Everyone associated with it has."

"That doesn't make sense, not if Sinclair Pharmaceuticals is planning to continue the work."

"They aren't," Kader said. "According to Olsen, the negotiation between the university and Sinclair has been terminated."

"Why? The university could have recouped some of its expenses." I couldn't believe I was advocating for Sinclair. I didn't want other people doing Russ's and my research.

"Olsen didn't know why. Signing the NDA saved his retirement benefits."

I leaned forward with my elbows on the desk. "What is happening? Why are they playing hardball?"

"There's some additional information in the notes, but please start at the beginning. The information goes back to before the gathering. I plan to follow a few more leads. In the meantime, I'm hoping that a second set of eyes, especially those fucking blue ones staring at me right now, the ones attached to the smartest woman I've ever known, will see something I've missed."

My cheeks rose as my hands lifted to cover them. "I'm glad you asked me. I like helping. I feel so useless."

"Doc, you're not useless, ever. And you're fucking sexy. I'll call you back tonight. Make as many annotations as you want. I want to know your thoughts on everything."

"Okay. My thoughts are that I miss you."

"Your thoughts on my notes."

I nodded. "Your timing is great. I just told myself I needed to be productive today and not spend the day missing you."

It was Kader's turn to smile. "You can miss me along with helping. The sooner we figure this out, the sooner I'll be back."

"I thought you worked alone."

"Kader did for the most part." He spoke of himself in third person. "There's Jack, but he doesn't know all that I do. Whoever the fuck I am right now likes having you as a partner."

"Jack has to have a clue. I mean he didn't enter that shed with various gun safes and not suspect that you do something with guns and weapons."

"I'm not talking about Jack now," he said. "I'm talking about you. I don't want to do this assignment alone. I want to get back to you."

My head was nodding as my smile broadened. "I want that too."

"After you hang up, go down to the office. There will be a folder on the main screen that is titled 35-IILC. Click on that— nothing else."

"If I click on something else will the house tell on me?"

"35-IILC."

"She knows my name."

Kader's attention seemed to be pulled away. His gaze diverted to the side.

"Kader?"

His green gaze returned. "Laurel, I need to go. Tell me you'll spend the day reviewing my notes."

"I will. Stay safe."

"You too. No doors."

"Okay."

Less than an hour later, I was showered, dressed, and walking to Kader's office with a cup of fresh coffee in hand. Pausing in the living room, I stared out at the view. It was different from this direction, not of the ravine, but the prairie, complete with rolling hills and the mountains in the distance. The earlier fog was gone and the air was as crystal clear as the sky.

As I neared the far end of the room, I was able to see the crushed-rock driveway that led to the outbuildings. Wrapping my hands around the coffee mug, I spoke, "Missy, can you hear me?" I wasn't certain if I needed to be near a screen.

"Yes, Dr. Carlson, I can hear you."

"Is the house secured?"

"Yes, the house is secured."

"What about the outbuildings?"

"There are twelve other buildings on this property."

Twelve?

"Are all twelve secured?"

"There are seven buildings near this house."

"Are the seven buildings near this house secured?"

"Yes, they are secure."

"Where are the other five buildings?"

"The other five buildings are located near the entrance to the property."

"Are those five buildings secured?"

"The other five buildings are currently off-line."

I stood taller. "And you can't tell if they're secured or not?"

"No, Dr. Carlson. I could call Jack if you'd like."

A chill fell over my arms as I recalled my one encounter with Kader's ranch manager. "No, that won't be necessary. Please inform me if anything with this house or the seven buildings near this house changes."

"Yes, I will notify you."

I tried to recall the layout of the land that Kader had shown me from the airplane. "Missy, do you have an aerial view of this property with all the buildings?"

"Yes."

"May I see it?"

"Would you like it to appear on a screen or for me to print it for you?"

"Print it, please."

As I stepped into Kader's office, the printer came to life. Instead of one page, it was four, a puzzle for me to piece together. Staring down at the four sheets, I saw the house Kader called Jack's as well as the building he mentioned housing seasonal ranch hands. The other three buildings were large, larger than either the house or bunkhouse.

I could assume they were barns, but would that be right?

Sitting in Kader's chair, I brought his monitor to life. The only file on the home screen was labeled as he'd said: 35-IILC.

Clicking, I waited as the document opened.

The text was formatted similar to a diary, listing date and entry. The first date caught me off guard. February 1st. I commented off to the side. *I thought you said you took this case a month ago?*

KADER

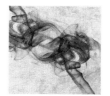

*M*y offer to purchase the illegal sale of Laurel's research and development was approved. I stared down at my phone as the information came through my tight network of firewalls and virtual servers. Keeping my identity hidden was the goal. Thus far I'd succeeded. And yet it was at moments like this that I hated the delays in transmissions.

I sent a message back.

SENDING AGREED-UPON PAYMENT. TRANSACTIONS HAVE BEGUN.

Taking a deep breath, I looked back to the dark screen, the place where Laurel had been in all her just-awakened splendor. Add the extra pinkness to her cheeks from the cool air while she'd been on the balcony and she was a goddess. If I were back at the ranch, the urge to take her back to bed would be too powerful to ignore. That was why I was 1500 miles away and why I didn't have a 24/7 screen running of her presence in the house.

Once this damn assignment was completed, I wanted to imagine that spending twenty-four hours a day in bed was in my future. That thought was the carrot I dangled for myself, a reward for success. I also knew it probably wouldn't happen. Not that I'd fail. I wouldn't. It was that Laurel Carlson had bigger plans for her life than to live on a secluded a ranch in Montana. The woman who'd claimed my heart long before she was a woman had a gift. It was her willingness to learn, her knowledge, and unmatched determination. Her gift was why I hadn't returned her letters years ago, why I'd walked away from the best person to enter my life.

While I didn't want to give her up again and the thought made me physically ill, I knew it was the right thing to do. No matter what happened, I was determined to find a way for her to continue her research.

I looked up as a new message appeared on the screen. While nondescript, it was the same icon Laurel had seen a few days ago. The message appeared as I clicked.

YOUR TIME IS RUNNING OUT.

I'd promised evidence of Laurel's death within forty-eight hours. I'd given my word. In the past that had been enough; never before had any employer required a body. If it was specified upfront that the body was to be found, it was found. Otherwise, I worked at my own discretion. While it wasn't laid out on the screen, something about these messages screamed insecurity. My gut told me that I wasn't the only one whose time was almost up.

I replied.

THE MAN IN THE PHOTO HAS BEEN IDENTIFIED. MY TARGET WAS ELIMINATED. BECAUSE THIS WASN'T REQUESTED PRIOR TO HIT, HER BODY IS NOW UNRECOGNIZABLE. ALTERNATIVE EVIDENCE WILL BE MADE PUBLIC SOON.

I hit send as my network continued to run string after string of data in an effort to localize the geographical location of the person claiming to be my employer. The dark web was vast, its edges far-reaching beyond the borders of our country or any country. It held no limit anywhere on the earth. Pinpointing the location was similar to searching for a virtual needle in the haystack. Sequence after sequence spun, each replacing one element within the string.

To ensure the security of the dark web, layers of input were encrypted. If our correspondence had been on an unencrypted server, I would already have latitude and longitude as well as street address if one existed. I'd been running the search since I received the message nearly two days ago. Progress was being made, but at the rate it was going, I doubted it would occur before it was time to produce my proof.

A quick check of the time told me that it was time for me to make my next face-to-face visit. While this was not usual operating procedure for me, this was not my usual assignment. There was no doubt, killing was fucking easier than keeping someone alive.

It was time to question Dr. Carl Oaks, the dean of the university. Something felt off about him and his role in this whole thing. He could be oblivious to what was happening around him, as Laurel had been. Then again, his assistant, the woman who'd worked for him directly for over a decade had attended the hotel meetings with Cartwright and Moore.

It was something that Olsen said last night that was eating at me.

According to Olsen, Dean Oaks had been the one to tell him the research was to cease. Olsen believed it was due to funding. Yet he never said that was confirmed. I needed to learn why Oaks wanted the research stopped and why he'd said that as long ago as last July, nearly a year ago.

Since in-person interviews weren't my forte, I'd spent the entire night wading through Oaks's and his assistant's emails and phone logs. Not only were they clean, they were fucking squeaky clean, as if someone with a great deal of knowledge had scoured them.

The question was who and when?

Olsen had also mentioned that Oaks ran the university like one of his ships. From that statement, one could assume that Carl Oaks had been navy. While his military service had been easily confirmed, I recognized a whitewashed record when I saw it. Details were lacking. Carl Oaks had reached the impressive rank of rear admiral before retiring with twenty-three years of service. After retirement, he spent six years at a university in Maryland as the dean of the school of finance before accepting the position as university dean in Indiana.

I wanted to find out if he could be the man with the knowledge to sanitize his correspondence and access the dark web with the offer of the research and development for Laurel's formula and compound.

Being Saturday, Oaks's routine meant he would go to a neighborhood diner for a light breakfast and then spend the morning at the driving range. The man was a dedicated golfer. Any Saturday when the sun shone he could be found at the same range. His only deterrents were snow and lightning.

A smile came to my face, if for only a second.

I had another reason for him to miss his weekly date with a bucket of balls—me.

An hour later, outside a small but busy diner in Carmel, I scanned the parking lot.

I'd secured a space beside his Mercedes CLS sedan. As I was about to slip from my rental car, an alarm vibrated on my phone telling me that Olsen was making a call. The minor adjustment I'd made to his phone's software allowed me to be kept apprised of his calls.

Up until now, he'd been quiet.

I sat taller.

Fuck.

Olsen had just made a twenty-six-second call to a number my program recognized.

It appeared I wasn't the only one who wanted to talk to Dr. Oaks.

My plan had been to slip into Dr. Oaks's car and redirect his morning travels.

Holding my phone to my ear, I waited for Olsen's call to replay while watching the entrance and exit to the diner.

"Carl, this is Eric. Call me back immediately. We have business to discuss."

My nostrils flared as I exhaled. "I let you live, asshole. Don't disappoint me."

My breath caught as the dean of the university exited the diner. He wasn't alone.

Fuck.

I recognized the man with him immediately. He was Officer Stanley, one of the fake policemen from Laurel's home. For the next few minutes, Oaks stood in the open lot, speaking with what appeared, due to his gestures and body language, to be determination to make his point. From my vantage point, the former Officer Stanley wasn't saying much in rebuttal, mostly nodding his head to Oaks's comments.

Finally, Dean Oaks turned my way and began walking toward his car. His eyes narrowed and head shook as he approached, yet he wasn't noticing me or my car. With his hand on the door handle, my phone vibrated seconds before Oaks pulled his phone from the pocket of his light jacket. Still standing between our vehicles, his lips were slightly out of sync with the call coming through my software.

"I got your message, Eric. What the hell were you thinking? We have no business to discuss. Never call me again." Oaks glanced around the lot as he opened his door and sat behind the wheel. He started his engine and began to back out of his parking space.

"I-I figured it out," Olsen said. Even without my knowledge of whose phone I'd bugged, I'd recognize the same voice from last night.

Oaks's car pulled back into the space. From my spot, I saw his hands release the steering wheel. "Eric, the paperwork isn't finalized. I suggest you don't push whatever agenda you think you have figured out or you won't see a fucking penny of your retirement."

"I will. I consulted an attorney yesterday. She knows most of what happened. I'm vested. I've done the time. There's nothing you can do to my retirement. And for the record, if you attempt anything that will change that, I'll be the one eating popcorn as the university burns to the ground, taking you and your career with it in flames."

"I don't know what you're talking about."

Though difficult to assess through the darkened windows, Oaks's posture didn't reflect his confident tone.

"I think you do," Olsen said. "You see, I'll have a ringside seat because I'll be the one with the match."

"Eric, you're losing it. That's the real reason the university had to relieve you of your position. Don't make us go public about your mental debilitation."

"You killed them both and now you're selling their research on the black market."

"Delusions don't become you."

"Last night..."

I held my breath waiting to hear the rest of Olsen's sentence.

"...I thought I was next. I thought you'd decided that firing me wasn't enough. I thought my life was over. That gives a man a new perspective. I want a cut."

"Eric—"

"The last bid I heard about was over a billion. I want my share. I put years of my work into that department. Hell, I want Russell's and Laurel's shares too."

"You think I know what the hell you're talking about?"

"I wouldn't be talking to you if I didn't."

"Who have you spoken to about this crazy theory?" Oaks asked.

"Right now, no one, but, Carl, I know this is life or death. I have a backup plan. If that plan goes into effect, you're going down."

"Seriously, Eric, are you off your meds?"

"I have proof of everything I'm saying."

My eyes widened, unsure if I was more upset at Olsen

because I'd let him live and he'd successfully lied about what he knew, or at myself for believing him because he believed in Laurel. It was another example of how she was affecting my decisions.

That had to stop.

My jaw clenched as I contemplated my next move while the two of them continued to talk.

"I don't know what you have," Oaks said, leaning back against his seat. "But this isn't a conversation for the phone. How about I come over to your house?"

"No. I'll meet you in a public place."

"When and where?"

"I'll give you an hour. I know your routine, Carl. Near the driving range where you frequent, there's a small park. I'll be sitting on a park bench people-watching. This time of year, places like that are swarming with all the people suffering from cabin fever and itching to get outside. It's even filled with families. Too many people for anything other than a discussion."

From my angle, I could see Oaks's shoulders straighten. "I'll meet you, not because I know a damn thing about what you're saying, but because I'm concerned for your safety, Eric. You're coming unhinged."

"No more than an hour." The call went dead.

Well, fuck.

Instead of putting his car in gear, Oaks hit a button on the screen upon his dashboard.

I lowered my phone to my lap as I watched his lips move and hands beat against the steering wheel. Whomever he was speaking to was getting an earful. I just wished that were me.

A few minutes passed. As they did, I sent a message to my network to put an active trace on Oaks's calls. I wanted to know who he was speaking with. Before I was done, the engine of Oaks's sedan turned off and the driver's door flung open.

Still paying no attention to the car parked beside him or me, the large man inside, after slamming the door, Oaks marched past my rental car and headed back into the diner.

I had two choices—wait to see what was happening here or stake out the park where their meeting was about to occur.

LAUREL

I sat back against Kader's chair and massaged my temples, flexed my fingers, and inspected my bandage. Hours of staring at the computer screen had me more confused than reassured. It pained me to think that I'd lived so naïvely, sailing through life, work, and even possible relationships totally oblivious to the world around me.

Kader's notes contained the dates and times of each entrance and exit to the hotel room in downtown Indianapolis, as well as the names of those present. Other than hotel staff, the room was only accessed by Russ, Stephanie, and Pam, with the exception of Sinclair's one visit.

I racked my brain, trying to decipher dates.

And then it occurred to me. I could access my data history on the laptop Kader had set up, all the information from my and Russ's flash drives. Since I couldn't take Kader's computer to the dining room, I went to the dining room to retrieve my new laptop.

As I was collecting all my notes and closing the laptop, I

stilled. My hearing strained as the floor vibrated beneath my stocking feet. The sound and sensation reminded me of when Kader flew over the house.

I rushed to the window, hoping to see his blue and white airplane.

Scanning the blue sky, I felt disappointment wash over me. Other than a few fluffy white clouds, the sky was clear and free of airplanes.

Maybe I just missed it, I thought.

With all my things in hand, I went back to the office, and yet my mind was on the sound I'd heard. I pushed a few keys as I'd been shown and called the only person I knew how to contact. After a few beeps, it was clear Kader wasn't going to answer. I clicked the icon to leave a video message. Plastering a feigned smile upon my lips, I looked at the darkened screen. Finally, my own image appeared.

"I'm sorry to bother you. Did you return already? I thought I heard your plane." My breathing caught and pulse took on new speed as the sound returned. I looked up toward the ceiling and back to the camera. "There it is again. Do you hear that?" I stood and rushed toward the windows. Again there was nothing but the usual view. Making my way back to the chair, I sat with a sigh. "I wish it was you. I guess it's someone flying over the ranch." I shrugged. "Maybe it's Jack. Never mind. When you get a chance, please call. I have a few questions about your notes. I..." I took a deep breath. "...can't wait for you to return. I miss you." I hit the button to disconnect before I added the sentence about love.

If the declaration was difficult to voice, did that mean it wasn't true?

Leaning back, I gave that more thought.

Mason Pierce was my first love. When we were teenagers,

the declaration was easy to say and even better to hear. Closing my eyes, I remembered the first time love was mentioned. Of course, I'd thought it. I'd doodled it on my school notebooks—Mason plus Laurel. I'd even told my friends about him. Most of them thought it was crazy for me to like a boy I only saw a few times a month. After all, there were plenty of boys at our school.

That had been true, but none of them were Mason Pierce. They didn't have his intense green-eyed stare, the one that made me feel wanted and admired.

The dichotomy of our lives was evident from our first meeting. Yet instead of creating an impassable chasm, the diversity drew us to one another. Mason was unlike any of the boys I knew. We'd been only preteens when we first met. My life was consumed by school, friends, family, and piano lessons. Disappointments came and went with mundane tragedies that were forgotten the next day. When my parents forbade me from attending my first concert with Ally, I thought life was over.

Getting to know Mason opened a world to me that I never knew existed.

He never complained about his life—caring for his sisters or missing meals. Instead, he'd talk about it like it was an adventure. He was the hero in the story, the one who saved the day. That was how I saw him. If I were honest with myself, it was how I saw him still.

He could claim that he was a killer.

Even before realizing his identity, I saw Kader as my hero.

The Mason I'd loved disappeared from my life. Maybe, just maybe, I was afraid that if I proclaimed my love for him again, he would again disappear.

Once more the floor beneath my feet vibrated. Instead of waiting for the sound, I ran to the windows and peered upward. The rumbling grew louder.

Damn it.

I knew I wasn't supposed to go outside, but if I wanted to see who or what was flying over, I needed a better angle. Still in my socks, I rushed toward the front door. With my hand on the handle, I looked up at the ceiling. "Missy, don't tell Kader." I didn't wait for her answer.

Opening the door, I purposely left it ajar as I stepped onto the porch.

The rumbling I'd heard was fading. It seemed to have gone the direction of the ravine, toward the entrance to the property.

If I waited long enough would it come back for a fourth time?

Sitting on the top step of the porch, I lifted my face to the sunshine. Its warmth radiated over my skin. Squinting my eyes, I peered out at the open land. In the distance, the breeze moved the long grasses, one direction and then the other, as if instead of green vegetation, it was a green sea with waves flowing this way and that.

Though the sun offered heat, a cold chill settled over me, reminding me that I was totally alone, a singular soul in all this vast space.

Please hurry back, I thought as I stood. It was as I was about to turn back to the house that something caught my eye.

The mud from yesterday morning was mostly dried, yet near the edge of the porch were distinguishable footprints, more accurately, boot prints. After a quick check of the still-open door, I slowly descended the front steps. Once I reached the ground, it was evident by the way my shoeless feet weren't sinking that the dirt was now hard and dry. The wearer of the boots must have stood out in this area earlier today or later yesterday.

That was it.

It was yesterday when Kader and Jack had been talking.

I took a few more steps and crouched down, running my fingertips over the dried mud. As I did, my mind filled with contradictory arguments for my earlier assumption.

Jack had been here immediately following the storm. At that time, the ground was so saturated, it was doubtful the prints would remain. More than likely, the slick mud would quickly have flowed, filling in the void. And while Kader was a possibility, the print before me was too small.

I had seen his boots, watched as he'd slid his feet into their depths and as he'd removed them. My heart had pounded as he exposed his colorful and muscular shins and calves if only for a moment, a glimpse.

I ran my fingertip again over the boot print. Standing, I moved my stocking feet to its side.

The print was closer to mine than to Kader's.

I tried to reason.

Maybe as the dirt dried, the print changed in size. There were impression materials that did just that, expanding or contracting.

Wrapping my arms around my midsection, I pivoted, turning a slow circle and taking in the land. While the prints were present, they didn't appear to lead in any direction, as if someone had stood at this point and then evaporated. I studied the house.

There was no advantage to this viewpoint, no windows to peer inside. Only the front porch and the large window above the doors could be seen. That window was too high to see inside.

Though I searched, nothing appeared to be unusual. The only sound was that of the breeze and the rustling of the grass. I began to take a step toward the side of the house when I stopped. Looking back at the porch, I ensured the door was still open.

What did I expect to find?

More prints.

The small-footed individual who left the prints.

And then what would I do?

"You're being paranoid," I said to myself. "It could have been anything. Maybe they aren't really boot prints. Maybe the rain simply pooled.

My counterargument wasn't as convincing as I climbed the steps, walked onto the porch, and stopped in the doorway. Spinning back to the outdoors, I could see various smudges of dirt appeared more pronounced.

"No," I said aloud. "If someone would have been here, Kader's security would have alerted me." Besides, there's no advantage to being on the porch. There was nothing to see.

My reasoning didn't stop my building anxiety.

By the time I reached the foyer and closed the front door, my pulse thumped in my veins and my breathing grew shallow.

It was simply my imagination, I repeated on a loop in my thoughts.

Scanning the entry, I peered up the staircase to the landing and beyond the archways to the various rooms and hallways on the first floor.

"Missy, please tell me that I'm alone in the house."

"If that is what you want."

"I do," I said.

"You're alone in the house, Dr. Carlson."

I looked up. "Did you tell Kader that I went outside?"

"You asked me not to tell."

"I did. Did you tell?"

"Yes, a message was sent."

KADER

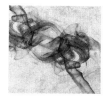

*T*he tracker that I'd placed on the bumper of Oaks's car was visible from the app on my phone. By its estimation we only had about ten minutes before Oaks would arrive at the park where Olsen had told him to meet. His instructions were specific enough that it didn't take me long to find him, the man who last night I'd allowed to live. One more glance at my phone told me I had a video message from Laurel and a notification from the house.

Fuck.

My thumb hesitated, levitating over the icon as I looked up, watching Olsen from a distance behind him. He may have called for this meeting, but by the way his head was moving nervously from one side to the other, he didn't radiate confidence.

Hoping I was making the right decision, I closed the two alerts and focused on my subject at hand.

Waiting for a woman with a stroller to pass the park bench, I approached from behind. Olsen tensed as I stepped around and lowered myself to the seat beside him. With my vision staying straight ahead and my hands tucked into the front pockets of my jacket, I said, "You lied to me."

Before he could respond, I turned toward him. His cheeks paled and despite the spring temperatures, his forehead glistened with a visible coating of perspiration. His lips parted, yet no words came forth as his eyes flickered with recognition of not only who I was but of what I was capable of doing.

That's right, just like the one in a nightmare, this boogeyman is back.

As soon as his gaze met mine, his chin dropped and eyes lowered. "H-how...? Did...you know...? I'm here?"

It wasn't a complete question, yet I ascertained his meaning. My head shook as I spoke low. "No, Dr. Olsen, you are asking the wrong question. It's a shame really. I offered you an opportunity to live and to enjoy life. I asked only one thing in return, the truth. I offered you a future and you squandered the opportunity."

"No." His head shook. "From what I can recall of last night, I never lied to you."

"You told me that you didn't know anything else."

"I didn't lie."

"And yet you claim to have evidence of deaths and black-market sales."

His head tilted before his tone turned indignant. "You're listening to my calls?"

"Not your biggest concern at this moment."

Tears filled his eyes, the droplets teetering upon his lower lids. "When I first saw you, I thought you were going to kill me. I thought Carl hired you like he hired others to kill Laurel and Russell. When I woke with scattered memories of last night, I realized that even though you didn't kill me, I wasn't long for this world.

"Don't you see? If I die too soon, my wife and family may be left with nothing. He will do all he can to take it away, to punish them in my stead. That's why this morning I decided I had nothing to lose. I would leverage my suspicions."

Suspicions. This was fucking suspicions?

I looked at my phone. "You have seven minutes until Oaks arrives. Give me every fucking detail before then. You're also going to wear a wire during your conversation with him."

His head tilted. "Are you law enforcement? FBI or something?"

The tips of my lips curled upward a bit. The last time I'd been asked that question, I was working for *something*—for the Order. That wasn't the case today. This was *my* assignment, my own choice. In this role, I didn't follow orders. That minor detail in and of itself had Eric Olsen's future at a pivotal juncture.

Kader—the determiner of destinies.

"Six minutes," I said. "First, give me your jacket. Second, start talking. Spill everything you know."

"Why my jacket?"

Removing my hand from my coat pocket, I extended it, opening my fingers and exposing my palm. The device I held within was similar to the one I'd placed in Laurel's bra. "This is the wire I mentioned. I'm inserting it into the lining of your jacket. Once it's in place, don't take the jacket off, and I'll be able to hear all that's said."

Exhaling, he lowered the zipper and pulled his arms from the sleeves. Beneath the jacket, he wore a slightly wrinkled button-up white shirt and a dark blue tie. For the first time, I noticed his blue trousers and black loafers.

"Formal for a Saturday."

Olsen shrugged. "I lived for work. I dressed for work. This is what comfortable is for me."

I nodded as I worked to insert the device in the lining. "Talk."

"I-I don't know what to say. This isn't fact. It's assumptions." He scoffed. "Like a gambler desperate for a win, you could say that I'm using what I know and betting on the come."

"What do you know and where did you get the assumptions?"

He sighed. "I know that Oaks isn't the great man he pretends to be. I don't have proof, but I think he'd sell his own mother for the right price."

"He sold you out?"

"Everyone and everything. He sold out the university, the department, Russell, Laurel, the research, and me."

"You said he stopped the deal with Sinclair. So how is he benefiting?"

"He is, not the university."

"Talk."

Olsen fidgeted on the bench, sitting taller only to lean down, placing his elbows on his spread knees. With his gaze out to the walking trails before us, he began, "Not too long ago, I over-heard something that at the time, I didn't quite understand. It was about bids on the research." He looked down at his hands. "At first I thought someone was counterbidding Sinclair Pharma-ceuticals. This conversation I heard happened after normal hours. Most of the people who were still with us had gone home. I was in one of the labs trying to recover data." His head shook. "It wasn't for anything bad. I thought I was recovering the data for the sale to Sinclair, to help the university. Even though I wasn't happy about the idea, mostly because I knew that wasn't what Laurel wanted, I was doing what I was asked to do."

"Stay on track."

Sitting back up, he inhaled. "I am. This happened not long

after Laurel and Russell disappeared; Carl had asked me to bring him everything I could find on their research and development. We all knew that Russell and Laurel had some secret way of separating their data. To keep it safe, they'd said." He sighed. "Their plan didn't work. Well, it did in a way. The data I found was incomplete. So I guess they kept the research safe. I don't believe their plan kept them safe."

"Go on."

"That evening, I'd found some early data from the clinical trials. The files were large. Copying them to external storage took time. While I was waiting for it to download, I turned off the lights." He looked over at me. "I haven't been sleeping well. I thought I could get a few minutes of shut-eye."

The dark circles and bags under his eyes confirmed his statement.

"Who did you overhear speaking?"

"At first I wasn't sure. I think I'd dozed off. I woke at the sound of the door shutting. It was the hushed tones that caught my attention. I don't think they knew I was there. They never turned on the light."

"You didn't recognize the voices?" I asked.

"Partially. I recognized Stephanie's voice. The other person was less familiar."

"Your time is running out," I prompted.

"I could see them. There was a light on in the hallway coming through the window. When I saw the other woman, I knew who she was." His eyes widened. "The other person was Pam, Pamela Browncoski, Carl's longtime personal assistant. She's usually at the administration building, not in our building and especially, not in our labs."

"And you think she was representing Oaks?"

He nodded as his Adam's apple bobbed. "I think she was.

You see, Stephanie was questioning Pam about accepting an offer. She, Stephanie," he confirmed, "mentioned a number in the billions. Pam told her to be patient, saying that *he* wasn't ready to settle." Olsen emphasized the pronoun.

"And you believe that *he* was Oaks?"

"I assumed. As I said, these are speculations."

"Why did you say that you think Oaks hired someone to kill Carlson and Cartwright?"

"Again, supposition. They both disappeared—vanished." Olsen wrung his hands in his lap. "As I said last night, I don't believe the rumors people have been spreading, speculating that Laurel and Russell took off with the research. And..." He looked up from his hands. "When I overheard that conversation, Pam mentioned something about him wanting to recoup the money he'd spent to clear the way."

Clear the way?

"And Stephanie?" I asked.

His head shook. "She didn't seem fazed about Pam's concerns. She was emphatic that their time was running out."

"Whose time?"

Olsen shrugged. "I would assume hers, Pam's, and Oaks's."

I handed Olsen his jacket.

As he put it back on, he added, "Stephanie mentioned another sale had been posted as reason for them to hurry and take the money."

"Another sale of...?" I asked, knowing damn well that it was my listing.

"I assumed Laurel and Russell's research and development."

"Who would have that information?"

The tears came back to his eyes. "Russell or Laurel. But..." His head shook. "I won't believe it's her." He briefly turned my way. "Maybe what she said isn't true. I don't know how to look for illegal sales...*do you?*" he added.

"So others believe that they could be alive?"

"They say they do...I don't know anymore. There is one more option."

"What...?"

Before he could respond, my phone vibrated, alerting me that Oaks was close. Standing, my height eclipsed Olsen from the warming sunshine. Nodding, I said, "You're probably right."

"I am? About what?"

"You're a dead man walking. Go out with glory. Push Oaks and let me hear what he says."

"Can you? Are you someone who can stop him?"

I nodded.

"My family...?"

"They won't be penniless if you help me."

For the first time during this encounter or last night's, Olsen's gaze met mine and instead of averting, remained. "You said I can't trust you."

"What choice do you have?"

KADER

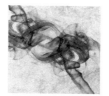

My new parking space allowed for a view of the larger parking lot closer to the main road as well as the park bench where Olsen waited. That wasn't all that I could see. There were walking paths filled with people of all ages as well as dogs of various sizes being walked on leashes. There were also soccer fields in an assortment of lengths with goals sized to match, a large expanse of them off to the side. Along with being outlined in white paint, the fields were surrounded by families. Within, children in bright-colored jerseys ran in pods, chasing a black and white soccer ball.

For a man out of his league, Olsen had made a smart decision to meet Oaks in such a public arena.

I nodded as in the distance, Oaks emerged from his Mercedes. Truly for this area, the make and model of his car didn't stand out in any way. This bustling metropolis just north of Indianapolis was primarily inhabited by those who earned far above the median income. Even this park showcased the dichotomy with the inner-city hellhole where I'd taken Laurel.

Instead of hurrying to Olsen, Oaks stalled, pacing near his parked car.

"What are you waiting for?" I asked softly.

My phone was tuned into Olsen's wire. The only current sound was that of his racing heart. Because the device wasn't as close to his body as Laurel's had been in her bra—fucking white bra—it didn't provide me with a readout of Olsen's heart rate. However, if I were to guess from what I'd observed last night and today, he was close to blowing. The pressure in his older veins was growing higher by the moment, more than likely approaching a dangerous level. If the man were a pressure cooker, the red warning light would be flashing and steam would be screaming at a high-pitched level.

Whether I cared one way or the other about his future, if I were a betting man, I'd put my money on his imminent demise. However, with the way he was sweating and fidgeting, that destiny might not be delivered by an assassin's hand. Eric Olsen could simply keel over of natural causes brought on by unnatural circumstances.

My attention went back to Oaks. Just like at the diner earlier today, he was no longer alone. The fake Officer Stanley was again with him.

After that man helped to take Laurel from her house, I was unsuccessful in getting a hit on facial recognition software for either Stanley or Manes, and ashamedly, I'd let it end there. Seeing Stanley again with Oaks, I made a mental note to go back and learn both men's true identities. I could start with Oaks's phone records. That information was currently accumulating.

After a few moments of talking, Oaks left Stanley in the parking lot and began his approach toward Olsen.

My gaze went between Oaks and Stanley.

Why is Stanley here, Dr. Oaks, if you aren't taking him to the meeting?

The hair on the back of my neck stood to attention as I considered the possibilities.

Stanley was here either to protect Oaks or facilitate Olsen's demise.

As I'd done earlier, Carl Oaks didn't speak until he sat down beside Olsen.

"I'm worried about you, Eric," Oaks said, his voice confident and lacking concern.

"You met with me. That means you agree that I deserve a cut of the payday you're getting from my department's research."

Their voices resonated within the interior of the rental car, clearly coming through my phone.

"You no longer have a department," Oaks retorted. "You no longer have research. You brought me everything you could find. I don't know what you're talking about with a payday."

"I copied everything."

Fuck. What are you thinking?

"Copied?" Oaks asked. "What?"

"I also lied. Russell and Laurel had one other person they trusted with their data." Olsen sat taller. "Me."

"I told you that the research needed to end. You didn't listen." Oaks's tone grew harsher as his volume decreased.

"Give me a cut of what you get and I'll take down my offer to sell."

What the fuck?

Oaks turned toward Olsen. "You son of a bitch. That's you?"

"You thought it was Russell and Laurel?"

"Are you working with them?"

"You know that isn't possible. Tell me who you're working with," Olsen prompted.

"Let's say you're right, that I know about a sale of the research," Oaks said. "I always intended to include you, Dr. Carlson, and Dr. Cartwright. They took off too fast. Tell me where they are and how I can reach them. We'll work this out."

"You can't reach them. You had them killed."

"You're delusional. I wouldn't even know how to do that."

"Really, Carl, you're going to play dumb, a rear admiral who worked in naval counterintelligence. With your background, the ins and outs of that dark world would be easy for you to navigate. You would know how to contact a contract killer. You would know how to post on the dark web."

My mind raced with the new information. Carl Oaks had a history in naval counterintelligence. I'd known he was navy. That was why his record was whitewashed.

Oaks shook his head. "You've read too many thrillers or watched too many movies. My experience with the navy was a long time ago. And in case you missed the part about the navy being us, I wasn't the criminal. I worked for the good guys. Besides, that world passed me by. I'm woefully behind in current technology. You're talking to the wrong man."

In the distance, Stanley had his back toward the park bench, with his phone to his ear.

Are you on a call or are you doing the same as me and listening?

"Five million," Olsen said, "and I'll take down my offer for another sale."

Five million. You idiot. You're too low. He must see it as a bluff.

"Five million," Olsen went on, "and I'll go away. I'll leave you alone, leave the university alone. I won't push to expose Russell's and Laurel's deaths."

"Eric."

Olsen handed Oaks a piece of paper. "Here's my bank

account information. The money better be there in forty-eight hours or I'll take this story public."

Fuck. Did you just hand him account information to your bank?

I was right; Olsen was out of his league.

You're playing a game and you don't even know the rules.

"You'll take fake news public?" Oaks asked.

"I told you that I have evidence, incriminating evidence. Imagine the headline. University dean is suspected in the disappearance of two tenured professors after he personally halts research for personal gain. Once the evidence of their deaths is made public, there will be no turning back the carnage to you and the university."

"Evidence, what evidence?"

Olsen handed Oaks something from his jacket pocket.

"What is this?" Oaks asked as he stared down at what appeared to be a photograph.

"It's a still from one of the main elevators in our building. That's your goon Harding with someone else and Laurel. It was taken during the early morning hours of the day she disappeared. I suspect he killed her. I would wager that he was doing what you'd ordered him to do."

Harding?

Before I left Indianapolis with Laurel, I'd checked the university security. The surveillance videos had been scrubbed. There were no videos of the three of them entering the building, the elevator, or of what happened in the basement. Yet the photo from the person who claimed to have hired me was also a photo from that night. And now Olsen had one.

Had Eric Olsen hired me?

Was he the one desperate for evidence of Laurel's death?

Had I been in the presence of the person who wanted Laurel dead, twice and let him walk?

My gaze went back to Stanley, or rather, Harding. As I scanned the parking lot, my skin prickled. He was no longer standing where he'd been. I couldn't spot him anywhere. It was as if he'd disappeared.

Where did you go, fucker?

Oaks stood. "We're done, Eric. You're losing it. You don't have the proof you claim." He lifted the picture and crumpled it in his fist. "This grainy photo means nothing. It could have been taken at any time on any day. There's no timestamp. The police and FBI have searched the university's security and found nothing to help in the search regarding Carlson's and Cartwright's disappearance or anything incriminating in any way. This photo was manufactured."

Olsen stood. "It's real."

"Then where did you get it?"

"I found it."

"Right." Sarcasm dripped from his one-word response.

"I did. I found it and another picture. They'd fallen under a cabinet near the scanner in my—what used to be my—department. I think someone dropped them."

Oaks stood taller. "What other photo?"

Olsen sat back down, his shoulders straight. "No way, Carl. I have it hidden."

Oaks shook his head. "I don't believe you." He tilted his head toward the parking lot, where Harding had been and then back to Olsen. "We're done."

"We aren't..."

The muffled crack of a single gunshot echoed through the car as the transmitter in Eric's jacket went silent.

Fuck!

I startled, pushing back against the driver's seat as Eric Olsen slumped forward on the bench, his chin falling to his chest, and his mouth opening. Even from my distance, I could see dark crimson fluid seeping through his jacket.

"Fucking hell," I mumbled.

Oaks nodded before straightening his neck and continuing his stroll back to the parking lot. With one last look toward the park bench, he opened the door to his car, looked around, and lowered himself inside. Backing out of the parking space, his dark sedan merged into a line of similar cars waiting to leave the park.

"I'm taking you down, motherfucker."

A woman's scream brought my attention back to Olsen as a crowd began to gather, phones in hand. No doubt the police had been summoned and would soon arrive.

Backing out of my space, I entered the line of cars leaving the park. There was a real phenomenon that law enforcement embraced. Pictures of a crime scene upon their arrival often revealed the killer. The urge to stay present and be voyeur as the police arrive was real. That was why it was time for me to disappear in plain sight.

For once, this time I wasn't the murderer.

A few miles away, I pulled into a parking lot. The program I'd set to trace Oaks's calls was supplying me with various numbers and locations. I would need to enter them into another program to retrieve names. Though I couldn't hear his conversations, I did have information.

My chest tightened. The time of the call corresponded to Oaks's departure from the park. It wasn't the number that caught my attention, but the GPS locator.

Fuck.

LAUREL

*a*s the sun lowered, filling the horizon with beautiful hues of purples and pinks, the temperature outside also dropped. It wasn't that I had gone back outside after I'd earlier tried to see the plane or that it was particularly cold inside Kader's home. It was that I could feel the coolness inside me. When I was young, my grandfather would say he could feel weather change in his bones. I never understood that saying until tonight.

Staring out at the darkening sky, a deep chill settled in my bones, snaking through my skeletal system and leaving a wake of goose bumps upon my skin. I needed a change of scenery. Anything was better than spending another minute in the industrial gray of Kader's office, staring at computer screens while comparing dates from his entries with Russ's and my editing history on our flash drives.

Entering the kitchen, I flipped a switch, bathing the room in golden light, and began my quest for dinner.

The inner chill combined with loneliness as I foraged

through the refrigerator. Preparing our evening meal had become a team effort. Without Kader, I wasn't a team.

My gaze went to the small screen over the counter, wishing for the millionth time that it would beep or ring or do whatever it did when he called. Even though I'd left him a message about the plane nearly five hours ago and I'd opened the front door, I had yet to hear from him.

My urge was to speak out to the house, but truly, each time I communicated with it, I was left with a strange, surreal sensation. Kader had told me that he could go weeks without talking to another person and that was why he'd named the artificial intelligence—AI—in his home. Now after only about twenty-four hours of seclusion, I understood his thought process. That didn't mean that carrying on a conversation with a house didn't creep me out.

It did.

In my old life, the one before the gathering—scratch that, after all I'd learned today, I realized it was the one I *thought* I had —I lived alone. That said, I also worked five to six days a week at the university, interacted in the community by shopping and the like, and spent time and communicated regularly with family and friends.

My current situation grated on my last nerve. This wasn't the same as before. This was a bubble I itched to pop.

I'd stand in the foyer and scream if I didn't think the house would question my actions.

Sitting at the kitchen table, I took a sip of wine and moved the food I'd prepared around my plate. While I should be starving, I wasn't. Even what I assumed was an expensive bottle of wine held no appeal.

Pushing my plate away, I brought my notebook forward and

began scanning my notes. I had a list of observations and questions for Kader.

His first notation had been dated February 1st. As I began to read, I realized that the information he'd gleaned went back to that date; however, it was another two weeks before he was hired. For the most part, I could pair observations such as comings and goings at the hotel with particulars like Russ entering observations from the clinical data. Of course, that added another layer of doubt.

Were his observations accurate or contrived to cover his visit to the hotel?

One of the discrepancies that played over in my mind, one I couldn't confirm or deny, occurred the last night we were all together on the fifth floor. According to Kader's notes from watching security footage from the university, Russ left the offices after me. Despite the inability to confirm it, in my memory, when I'd spoken to Stephanie, she'd told me that he had been there when she left.

It was the night Russ had promised me a rain check for dinner, the night he'd arrived at my house and tried to get me to leave with him before the fake police arrived.

If my memories were correct, Stephanie had lied to me. That thought was another knot in my stomach, a twist confirming that she was hiding something from me. Little did I realize it was her relationship with Russ.

Where had he been between work and his arrival?

Where had Stephanie been?

Were they together?

Those were some of the questions I had for Kader.

Beyond the windows the sun had set, disappearing beyond the mountains.

My thoughts drifted from what I'd been reading to the boot

prints I'd found outside. If I'd walked around the house to the areas with windows, would I have seen more boot prints?

Tucking my lip below my front teeth, I scanned the casing around the large kitchen window. From within, the panes were clear, unobstructed by blinds or curtains. It made sense that in the middle of nowhere, window coverings weren't a necessity.

I couldn't help wonder, though, what if they were?

Though my mind told me that I was being paranoid, I couldn't shake the sense that I was being watched.

Maybe it was by Kader. That was it, he was watching from wherever he was, just as he'd done from his office. That thought lifted my cheeks, bringing a smile to my lips.

Unfortunately, the idea was fleeting as I now stared at my reflection upon the pane.

The small hairs on my arms and legs stood on end, little lightning rods buzzing with energy.

Mentally, I searched the house. Yes, the bedroom had blinds to cover the windows and door. I could go upstairs.

"You're being silly. The house is secure."

Kader had promised security. Even though I could ask Missy the status again, I knew what she'd say. She'd tell me everything was secure and that she'd vowed to alert me if it wasn't.

Taking my plate to the sink, I looked down at my bandage and decided cleaning the kitchen could wait. Instead, I retrieved my glass, adding a bit more wine, and my notebook and headed toward the stairs. As I turned off the lights, I spun back toward the windows and held my breath.

If someone were out there, would I see them?

The rush of my pulse thumped through my veins as the darkened scene came into view. From the movement of the trees, it appeared the wind had picked up since I was outside earlier. And yet there wasn't a person or a set of eyes staring back. It appeared as it had since I'd arrived, a vast area of land.

I let out my breath and headed upstairs. Each light switch I passed, I turned off. It wasn't until I made it to Kader's room and, in the darkness, scanned the empty balcony beyond that I closed the door and then the blinds. Once safe inside, I turned on every light, illuminating the room until it shone like a billboard on Times Square.

The illumination combined with the seclusion created by the blinds chipped away at the cold sensation that had prickled my skin downstairs. Wrapping my arms around my midsection, I inhaled and slowly turned, scanning all about. The bed was made, but mussed from where I'd sat earlier. The bedside stands each contained a glowing tall lamp. In one corner was a smaller version of Kader's desk, complete with screens where he could contact me. The dressers, closet, and attached bathroom were, like everything else within the house, unchanged.

Removing the bedspread, I wrapped it about my shoulders and climbed onto the bed. With the pillows piled behind me and my glass of wine on the bedside stand, I resumed my review of notes.

At some point, sleep had overtaken me. I woke with a start, my breathing shallow and heart beating wildly as I peered about the room. It was still as bright as midday, each light shining brilliantly. I pushed myself up against the headboard and wrapped the bedspread tighter while trying to convince my pulse to find a healthy rhythm.

What had awakened me?

I strained my ears, yet nothing registered.

The clock on the bedside stand told me it was near midnight when beneath me the bed vibrated along with the windows hidden by the blinds.

My body froze in place as my eyes closed, and I listened to the growing rumbling, certain that once again it was an airplane I heard. Louder and louder it came, closer and closer.

If I went out onto the balcony, would I see it?

I hadn't seen it in the light...what made me think I could see it in the dark?

It was then I turned toward the door, the one to the hallway. It was unlocked. Not unlocked, unlockable. My gaze went to the dresser near the door.

With the rumbling now gone, I forced my legs to move, to take me from the bed to the floor. Leaving the blanket behind, I went to the dresser, leaned my shoulder into one side, and pushed. While it budged, mostly my feet slid on the hardwood. Slowly, inch by inch, I pushed until the tall dresser blocked the door, stopping it from opening.

Back to the bed, I pulled my knees to my chest and wrapped my arms around them, hugging my thighs against my breasts. With each passing second, my gaze stayed fixed on the dresser and the door behind.

A million thoughts cascaded through my mind. Why hadn't I gone back to the office? That's what Kader had told me to do. Why hadn't he returned my call? He'd said he would.

Climbing down again from the bed, I went to the computer in the corner. Shaking the mouse, I waited for the screen to come to life. My wrist twisted vigorously, yet nothing happened. Even the small light in the corner wouldn't come to life.

My hands began to tremble as my fingers typed, pushing the keys of the keyboard.

Nothing.

My breath caught as the door to the bedroom moved, colliding with the dresser.

I searched the room for a place to go, anywhere to get away.

There was only one option, one that was probably thirty to fifty feet aboveground.

Opening the blinds, I turned the handle and stepped out onto the balcony. The ground below was shrouded in darkness, yet I'd seen it during the day and knew that jumping was insane. I peered back as the dresser continued to move forward.

Fight or flight.

With my hands on the railing, I lifted myself up as the night wind whipped my hair around my face. Swinging my legs over the rail, I held on, refusing to surrender to the unknown, not after everything Kader had done to save me.

I closed my eyes and leaned forward, my upper body teetering over the expanse. The decision was made. Taking a deep breath, I prayed for a safe landing.

Just as my hands loosened their grip, my arm was seized.

"No," I screamed into the wind.

LAUREL

A powerful force and unbreakable hold.

With my body suspended high above the ground, gravity was on my side. All I had to do was fall. And yet Einstein said there was no such thing as gravitational force. He claimed instead it was the curving of spacetime—that energy told spacetime how to bend, and the bending of spacetime told objects how to move. According to him, the amount of bending was directly related to the object's energy. The object with the most mass had the greatest effect.

That wasn't me.

I planned on the greatest mass being that of the earth below.

Apparently, the man behind me superseded the earth's energy, slowing, stopping, and reversing my fall, pulling me back until I was no longer dangling tens of feet above the ground. The large hand wrapped around my upper arm gripped tighter until my collision wasn't with the land below.

My body was pulled back onto the balcony before crashing against a hard broad chest.

"What the fuck are you doing?" Kader asked, his tone hushed yet forceful.

My arms wrapped around his torso as my chin fell, burying my face in his jacket. Warmth radiated from his being as his sheer bulk sheltered me from the night wind. The dam I'd constructed over the last day, the one holding back emotions, burst. Like a raging river, relief flooded my circulation, weakening my knees and giving power to my current of tears. Bubbling and erupting from my throat, the salty mix covered the leather of his coat as my body shuddered in his embrace.

Even with the whipping wind, my senses filled with Kader, the hardness of his body, strength of his hold, even the scent of his bodywash and cologne. Like a ship lost at sea, in his arms I'd found my harbor. Despite our metaphoric raging storm, I was suddenly and unexpectedly safe.

Holding my chin between his thumb and forefinger, he lifted it higher until his intense stare was all I could see.

"Laurel, I told you to go to the office."

I nodded as best I could in his grasp. "I-I know." My words hiccupped with emotion. "I'd spent all day there. I thought..."

"You thought a dresser would save you, or maybe it was a good idea to plunge to your death?"

"I was hoping that death wasn't part of the equation." My back straightened as I leaned away. "I called you. You said you'd call back."

"I did."

"No, I've been waiting all day." I gestured toward the bedroom. "I have so many things I want to talk to you about."

"I do, too. I did call." His volume was still hushed as he reached for my hand. "Come with me."

The word *where* came to my mind.

That was where the word stayed, never making it to my

tongue. The truth was too obvious. Our destination didn't matter. I would go anywhere with Kader. I would go to the highest mountain or the deepest valley. After slightly more than twenty-four hours without him, I knew without a doubt that I'd follow this man to the ends of the earth.

As we passed through the bedroom, I stopped, slipping on my shoes and grabbing my notebook. When Kader's brows rose in question, I said, "You told me to take notes. I did."

His lips curled and green eyes sparkled. "You mean you are capable of listening to me and following directions?"

"I am. And when we're safe, I will prove that to you."

When I stood, Kader came closer, wrapping his arms around my waist and pulling me nearer until our hips met. "Prove it to me? Anticipate a strenuous test to demonstrate your capabilities."

A long-absent smile came to my lips. "You should know that I'm an excellent test taker."

"I seem to recall a near perfect college admissions exam."

I shrugged. "It was perfect. My dad told me not to brag."

"This test I have in mind requires more than your incredibly high intellect."

Tossing the notebook back on the bed, I lifted my hands to his broad shoulders. "Hmm. Are you suggesting there's a physical-agility component?"

"Yes, that's exactly what I'm suggesting."

Rising to my tiptoes, I brushed my lips over Kader's. "Please don't leave me again."

"I can't promise that, Laurel. Now come with me. I have something to show you."

"Oh, part of my test?"

"I wish."

I laid my hand in his. Kader stopped, turning my hand over and inspecting the bandage.

"I'm sorry."

I shrugged. "It's fine."

His fingers wrapped around mine. "This doesn't hurt?"

"No. I like it."

Hand in hand, we made our way down the staircase. Instead of heading toward the office, Kader led me toward the front door. My feet stalled. "Wait."

"What?"

"There were footprints out there," I said, the memory chilling my skin.

"Footprints?"

"Boot prints. I saw them late this morning."

"They were probably mine or Jack's," he said.

I shook my head. "I don't think so. They were too small."

His neck straightened. "First, I should be upset that you were outside."

"You could be, or you could consider who would be outside your house with small boots."

His nostrils flared as he stood unmoving.

It was as if I could watch the wheels turning in his mind.

"Grab a blanket and pillows from upstairs."

"What?" I asked. "We were just up there."

"I'll get food from the kitchen." His volume rose. "There's a camper in one of the outbuildings. I use it when I spend days on end out on the ranch, checking the fence lines. It's easier than returning every night."

"Doesn't your camper have a bed?"

"Hurry," he said.

Letting go of his hand, I took a step toward the stairs and just as quickly, I turned back. As I'd done so many times since this mountain of a man came into my life, I scanned him from head to toe—his tethered hair, thick neck, broad shoulders, muscular frame, and powerful long legs, all the way to his black boots. As I did, I marveled that he was part of my life—that I was part of his.

Not only was I amazed that we were reunited, but that despite life's twists and turns and the decisions we'd made along the way, we'd found our way back to one another. With this man, I had a sense of wholeness. "I don't want to be away from you."

"Three minutes, Laurel. Hurry."

"Kader..."

"Laurel, we need to hurry. It can wait."

My tongue darted to my lips. "You said something on the call, but I didn't. I want to say it."

His cheeks rose as he nodded. "I know. I fucking know."

I walked back to him. "Then let me say it." When he didn't respond, I vocalized what had been on my mind. "I love you, Kader, or Mason, or any other name, I love *you*. I always have and being with you now, the emotion is so overpowering...I can't believe it's real."

His finger came to my cheek. "It's real. I feel it too. That other name is Price, Edgar Price."

"Edgar?"

He shrugged. "Price was close to Pierce and well, Edgar was a pilot in the Or— arrangement where I worked after I was...we were friends." He sighed. "Laurel, hurry. I'll tell you what I can in time, but first, we need to get out of here."

My grin returned as I made my way back to the bedroom.

Mrs. Edgar Price. Hell no. Dr. Laurel Carlson-Price. Dr. Laurel Carlson-Pierce.

I didn't care which it was.

It seemed that I was no longer the schoolgirl doodling *Mason*

+ *Laurel* in the margins of my science notes. I'd progressed beyond that. I was a grown woman doodling names in my mind.

All the warm feelings from downstairs vanished and a chill came over me as I tried to enter the bedroom. From within, a cool wind howled; its force resisted the opening of the door. Pushing the door inward, I hurried around the misplaced dresser, stepped to the open glass door, and shut the door to the balcony. Immediately, the air stilled and quiet filled the room.

I turned back, scanning from corner to corner.

Didn't we close the door before we went down?

Maybe we didn't latch it?

My arms wrapped around my midsection as I continued my assessment of the room.

Nothing had changed. Even the dresser was still askew.

"Stop being paranoid," I said. "Kader's back. Everything will be all right."

As I reached for the blanket, the one I'd had wrapped around me, I remembered the notebook. I recalled it but didn't see it. The notebook was no longer on the bed where I had tossed it just a few minutes ago. Crouching down, I looked to see if it had been blown onto the floor. Ducking lower, I peered under the bed.

Nothing.

That sense of dread, the one that felt like eerie music should be playing in the background, prickled my flesh as I stood. Keeping an eye on every connecting door, my gaze continued to search as I gathered the blanket and pillows as Kader had said. Pausing at the dresser, I opened the middle drawer and gathered the flash drives. After I'd uploaded their content onto the laptop, I'd stowed them up here. Another glance around the room and I hurried back toward the stairs.

"Laurel." His deep voice came from the foyer. "Hurry."

Standing near the doors, Kader appeared nearly as I'd left him, except now he had the strap of a duffel bag over his shoulder. My shoes gripped the steps as I rushed down the stairway. Nearing the bottom, I met his eyes. As our gazes connected, my stomach twisted.

Something was off. There was something different in his green-eyed stare.

I tilted my head. "Camping?"

He nodded, yet he didn't speak.

"Have you seen my notebook?" I asked.

"You'll love the spot near the river. It's one of my favorites."

I squinted. The shake of his head was almost imperceptible. *Almost.*

Taking the pillows from my hand, Kader hugged them with one arm as he opened the front door and led me into the night.

LAUREL

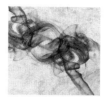

I walked close to Kader as we made our way between
the outbuildings. While the night wind continued to
howl, other than our footsteps, we remained silent. Coming to a
stop near a building I'd never before entered, Kader lowered his
face to the sensor, allowing it to scan his eye. The door opened
with a beep.

As we stepped over the threshold, Kader turned on the overhead lights. Unlike the building with the gun safes, this one was
larger with multiple elongated rectangular lights illuminating the
collection of vehicles within. The concrete floor before us was
filled with a variety of trucks, a pull camper, an RV, and multiple
smaller all-terrain vehicles, such as ATVs, motorbikes, and even
snowmobiles.

"Kader?" I questioned softly.

His finger came to his lips as his head shook one time.

Biting my lip, I nodded.

With my hand in his, Kader led me toward the far end of the
long building. My feet hesitated as we passed the large RV and

then the camper. We came to a stop at a familiar vehicle. It was the old truck, the one we'd driven from Indiana.

My eyes widened and nerves tingled. Again, Kader's finger came to his lips. Opening the driver's side, he threw the pillows, blanket, and duffel bag behind the seats. Helping me into the other side, he hit a button on a panel. The large garage door began to lift as he got into the truck and started the engine.

It was as the door moved higher that it began to hesitate.

"Is it going back down?" I asked, my eyes wide.

"Buckle your seat belt," Kader said as he revved the engine. Reaching behind the seat, he pulled the plush bedspread forward and tossed it my direction. "Cover yourself with this, all of you. Hurry."

My hands shook as I followed his directions. With the blanket over me, I pulled it toward my face.

The truck rocked, forward and backward, until the door lowered closer to the ground.

"Now," he shouted, "cover your face."

The world visually disappeared as the noise level heightened.

The cab vibrated, my breath caught, and my eyes closed as the old truck moved forward. The impact threw me back against the seat, the seat belt tightening, as his foot flattened over the gas pedal, pressing it to the floor.

Once we began to move faster, the old truck skidded upon the rock drive, sending pellets flying. Letting out a breath I hadn't realized I was holding, I removed the blanket from my face. My first concern was for the man beside me.

Was he injured?

Kader's back was straight and fingers blanched, yet he was safe. The windshield was intact and the cab of the truck wasn't compromised. My head twisted about, surveying the damage we'd caused. I gasped, seeing the garage door shattered with shreds of wood and metal splintered in our wake.

"What's happening?" I asked, unsure if I'd spoken aloud.

Taking his phone from his coat pocket, Kader lowered his window and tossed it onto the rocks below.

"You're scaring me."

He still didn't respond. The wheels continued to bounce as we drove through darkness. Instead of heading the direction we'd come when we entered the ranch weeks ago, the way toward the entrance and Jack's house, Kader turned the truck into the night onto the vast prairie. Without headlights it was difficult to differentiate land from sky.

I strained to see the terrain before us, frightened that we'd accidentally come across a ravine or gorge, postponing the plummet to my death instead of rescuing me from it.

After what seemed like hours but was probably less than thirty minutes, Kader brought the truck to a stop, shifted to park, and sighed. Turning to me, he said, "I'm so fucking sorry."

"What is going on?"

With only the light of the moon, I watched as Kader's head shook and he reached toward me, unlatching my seat belt. "Come with me."

I nodded, again certain that the destination wasn't as important as being with Kader.

Stepping out of the cab, I immediately noticed the decreased wind. Looking up, I saw how the night sky sparkled, the perfect black velvet covering sprinkled with glowing diamonds. As I took in the darkened landscape, it appeared that we were in a valley, a bowl. It was the land's topography that was protecting us from the wind. When I turned back, Kader had the pillows and blanket in the bed of the old truck.

With his hand extended, I laid my fingers in his palm. His long fingers closed as he tugged me up to the truck's bed.

"This is your idea of camping?" I asked as we came closer.

"No. This is my idea of running."

"From who? Why did we splinter the garage door all to hell?"

Instead of answering, his green stare washed over me, over all of me.

"Come here, Laurel. I fucking need to be sure you're safe."

Removing his jacket, Kader draped it around my shoulders. As he did, his large palms skirted my arms from my shoulders to the tips of my fingers. His eyes widened as he traced from my cheek to my neck and collarbone. It was as his fingers splayed over each side of my waist that my insides came back to life, remembering what this man was capable of doing.

"I want to fuck you." His declaration rumbled through the cool night air.

"I-I..." I peered up at the vast diamond-studded sky and back to him. "I want that too, but I need to know what's happening."

Kader nodded. Wrapping his arm around my shoulder he brought me close. With the bedspread wrapped under and over us, I laid my head over his shoulder. Beneath my ear, his heart sounded out a pattern—a story in Morse code. Though I didn't understand its meaning, the strong, steady beat helped my pulse return to normal.

With too many thoughts racing through my mind, one dominated. I lifted my chin and stared up at his chiseled jaw, high cheekbones, and furrowed brow. "Kader, are we safe?"

"We will be."

I sat taller. "You said you would call, that you did call, but you didn't."

"I did. I couldn't get through. After noon Indiana time, the house went off-line."

"B-but I thought it was fail-safe?"

His jaw strained. "I fucking did too. It has been since I rigged it."

Thoughts came and went in rapid succession. "I-I haven't spoken to her since about that time." My gaze met his. "She calls me by name."

"Her? Who?"

"The house, Missy, the last time we spoke was after I went outside. Also, she addresses me as Dr. Carlson. She also knew I was officially missing and offered to call the authorities."

Kader's body stiffened. "When?"

I tried to remember. "It was last night, the night you left. She said she knew my identity because of my fingerprint."

"Fuck, Laurel. You need to tell me those things."

"I wanted to tell you a lot of things. I left you a message."

He shook his head. "I received it, but it was scrambled. The last message from the house said that everything was secure and no doors had been breached."

"When?"

"Not long after your message."

"I did breach a door, the front door. I kept hearing a plane. It sounded like yours. I went outside to see." My head shook. "I didn't see it. That was when I saw the boot prints."

Kader's jaw clinched tighter, straining the muscles in his cheeks.

"And my notebook," I went on. "It was on the bed, but when I went back, it was gone."

Taking a deep breath, he ran his free hand over his hair. "This is fucking nuts. I think someone infiltrated my system. How the hell does someone infiltrate a fail-safe protected system?"

"I don't know. From all I've learned lately, nothing is fail-safe, nothing is secure." I let out a long breath. "I was so naïve."

Kader hugged me tighter. "I'm sorry this has happened, all of it."

When I lifted my chin, my eyes were moist, yet my lips were curled into a grin. "Then we wouldn't be together."

"You'd have the life you deserve, the one you've worked so fucking hard to have."

"You said I'd get that back. I want that but not as much as I want to be with you."

His head shook. "In the middle of nowhere Montana, in the back of a truck, on a cold spring night?"

I draped my arm over his torso. "Those are two separate things. It's not the *where* I care about. It's the *who*."

Kader took a deep breath, his chest rising and falling. "Laurel, I learned a lot in Indiana. Not enough."

"Not enough to be sure I'm safe?"

His head shook. "No. This is bigger than it looks."

LAUREL

While Kader's words induced fear, his presence made the words tolerable.

"How big?" I asked.

"Bigger than you and Cartwright, bigger than the university and Sinclair Pharmaceuticals, and bigger than what I've learned in Indiana."

"Please tell me what you've learned."

He let out a long breath. "Going back, as I told you before, I spoke to Olsen. I thought I trusted him and he'd been truthful."

"You thought?" I asked.

"That was the other day. This morning...probably yesterday by now...he called Oaks."

"Dean Oaks? What about?"

"Long version or CliffsNotes?"

"CliffsNotes."

"I'll try not to repeat what I told you on our last call, but I want to keep it chronological."

I nodded.

"Olsen believed that Oaks was behind everything, starting with ending the research. According to him, Oaks first mentioned ending the research last summer."

With each word, my head shook in disagreement. "No, Eric never said anything—"

Kader's finger came to my lips. "The CliffsNotes aren't short, Laurel. Just let me talk."

I nodded under his touch, marveling that even in the middle of a deep valley, with my life imploding in all directions, simply being in Kader's presence steadied me. It was as if I could hear what he was going to tell me, not because I welcomed the information, but because I wasn't alone.

"And then he called him into his office the end of last year and said the research had to end and the lab had to close. Period." Kader continued, "When he again didn't elaborate on the reason for his decision, Olsen believed it was due to funding. Olsen talked to other deans and decided to push the investor route."

"So that was all him? He'd brought up the excessive spending, but Russ and I were under the impression it was Oaks who pushed."

"According to Olsen, Oaks never specifically cited spending and expenses as the reason. That was another of Olsen's assumptions." With a grin, he added, "Just so you know, each time you interrupt me, I'm adding a new exercise to that agility test."

My cheeks rose as my hand came to rest upon his broad chest. "You really suck at the scary persona. Testing or requiring additional sexual dexterity isn't a deterrent."

"For the record, that's three interruptions."

Before I could respond, Kader continued, "Oaks wasn't happy that the research was continuing. He gave Olsen an ultimatum, saying that no matter what, all of it would be discontinued after this semester. And because it was incomplete, nothing would be published. The university had the rights to the data and it would all be buried as if it hadn't happened."

Just like the project I'd been involved in during grad school.

My mind swirled, a cyclone of dates and instances. The revelations sickened me as well as the success of the plan. It may not have happened as Dr. Oaks ordered; nevertheless, Russ's and my research was now stopped. The end goal was the same.

"After you and Cartwright disappeared," Kader went on, "Oaks asked Olsen to compile all the research and development data he could find and he did. Olsen thought he was pulling the data together for the sale to Sinclair—which doesn't make sense now since that sale was stopped. Olsen said he was shocked when Oaks pulled the plug."

"But why stop it? The university could have recouped—"

Kader's finger stilled me again. "Four."

Inhaling, I allowed the fresh night air to fill my lungs before exhaling.

"Not selling the research goes along with discontinuing it. I just don't understand why. I think I told you," Kader went on, "but according to Olsen, Oaks was also the one who pushed Olsen's departure from the university, making him retire or he would lose his retirement buyout."

"Yes, and you said Dean Oaks made Eric sign an NDA."

"Sound familiar?"

"It does. It sounds a bit like that project during graduate school."

"That's what I thought of too. Well," Kader went on, "this morning Olsen called Oaks and basically demanded a meeting, claiming he knew everything."

"Why? What everything?"

"Laurel, I'm losing count."

I shrugged. "Five, unless you count the NDA discussion."

"Too fucking smart for your own good." Kader shook his head as he tugged me closer, the warmth of his embrace my shield against his discoveries. "I spoke to Olsen for a few minutes before his meeting. He added to the story he'd told me before. He said he'd overheard a conversation between Oaks's assistant and Stephanie Moore. This happened after you and Cartwright disappeared. He heard Stephanie tell Pam that their time was running out and the highest bid needed to be accepted. Pam replied that *he* wasn't ready. He wanted more money to recoup his expenses."

My stomach twisted as the blood drained from my cheeks. I sat upward. "So Eric is saying that it was Dean Oaks? He was the one who paid to have me and Russ killed?"

"I still don't know if there was a contract out on Cartwright. He was involved in the hotel meetings, remember?"

I did. I'd been looking at the dates all day.

"What did Stephanie mean that the time was running out?"

"I'm not sure. Maybe someone discovered the second listing. Besides..." Kader shook his head. "...I haven't been able to confirm that Oaks is the one who hired me. I'm getting closer to tracking the cryptocurrency transactions. It's usually anonymous. What's helping now are the number of transactions."

"I hate that you spent so much..." I didn't finish the sentence, instead exhaling.

"I'm doing my best to track it. It isn't as simple as it sounds. Each transaction takes a different route through the hidden dark web, passing through multiple firewalls, shells, and phony institutions. It's the final destination I want. If my program is correct, they appear to be ending at a depository in the Cayman

Islands. That's not an extraordinary destination. A lot of Americans use the Caymans to hide money. Connecting it to Oaks or anyone will take more time."

"Would it be extraordinary if Dean Oaks had a home on Grand Cayman?"

He inhaled. "I should have found it."

"You can't know everything. And to make it more difficult, the home isn't in his name. I remember talking to his wife one time at a cocktail party. She was on her third or fourth glass of wine and in the mood for sharing. She said something about leaving Carl and going to the Caymans. She said why not, reasoning that unlike the house in Indianapolis, the house there was in her name."

His brow furrowed. "Same last name?"

"No. She didn't change her name because she outranked him in the navy when they met. She retired after they married, and he went on to accomplish bigger and better things. I always got the feeling it was a bit of a sore subject for her. He got the awards and honors; she stayed home with the children and played the role of admiral's wife." I shrugged. "Their children are grown now and live all about. I think she feels she missed an opportunity...anyway, she retained her last name—Givens, Edith Givens."

"Funny, Oaks never mentioned family," Kader said. "Olsen, however, was concerned about his wife and family. He said more than once that he was afraid Oaks would have him killed just like he did you and Cartwright."

My eyes opened wide. "Isn't that confirmation?"

"No. Not when it comes to Olsen. He made many unsubstantiated claims. When I asked for proof, Olsen said it was speculation. Until..."

"Until what?" I asked.

"Until he tried to capitalize on those same speculations. I placed a wire on Olsen for his meeting with Oaks. He told Oaks he wanted a cut of the money for the sale of the R&D. Claiming he had the proof, he pushed Oaks. When Oaks asked for proof, Olsen showed him a picture of you and the fake police in the elevator at the university."

My neck stiffened. "I thought you said the security feeds were spliced or cleaned by someone else."

"They were. Interestingly, Olsen knew the name of one of the fake policemen. He said his name was Harding and that he worked for Oaks. As if to confirm that bit of information, Harding was also with Oaks at breakfast and again at the rendezvous point."

I pressed my lips together, fearful of hearing more yet unable to stop listening.

"I don't believe Olsen recovered the photo from the security footage," Kader said. "The day after I took you from the elevator, nothing was on the university's security footage. I don't believe he could access or erase it." He shrugged. "I'm not even sure if Olsen showed Oaks the same photo as the one my employer sent me. I only heard his description; nevertheless, it sounds similar."

"So it wasn't Dean Oaks who sent that message to you. It was Eric?" I asked as a lump came to life in my throat.

"I don't think so. He said he *found* the photo near a scanner in your department. I believe Olsen was pushing his luck by pressing Oaks. By Olsen's own admission, he was piecing together clues without any real evidence."

"He found it in our department? There were multiple scanners and printers." My eyes opened wide and my hands came to my cheeks. "Oh, if Dean Oaks *is* guilty, Eric needs to be careful.

Can you help him? I know you say I'm too trusting, but I don't believe he's the one. First, if he had that kind of money, he wouldn't be so worried about his family. Second, he believed in us."

Kader let out a long breath.

KADER

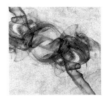

The look on Laurel's face, her expression of trust and concern, tore at my insides. I'd been there when she'd seen Cartwright's body. This wouldn't be as traumatizing. Nevertheless, it was still another colleague dead.

"Kader?" she asked, her big blue eyes pleading.

My lids lowered as I took a breath. "He's dead, Laurel. Eric Olsen pushed too hard."

In my grasp her body stiffened.

"How?"

"Gunshot. Right the fuck in front of me."

"You didn't..."

My head shook. "No, I didn't. I had the opportunity to end his life the night before. I didn't. By the way he slumped forward, the trajectory of the shot came from behind. Oaks was to his side."

Again, her eyes were wide. "So the shooter was trying to get him too?"

"No," I replied confidently. "Oaks stood, gave the signal, and before I could move, Olsen was gone. Oaks simply turned away and left the park. He fucking knew what was happening. He called for it, essentially as guilty as the fucker who pulled the trigger. Olsen didn't have a chance. He signed that death warrant the minute he pushed Oaks."

"A park? They were at a park. Didn't people hear the gunshot?"

"A silencer doesn't really silence, not like in the movies," I explained. "However, if you add to that somewhat-muffled sound with cars coming and going, kids playing and screaming, babies crying, dogs barking, and whistles from referees blowing..." I thought she was getting the point. "There's a lot of noise competition. People rarely assume the worst. Instead they make rational excuses such as a car backfiring."

Lowering her head again to my shoulder, Laurel sighed, her body losing its rigidity. I reached for her chin and brought her beautiful gaze to mine.

"Tell me what you're thinking."

She sighed. "I'm not even sure. I'm trying to remember."

"What?"

"Everything and nothing," she said, her eyes glistening in the moonlight.

"I think Olsen was an honest man who feared for his life and his family's future. He risked everything to get more for them. Some could call that greedy."

Though they'd been closed, Laurel's eyes popped open. "Kader, that's what Russ said about Dean Oaks, that he was greedy."

Like an extremely slow-moving game of Tetris, the pieces were clicking.

Cartwright said Oaks was greedy. Cartwright was at the hotel meetings. I wasn't going to bring it up again to Laurel, but my gut told me that Cartwright was in the thick of this with Oaks. My question remained—what got him killed?

"I fucking wish we had a better shot of the person who entered your house with Cartwright."

"The picture blacks out too soon."

As if the person knew my system.

That thought brought back the itching to my skin. I fidgeted on the truck's hard bed.

Like the person who has breached my house.

"I also wish I could recall the notes I took," Laurel said.

Leaning my head against the back of the cab, I closed my eyes. "Maybe we should sleep and resume this in the morning?"

Laurel curled closer, her arm stretching over my torso beneath the blanket. "I agree, but..."

My eyes opened as she peered upward.

"...you said you'd call. I have so many more questions. Why was the house off-line and why did you say we were camping when we are in an open truck bed? Why did you crash your own garage?" She sat up. "Why did you throw your phone?"

"Laurel, I don't want to..."

...scare you.

...tell you.

...voice my thoughts.

I didn't know how to finish the sentence.

I bristled as my mind wrestled with the evidence.

Was my evidence any more concrete than Olsen's?

"Kader, tell me."

"It goes back to the fail-proof security in my house. I thought it was odd when I couldn't reach you and when your message to me was scrambled. I told myself it was due to a storm. I was too busy with Olsen to check the radar and some-times the weather can get pretty violent here."

Her head shook. "No, it was windy, but that's all. No storms since the other morning."

"After Olsen called Oaks, I began running a search backdooring into his cell phone provider, tracking his calls. I couldn't listen in, but I could determine the other phone number, location of both callers, and length of call."

I closed my eyes momentarily, recalling the GPS locator's readout on the recipient of the call Oaks made after Olsen's death. Just like when it appeared, my chest tightened. "I immediately tried to call you. I tried to call Jack. Everything was down. I couldn't reach either of you."

"I was never far from a screen. I kept waiting."

"The calls didn't go through."

"Why?" she asked. "What did you want to tell me?"

I reached for her hand and squeezed. "I wanted to fucking tell you to get to the office, to the safe room."

"Why?"

"The person Oaks called after Olsen was shot wasn't his goon. The call didn't originate and end in Carmel, Indiana. The coordinates on the phone that received the call came up as this property." My words came faster as I vocalized what I'd seen. "You see, this place isn't really a location—there is a city listed on the address, but in reality, my property isn't within its limits. The location came up as latitude and longitude." I pulled Laurel closer. "Fucking here. I know every goddamned inch of this land."

"Pretending to take the camper? Running into the door?" she asked.

"I trust my gut."

She nodded.

"We were being overheard. Everything I said about the camper and the river was to send whoever it is in the wrong direction." I gestured toward the truck. "This is a piece of shit. I had no intention of keeping it. I just bought it for the assignment. I have been a bit busy and haven't had time to dispose of it. Every other vehicle in that garage is microchipped. For lack of a better explanation on why we took this one, it isn't chipped. It isn't traceable."

"Your phone?"

"Same thing. Someone could rightfully assume we're out here on the property, but the exact location can't be electronically verified." I took a deep breath. "Laurel, I don't know how it was done, but the house, my security, it's been infiltrated. Although it doesn't fucking make sense, it's the only plausible explanation."

Sitting up, Laurel asked, "Is someone after *you* because of *me*?"

"Oaks isn't that smart. His goon isn't that smart. He's a fucking good shot, but I can't believe that either one of them could get back to me even if he is the one who hired me."

Her hand began to tremble. "So that means whoever is here on this property is here for *me*. How do they know I'm here? I have nothing—no phone or anything. I promise I wasn't online. I've done everything you said."

Cupping her petite hands in mine, I softened my tone. "I believe you, Laurel." My head shook. "I don't know how you were found. We've taken every damn precaution and now we're running blind. We can't go back to the house. I could try to make it to Jack's, but the sensors I've placed on the land need to be avoided. Every fucking thing I did to protect this property has now potentially turned against us."

"Shouldn't you tell Jack?"

"I should." I took a deep breath and sat taller. My gaze scanned the crests of hills surrounding us. We were in a bowl. I'd come here on purpose. No one could approach from any direction without being seen. "Tomorrow, I'll move the truck and hide it as much as possible. It's roughly a four-mile hike to his house. The land isn't perfectly square, and with the topography and avoiding the sensors it will take a while. You'll be hidden. I'll go as soon as the sun rises and get back as soon as I can."

Laurel jumped upward. "You are not leaving me again. No."

"I'm keeping you safe."

"Then keep me safe with you. I'm not asking. I'm telling you. You're not leaving me."

Inhaling, I ran my hand over my hair, my mind filling with possibilities. I didn't want to believe that Jack was compromised in any way, yet I couldn't shake the feeling, the feeling in my gut. It was an instinct that rarely failed me.

He was my only team, only confidant.

I hoped this time it was wrong.

Over the years, I'd risked my life for Jack, for Commander Jackson. It wasn't a one-way arrangement. He'd done the same. I'd put my life on the line for him and he'd done the same for me. That loyalty was not only ingrained but had been tested. There was only one thing bigger than our fellow team member in the Order.

One thing.

The Sovereign Order.

The good of the country, the republic, and the democracy.

There was no fucking way the Sovereign Order was involved in this assignment.

When called upon by them, I'd answered. Jack and I still answered their call. Edgar Price wasn't contacted via ex-Commander Jackson to kill Dr. Laurel Carlson. Even the thought of that made my skin crawl. No, this was a random assignment Kader had accepted on the dark web.

Not even remotely the same.

Pulling the blanket with her, Laurel sat up, cupped my cheeks and shimmied over my lap until she straddled my legs. Leaning forward until her nose was before mine, she stared into my eyes. "Tell me what you're thinking," she asked.

Had she asked, or was this gorgeous, trusting, and brilliant woman demanding the truth from me as I had from her?

"Laurel, I'm the one who makes the demands."

"Most of the time."

I lifted my hands to her hips, splaying my fingers.

The air rippled as a low, guttural sound emerged from my throat.

With every ounce of self-control, I fought the need to pull her down, push her against me, and feel her blue-jean-covered pussy grinding over my cock. Forget the damn blue jeans. The way she was moving, not humping, just rocking enough to fucking scramble my thoughts and redirect my circulation was going to ignite the denim until there was nothing between us.

LAUREL

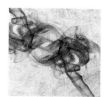

I allowed Kader's jacket to fall from my shoulders, for the cool night air no longer registered. With my knees on either side of his thighs, I reached for the hem of his shirt and pulled it upward. With only slight hesitation, Kader lifted his arms, allowing me to slip it over his head. In the silver moonlight, his tattoos took on a spectacular glow, the colors losing part of their shine while the black outlines and shapes came more into view.

Sitting back, I ran my fingertips over his chest. With each swoop of my touch, his grasp of my hips tightened. His fingers dug deeper and the muscles beneath the inked masterpiece tightened as he fought his need to stop me.

When our eyes met, I reached for the hem of my shirt and pulled it up over my head. I'd promised him a striptease when he returned. This might not be what either of us had in mind, but it was working. As I unclasped my bra, allowing it to fall forward and the straps skirted over my arms, the air around us filled with a long hiss.

It wasn't the rattlesnake he'd warned me about, the one he'd mentioned to scare me. No, there wasn't a dangerous hissing serpent in the grass nor had one slithered into the truck. The hiss came from the handsome yet sometimes frightening man beneath me, the one whose cock pushed against his zipper, the hardness pressing against my core.

Rolling to the side, I slipped my feet from my shoes and wriggled out of my jeans and panties.

When I turned back, I momentarily wondered if the zipper had lost its battle or if Kader had freed his giant cock. Neither answer was wrong; both were right. I didn't care how it happened, only that his thick rod was standing erect, its length and increased circulation weighing it down.

Leaning forward, I wrapped my hands around his girth and licked the pre-cum from the tip.

"No fucking way," he growled as he palmed my hips and lifted me over him. "I'm coming in that warm pussy."

Peppering his bare chest with kisses, I positioned myself over him until my hands were upon his broad shoulders.

Holding my hips in an unbreakable vise, Kader forbade me from lowering myself and taking him inside me. My heady breaths became quicker as he leaned forward, his mouth seizing my nipples, kissing, licking, and biting. With each ministration my circulation sped faster, my breasts became heavier, and my nipples drew tighter. Those weren't my body's only reactions as I wiggled against his hold. My wet core clenched with need, yet he wouldn't allow it, keeping me lifted high enough to tease me with his hardness and still not fill me.

"Please," I pleaded.

"Are you ready for me?"

"Oh." I didn't have time to answer before his grip of my hips shifted and I was pulled down, my core sheathing his cock.

My back straightened as I sucked in a breath. It was as I exhaled that my answer came in between panting breaths. "So ready."

"You're fucking amazing," he growled as he began to raise and lower me.

I was on top, but this was his show. He was the director and producer, the one in control of every aspect of the production. Oh, I was his chosen starlet. That alone gave me a sense of worth and a feeling of power. In reality those emotions were part of his illusion. Like the master craftsman he was, Kader would take me to the precipice, loosen his hold, and allow me the freedom to move and to ride as my body came closer to coming undone. My nails tightly gripped to his broad shoulders, the rougher surface of his skin saving him from injury.

The tightening grew painful, the need overwhelming as the finale came into view.

With his neck strained and his beautiful colors on display, Kader would call cut to the production, keeping me from the prize. It was the game he enjoyed playing, his way to control every aspect from our position to my orgasms. It wasn't as if he were closing the curtain on the show. No, he was simply redirecting my movements, calling for a redo until he once again had me at the edge.

Even surrounded by the dark, cool air, my skin slicked with perspiration. Beneath Kader's tattoos, his muscles tightened and pulsated. It wasn't until my mind could no longer hear his commands and my body was strung too tight to stop my implosion that he pulled me lower, closer, stretching my thighs to the point of pain that we both finally came undone.

Collapsing over his massive chest, his embrace surrounded me, holding me secure. Though my eyes closed and my energy was depleted, my body continued to quake and my muscles within quivered. The sound of our breathing filled our ears as skin to skin, our hearts beat against one another.

I don't know how much time passed before we turned, rolling onto our sides and breaking our union.

Kader's finger pushed the tangled strands of my hair away from my face. "I'd give up everything to keep you safe."

Tears came to my eyes as I lifted a hand to his cheek. "I don't want you to do that."

"Laurel, you said it yourself. It's not the where. It's the who—and you are her. There's nothing here—not one damn thing—that's more important than you, than your dreams and future."

"That's not true," I said as the earlier lump grew in my throat, choking out more of a response.

"It fucking is."

"I love you and you've said you love me. That means this isn't one way. You want what's best for me and I want what's best for you, too. I couldn't...I wouldn't ask you to give up any of this. This land is you, wild and untamed, dangerous and beautiful. It's a rush of nature, a contradiction in qualities—callous and harsh yet peaceful and calming. This is where you belong."

Kader sat upward and pulled the blanket around us. As he settled against the pillow at my side, looking up to the vast sky, he said, "When I came here, I didn't know where I belonged. I didn't remember anything." He turned until we were again nose to nose. "I wasn't sad."

"Good. I don't want to think of you sad."

His head shook. "I wasn't." His palm came to my cheek. "I also wasn't happy. I was present. I can't explain it. Danger didn't scare me. Send me in to an impossible situation and I didn't worry about mortality, only success. Close calls didn't cause my heart to race. I succeeded or failed, mostly succeeded. I didn't rejoice or mourn. There was a reassuring sameness to every day and every situation. Even sex did little to change the constant equality." He shrugged. "I guess it felt like relief. Nothing, fucking nothing like it is with you. I want you so badly it hurts. It's also dangerous. Before, I never would have done what we did tonight."

"Have sex in an open truck?"

"No, Doc. Run. Tonight I ran. I was so fucking scared. All the way back here from Indianapolis, I imagined a million scenes. None of them were good. I couldn't reach you. I had images of finding you dead, hurt, anything..." He ran his finger over my cheek. "...but the way you are this moment."

My cheeks rose. "I'm a mess at this moment."

"Freshly fucked is the perfect mess. To me, you are radiant."

The flood of endorphins from the high Kader had just taken me on began to fade as my education and research came back into focus. "Are you saying that before remembering who you are or were, you'd lost your fight-or-flight impulse?"

Kader's eyes narrowed. "What have I said about analyzing me?"

I sat up, my hand on my pillow as the cool breeze blew over my skin. "I'm really not."

"Bullshit."

Tugging at the blanket, I brought it over my chest as new ideas filled my cyclone of thoughts. "Your memory, how did you lose it?"

"Laurel."

"Mason, you had a life and a family. From what I read after you died, you were a war hero whose last known address was Chicago. You had left the military with honors and went on to college to earn a degree." I tried to think back. "I can't remember your major, but I think it had something to do with computers. You also worked for a real estate investor...I don't recall the name." Since he wasn't stopping me, I continued, "The fatal injury you sustained wasn't in the military, and yet somehow the past I just mentioned all disappeared from your memory. I'm asking how?"

He turned and exhaled, his gaze pointed unblinkingly toward the stars. "Computer engineering and the company was Sparrow Enterprises."

I'd heard that name before.

"Do you remember Lorna?" he asked.

"I do."

"I do now too. When you're safe, I would like to try to find her if she's still...alive." He exhaled. "If she isn't, it's my fault."

I leaned over him, my breasts flattening over his hard chest. "She was. She was the one who contacted me when you died."

His green eyes came my way. "Was she still living in Chicago?"

"I don't know. Her letter came with no return address. There wasn't even indication that the envelope had been processed at the post office. No stamp. No postmark. I'm not sure how she even found me. It was weird, almost like the letter was magically placed in my mailbox."

Kader's lips curled upward. "There aren't many people who could do that."

"I thought it was odd."

"Not many, but there are a few. I wonder if she's still with them." He sighed, his smile fading. "They probably fucking hate me. If they don't, they will when they find out I didn't die."

There was something in his gaze, a faraway look that saddened me, making me want to do anything in my power to take it away. "I'm glad you didn't die, and I don't hate you."

His hand came to my shoulder as he pulled me closer. "If you do, you have a strange way of showing it. I especially like the thing you do with your hips just before your toes curl."

"Who is them?" I asked, ignoring the heat in my cheeks.

"People I once knew."

Sighing, I laid my head on his shoulder.

As we stayed that way I listened to his breathing, the beat of his heart, and the breeze. Perhaps as we lay in the calm, I should have been thinking about the people he once knew. Maybe he was. I wasn't. Instead, it was my life's work that came back to me.

It was possible for a traumatic event, such as an explosion, to result in amnesia brought on by either physical brain damage or psychological coping. The origin often played a role in the severity. It was also possible that the amnesia could erase all past memories. Yet it seemed unlikely that amnesia of either origin would interfere with the hyperarousal or acute stress response known as fight-or-flight.

That response was inherent and wasn't limited to humans.

Animals of all intellectual capabilities innately possessed the same physiological reaction to perceived threats. It wasn't a learned response, not something that could be taught or forgotten. Lab rats separated from all contact at a very young age still possessed that particular reaction—a fear of threats.

The reaction was chemical, the body's response to the adrenal medulla's secretion of catecholamines, particularly norepinephrine and epinephrine. Hormones also played a role in the body's response to stress. Memories were capable of spurring the chemical secretion. Yet the opposite didn't apply. Even without memories, the secretions occurred.

The only way the response could be overridden was by suppressing the secretion, perhaps with physical alteration of or damage to the adrenal medulla located in the adrenal glands.

While that would suppress the fight-or-flight response, it wouldn't cause the loss of memories.

These were two related but separate bodily functions. Memories were produced and stored in the limbic system within the brain, more specifically the hippocampus. The reaction to perceived dangers such as the fight-or-flight reaction was brought on by secretions from the adrenal glands, located at the top of each kidney.

The side effect of losing that reaction as it was connected to traumatic memories was what Russ and I had been trying to avoid in our research. That was why we didn't want the traumatic memory gone. We wanted to soften the body's psychological and physiological reaction to the memory, not curb a person's ability to sense danger.

Thoughts of our work lulled me to sleep as Kader held me close.

When my eyes opened, the sky above us had begun to lighten. It wasn't the sunlight that woke me. It was the rumbling. My skin prickled as I listened.

It was the same yet different.

I shook Kader. "I hear a plane."

KADER

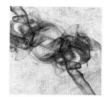

*J*umped up. The cool morning air upon my skin reminded me that I'd slept shirtless. For the first time I could recall, that wasn't my priority. Nor was the fact that I'd slept in the back of a fucking truck bed, closing my eyes and falling asleep, something I hadn't done the entire time I was in Indianapolis.

Running my fingers through my now mostly loose hair, I removed the tie. Sliding it over my wrist, I listened to the sound that had woken Laurel. Blinking, I squinted toward the rumble and stared upward, searching the whiteness. Yesterday's warmth combined with last night's cool had worked together to give us the perfect cover. We weren't hidden beneath trees as I'd planned; we were hidden in a bowl filled with fog.

"Do you hear it?" Laurel asked, pulling her shirt over her head, the rest of her clothes now also in place.

"I do. It's not a plane."

Her lips formed a straight line as she too tilted her face upward toward the sound. "I think you're right. It sounds different than yesterday." Her eyes opened wide. "Is it a helicopter?"

After I pulled my shirt over my head, covering my chest, torso, and arms, I reached for Laurel's hand, trying my best to sound calm. "Yes, that's what it is. And it's flying over my land. That means only one thing." I didn't wait for her to respond. "It's fucking looking for us."

We both hopped down from the tailgate.

"What are we going to do?" Her eyes darted all about. "This fog won't last forever."

"No, but damn." I looked up as my cheeks briefly raised. "We couldn't have asked for a better cover." The whirring grew closer.

Laurel grabbed my arm. "Will they come down here?"

"Not without reason. Fog is one of the worst conditions for chopper flight. Pitch black is better. If they could track us here, they might, but they can't. No phone. No chipped vehicle. We're fucking invisible. Unless..."

"Unless what?"

"They have thermal infrared sensors." I was thinking the way I would on a mission, anticipating the worst-case scenario from my enemy. "Our saving grace may be the larger mammals on this ranch. Not only the horses, but in the wild we have—"

"You told me about the large cats and black bears."

"There are also bison, deer, and bighorn sheep. Heat alone won't make a seasoned chopper pilot risk the fog."

Her eyes closed as she exhaled and leaned closer. "You know, you keep doing it."

I wasn't fucking sure what I was doing. We were hiding in a fog basin and now there was a helicopter searching my land. "I'm not doing anything except fucking up your life."

"You're saving it," she said matter-of-factly. "Because of you, I have a life."

Going to the truck bed, I lifted my jacket and wrapped it around Laurel's shoulders. The black leather enveloped her petite frame. Taking her hand again, I scanned the valley. The dense fog swirled around us as the rumbling of whirling blades lessened, moving farther away. While the increased distance reassured me, the whole idea of someone searching my land with a plane or helicopter had me on edge.

Each instance, each breach, each new invasion felt more and more like the Sovereign Order.

"Laurel, there's a patch of pine trees just a bit north of where we are, still in the basin. We can hide the truck there. I brought some food, a few protein bars. We'll eat. After that, I'm headed to Jack's. I'm torn between being worried or being leery about him. Something is fucking off, but no matter what, I owe him."

"I'm going with you."

My arm snaked around her waist as I pulled her close. In my arms was where I wanted her. I wasn't certain if it was where she belonged or not, and the longer she was with me, the less I cared about the right- or wrongness. "All I have with me is one gun with limited ammunition. I should be able to get more at Jack's as well as work on getting us off the ranch and away. Right now..." I let out a breath as I stared down at her fucking blue eyes, so full of unwarranted trust. "...I'm fucking scared and I don't like it."

Her petite hand came to my chest, resting on the front of my shirt. "I was thinking about this last night as I fell asleep."

"A plan to get us off the ranch? Do tell."

"No." Her cheeks filled with a blush of pink. "You being scared."

I sucked in a breath.

"I'm not analyzing."

"Then what the fuck are you doing?"

"What I do. You said you didn't want to take my life away. This is what I do. I deal with memories and responses. Let me keep doing it."

The clouds around us shifted, swirling in the morning breeze as the sun's rays brightened the glow of the whiteness. It wouldn't take long for the fog to dissipate. "Hurry the fuck up."

"I don't believe that your memory loss *and* your absent fight-or-flight response were physically or even psychologically related. It is unlikely and clinically doesn't seem possible."

Letting her go, I took a step back and turned. With each pivot within my 360-degree spin, I inhaled and exhaled, my mind filled with the days, weeks, and months after the explosion. My hands fisted as I recalled the horrendous and excruciating pain as my charred skin was debrided. Those were memories I didn't want, and yet with the realization of my identity, they'd returned. It wasn't only the physical torment, but the psychological. And then I recalled the peace when it finally faded. Not remembering the losses had been easier and allowed me to concentrate on my duty for the Order.

When I was again facing her, I exhaled. "Laurel, we don't have time for this. Maybe I just fucking didn't want to remember."

Laurel's head shook. "I don't know what happened, but I have a theory."

"You have thirty seconds, and then I'm moving the fucking truck."

She came closer, lifting her hands to my shoulders. The returned memories made me want to stiffen, to back away from her touch. Clenching my jaw, I remained still.

"Does this bother you?" she asked, looking from my eyes to her hands.

"No." My answer wasn't a complete fabrication. I liked

Laurel's touch, that she would touch, and that she did. I liked the way her gaze connected to mine. Everything about her was the opposite of bothering. The fault fell with me.

Her blue eyes stared up at me. "Last night you said that since the return of your memories and true identity, your fight-or-flight has returned."

I nodded.

"The return of your memories isn't the only thing that's changed."

My brow furrowed.

"Something else changed, Kader, Mason..." Her lips curled upward. "...Edgar." The air filled with her giggle. "Sorry, that one is going to take me a bit to say with a straight face."

"He was a good man."

Her smile faded. "Oh, I'm sorry."

My shoulder shrugged. "The mission succeeded, the loss of a team member was inconsequential in the fight as long as the goal was achieved. Edgar died a hero, one that no one would know, read about in history books, or even see his picture on the news. When I had to choose a name, it seemed...appropriate."

Moisture filled her blue orbs. "Okay, Edgar. I'll call you by whatever name you choose."

The sun above continued to shine, warming the ground and threatening our invisibility shroud. "Hurry up with your theory."

"Think about it. What else has changed in the last, say, month...or more specifically, the last few weeks?"

I wasn't certain where she was going. "Only every fucking thing."

"Why?"

The reason was fucking in front of me, talking to me, goading me on. "Do you want me to say it's you?"

Her blue eyes widened as she nodded. "Yes, that is what I want."

I reached for her waist and pulled her close. "It's you. Every goddamned thing is you. My world is turned upside down because your fucking gaze stared at me through the damn computer screen. Nothing has been the same since."

Laurel nodded. "That's it. That's the answer."

"What? I'm running like a fucking coward because of you?"

She shrugged. "First, whoever you are and whatever name you choose to use, you are not a coward. Second, the hyper-arousal or acute stress response known as fight-or-flight is chemical. Everyone has it. It's what has kept you safe and alive your whole life. It was what allowed you as a kid to steal food for you and your sisters and not get caught. It kicked in when you thought Lorna was in danger, and that chemical reaction enabled a scrawny teenager to stand up to a grown man."

I fucking hated that she knew my past and at the same time, there was comfort in her knowledge, in our connection, a sense of sharing without saying, understanding without explanation.

"You had it; I don't believe that after your accident it disappeared." Her front teeth tugged on her lower lip. "I remember the first time I saw you as you are now—no, the second—when you confronted Sinclair at the gathering. Your composure was part of what drew my attention to you. It's my theory that you, Kader, never lacked that chemical reaction. You learned to temper it. I mean, others do, soldiers, law enforcement, firefighters, bodyguards..."

"I'm not a fucking hero."

"Those are people who put their lives on the line. What you do is also dangerous. It would make sense that people in your line of work also learn to control it, to override the reaction. By doing so, it allows you to feel infallible and invincible. It allows you to face danger and succeed. That's what you've told me. What would happen if you didn't succeed?"

"I'd succeed the next time."

"What if there wasn't a next time?"

My fingers held tighter to her hips as my heart began to beat faster. "This is fucking analyzing."

"What if you didn't get another chance? What if, like your friend Edgar, you didn't return from an assignment or a mission?"

"Then I didn't. I didn't fucking care. I lived for assignments. I moved from one to the next. Even here with Jack, nothing mattered. I mean, I give a shit about this land, but not really. I give a shit about him, but I know he's capable without me." Her meaning came through as I nodded. "None of that is true any longer."

"What?"

"I didn't care—past tense—because if I never returned, there was no one to miss me, no one I'd miss." I swallowed. "And now..."

Laurel looked down from one of my hands to the other and back up to my eyes. "I would miss you."

Exhaling, my eyes closed as I lowered my chin. "So yes. Last night I walked away from Indianapolis without confronting Oaks and finishing this assignment because I was fucking scared."

Her head shook. "For yourself?"

"Not even slightly."

"For me?"

"I can't lose you, Laurel Carlson. I won't lose you again, and I will kill any motherfuckers who think they can get to you."

"That doesn't make you a coward. It makes you a protector.

Like the boy who protected his sisters, you're a man who protects the person he loves. It's scary."

"See," I replied, "that's where you're wrong. I scare people, not the other way around."

"I believe you. You aren't scared of those people..." She gestured to the fog. "...the ones trying to hurt me and you know what?"

"What?"

"Neither am I because I know you won't let anything happen."

I swallowed as I stared at her trusting gaze. "Was that theory supposed to fucking help? If it was, you screwed up on this analysis. All your theory did was make me see how badly I want to wrap you in damn Bubble Wrap and hide you away. Taking you with me isn't the answer."

"It is, Edgar. It is. Even though my adrenal glands should be flooding my bloodstream with catecholamines and I should want to fight or flee, I'm tempered. That isn't because I face danger without reservation. I don't. I'm a woman who carried pepper spray with her to the grocery store. I'm tempered because I trust *you*. The only part of this situation that scares me is losing another person I love." Her hands came to my cheeks. "You are at the top of that list. Keep me with you and let's get Jack and get the hell away from here."

JACK

Nearly forty-eight hours earlier

The reprieve Pierce and I'd enjoyed from the Sovereign Order wasn't without cost. Pierce had no clue of the extensive correspondence I still had with the Order. It wasn't like we'd joined the fucking Boy Scouts and one day decided we were too cool, throwing away our blue uniforms and replacing them with football jerseys.

The Order didn't work that way. It also didn't forget.

Investments.

That was what every member of the Order was considered, an investment for the greater good. Not all of us were brought back from the brink of death as Pierce had been. Others were brought back from psychological terrors and others from more self-inflicted defeats. Mine had been a failure to follow command. It had the potential to become a scandal capable of stripping me of all military honors, the repercussions of which could leave a dark stain on my great military family. I was the youngest in a line of career military.

The day I agreed to enter the Order was the day I officially died. The woman I'd left stateside, my parents, siblings, and even my grandfather—still alive at the time—were notified of my demise.

The option to inform them of anything different was taken from me without consideration for the consequences. They would learn of my death and I would continue, or they would learn of my death and they'd see me in a box. In that reality, my choices gave me an opportunity to right the wrong I'd committed. As I was often reminded, it was an honor bestowed on few.

Court-martialing was off the table. That would require testimony. It would shine a light, making both my crime and the actions of others known to more than the few. That spotlight would also have brought shame on my family. That option was eradicated from the equation the moment I gave my life to the Sovereign Order.

I continued to take breaths as my remains were gathered, sealed in a military vault, and sent back to the States. The Sovereign Order's gesture gave my family something to see and mourn, offering them closure as they said goodbye to the man who died as a hero.

Nothing prepares a man or woman for the intense transition of entering the Order.

Physical and psychological training superseded anything I'd endured in my first life. Grueling repetition as my body became stronger and my mind focused on the only thing that mattered. The three words were synonyms for the one true meaning.

Country.

Republic.

Democracy.

The crime I'd committed was buried. The man I'd killed lost forever.

I later learned it had been my commitment to country over

rank that earned me the honor of entering the Order. The battle had been fierce and casualties great. I'd followed orders and taken my battalion into dangerous conditions. We were ready. We were elite fighters.

It wasn't until it was almost too late that I realized we'd been set up, sacrificed. It wasn't until I stared my motherfucking lieutenant in the eye that I knew...

He'd sold us out.

I wasn't certain why.

I'm still not.

Had he been promised honors from his superiors or had the enemy gotten to him?

None of it mattered as explosions erupted all around and the night sky filled with the all-too-familiar fireworks. The colors in the sky were wrong. The signals indicated that we were the enemy. I'd heard the scenario too many times.

Friendly fire.

What was going down wasn't fucking friendly. It was a setup.

I had the choice.

I chose the death of a superior. I chose his death over that of the men and women in my command. It was a long shot, but one that could potentially save lives even if the reality cost me my career. It was a decision that came easier than I imagined.

Seventy-five percent of my men and women returned to base.

Our lieutenant didn't.

The troops returned under my direction as I was second-in-command.

The MPs arrived at my bunk that night.

A week later, I died. Ironically, I'd been the casualty of friendly fire.

Simultaneously, I was reborn.

The process took time. Physical changes occurred. It took

months of surgeries to become no one, no one who can be identified, and no one who will be missed.

The transition seemed like a lifetime ago because it was.

Over two decades had been given to the Sovereign Order. During that time, I'd made my way up the hierarchy of command in a way that would have made my father and grandfather proud had I been able to share.

My life wasn't without darkness.

Many things could be beaten into and out of a man.

A love for and dependence on alcohol wasn't one of them.

Even in the driest of countries, alcohol was obtainable. One simply needed to have a desire that exceeded reason.

Oh sure, there were twelve-step programs. Each time I considered entering, I stalled out on step four. A searching and fearless moral inventory was nearly impossible to do when your life was based not on moral decisions but commands, when taking a life was as easy as taking a drink. An inventory on a life reborn in service and order didn't yield awakening. It revealed the extent of vast darkness better left unexplored.

Stepping away from the team as Pierce and I had done almost half a decade ago was the closest thing to freedom either of us would ever experience. It was a delicate balance. The Order had rewarded our loyalty, secrecy, and service. Yet we were not free.

The assignments still came. They were few and far between but usually significant.

To experience a life outside of the Order, I relinquished my position. That meant I was no longer in tune with the overall assignments. I didn't know the newer recruits. I had one mission, to correspond and accept orders for Pierce. His ability was legendary. And while he had the option to pass, it was my assignment to assure that when necessary, he didn't.

The communications between me and the Order that occurred were buried deep on the web.

The Sovereign Order existed where other branches of the intelligence community had yet to go. We were a part yet separate. It wasn't unusual for the Order to limit the information that the other agencies obtained. While members of their teams sat secluded in an underground vault redacting information that would be disseminated, what they didn't realize was that the Order had redacted it first.

The well-known branches of the intelligence community didn't acknowledge that we existed. To do so would be to admit that since before the Second World War, our own government had successfully operated a subversive elite group of teams who only answered to Top, the head of all teams.

Pierce—now Price—and I were no longer in the larger loop. We were only informed about assignments that involved us.

Earlier this morning, I'd driven up to Price's base, ready to tell him that I'd received some unusual messages, ones that didn't make sense. I planned to inform him that I anticipated an upcoming command.

Finding the woman in the outbuilding threw off my game and erased my message.

A sex toy.

Really?

That wasn't like the man I knew. It wasn't like the man I'd known since he entered the Order.

I was well aware of his talents and that he sold them to the highest bidder. While I'd done my part to keep that part of our new lives hidden, I couldn't be certain of what the Order knew. And yet having a woman here on the ranch was completely unexpected and unprecedented.

Once I'd made it back to my house, I'd begun my research,

detailing her features as well as an estimation of her particulars: age, height, weight. My system was searching databases when it all stopped. Electricity still flowed, yet my entire system locked. Going out to the barns near the corrals, I accessed the safe room, the one with the server, temperature controlled and protected; our system would be the envy of many high-tech giants.

Nothing was out of order. Whatever was interfering wasn't happening because of something on my end.

Logically, I could have said it was the storm from earlier this morning.

My mind refused to accept such a simple answer.

It was as I was walking back to the house that I saw the SUV approaching.

The ranch hands weren't due for another week. The managers who'd worked for me for years had a code to enter the ranch. I hadn't activated the code. No one should be able to brazenly enter.

My shoulders straightened as I reached for the pistol, the holster strapped to my back. Releasing the safety, I held it at my side as the SUV came closer. With the darkened windows, I had difficulty seeing within.

After the SUV came to a stop, the door opened.

I lifted my pistol.

No one came onto this property without permission.

Small black boots became visible below the opened door and then ankles and calves covered in tight denim.

What the fuck?

This was a woman.

It was as she stepped to the ground that her face came into view.

I lowered my gun.

"Morehead," I said, "what the fuck are you doing here?"

I hadn't seen her in years. She'd been a recruit on another team within the Order before Pierce and I became our own team. While we'd only met a few times, I recalled her potential. The Order had been fortunate to acquire her, a scientist and a soldier. She was the new face of the Sovereign Order.

"Commander Jackson," she said, taking a step my direction.

"Not any longer."

"That's right." She came to a stop before me. "I always hoped to be assigned to your team."

"Not much left."

"Not because you're not good but because you are."

I inhaled. "A personal visit is highly unusual."

"Commander, the Order believes your team has been compromised."

"In what way?"

She nodded toward the pistol still in my grasp and then looked up at the blue sky. "Promise not to shoot me?"

I shook my head as I latched the safety and placed the pistol back in my holster. "The Order doesn't make house calls."

Her smile broadened. "It also doesn't deploy teams of two. I believe we both know that the Order makes exceptions."

"What exactly can I do for you, Morehead?"

"This ranch is lovely. I've been traveling for a bit. How about a glass of lemonade and we can talk shop? I believe we can work together to help the Sovereign Order."

Nodding, I waited as she approached. "I thought I heard something about you and a long-term assignment?"

Infiltration was not the Sovereign Order's usual modus operandi. It was risky to have a member out in the world even under a pseudonym. Of course, creating alternative identities was one of the Order's specialties. Nevertheless, out in the world for a length of time created unlimited opportunities for a cover to be blown or a member to forget the rules.

Get in and get out. That was what the Order usually did.

To assign a member a longer post required a highly sensitive situation and extremely skilled member. Only members with the right knowledge and ability were given long-term assignments.

"You have been kept informed," she said.

"Not really..." As we walked up the porch steps I tried to recall the source of information. "It was mentioned a few years ago, mostly in relation to your ability as well as appearance." I lifted my hands. "In regard to your ability to look younger than your years and training."

"That has helped." She smiled. "Having a good memory pays off in this line of duty."

"Your talents precede you, Morehead. Even though I'm no longer in command, I hope the Order has utilized those." I opened the door to my house.

"It's not my name, but yes. I'm currently a dissertation away from my doctorate. The Order is very interested in what I know. I'd say my future is bright."

"Good for you." I gestured toward the kitchen table. "Lemonade you said?"

"Unless you have anything stronger. It's been a long trip and my work has just begun."

LAUREL

Present day/time

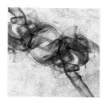

*W*e moved as if Kader's land was littered with land mines. Nothing was a straight line as we walked about his property, purposely avoiding the sensors he'd installed. The entire time his neck was straight, shoulders broad, and jaw set. Every crunch of underbrush and every broken twig caused his head to turn and his vision to scan.

There'd been no sign of another aircraft, no plane or helicopter, since we'd climbed our way out of the fog-filled basin. If we weren't in mortal danger, the beauty of his land could be better enjoyed. The feeling as we exited the cloud bank and moved above it was unlike any sensation I'd had. It was as if we were standing above the clouds on the rim of a giant crater.

Since then, we'd moved to lower ground, to tree lines and edges of ridges, our presence hidden below the rocky ledges. I wasn't certain how long we'd been walking, only that my legs and feet were unaccustomed to strenuous exercise. While I used to run, ever since I'd awakened in the basement of that disgusting house, my exercise came mostly in the way of sex. I wasn't complaining, other than that it wasn't proper training for hiking with a fifteen-pound jacket and tennis shoes on rough terrain.

As I stopped and looked up at the blue sky, I appreciated that at least the sun was out and the temperature was warming. "How much farther?" I asked as my hands came to my hips and I inhaled.

"We're approaching Jack's area from the far west edge of my property."

"And no one can see us?"

Instead of answering, he continued with his plans. "There's an old shaft that was constructed a long time ago that opens into the base of the ravine. If we can get down to that opening unseen, we can move underground, safe from visual as well as thermal sensors." He shrugged. "It's an old maze, but if I can keep my sense of direction, there is one vein that leads to a barn near Jack's house. All of the ends—exits and entrances—were blocked years ago. That was long before we lived here. I'm certain that given the right motivation, I can either break the wooden barriers or pry open the locks. I've been racking my mind trying to recall the old blueprints I haven't seen in years."

My skin prickled. "Shaft? Would this be like an old coal shaft? That doesn't sound safe." My thoughts went to spiders and snakes and all the dangers Kader had mentioned, trying to scare me a few weeks ago. "What about bugs?"

"We're bigger than the bugs, and they didn't mine coal here. They mined quartz. By the late 1800s this state had a significant number of quartz mines."

"That still doesn't tell me they're safe."

Kader reached for my hand. "If my land is being watched, I don't think it's possible to approach Jack's house and the other buildings near there unseen. This is all my own damn fault. Anyone coming from the roads would enter there first. We set up the security that way. It wasn't that we forgot about the mining shafts, only that to enter them, you have to be on the property. It didn't seem necessary to add more security to them."

He swallowed as he ran his hand over his hair.

There was something in his expression.

"What are you thinking?"

He exhaled. "I'm thinking that if the rain the other morning combined with the spring runoff from the mountains flooded the entrance, we've lost the option. Hopefully the water hasn't made it into the shafts."

My head shook. "No, Kader." It seemed that *Kader* was the name I reverted back to when my thoughts were all over the place. "People die in flooded caves and mine shafts. And what does late 1800s mean specifically?"

"I think I saw 1870 on a blueprint once."

I leaned closer and looked up at his face. From my new angle, the few days' beard growth was visible on his neck, chin, jawline, and cheeks. Higher, his green eyes sent their laser stare to me. With a nod, I laid my head over his chest and took comfort in the steady sound of his heart.

Kader's arms wrapped around me. "Laurel, we're blind out here. Technology has been my friend for as long as I can recall, even earlier than I used to recall. This is survival 101. My house has been infiltrated, for certain, my surveillance system. I don't know if anyone else was inside it, but the loss of your notebook has me concerned. The only reason we were allowed to enter that garage was because the person or persons responsible thought we were taking the camper to the river. They were allowing that because they believed we were leaving a trail so they could find us. Us leaving in the truck wasn't part of their plan. That's why the garage door closed. This system was not only supposed to be fail-safe, but it was created with the ability to anticipate."

He leaned back and lifted my chin. "I programmed it. That means it anticipates *my* next move and all that I thought to add. For that reason, I now have to push aside my first thoughts and rely on my gut. If I'm right and we're being hunted, this is guerilla warfare. I also don't know how many people are involved."

With each of his sentences my knees grew weaker and my empty stomach churned. As tears filled my eyes, I asked, "Why? Why is this happening to me? The research is stopped. Russ is dead. Eric is dead. I'm missing..." A thought occurred to me. "You were supposed to produce proof of my death. Did you?"

"I planted the evidence. Your shirt, the one with the blood, and your damaged cell phone should soon be discovered in a large trash bin on the university's campus. It's not evidence of your death, but it leads to the theory of foul play versus simply missing."

I looked down at my palm. The bandage from yesterday was dirty, yet the wound beneath was still as clean as it could be. Yesterday, it was evident that the healing was progressing well. Letting out a breath, I mumbled, "My poor parents."

Again Kader reached for my chin. "Stay focused on here and now. I realize it's difficult not to think about them, but right now you must think about you."

A lump came to my throat. "You think I'm being emotional again."

His head shook. "No. Now that I remember that I had a family, I get it. I do. I guess in a way, Jack is family. That's why I can't leave him behind. I need to get to him before we get out of here."

It wasn't that long ago that Kader couldn't comprehend my

connection to my family. The change in his insight was just another example of how his life before was coming back and infiltrating his decisions.

"Okay. If you trust him, I do too."

"I don't have any other choice. He's stood by me for years. He's the closest thing I've had to a partner since...Mason died. He's smart. Together we've been unstoppable. I should have told him the truth the other day when he came up to the house."

"Then let's get to him."

As we were about to move toward the ravine, another low rumbling filled our ears. Instead of causing fear, it made my cheeks warm with embarrassment. It wasn't an aircraft but my stomach.

Kader's lips moved upward to a grin. "And food. Jack has food."

"You're making this more appealing."

Following Kader, we came to the least-steep incline leading down into the ravine. Rocks and soft dirt slid under our weight as we climbed lower. Through it all, Kader continued to scan the horizon, searching for anyone either by sky or land.

Near the bottom, the river raged, soaring over rocks and extending beyond its banks. The small saplings peering out of the river gave me some indication of how it should be, when the winter snow wasn't melting and the rain hadn't fallen in buckets.

"The river flows off the land. I believe they'd bring the quartz here and use the river to transport it."

"Where's the mine shaft?" I asked, looking upward at the steep hills. From our position, we were too low to see the house or have any indication of direction.

"This way," he said, tugging me along.

While the opening was blocked by vines and trees, it was thankfully higher than the waterline. Once Kader pulled the vegetation away, the barricade was nothing more than a large wooden planked door, one that time had weakened with moisture and rot. The lock consisted of two links of a large rusted chain with a corroded key-opened padlock holding the links together.

Kader didn't need to pick the lock. One kick of his boot, and the planks gave way. A few more kicks and the opening became large enough for one person at a time to enter.

"What about a flashlight?" I asked.

"Let me go in first."

My lip disappeared behind my teeth as I stood back, watching his large frame push through the opening he'd created. With each passing second my heart raced. I scanned the blue sky, hopeful it wouldn't be the last time I saw it.

Small spaces had never been my thing, yet I didn't have an irrational fear. No, the concerns racing through my head were completely rational. What we were about to do was not.

A glow flickered within the opening.

"Laurel, come on."

One last look up. As I stepped inside, I stopped.

"What is it?" Kader asked.

"I think I hear the helicopter again."

KADER

took a deep breath of the dusty, stagnant air. The shaft had not been created for men my height. I had to stoop, the ceiling too short for me to stand erect. Thankfully, upon entering, I'd found a few abandoned tools. Quite possibly some of these antiques could have been abandoned where I'd found them for over a hundred and fifty years.

I handed Laurel the coal torch. "Hold this and try to shine it ahead of us."

Her hands shook as she gripped the rod. "How did you do this?"

"Coal and a stick ignited with an old flint lighter."

"Kader," she shrieked.

My gaze followed hers. With the light of the torch, our path shimmered as spider webs draped from wall-to-wall created intricate patterns and the ground appeared to move. It was an illusion caused by the shimmering webs and the scattering of spiders and other insects running from the light.

"Don't worry," I tried to reassure. "They don't want to see us any more than we want to see them."

"I'm not worried about them *seeing* me. I'm worried about them *biting* me."

"We'll make noise and move at a steady pace. The hobo spiders are the most dangerous, but they're not aggressive. They'll only bite if they feel threatened. We aren't threatening them."

"I-I can't..." Her face paled in the light of the torch as her head shook vigorously back and forth.

"You can." I worked to keep my voice calm. "Doc, you've got this. If you heard the helicopter out there, now is the time to get to Jack."

"I'm scared."

"Then that shit you said is working. Glad to know you're secreting...whatever you said."

"Catecholamines, and now isn't the time to remind me of fight-or-flight because I choose flight. I choose turning around and getting the hell out of here."

"Stay with me, Laurel. Cover your hair with my jacket and stay right behind me in my wake. They'll run from my footsteps and I'll break through the webs."

It wasn't the worst conditions I'd ever experienced. My thoughts were now filled with more than before, not only missions for the Order, but places I'd been in the army as well as Chicago. With each thought, I fought to push it away and stay focused on here and now.

Mostly I was successful, but the memories were there, coming back at supersonic speed.

Though Laurel's expression was pained, her forehead furrowed and lips drawn tight, she nodded before handing the torch back to me and moving my leather coat so that it also covered her head. Reaching out, I pushed loose strands of her dark hair under the leather.

"This gives the spiders fewer places to attach," I said with a feigned grin.

"That isn't helping."

I handed her back the torch and began moving forward. The ground beneath the souls of my boots and her shoes was damp yet not saturated as I'd feared. The incline moved higher as the ground grew both dryer and harder. Braces still standing that had been erected a century and a half ago creaked. Others were strewn over the floor, fallen and damaged by time.

It was as we came to the first fork that I hesitated.

"Kader?"

The ability to recall particulars was something I'd perfected in the Order. When we went on a mission, we carried nothing that could be identifiable. All information had to be retained mentally.

The blueprint appeared in my mind. While I'd seen and studied it, I'd never investigated the shafts myself. If I recalled correctly, according to those plans, we needed to take the shaft to the right, and yet my sense of direction urged me to go left.

Though my gut rarely let me down, Laurel was right. Where she was concerned I was off my game. This was a time to trust my memory.

"The blueprint says right," I said, turning back to Laurel. The path behind her was pitch black, indicating how far we'd traveled from the opening in the ravine. "We're going right."

"I'm staying with you."

The decision was correct.

It was as we neared what should be the opening within the floor of one of the barns near Jack's house that we found ourselves face-to-face with a roadblock. Rocks, dirt, and rotted wooden braces filled the shaft, leaving a small opening near the top. Leaning inward and peering above the debris, a ray of light shone, streaming down from above.

"I would guess that all the construction aboveground caused this part of the shaft to give way."

"Should we turn around?" Laurel asked.

"We're too close. Let me see if I can move some of this so we can get through."

"Will the ceiling hold?"

It was the same question I'd posed to myself as I scanned the integrity of the braces over our heads. I turned to Laurel. "I am getting you out of here and to someplace safe. We're not fucking dying in a mine shaft."

By the light of the torch, her blue eyes shone, their gaze staring right at me. While her cheeks were streaked with dirt and my leather coat was covered in dust, she was the most beautiful woman I'd ever known. "We are getting out."

"I trust you."

It was such a fucking simple statement and yet it overwhelmed me. Staring at the man hired to kill her, Laurel Carlson trusted me. Pulling at the loose rocks and chunks of dirt, I peeled away the pile of debris, piece by piece. The remaining brace creaked as dust and sand filtered down from the ceiling above us. When the opening was large enough, I offered Laurel my hand.

"Come here, let me help you."

"I'm not going through that place without you."

"Not the time to argue, Doc. I'm not going through and leaving you behind either. Climb and let me watch that sexy ass go through that opening. I'll then hand you the torch and follow."

The opening was large enough for her petite body; however,

the debris was spread out. Bit by bit, she crawled, her back against the ceiling and stomach on the rubble.

"I see the opening." Her voice was muffled.

"Can you get down?"

"I-I think so."

In the dimness beyond the opening I heard a thud. "Laurel, are you all right?"

"I am, but I don't think I can reach the torch."

"I need to remove a few more rocks for me to fit. Wait where you are."

"Good advice," she replied. "It's dark over here, but not like over there. There's light coming from up above. I think it's the entrance. I think we're here."

"Keep talking to me," I said as I widened the opening, rock by rock, clump by clump. My skin coated with sweat as I continued to work, listening as she spoke. I didn't care what she was saying, only that she was speaking."

"Tell me something, Laurel."

"I'm scared."

My fingers ached as I dug at the debris. "No, something about you. Something about us. I just want to hear you speak."

"Oh, okay. Let me think..."

"Keep talking, Doc."

"I remember the first time I went with my dad to that Boys and Girls Club, the one you went to."

I inched closer as the board above me creaked. "Tell me."

"The lady's name at the desk was Miss Betsy..."

I was fucking strong and yet it took every ounce of energy to push forward, the rocks below ripped at my jeans as the wood and rocks above tore at my shirt. I didn't care. Pain didn't register. Getting to Laurel was my only concern.

Though I'd left the torch on the other side of the rubble,

through the dusty air, I saw her, the stream of light shining down, illuminating the dirt and webs around her. Like an angel in a heavenly light, she was there. Her voice was a song bringing me closer.

Inhale.

Exhale.

I repeated the process, yet each time was more difficult. I couldn't fill my lungs.

Black spots danced over my vision as I blinked, concentrating on Laurel.

The pressure on my back and torso increased. My mind told my body to push forward, to move, yet my body couldn't comprehend.

"Laurel..."

LAUREL

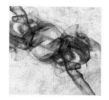

"*K*ader!"

He'd been in the opening. I heard him pushing through and seen the glow of the torch around him. Now it was only dark.

Why had it all stopped?

With only the light streaming from above, I climbed upward, toward him, pulling at the rocks, digging my nails and fingers into the debris as I ripped each obstacle away and threw them behind me. It was as I reached the top that my sore hands found his face with his head down.

Panic flooded through me as I continued to dig at the earth, pulling and speaking, calling his name. "Don't you do this. Don't you leave me now. You promised. You promised me letters. You didn't write them. You're not getting out of this promise, Mason Pierce. We're getting out of here."

I reached for his cheeks, cupping them in my grasp and pulled my body closer. In the stagnant dusty air, I came nearer, searching for the gust of his breathing or the beat of his pulse—for any sign that he hadn't left me.

Under my touch, his skin was warm and sticky, covered in moisture, perspiration and blood.

"Talk to me, damn it." I brought my lips to his. Instead of kissing, I suctioned mine over his and blew.

I was aware that this wasn't the right position for mouth-to-mouth or if his lungs could inflate with the pressure. I couldn't get to chest compressions if I needed to. Stretching my arms, I reached farther until my fingers trailed over his wide neck. Holding my breath, I waited. His carotid artery pulsated. Closing my eyes, I concentrated, verifying that I wasn't imagining the pulse beneath my touch.

Thump.

Thump.

It was real. It was there.

One of his large hands was extended. Gripping it with both of mine, I pulled. "Mason. Mason." I continued to call his name as I pulled, his large body not budging. "This isn't happening. You are not going to be stuck here. I love you. You have to stay with me."

Again, I dug at the debris. With time and effort, the pile beneath him lowered. Unfortunately, gauging by the light of the torch behind him, as the debris lowered so did the ceiling above.

Kader was sandwiched between.

Dig.

Pull.

Breathe.

I struggled for my own breath in the musty air as tears erupted, coating my cheeks as my nose ran. My muscles ached and fingers bled as I grew more frantic. Finally, I stopped, my body trembling, breathing ragged, and chest heavy with over-whelming sorrow.

Grief.

Disappointment.

Failure.

My chest quaked as sobs bellowed from within me.

The thought of me dying in this shaft was out of reach. I didn't care about myself. It was the knowledge that I'd failed him when he'd risked everything for me. Holding myself, my chin dropped to my chest as the tears continued.

Without Kader, there was no reason to go on.

It seemed too unfair.

Kader had been right about fate.

It was a vindictive bitch.

I'd been naïve to believe that fate was the fruition of what was meant to be.

I'd been naïve about everything and now it was over.

We hadn't found one another because it was meant to be.

Hell no.

We'd found one another for it all to end in a dark tunnel.

Landing my lips on his forehead, I softly kissed his skin. "I never stopped loving you. I won't now."

More tears blurred my vision as I climbed down the pile of rubble. My foot slipped sending me tumbling as the rock below me broke loose. I scrambled as an avalanche of debris shifted, creating a wave of rocks and dirt. Instead of fleeing, I fought the current, climbing back upward toward the lowering peak until I found both of his arms and pulled with all my might.

Freed by the movement of the earth below him, Kader lurched forward, his weight too much as we both plunged to the hard ground below. Freed from the pile and ceiling, we were now trapped, the ceiling collapsing the tunnel behind us. Not only that, I was trapped by him, his massive torso on top of me as I lay face up, his shoulder over my face.

Pushing upward, I wiggled, inching higher until my face was freed.

Gasping for breath, greedy for anything I could inhale, my lungs filled with the dusty air.

"Mason," I called, my free arm rubbing over his back. "Kader, you have to wake."

His pulse still thumped under my touch and his chest, pressed against mine, moved. All at once he coughed as his body tensed.

"Laurel." My name came between coughs racking his body as he pushed up from the hard ground, freeing both of my arms.

I reached up, cupping his cheeks in the darkness. "I'm here." My declaration came between sobs.

As his coughs echoed off the walls and ceiling, dust and sand pelted us from above.

"What the fuck?" In the dimness, he moved, sitting up and tugging me to him. "What the fuck happened?" he asked.

"I don't know. You were crawling through the opening and just stopped."

His inhale stopped as he groaned. "My chest fucking hurts."

"Can you move, like get us out of here? Or tell me how and I'll do it."

My eyes had adjusted enough to see that Kader had twisted his neck, craning it back and peering toward the collapse behind us.

"The fucking shaft collapsed. How did I get out of that?"

"You're not letting me go. I'm not letting you go either."

His hands came to my cheeks as our lips met. "I fucking love you, Laurel."

"I love you. I always have. Now get us out of here."

"You were bossy as a girl too."

"I'm still a girl."

"No, you're all woman."

Brushing off my clothes as if it would help, I stood. "This section is taller." I looked up. It was too tall, probably ten or more feet. "I don't think that even you can reach that opening up there."

With minimal groans, Kader stood and lifted his hands. "I'm close." He looked around. "If I could just stand on something, I could reach it."

"What about me?"

"I think you're too short," he replied with a smirk.

"Thanks. What if you lift me up?"

"And what do you plan on doing?"

Reaching down I lifted a large piece of rock, holding it with two hands. Gripping the end, I assessed the size and length. "I could hit the boards with this."

"Or drop it on my head."

"I won't drop it. Those secretions are happening right now and I'm ready to fight. Lift me up. I'll smash the wood like you did with your boot."

"Laurel."

"Lift me now," I demanded.

His hands came to my waist.

"Am I too heavy?" I asked when he hesitated.

"No, I'm just thinking about what's above. It could be anything. Something could come falling down."

I pointed upward. "I see light. I'll aim for that spot. If light is getting through, it's clear."

After a sigh, the pressure to my hips increased and my feet left the ground. Swinging the rock over my head would create the most amount of force. Yet it wouldn't be stable. I could easily drop it on Kader's head as he'd predicted. My most controlled movement would be upward from in front of me, the way my dad taught me to shoot a basketball before my arms were strong enough to shoot the correct way.

He would tell me, "Hold the ball between your knees. Using your legs and arms, push it up and toward the basket."

Gripping the rock, I imagined that outdoor hoop Dad placed in our driveway. Clenching my teeth and closing my eyes, I hurled the rock upward, imitating the childhood free throw. As I held tight to it, the rock collided and wood cracked.

"Well, fuck," Kader said. "Do it again."

Taking in a deep breath, I again pitched the rock upward. This time the wood gave way, splinters raining down.

"One more time and let me climb up," I said.

"Whoa, Wonder Woman, just a minute."

He lowered me to my feet and pulled me close. Even though both of us were hot, dirty, and covered in sweat and blood, I leaned into his torso. His arms surrounded me. "I fucking hate you going up there without me. What if someone..." He didn't finish.

"What's our choice, Mason? Tell me what to do once I'm up."

"It's not your job to be brave. You're the brains."

"Now who's sexist? Besides you have the brains too. What will I find to get you out?"

He nodded. "I have an idea."

A few minutes later, I slowly lifted my head out of the opening, peering around and taking in the structure around the broken barrier. Large wooden pillars reached up to rafters high above. Stacks of straw or hay blocked my view in one direction. Another way, there was a wall and yet from somewhere the building was filled with natural light.

"What do you see?" he asked.

"Nothing except bales of straw, a wall, and some posts."

"No people?"

"No."

"Try to grip something besides the edge if you can. The wood's old and will probably break. Get ready, I'm going to push."

I grasped for anything, as Kader pushed and I pulled. Once my body cleared the opening, I leaned back against the straw, catching my breath and taking in the fresher air.

"Look around for something I can use to pull myself up," Kader said from below.

"Okay. Stay there."

"Sure, Doc. I'll do that."

Beyond the straw I found a wall covered with different supplies. Hanging on nails were ropes. Some were rough while others were smooth. I reached for one of the smooth ones and went back to the opening. "I found a rope."

"Perfect."

My gaze darted around. "Let me tie it to this pole and see if it's long enough to get to you."

The knot I tied wouldn't pass any sailing or cowboy inspections; nevertheless, it was big and strong as I tugged over and over again before tossing the length down into the hole.

"Can you reach it?" I asked.

"I've got it. Stay away from the edge," Kader yelled.

The rope pulled taut and the pole creaked as the air filled with grunts. The noises came closer until his long hair and green eyes appeared above the opening.

I let out a long breath as he did the same as I'd done earlier and pulled himself to safety.

Once we were both standing, I smiled. "Maybe Jack will let us use his shower."

"You're still beautiful," Kader said, his finger going over my cheek.

I reached for his hand. "You hurt your hand."

Kader did the same, turning my hands over in his grasp. "Look at yours."

Dirt and blood combined on our palms and fingertips. "I don't care. Please, get us out of here."

Kader took my hand and led me toward a closed door. We stood in place, listening for the sound of anyone. The door and pulleys creaked as he pulled, sliding it open enough for us to exit. Horses nearby whinnied at the new sound and our invasion of their territory.

"That's a good sign," Kader said.

Not being well enough versed in horses to comment, I nodded. The beautiful creatures came our way to the edge of the corral, curious to see who was invading their space. Tall and proud, their black manes blew in the breeze and their brown coats shimmered in the sun.

"I'm not sure if we can get into his house."

"The security?" I asked.

"Yes, if it's programmed against me."

"Missy, your house, told me the other day that the buildings down by Jack's were off-line."

Kader's brow furrowed. "Why would she say that?"

"I asked if everything was secure."

"When was that?"

I tried to remember. "The first morning you were gone."

"She said these buildings were off-line a day ago?"

"Yes."

He shook his head. "None of this fucking information came

to me in Indianapolis. I should have known what was happening."

I reached for his hand. "We can't change that now. Let's just please get away."

Quietly, we scurried toward the back of the house, keeping ourselves as low as possible. I followed as Kader led me around to a back porch. Stepping onto the wooden stairs, we moved gingerly. With his hand cupped over his eyes, he peered through the window.

"I don't see anyone."

Kader reached for the door handle. "Try not to touch anything."

KADER

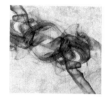

*O*pening the kitchen door, I peered inside, taking in each inch of the room. In all the years we'd lived here, I'd never entered Jack's home without knocking or without his knowledge. Yes, I'd purchased the land—Edgar Price had. However, that didn't mean we both didn't deserve our space and privacy. Jack had always respected mine and I'd respected his.

While my current actions went against that philosophy, my gut told me not to announce our presence.

Together, we stepped inside. Each movement, each sighting, had my senses on high alert as if every nerve was firing, bringing the short hairs at the nape of my neck to life and tingling my skin. Each sense was intensified.

Sound—there was nothing.

Sight—I scanned the counters, the walls, and each surface.

Smell—nothing distinguishable.

My neck stiffened. It wasn't because of what I smelled but what I didn't. I turned, my gaze going to the clean and empty coffee pot. That may seem like a strange observation, but it was just past noon and Jack was known for his perpetual coffee drinking, well, until the stronger drinks began.

Back at the kitchen table, two of the four chairs were askew. Not so much out of place, but not in place.

Two?

My stomach twisted.

On the surface, near one of the chairs was a glass, a tumbler, with a small amount of light amber liquid. I didn't need to lift and inhale its aroma to know what it was. After the coffee was done, Jack liked his whiskey on the rocks. The amber was clearer than normal due to melted ice cubes.

I hadn't known him to begin drinking early in the day since we stepped away from the Order. He said it proved that he was in control of the alcohol and not the other way around. Then again, once the whiskey began, I never remember him leaving any in the glass. Jack always finished his drink.

"Look," Laurel whispered, tilting her head toward the sink.

Within its depths was another glass, upside down, taller than the tumbler, and rinsed clean.

Had someone else been here?

As a rule, we didn't have company on the ranch, not until the ranch hands came on for the season. While they were present they—especially the managers—often joined Jack in this kitchen after a long day. The table that now appeared to seat six would have leaves added. Whether they were discussing the day, the cattle, the horses, or sharing a pot of chili, Jack had an easiness about him that welcomed camaraderie. While I was more of a loner, Jack had a way with people. That was why he'd succeeded as a commander. He could be gruff, yet he found a way to connect to the men and women under his command.

I don't think his admiration for alcohol hurt. He always

enjoyed having someone with whom to imbibe. Unfortunately for him, I wasn't much of a drinker.

Laurel moved her hold to my lower arm, her grip tightening as her blue eyes widened. "Two glasses?" she asked in a whisper.

"They could both be his."

She peered back at the chairs.

I shrugged and spoke, continuing to keep my voice low. "We'll do a sweep of the house. If he's not here we'll check outside. I know where he kept emergency supplies. We'll get those and although I hate to go without him, we'll leave."

"What if the helicopter person is here or gets back?"

Bending down, I removed the gun from my ankle holster. "Stay close."

Though her grip of my arm trembled, Laurel nodded.

With only one floor, Jack's home wasn't as large as mine. That was the way he wanted it. He said he didn't need much room. He joked that compared to his quarters at the Order, this was a fucking McMansion.

Individually, we'd both accumulated a generous amount of funds. While his had mostly sat in accounts, I'd been the one to invest and grow mine. That didn't mean Jack didn't have a substantial amount. After all, he'd been with the Sovereign Order much longer than I had.

While I grew money, Jack's talents with growing were centered more on the care of livestock, horses, and crops. After we'd moved here, he allocated some of the land to grow our own straw and hay. No, they weren't the same thing.

Together we moved from room to room. Living room, bedroom, baths, out to the four-season room, with each step, my gut churned.

The entire house was spotless.

Nothing besides the two glasses was out of place.

Jack was many things and good at many things.

Cleaning wasn't one of them, not unless it was a job—similar to what I'd done at Laurel's.

That was the feeling I got as we looked around.

This house had been cleaned, sanitized.

Fuck.

Why?

With a sense of dread, we approached the only closed door within the house, the one to his office. I'd been in there many times after he'd received a summons from the Order. It was where we strategized and reviewed the intel.

My office was for my work.

His was for ours.

Closing my eyes, I turned the knob and pushed the door inward.

Instinctively, I held my breath. The stench caught in my throat, rendering me unable to swallow or inhale. At the same time, I shifted, blocking Laurel's view.

Fuck. Oh, Jack.

I only saw for a moment, yet the memory would be etched forever.

How many dead bodies had I seen?

How many had I killed?

I couldn't come up with an answer, and yet seeing my commander, teammate, friend ladened my chest with heaviness. His leather chair sat as an island in a crimson pool. The hard tile floor didn't allow the life-giving fluid to saturate, instead keeping it upon its surface.

His head was back and arms dangled from his sides. On the floor to his right within the crimson puddle was a pistol I recognized immediately. It was Jack's, the one he always carried. By its presence as well as the splatter dotting the wall behind his chair, the gunshot was meant to appear self-inflicted.

There was one more clue.

The paper upon his chest with large scrawled writing: *MY LAST COMMAND. CLEAN THIS ONE UP, TOO.*

What the fuck?

Too?

The count was too high.

Each job, each cleaned scene ran through my thoughts, the reel ending with Cartwright. That was the last, but definitely not the first. The protein bar I'd eaten earlier threatened to make its way back up or maybe it was bubbling bile from my churning stomach. Retaliation came to life within the caustic concoction.

I was a fucking killer and that was what I wanted to do.

I spun back to Laurel.

"Oh no. What?" she asked.

At the sound of her voice, the sight of her simple beauty, even covered in dirt and grime, my focus changed. Revenge would come after she was safe. "We need to get the hell out of here, now."

"Is it...is he...?"

I closed my eyes, pulling the door shut. When I opened my lids, her blue orbs were staring up at me. "He's dead. It's hard to say for sure without getting closer, but I'd say it didn't happen today."

"This is all because of me."

"I don't think so anymore. I think I'm the next target." This was the fucking Order and I knew it. What I didn't understand was why.

Tugging her hand, I no longer gave a shit about noise. This was a race against the clock, and right now the clock was in the lead. Flinging the front door open, I stopped and surveyed, contemplating our next move. We could take one of his vehicles, but they too were chipped. The plane would be fastest, but it was up at my place. It was also easily traceable. If we were suddenly fighting against the Order, we had no place to hide. Their teams were vast and omnipresent.

My heart continued to thump in my chest.

Jack was my connection, my commander, and my friend. Without him, Laurel and I were alone against a virtual army.

No, the Sovereign Order was not the army or any other monitored branch of the military.

It didn't operate under the Geneva Conventions. The rules of conduct didn't apply regarding a perceived threat. An order was an order, an assignment, an assignment. The reason wasn't to be questioned. A member's only mission was to fulfill the duty for the country, republic, and democracy.

I couldn't fathom how either Laurel or I was a threat to the above.

Nevertheless, there was nothing to stop them from killing Laurel if I was the target, or me, if she was. They outnumbered us and that fact alone could be our death sentence.

My heart was heavy with the knowledge that it had been Jack's.

There was no fucking way anyone besides someone from the Order was responsible. Jack didn't kill himself. Jack didn't order me to clean up his body. This was more than his death. It was a message.

"Come with me," I said.

KADER

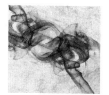

*R*age caused my blood to boil. The message upon Jack's chest was for me and only me. I had done every assignment Jack had brought to me over the last few years. There were a few I postponed, needing to complete my own work first. Yet I'd never let them down and always done my best to succeed. Jack had too.

We'd given up our lives for the Sovereign Order and now they'd taken Jack's.

He fucking deserved better.

The memory of misleading him a few days ago ate away at me.

He deserved better from the Order and from me.

"Mason," Laurel whispered, "I'm sorry about Jack."

My head shook as I tried to refocus "I can't concentrate on that. I have one goal and that's to get you to someplace fucking safe."

"Where is that?"

I didn't answer because I didn't have one.

Instead, as we stood at Jack's front door, I scanned the grounds before us, scrutinizing each inch of landscape. The entire scene seemed eerily still. The corral we'd recently passed was empty. The gates were programmed as were feeders. With the horses moved out to pasture, even the wind refused to blow.

Stepping forward, something outside caught my attention. Taking Laurel's hand, we stepped off the path into the grass until we reached the edge of the crushed-stone drive. "Look," I said, pointing to the first stepping-stone leading to Jack's house.

The boot print was a partial, yet it was enough to gauge the size of the boot.

"That's like the prints I saw up by your house," Laurel said.

"Are you sure?"

"I am. Did Jack have uncommonly small feet?"

I shook my head as I crouched down and ran my finger over the dried mud. "No, this is small, and it's mud. Whoever it was had been walking somewhere else before coming here." I stood up and looked around. "They didn't step in mud on the drive."

"The barn floor was earth. Maybe it was still wet."

"When did Missy say these buildings went off-line?"

"She didn't say when," Laurel said. "She said they were off-line and that was Saturday morning."

I was relatively certain from the scene in the office that Jack was dead by then, maybe even Friday evening before I left the ranch. That would mean that I'd left Laurel alone with a trained assassin on the property.

If that were the case, I was definitely the target.

"Come on," I said, leading her to the place where Jack hid supplies—emergency supplies.

As we passed by each building, I scanned the entries for any sign of intrusion. The problem that wouldn't let me go and had my nerves on overdrive was that if this was a member of the

Order, he or she was as well trained as I was. Hell, if that person hadn't wanted me to find Jack's body, I wouldn't have.

It was definitely a message.

Nearing the door, an unwelcome noise came from a distance. My neck straightened. Laurel had heard a plane. We'd heard a helicopter. This was neither, which was a fucking problem. The high-pitched whine didn't belong to a large craft. It was a drone.

Fuck.

I pulled Laurel against the side of a building, under the eave. Though my heart was beating wildly, I did my best to sound calm. "Stay still."

"What if they have the thermal infrared sensor you talked about?" she whispered.

"Then it's better that we're out of the building. We could be an animal."

We waited as the whine grew louder, circling each building, before dimming, moving down the long dirt-packed drive toward the entrance.

Hurrying into the barn, Laurel's nose scrunched. "Oh."

This wasn't an outbuilding like I had up by my home. This was an actual barn where horses were stalled.

I lifted my hand to my nose. "Yes, I'd guess the stalls haven't been cleaned for a few days."

"Oh, the poor horses. They probably need feed too."

"Stop worrying about everyone else," I scoffed.

"But they can't take care of themselves."

"Jack had an automated system that allowed him to handle so many tasks. As long as the feeders have food, they're fine."

"But if they're off-line...?"

I shook my head. "Stop. It's not connected that way. He wanted it fail-safe even when storms affected the electricity or there were problems with the internet. They're fine."

"Are you just saying that to shut me up?"

"Doc, I don't want to shut you up. I love your concern and inquisitive mind. I want to keep all of that. First, I need to get you to safety, and then I'll worry about the horses."

Stepping through dirt and straw, I led us to the back of the barn and a tall set of shelves filled with grooming tools and bins of feed. To the bystander the shelves appeared permanent. They weren't. It was an illusion.

In reality they were on a hidden track, allowing for their movement.

"Stand back," I said, gripping the shelf and pushing.

With little resistance, they moved, revealing a hidden door within the wall.

"Oh, this is all very History channel with hidden passageways," Laurel said.

Spinning the old padlock between my thumb and finger, I entered the combination. No fancy eye scanners, no communication with Missy, this was as basic as it could get: a hidden door and a combination padlock.

"Jack was smarter than shit. He could program the whole fucking ranch to run with little input. He could track down a target. He was also old school when it came to safety. I used to think he was just old and paranoid. Now I'm fucking glad. If he were still alive, I'd thank him."

"Me too."

Once unlocked, I slid the hidden door, causing it to disappear into the wall.

There was nothing fancy or high tech. The room was a reinforced box with no windows and a single bulb with a pull string for illumination. Along the wall were cases with firearms of all sizes.

"Why did he come up to your place for a gun if he had all of these?" Laurel asked.

"He asked for a particular one." I pointed. "That one."

"Is it different?"

"They all have their uses."

Taking another pistol, I placed it in the band of my blue jeans and stuffed the ammunition into the pockets of my coat, the one Laurel was still wearing. "I'd feel better if you were carrying too."

Her head shook. "No, you wouldn't. Listen, I'm not against it. I don't want one unless I know how to use it. I don't."

"Shooting range is on our list of things to do," I said. "We'll do a rain check for now."

Laurel's eyes filled with tears. "No rain checks, Mason. I promise you that if you take me, I'll go to a shooting range. No rain check."

Recalling Laurel's words after finding Cartwright—that he'd promised her a rain check, I reached for her hand. "Then we'll call it a date, Dr. Carlson."

Her lips turned upward. "I would love to go on a date with you."

I lifted a metal box and placed it on a higher shelf. "This is what I hope Jack kept supplied and charged." As I spoke, I opened the box. Letting out a sigh, I pulled out multiple basic cellular phones, the kind that could be purchased at a big-box store or a gas station. Most importantly, the kind that weren't registered to a user or chipped with a GPS device.

"Oh, we're not disconnected any longer," Laurel said, her big blue eyes peering at me through the dirt on her cheeks. "Mason, who can you call?"

My already-churning stomach did another flip. A few weeks

ago, I would have said no one, there was no fucking person to call
for help against the Order. That had changed. Along with remembering who I was, I now recalled what I was and what I did.

I'd pledged my loyalty to a man, a family, a different kind of
order. I hadn't broken that vow; it had been taken from me. I
just hoped that somehow I could make him see what had truly
happened.

"There's only one man—make that three—who can help us
out of this. The questions racing through my mind included are
they still there, will I be able to reach them, and will they help."

"You said you work alone."

Thinking of Jack, I sighed. "I guess I wasn't completely
alone, not like I am now."

"I'm here," Laurel said, "even if I'm no help."

"This is all for you. If it weren't, I'd be searching this property for Jack's killer. I plan on doing that. First, I have to get you
to safety, and there's only one place that comes to mind."

"Where?"

"Chicago." I turned on the phone. A telephone number that
had been missing from my brain for nearly seven years came
back with amazing clarity.

Did it still work?

Would it lead me to the one man who could help me?

I took a deep breath and began entering the number. "It's
now or never."

LAUREL

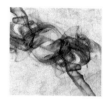

*W*rapping my arms around my midsection, I watched as disappointment settled over us, dimming the one light bulb and covering us in its gloom. Anguish materialized as small lines on Mason's face and concern in his green eyes. The man, the one who when I first met had no emotions, now had them in excess. They emanated from him in waves.

Exhaling, he shook his head and tossed the phone to the shelf.

"What happened? Didn't it work?" I asked.

"The phone worked. It must be the number. I fucking know it *was* right. It didn't connect. Some damn recording." He shook his head. "Of course, it didn't fucking work. It's been too long, too many years. I don't even know if..."

"If?"

"I want to think they changed it, not that anything has happened to them..." He stared off into space.

I reached for his arm. "If this person lives in Chicago, can't you find him?"

"It's not that easy."

"The company you worked for, that real estate place, maybe someone there could help."

"Laurel, so many worlds exist that you don't understand." He ran his finger over my cheek as his Adam's apple bobbed. "It's better that way."

"Mason, I understand more than you know."

He nodded. "I didn't say you weren't fucking brilliant."

"Then tell me what you're talking about."

His head shook. "I've already done too much of that and showed you too much. I won't do more." Stepping away, Kader's hand went over his hair, his long fingers combing through his locks as his massive body spun in place. Beneath his ragged shirt, his bicep bulged. Cords came to life in his neck and his chiseled jaw clenched. "This..." He didn't finish.

Going to him, I laid my hand over his chest. "...will work out. I trust you."

"Fucking don't."

"Why? You haven't failed me yet."

"I haven't failed you?" He reached for my hands and turned each one palm up. "You're hurt, dirty, and bloody. We're trapped in a barn filled with filthy horse stalls. Jack is dead. I wanted to save you, to save your formula, and find out who hired me. All I did was put you in harm's way."

"Tell me what you mean."

"Laurel, it's not you that they're after. It's me."

"What? Why?" I asked, my gaze narrowing.

"That's it. Fuck yes." His green eyes sparkled with whatever revelation had just occurred to him. "Stay here. I'm going back into Jack's house."

My head shook as I reached for his hand. "Why? What are you going to do?"

"I know who killed Jack. Not the person but the organization. I'll contact them and negotiate: me for your safety."

"What the hell does that mean? If it means you're planning on giving yourself up to some organization that killed Jack, you're crazy. That isn't happening."

He stood taller, his neck straightening as he exhaled. "Laurel, I made a commitment, as did Jack. I don't know why they think I went against them or if they think Jack did. All I know is that the...this entity is capable of keeping you safe. Fuck, they can give you a new name, a new life. I know they can. They did it for me."

"I don't want a new life if you're not in it."

He reached for my shoulders. "I..." His Adam's apple bobbed again as he forced a smile. "Dr. Carlson, I don't know how I forgot you, but it won't happen again. You can be certain of that."

"Mason, stop." New tears came to my eyes. "What if they hurt you?"

"It doesn't matter. They may. They're fucking capable, but they won't kill me. That would be too easy. They want what I have. I was stupid to think I could break free. In the back of my mind, I think I always knew that wasn't possible. And because of me...Jack..." He let out a long breath. "I don't think I really cared what would happen until your blue eyes saw me through my screen. Before then, nothing mattered. Now something matters, *you*. I'll go back and do whatever they say, knowing that you have a life—a safe life."

I couldn't see as tears filled my eyes and I fell against his broad chest.

Slowly, his arms encircled me. "I'll think about you every day.

Know that. No matter where you are, I'll be thinking about you." He lifted my chin. "Don't let that stop you from having a life." His head tilted as a sad smile came to his lips. "I remember a young girl who talked about being a great scientist."

I swallowed the lump forming in my throat.

"We used to talk...up on the roof of the rec center under the stars. She told me that anything was possible. Through her, I was able to see the shithole my life was and believe it could change."

"Mason..."

"She had more dreams, that girl. She wasn't only going to be a great scientist; she was going to be a wife and mom, a super-woman capable of anything."

I sniffed as my nose ran and head ached.

"Follow those dreams."

"I-I..." I sucked in a ragged breath, forcing my words to come. "Please don't do this." I peered up through my dripping lashes. "Mason, those dreams included you."

"I'm sorry, but Mason died."

"Stop...who are these people?"

"Me. I'm part of them."

"They killed Jack. What if they don't negotiate?"

"They will." Mason released me and took a step back. "Stay here, Doc. I'll be back."

"No," I staggered toward him. "You said you wouldn't leave me."

"It won't take long. I know this will be a call that will be answered."

My eyes closed as my knees grew weak and my backside fell to the ground. The sound of the sliding door echoed through the room followed by another sound, one I presumed was the movement of the shelves being pushed back over the door. I let out a long breath, hugging my knees to my chest.

I wasn't certain how much time had passed. It seemed like seconds, yet it only takes sixty to make a minute. Maybe it was more. I wasn't certain of anything until the phone Kader had tossed onto the table began to ring.

My eyes sprang open. "Mason!"

The phone rang again.

"Mason!" I called toward the door.

Oh God.

Jumping to my feet, I wiped away my tears with the back of my hand and wiped it on my jeans.

Ring.

My gaze went between the door and the phone.

Ring.

I reached for the phone and hit the connect button. "Hello." My heart pumped faster as I waited for a response. "Hello, oh, please be there."

"Who is this?" the deep, demanding masculine voice asked.

Was this who Mason had called?

Was this who he trusted?

Or could it be that other group?

"Did this number call you?" I asked.

"You have five seconds and then this number will be blocked."

"Please, tell me."

"Yes, you called. Three seconds."

My head shook. Hell no, that wasn't all. My entire body practically convulsed as I held the phone tighter. "I didn't call you, not *me.*"

"Lady—"

"It wasn't me. His name is Mason, Mason Pierce." I spoke as fast as I could. "He said you were the only one who could help us. Please don't hang up." My eyes closed as I waited, praying that this person would listen.

"Hello?" I questioned.

The line went dead.

LAUREL

"**No!**" I called out staring down at the cheap cellular phone in my hand.

Mason.

I had to let him know before he called whomever he planned to call.

Stuffing the phone into one of my jean pockets, I pried my fingers between the door and jamb and pulled. The moment it moved, I let out a breath, thanking the heavens that it wasn't locked from the outside.

Despite their size and bulk, the shelves moved easier. I scanned the inside of the large barn. "Mason!"

Oh, please don't call those people.

My tennis shoes slipped on the straw-covered floor as I hurried through the barn and out into the yard. Just as quickly, I stopped.

"Dr. Carlson," he greeted.

The sinister tone to the familiar greeting sent chills down my spine.

I took a step back as I stared at the dean of the university.

It was as if time and space had altered. Confusion washed through me, changing everything I knew, everything I believed. The world was out of place.

Why would Carl Oaks be here?

"Mason!" I called, searching the driveway and yard as the breeze picked up, rustling the taller grass in the distance.

Dr. Oaks's shoulders relaxed as he took a step my way. "Thank goodness. I was told that I'd find you here. Your parents will be so relieved."

I took another step back. "Carl? What's happening?" I searched, looking around for Mason, yet he wasn't there. It was only Dr. Oaks. "Why are you here? Why did you come *here?*"

"Laurel, you've had us so worried."

My hands fell to my sides as I fought the urge to run my palms over the denim and confirm the flash drives were still present in my pocket. I balled my fists. "Carl..."

"Look at you," he said, his voice dripping with concern. "My God, are you all right? What has happened to you? Were you taken?" His eyes opened wide. "Did someone kidnap you? Is that how you got here?"

I peered down at my filthy shirt, the dirt on my jeans and shoes. Lifting my hands, I saw the dried dirt and blood. I looked back up. "You're here, why?"

"For you, of course."

"I'm fine. You can go."

"And leave you here?" he questioned. "I couldn't live with myself if that happened." He extended his hand. "Come with me, Dr. Carlson. I'll take you to the authorities and after they get your statement, we'll head home."

"Home?"

"Indianapolis." He pulled a phone from a pocket inside his jacket. "Here, use my phone and call your parents. I am sure they'll be as relieved as I am." He extended the phone my direction. When I didn't move, he added, "Don't you think they should know that you're not dead? That had been the rumor for both you and Dr. Cartwright." Carl turned his head from side to side. "Is he here too?"

I swallowed and lifted my chin. "No, he isn't here. I haven't seen him..." I shook my head. "...since Indianapolis."

Carl's brow furrowed. "Are you sure?"

"Yes, I'm certain."

"Was that before or after you killed him?" Carl asked, lifting his phone. "Come, you will appreciate my question better after you see this picture."

Acid bubbled in my stomach, creating a sour taste in my mouth. "I don't know what you're talking about."

He stepped closer and his large nose wrinkled. "It's a picture of Cartwright."

"Okay."

"Come, Laurel, take a look."

I took another step, wondering if I made it to that room if I could use a gun. I was an intelligent woman. I could do it. I would. Shaking my head, I said, "I don't want to see a picture of Russ."

"It's not very flattering. Let me describe it." Before I could respond, he went on. "You see, Russell is there on your floor, your bedroom floor."

I took another step back. "What are you talking about?"

"The two of you were romantically involved. He wanted to break it off and go to work at Sinclair Pharmaceuticals. You argued." His beady eyes came my way. "Damien Sinclair confirmed his offer. Dr. Cartwright accepted it and promised

he'd get you on board. You should know that I've given my statement to the police."

"You're mistaken."

Jack's front door opened, the screen door slamming as
Stephanie Moore stepped onto the porch. From my vantage
point, I scanned her up and down; my gaze fixed on her feet—
her boots.

Her small boots.

"Nothing is ever easy with you, Dr. Carlson, is it?"

"You...it was you," I said, staring at the woman who'd been
my assistant for the last two years. Her blonde hair was secured
back in a messy bun and her lean, athletic body was covered in a
sweater and stretchy denim leggings.

Her smile broadened. "Me. What was me?" Her eyes opened
wide. "Oh, I know. I know more than you ever gave me credit
for knowing."

"That's not true. I valued—"

Stephanie raised her hand. "My turn. Who am I? That was
your question. Let me share. I was the other woman fucking
your boyfriend and learning your secrets." She tilted her head.
"Sometimes on the same day. Yes, that was me."

My stomach twisted and hands trembled, yet I didn't move
forward.

Her nose wrinkled. "I'm not sure how you put up with it for
so long. I mean, the sex really wasn't that great, but he was
smart...and greedy, I'll give him that. He sold you out, you know."

"No, Russ wouldn't do that."

"Oh, that's right." She slapped her thighs with her palms.
"God, I'd forgotten how repulsively nauseating your Little Mary
Sunshine act could be."

My mouth opened in utter shock, yet nothing came out.

Stephanie went on. "Perfect Laurel Carlson with a doctorate in this and in that. So fucking smart and yet so damn stupid. You had the whole world on a platter and were the face of an amazing drug, one with unlimited potential." Her head shook. "Too much potential. Oh, and one you stole."

Stole?

"The thing was," she continued, "all you would have had to do was join us. After the government shut down your study, the data was gold. All it would have taken was for you to have gotten off your fucking perfect pedestal."

Government?

"He said he gave you a chance. Did he?"

I shook my head at her question. "He? Russ? What?" My vocabulary had been reduced to one-word sentences.

Her smile beamed. "I told you, Carl. He didn't. Without her, our cuts were higher." She laughed. "And he said you were greedy."

I thought back to what she'd said a minute earlier. "The government wanted our study to stop." It was a statement, yet the way I voiced it, the sentence sounded more like a question.

"Carl?" Stephanie said as she shrugged. "It's not like she'll be able to tell anyone."

Again my eyes searched for Mason. "Where is he?"

"Jackson?" Stephanie asked.

"No..." I hesitated, wondering what name to use. "...Edgar."

"Oh, if you mean the man who owns this property, he's a little tied up at the moment." She turned back to Dr. Oaks. "You were saying?"

"Laurel, you don't look well. Perhaps we could go inside?"

I shook my head. "That's Jack's house. We can't just go in."

Stephanie laughed. "I don't think he'll complain."

I turned to Carl. "What did the government have to do with our research?"

"You know how the government is…I didn't get much elaboration. I was only told to discontinue the funding and stop the research."

"The government? *Our* government?" I asked, trying to piece together what I knew with what they were saying. "They wanted it shut down and you sold it?"

Carl's chin rose higher. "I stopped the sale to Sinclair Pharmaceuticals."

"No, Carl, the sale on the black market. The one you completed. The one that made you over a billion dollars richer or is all of that money going to your wife. You did have the deposits go to the Caymans."

Dr. Oaks turned to Stephanie. "Where is he, the man who was supposed to do the job? You said he never failed. I should have just told Harding sooner…"

I sucked in a breath as that puzzle was solved. Carl was the man who hired Kader. He hadn't found my assassin by himself; he'd had Stephanie's help. "You hired an assassin?" I asked, not directing my question to either one.

"That sounds so dramatic," Carl said. "This…" He gestured between us. "…wasn't supposed to happen. It was really a simple plan. I'd shut down the research and make the government happy. Why not make some money on the side?"

"Why kill me, Russ, and Eric?"

Carl's lips pursed to the side. "Eric wasn't planned. He did that to himself." He huffed. "Who knew he had the balls?"

"Not me," Stephanie replied as if it wasn't a rhetorical question.

"Me and Russ?" I asked.

"Consider yourself unique," Stephanie said. "You were the only planned death."

Was that supposed to make me feel better?

"Cartwright confirmed you wouldn't sell. We couldn't have a whistle blower. Well, and he blew it when he went to your house."

"The night of the gathering?" I asked.

"No," she said. "The night you were supposed to die."

"I'd given up on her guy and called in a favor," Oaks volunteered.

"Russell didn't tell me that he went to you," Stephanie said. "I found out. That's when I talked him into retrieving the hard drive from your house." Her cheeks rose. "Cute idea to hide it behind a stone in your fireplace."

My fingertips came to my lips. "Oh my God. You were the person behind him. You killed Russ. You shot him."

"And it was so perfect to blame on you. Jealous lovers..." She tilted her head toward Carl. "...he even had the picture."

"Then when the police arrived," Stephanie said, "there was nothing. He was gone. Not one damn clue."

Carl looked to Stephanie. "I'm done. Let's get out of here."

My breath caught as Stephanie pulled a gun from behind her. I took another step back as she clicked the safety and lifted it, extending her arms.

"I'm ready for this to be done, too," she said.

I jumped and closed my eyes, wishing I had time to replay my life even in my thoughts. I pictured Mason, not as he is, but as he was when we first met. The image gave me strength as the air filled with the explosion coming from her gun.

LAUREL

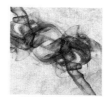

I waited for the pain of the bullet's impact.

Did death occur so quickly that it was painless?

Opening my eyes, I gasped as I took in Carl Oaks's lifeless body.

Holy shit.

"Oh my God," I said.

Stephanie shook her head. "That man was on my last nerve."

"So you killed him?"

She lifted her gun, pointing it at me. "I have more bullets."

"What about the money in the Caymans?"

A small smile came to her lips. "Another clue leading to him, and he was too dumb to realize it wasn't his account." Slowly she lowered her gun. "Good news, Dr. Carlson. It's not your time yet."

"Why?" I asked. "I-I mean, good."

"That hard drive. It was out of date." She tilted her head toward Jack's house. "He didn't write the current listing for the updated research. I knew as soon as I read it that it had to be you. That's how I knew you weren't dead, why I asked for proof."

"He?" I prayed it was Mason, that he was still alive.

She moved the gun. "Come with me."

"Where are we going?"

"Back up to his house."

Oh, she did mean Mason.

"I know you have the data. Give it to me and I'll let him live."

I nodded. "I have it."

While it was in my pocket, I hoped that by going up to the house, I'd give Mason more time. I wasn't certain what he needed time to do, but I hoped it would help. "Are we walking?" I asked.

"No, I have an SUV."

We pulled up to Kader's house like two old friends. That was the way we looked. As they say, appearances aren't always as they seem. We definitely weren't two old friends.

I looked down at my dirty hands, resting in my lap, where Stephanie had told me to place them. "Why aren't I tied up or something?" I asked. "I know I'm new to this dark, dangerous life, but shouldn't I be restrained?"

She looked my way and grinned. "Nauseating yet refreshing. It's too bad you won't be around for long."

I let out a long breath. "Why did you do this?"

"You didn't catch the part about the 1.2 billion dollars that is now completely mine?"

I weighed my thoughts, wondering how honest I should be.

"Go ahead. I can tell you want to say something."

"What about Pam?"

Putting the SUV in park, Stephanie leaned back against the driver's seat. "Damn, I didn't expect you to be so well-informed." She turned my way. "Don't worry about it. The money's all mine. My partners are gone. Pretty soon, I will be a memory." Her cheeks rose. "Not one of yours. Funny. Don't you think? Your goal was to erase traumatic memories and in reality, all it takes is a gunshot to the temple. No more memories."

One would think I'd be frightened. Maybe I was. Maybe I was past that. Or perhaps my goal was to get back to Mason. I wasn't confident in anything, only that keeping Stephanie talking was my best option. As long as I could hear her, I was alive.

She tilted her chin toward the house. "Nice place."

Okay, we were resorting to small talk. "It is."

Opening the driver's door, she said, "Let's go."

As I reached for the handle, I winced. The cut on my palm was again open and angry. Surely the filth of the mine shaft and barn weren't the most therapeutic. I lifted it toward Stephanie. "I know you're going to kill me, but maybe I could clean up first?"

"Do you have the up-to-date data?"

"I do."

"Here?" she asked with a tilt of her chin toward the house.

"Yes, but I'm not sure I can access it."

"Don't lie to me."

I took a deep breath and scanned the grounds, hoping for a miracle, but losing faith each minute. "I'm not. Someone messed with K-Edgar's security. Nothing was working last night."

"Let's go," she said.

I walked ahead of her and reached for the door handle. Before trying to open it, I asked, "How did you find me?"

"He was supposed to kill you. I didn't know much about him

only that he was supposed to be this man with unlimited talents."

My mind went where it didn't belong. That was all right. If I were about to die, doing so with thoughts of Kader's many talents going through my mind wasn't a bad way to go.

"I tracked him down. Once I did, I found your fingerprint."

"In the house?"

"In the database."

I squeezed the handle and pushed. The door didn't budge. Like a jolt of caffeine, my pulse quickened. "It's locked. I swear it's not me."

"No, I have it turned off." Stephanie pushed past me, and squeezed the handle. When it didn't budge, she reached for her gun. "Come with me."

"If she won't let us in, we can't get in."

"If the fucking research and development is in there, we're getting in."

I'd never really walked around the exterior of Kader's home. The way it was set on his property, all of the windows were high, even on the first level, the ground below them sloped. Stephanie pointed to the balcony that I knew was off of Kader's bedroom. Looking up was worse than looking down.

"There."

"Are you crazy?"

"Not the thing to ask a woman with a gun."

I again showed her my palms. "Even if I had a rope and was normally capable of such a thing, I couldn't do it now."

She let out a long breath. "Meet me at the front door."

My mind went to her SUV. "Okay."

"Don't even think about defying me. Jackson's dead. Pierce will be too."

Pierce.

Shit.

She knew his real name.

I nodded my head. "I'll be there, at the front door." I peered upward. "Can you get up there?"

"How stupid are you?"

I didn't answer.

"I was there last night when you closed the door."

"And you didn't try to hurt me?"

"I needed you for what happened earlier. You were my bait to get Oaks out here. Be there when I open the door."

"Stephanie, I don't care if you let me live. Don't kill him. He already died." I didn't wait for her to respond as I turned and headed toward the front door.

Sitting on the top step, I looked out over the land. The afternoon sun was still high and out on the prairie, the grass was greener than it had been when I first arrived. I lifted my face to the sun. Even through the dirt and grime, the rays warmed my skin.

I doubted I'd be able to overpower Stephanie, but as I sat there, I made the decision to try.

A rumbling like we'd heard this morning came into range. Squinting, I searched the blue sky for the culprit. It wasn't a plane or a drone. I was certain it was a helicopter. And then it stopped. Didn't fade, but ended.

A few minutes later, her voice made me turn. "Dr. Carlson."

"I thought you said you didn't have to share the money."

"I don't."

Then who was flying a helicopter?

MASON

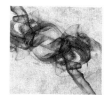

$\mathcal{M}$y eyes blinked open and my head throbbed.

"Laurel." My mouth felt dry as my tongue stuck to the roof of my mouth.

What the fuck?

I was lying on the floor and unable to move my arms. Twisting and turning, I assessed the situation. My wrists were bound, yet as I scooted over the tile, it was clear that I wasn't attached to anything. Whoever had done this must have hit me from behind and believed I'd either stay unconscious longer or not try to free myself.

Flexing my arms, I pulled against the restraint. As I did, my bicep ached.

I hadn't only been hit. Someone injected me with something.

I searched for a window.

How fucking long had I been unconscious?

The sun was still shining. Or was it the next day?

"Laurel, I'm coming." While I didn't say the words aloud, I screamed them in my head. The memory of her, every fucking memory came back as I unsteadily made my way to my feet and looked around.

This was Jack's house. I was in one of his bedrooms. Making my way to the door, I turned and reached for the handle.

Locked.

"Fuck this."

Taking a step back, I lifted my boot and kicked the door as I had the opening to the mine shaft. The sound of the collision echoed through the bedroom, yet the door remained intact.

Another kick and another.

I put my weight behind it and still the door stayed secure.

Leaning against the wall, I took a deep breath and reassessed. It seemed as though whatever I'd been injected with had me off-balance and not at full strength. Closing my eyes, I inhaled and exhaled. It was as I opened them that I noticed the window, the same one I'd just used to assess daytime.

While it seemed clear I wasn't functioning on all cylinders, that barely slowed me down as I tucked my head and threw myself through the panes. Glass and casing shattered as my body fell to the ground below and rolled on the grass. Shaking away the odd feeling of the drug, I stared up at the blue sky as the whirr of a helicopter came closer.

I scurried to my knees and feet.

This chopper wasn't flying low—it was fucking landing upon the lane in front of Jack's house.

No one entered my property and suddenly it was Grand Central Fucking Station.

Leaning against the side of Jack's house I watched, wishing I could get back to the barn for a new gun. It was too late. After the blades slowed and lowered, both sides of the helicopter opened and three large men stepped out, guns at the ready.

"What the fuck?"

This wasn't a team from the Order. We didn't announce our presence. We infiltrated, coming in quietly and taking care of business. These men were acting more like federal agents or the opposite, members of the underground.

No.

A strange flame of hope flickered to life.

I wanted to believe. For nearly seven years hope and belief were removed from my thoughts as well as my vocabulary. Maybe I was what I'd called Eric Olsen—a dead man walking. It wasn't like I could fight off three grown men with my hands tied behind my back, literally.

"Pierce," one man called.

I sucked in a breath and stepped from the side of the house.

"Raise your hands," the three yelled in unison.

"I can't." I spun showing them my hands.

While two men continued to keep their weapons trained on me, the third came closer. "Tell me who you are."

I lifted my chin. "Mason Pierce."

"I was told to ask you one question."

My head bobbed as I hoped my memories were truly complete. "Ask."

The man pulled his phone from his pocket. "The boss was specific." He looked down at his screen and back to me. "No pressure, but if you're lying he said to kill you on the spot."

I stood taller, my shoulders as broad as possible with my arms still bound. "Ask."

He read from his phone. "Did you think a rook could take a knight?"

My eyes closed and nostrils flared as I inhaled, filling my lungs with air. Behind my lids, I saw the chessboard. With the image came the realization of why I had chess pieces within my ink. Memories crashed like waves on a beach, one after another, a never-ending cycle as they came from the depths of my subconscious. Taking another breath, fighting to maintain a semblance of control, and doing my best to calm the churning sea, I opened my eyes and spoke to the man with the phone. "Are you in contact with your boss now?"

The other two men came closer, the barrels of their guns unabashedly aimed at me.

I stayed perfectly still.

"Yes."

"Tell him no," I said with my chin high. "Tell him he has it backward. If he would have sat the fuck down and finished the game, my knight most certainly would have taken his rook."

The man's eyes widened. "That's what you want me to say...to him?"

"Every fucking word."

Lifting his hand, signaling for the other men to stay back, the man with the phone sent the text.

Instead of receiving a text in response, the air filled with the shrill ring of the man's phone.

"Boss. Yes." He scanned me up and down. "Big. Hulk-big. Brown hair. Green eyes." He nodded. "Yes, sir." He turned to me. "He wants to talk to you."

I turned, again showing my hands. After the man with the phone snapped his fingers, one of the other men returned his gun to his holster and came my way with a blade in his hand.

A groan came from my lips as the binding gave way. Stretching my shoulders, I extended my hand.

"Same consequences," the man said as he handed the phone to me. "You lie, you die."

Gripping the phone, I brought it to my ear. "I fucking owe you, Sparrow."

For what seemed like an eternity, the line remained silent.

Finally, he spoke. Like a ghost from the past, his voice and tone reminded me of the way things had been and perhaps, how they could be again. "If this isn't you, you're dying again."

"It's me."

"We need to talk. Death isn't off the table."

My lips turned upward. "You always did think you were a badass."

"Time has passed. I am."

"I believe you," I said. "How did you find me? The call didn't connect."

"Reid called back and spoke with a woman."

Reid.

A woman.

Lorna.

I had too many questions for a phone call.

My chest tightened.

Laurel.

With my gut twisting, my eyes darted around, for the first time noticing a body lying in the driveway. Even from a distance I knew it wasn't Laurel. While that was encouraging, that didn't tell me where she had gone or who she was with.

Maybe she was still in the barn.

"Go with the Sparrows," Sterling Sparrow said through the phone. "The plane is on its way. I want to see you back in Chicago, yesterday."

"Sparrow, I know I have no fucking right to ask, but I need your help. I need a favor and you're the only who could help."

"If you're who you say you are, you're wrong. You're one of the few who has a right. What do you need?"

LAUREL

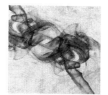

*A*s I led Stephanie into Kader's house, I searched desperately for a distraction, anything to keep her occupied while I learned more about Mason—where he was and how he was—as well as why there had been another helicopter. I stilled at the bottom of the stairs. "I need to clean up."

She scoffed. "This isn't a luncheon. Where is the data?"

"No, it's not, but I'm filthy and exhausted." I peered beyond the archways. "And hungry. Aren't you hungry?"

"Dr. Carlson, my patience is wearing thin. I have plans and spending the afternoon reminiscing isn't part of them."

The tears coming to my eyes were real. I wasn't looking for sympathy. She'd told me repeatedly that death was on my agenda. I just wanted to feel less disgusting. "Stephanie, you're going to kill me. Please give me ten minutes. I'll shower, change clothes, and come back down."

"What's to stop you from exiting the balcony?"

"Twenty to thirty feet and these..." I showed her my bloodied hands again.

"Let me see the data first."

"Why didn't the door open? I thought you'd overridden the system."

"It's working with a few adjustments."

What adjustments?

I exhaled. "Fine. It's on a laptop in the office."

"Connected to the house's IT system?" she asked.

My chin fell as I walked toward the office. "No. It's not connected."

"You're either dumb or trusting or both."

My feet stilled as my chin lifted and neck straightened. "What the hell is your problem?"

"My problem?" she repeated. "My problem is that I've spent the last two years suffocating under your watch. You're fucking trusting of anyone yet also no one. I could come and go from your house, get into your files, and yet you kept the important data just out of reach."

"My house?" I asked, my brow furrowed as my head shook. I didn't recall Kader saying she'd been in my house.

"Yes, Dr. Carlson. I frequented it regularly before Carl hired Kader. After that, I came just enough to learn his system."

"But he never saw——"

"Because I'm good. My training is newer. I knew what to look for."

"Is that how you turned off his cameras when you and Russ came to my house?"

"Imagine when Russell told me about the damn stone. The two of you have accolades for your intelligence and you hid the hard drive behind a *stone*." Her head shook. "There's no way to predict with you. And then here I ask about the laptop. There's no way for you to know I've searched his system, yet you confess the truth. It's like you're too smart for your own good and too stupid to lie."

"If I'm so stupid, why do you want my research?"

"I don't. Uncle Sam wants it. If they find out about the black-market sale, I can prove it wasn't me. My data is newer."

I turned toward the office, past the large fireplace in the living room, and stilled. Though I hadn't been in Kader's house long, it had a sense of home, one that having Stephanie here was fading. Walking down the hallway and stepping over the gray threshold, I had an idea.

Maybe I was too stupid.

Maybe I wasn't.

"It's in here," I said, moving farther onto the gray industrial surface. I pointed to the laptop.

"Boot it up. I don't know if I can believe you."

I thought I was too stupid to lie. While I thought those words, saying them didn't seem prudent.

Sighing, I sat, opened the computer, and hit the power button. As it booted up, I asked, "Why would the government care about my research?"

"They don't like it when people steal their intellectual property and claim ownership."

My neck straightened. "I didn't steal. You were there. You know we did this. Russ and I did this." I gestured toward the screen. "And the ownership isn't mine. It belonged to the university."

Stephanie shrugged as she sat before the laptop. "You might have gotten away with it if you hadn't called attention to yourself. That's why I've been stuck with you for the last two years."

"How did I call attention...?"

She lifted her hand. "Stop. Go, ten minutes. If you're not back here by then, you're dying in the shower. Your choice."

It was true my mind was mush, but that didn't seem like much of a choice.

I turned toward the door. Coming to a stop, I twisted, craning my neck back to her. Stephanie's attention was engrossed in the files I'd retrieved. My pulse kicked up a notch as I contemplated my next move.

"Do you want anything from the kitchen?" I asked.

Her eyes didn't leave the screen. "This is really it."

"Food," I said again.

"Shut up and just go. The clock is ticking."

A lump formed in my throat as I wondered if the *adjustments* she'd made to the house's technology would allow my plan to work or thwart it in its tracks.

What was the worst that could happen if I failed?

She'd shoot me. That was already the plan.

Had it happened? Had I become tempered as Kader had?

Taking a deep breath near the doorway, I lifted my finger to the raised bubble hidden inconspicuously near the door's casing. Willing my hand to stay still, I peered back at her as the red light scanned.

It was now or never.

"Secure," I said, quickly stepping through the doorway just before the reinforced door appeared.

"What the hell?" It was the last thing I heard her say before the metal door closed between us.

I let out a long breath as I fell to the floor. "Please, let that work." I looked up to the ceiling. "Missy, please keep the office secure."

I jumped to my feet as gunfire echoed, ricocheting like bullets bouncing within a tin can.

Holy shit.

Stephanie was shooting at the door.

Pushing away from the wall, I ran toward the front door, my tennis shoes skidding on the wood floor as I came to the door, squeezed the handle, and pulled inward.

My scream came from the depths of my chest as I was met with the barrel of a gun.

Before I could quiet the sound or slow my speeding heart, Mason stepped into view and without a word, wrapped me in his arms. We'd both been through hell and it was evident in both our appearance as well as our aroma. And yet in his arms, his heartbeat thumping in my ear, was exactly where I wanted to be.

I collapsed in his embrace. "Please don't leave me," I said, my body pressed against his.

"Who...?" he said, looking beyond me, directing strange men into his house.

I looked up at his green stare, the one I wasn't certain I'd see again. "It's Stephanie."

"Your assistant?"

"Yes, but she's more than that. Something about the government and..." The house echoed with the reverberation of more gunshots. "I wasn't sure it would work. She's in your office."

Mason smiled. "Locked in?"

I nodded. "I did the finger scan and then rushed out."

He looked up at the other men. "She's not going anywhere. The only way to open the doors is by the command of the person who locked it." He shrugged.

"Are you sure?" asked a tall dark-haired man.

"I am, unless my office is dismantled. Help me get her to safety..." He pulled me closer as his head tilted my direction. "...and then we can deal with Stephanie or whoever she is."

"Sir, the boss wants you now. With your and his permission, we can take care of this problem after we get the two of you to the plane. According to a text I received, it will be arriving soon."

I looked up at Mason. "The boss? A plane?"

He squeezed my shoulder, pressing me closer to him. "I have a few things to tell you. Let's get out of here."

"Are you sure you want to leave?" I didn't mean the trauma of the day; I meant his land and house, the place he'd come to enjoy.

Mason nodded. "I'm sure. I'm ready to go home."

"Home?"

"Sir," the dark-haired man said. "If it's okay with you, we'll leave Jimmy here to watch that room until you and the boss decide. Nick and I will escort the two of you to the plane."

"I thought you worked alone," I whispered as we scooted into an SUV.

"I hope not anymore."

After a drive back to Jack's, we stopped, and sitting in the middle of the lane that led to the front gate was a helicopter. I looked from the helicopter to Mason. "No, I don't think so."

Getting out of the back seat, he extended his hand. "Come on, Laurel, trust me."

A grin came to my face as I recalled the young man who said the same thing, taking me up narrow steps and onto a roof. I trusted him then and I'm bound to him now, trusting him with my body, life, and love. I placed my hand in his.

"Where are we going?" I shook my head. "Never mind, as long as you're with me, the destination doesn't matter."

The two large men said very little as they helped us into the helicopter. Yet whenever they spoke, it was with a measurable aura of respect, referring to Mason as *Mr. Pierce*.

With headphones in place, the helicopter lifted, its blades blowing the prairie grass as we rose over Jack's house, the bunkhouse, and barns. The higher we flew, the more of his land came into view. The ravine no longer was infested with dangers; instead, I saw it as our escape into the underground world of mine shafts. Higher on the ridge was Mason's house and outbuildings. Between and lower were pastures outlined with fences. It was truly stunning land.

When I'd first arrived, I'd equated its rough edges with Kader's—beautiful but dangerous. As he reached for my hand with the sleeve of his shirt raised enough for me to see his swirling colors around his cuff and I smiled up at his striking green gaze, I realized that the danger I'd perceived simply existed in the unknown. With each revelation of the man beneath the ink, the man he'd kept hidden—or was hidden from him—I became less afraid of that man and more fearful of losing him.

Over thirty minutes later, the helicopter landed at a private airport. Private was not meant to insinuate small. The various planes on the tarmac ranged from small ones similar to Mason's to huge monstrosities. Once the blades above stilled, the men opened the doors and escorted us out onto the sun-drenched tarmac.

A small cart came to transport us to the plane we'd been told was coming. It was as Mason squeezed my hand that I looked up to see his shining gaze. My eyes following the direction he was looking, I gasped.

"What the hell is that?"

The plane before us was like nothing I'd ever seen before. It was painted like a bird, a caricature that made the creature artistically fierce. With the gray head, white cheeks, and a black bib, it appeared predatory as the open beak covered the very front and its piercing dark eye surrounded the window to the cockpit.

Mason smiled. "It's a sparrow."

The steps descended before us with two women and a man standing at the top of the stairs. The man hurried down. "Mr. Pierce."

He nodded. "Yes, I'm Mason Pierce and this..." He tilted his head toward me. "...is Dr. Carlson."

My head snapped his direction at the use of my real name. Before I could question, the man who introduced himself as Keaton welcomed us aboard. At the top of the stairs, the pilot introduced herself as well as another flight attendant.

My mind was too scattered to retain their names or what was being said around us.

After he'd shown us to comfortable large seats and asked if we wanted anything to eat or drink, Keaton offered, "Mr. Pierce and Dr. Carlson, Mrs. Sparrow was made aware that you've had a rather difficult day. She wanted you to know that you're welcome to simply relax; however, once we're airborne, there's a shower as well as fresh clothes available for your use and a bedroom near the back if you'd like more comfortable surroundings."

Mason's brows raised. "Mrs. Sparrow? Mr. Sparrow's mother?"

Keaton smiled. "No, sir. Mrs. Sparrow is his wife."

After Keaton walked away, Mason leaned back and shook his head. "I guess I've been away for a while."

"Away from where?" I asked. "Are you taking me to paradise?"

"If I recall correctly, it's pretty damn close. I just hope we can stay."

MASON

I couldn't stop my pulse from racing as we came closer to our destination. Chicago's majestic skyline came into view through the windows, the lights and lake. Everything brought back memories, many coming at light speed. It was almost more than I could register. I had no doubt that it would take me time to remember everything. Not only that, I'd need time to remember how to be a part of a team, a real team.

I'd been alone with Jack for so long.

My chest ached at the thought of Commander Jackson dead in his house, killed in the line of duty, the duty of protecting his assignment—me. There were pieces of this assignment and how it had snowballed that were still out of reach.

One night, many years ago, Jack explained how he'd been added to the Order, how in the heat of battle he chose his troops over his lieutenant. While the military review board wouldn't understand, the Sovereign Order had. They saw his action as one that held country, republic, and democracy over chain of command—a chain of command that threatened the above.

According to the Order, there were times that warranted the three over the individual.

I wanted to believe that whatever went down with Jack, he did the same, choosing to protect his troop—me, believing that doing so was for the overall betterment of our cause.

There was more I needed to know about Stephanie Moore. I could and would do that, but now I hoped I wasn't alone. With what I recalled of Reid's abilities, I'd have help, help I was certain could exceed that of the Order. The problem was doing so without bringing attention to ourselves.

"Tell me again about..." Laurel gestured about. "...all of this, the people, and where we're going...and why you don't seem concerned that they know my name."

I ran the tip of my finger over her cheek. "This is a bubble. Your identity is safe and so is mine. No one violates the Sparrow trust and lives to tell about it."

Her blue eyes opened wide. "Is this like some secret—"

My finger touched her lips. "Doc, you're brilliant. I think you are smart enough to not ask too many questions."

"Should I be scared?"

"Are you?"

Laurel's head shook. "No, not as long as I'm with you."

Sitting back, I took her in, remembering all we'd been through since we woke in the back of the truck. Laurel Carlson was not only strong and smart—locking Stephanie in the office was ingenious—she took my fucking breath away.

"Thank you for being here."

"Even though my alternatives were vast, I'm with whom I want to be. The rest is icing."

Leaning my head back against the soft leather seat, I stared out at Chicago's lights as the plane began its descent. As I did, I recalled what we'd done, what Sparrow had provided since we came aboard. Even before that.

With the help of his men in Montana—yes, he had Sparrows scattered worldwide—we'd searched the barns and bunkhouse near Jack's place. After coming up empty, one of his men saw the tracks, leading from a rear barn up the road toward my house.

All the way up that drive, I again was plagued with images of Laurel as Jack had been. When we'd approached the house, I'd expected a knock-down, drag-out with whoever was responsible for Jack's death, Dr. Oaks's body, me being incapacitated, and Laurel's disappearance.

The best thing to happen was to open the door to her beautiful face.

There was too much evidence in support of the Order being involved for me to dismiss the possibility. That meant that Stephanie Moore was a part of the Order. If that were true, Jack could have known her, could have welcomed her into his home. In his position as commander, he was more acquainted with members of other teams than I.

Sparrow's support didn't end at the ranch.

Since getting airborne, both Laurel and I had showered. While I'd been able to shave and change into one of the fresh shirts, I was still wearing my ragged jeans and black boots. Not fitting into all of Sparrow's clothes reminded me of something I enjoyed. I was taller than he, not by a lot, but it was one of my advantages.

Laurel on the other hand, put on the clothes Keaton provided. Other than at the gathering, I'd never seen her in a dress, and while she was fucking sexy in one of my shirts, in what she called a simple gray shift and sweater, she was the most beautiful woman I'd ever seen.

Who was I kidding?

She was the most beautiful in anything and in nothing.

By the time we approached the landing, we had the opportunity to shower, eat a fantastic dinner, and place fresh bandages on Laurel's hands.

Turning hers over, I looked at the white bandage on her palm. "I'm so sorry."

Laurel shook her head. "I'm not, not about my hands. They'll heal because I'm alive, thanks to you."

"We're here because of you," I said.

"How's that?"

"You talked to Reid. That's what Sparrow said."

Her blue eyes opened wide. "The phone went dead. I thought the man didn't believe me."

"He spoke to you long enough to triangulate the call. That's why they landed the helicopter at Jack's. That's where you'd been."

She nodded. "These people you know...they have a lot of skills." Her gaze went around the cabin of the airplane. Currently, we were seated before a large TV screen on plush leather seats. "And a lot of money."

I swallowed. "I haven't been told and am quite honestly too nervous to ask, but there might be more."

"What?"

"Lorna."

Laurel sat taller as a smile brightened her face. "She's with them?"

"I don't know. If I asked and she wasn't, I was afraid I'd be worried and upset."

Laurel reached for my hand. "This *is* your home."

I brushed my lips over her forehead. "Only because you brought back the memories."

LAUREL

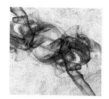

*a*s the plane, one of the biggest, most pimped-out planes I'd ever seen, touched down, I turned to Millie, the other flight attendant. "It's been a long day. What time is it here in Chicago?"

"It's almost eleven, Doctor."

I took a deep breath.

Mason's hand came over mine. "What's the matter?"

"Are we really going to his house this late at night? I mean, a man who owns a plane and can send a helicopter—"

"Doesn't like to wait," Mason interrupted. "And damn, this has been nearly seven years in the making. I can't believe he's married."

"And I'm wearing her clothes." I looked down at the gray dress, gray pumps, and white sweater. "So I'm just supposed to say, hi, thanks for saving us and oh yes, for clothes to wear?"

"I don't know what we're supposed to say. Go with it."

Though my freshly filled stomach was in knots, I nodded,

still unsure what the future would bring, where we would stay, what these people would be like, even if there was a chance to get the life I remembered back.

That seemed nearly impossible with Russ, Eric, and now Carl dead. I wasn't certain about Pam, and Stephanie was locked in the office at the ranch.

"Mr. Pierce, Dr. Carlson, there is a car waiting for you on the tarmac," Millie said after the plane came to a stop. "Have a nice evening."

Forcing a smile, I nodded as the cabin lost pressure and the door opened, stairs descending to the ground below. Standing at the top was as I imagined it was for dignitaries or royalty, a surreal feeling as a black SUV sat near the plane, a man standing near the driver's door.

Mason sighed.

"What?"

"It's a driver. I was hoping..."

Reaching for his hand, I squeezed. "Mr. Pierce, I would guess that making sure you are who you say you are is going to happen in a securer location." I looked up at his green gaze. "I'm not asking questions, but I am gathering suspicions that one doesn't simply walk up to Mr. or Mrs. Sparrow. We're still on trial."

Mason nodded. "You're right, as usual."

The driver introduced himself as Garrett and helped us into the back seat of his SUV. The rest of the drive was relatively quiet as he navigated the brightly lit Chicago streets. It had been a long time since I'd been in Chicago. While I was growing up in Oak Park, my parents would often bring Ally and me to the city for dinner, shopping, museums, or a play. Most of the time we'd ride the train into the city. It was another example of the difference in my childhood versus Mason's.

It was as the SUV passed a gate and began to descend down a lit tunnel that I reached over for Mason's hand. "Is it too late to turn back?"

His grin came my way. "It's been too late since I saw your picture. We were bound to the future we'd already set."

"And this is it?" I asked.

"I guess we'll see."

The SUV stopped outside an elevator within a parking garage filled with a variety of cars.

After helping us from the vehicle, Garrett said, "I'll escort you up. Mr. Murray is waiting."

Though Mason nodded, I felt his body tense.

Looking up, I wanted to ask who Mr. Murray was and why it wasn't Mr. Sparrow. I had many questions, yet the cloak of secrecy that seemed to envelop the world we'd entered kept them all neatly quieted on the tip of my tongue.

The elevator stopped at the floor marked 2. The doors opened to a stark cement wall with a sensor beside a steel door.

"Mr. Pierce, Mr. Murray said to enter, that your handprint will open the door."

We both stood straighter as I fought the rush of tears prickling my eyes. I flashed my gaze to Mason, feeling his sorrow, his overwhelming regret. If this were another test, he couldn't pass.

When he didn't speak, I did. "Garrett, can you please call Mr. Murray?"

"Ma'am, I was told—"

Without speaking, Mason turned his hands, showing Garrett the scarred, callous surface.

"His handprint won't work any longer," I said. "Please ask Mr. Murray to allow us entry to explain."

Instead of calling, Garrett typed a text and nodded. Less

than a minute later, to my relief, the steel door slid sideways disappearing into the wall. As it did another large man came into view.

His legs were spread, his hands behind his back, and his expression was less than welcoming. With radiant dark skin and short dark hair, his deep brown eyes glared, not at me but at Mason. The silence lingered, broken only by the ding of the elevator as Garrett wisely disappeared before the sliding of the door, closing us within.

Behind this man, I could see that we seemed to be in what appeared to be a technical epicenter, one that dwarfed Mason's in Montana. And while it was spectacular, it didn't command our attention the way the man's menacing stare, the way his biceps bulged below the sleeves of his shirt, and the way the tightening of his jaw, causing the cords in his thick neck to pop to the surface, did.

Such as the difference in the offices, I too was dwarfed by these two mountains of men. It was as if all the men around this organization were tall, built, and intimidating. Yet my concern wasn't for me, but for Mason.

Mason's chin rose. "Where is she?"

The she was Lorna.

"You look...different."

"I do. Now where is she?"

"She fucking mourned her brother once. I won't let her do it again."

"Not your choice. It's hers."

Mr. Murray shook his head. "Suddenly you believe she has a say."

"No, Reid, it's taken me seven fucking years." He lifted his hands, revealing his scarred palms. "I have a lot to explain."

"Then do it."

"First, tell me, is she here?" Mason's head tipped upward. "Is she safe?"

Reid relaxed his stance and brought his left hand forward, revealing a platinum wedding band. At the same time, Mason's tension broke. He exhaled, lowered his chin, and shook his head. It took a moment before he lifted his chin and met Reid's gaze. "I was wrong."

"About a fucking shitload of things. What specifically?"

"You. They don't make better men. I can never thank you enough for taking care of my sister."

"She's my wife. It works both ways. And for the record, I didn't do it for you."

"You're right. I want to see her."

Reid's head shook. "Not yet. Sparrow wants to see you first."

Mason took a deep breath. "I figured." He turned to me. "Reid, this is Laurel Carlson. If you ask Lorna, she should remember her."

"You're the one she wanted to tell about..." Reid said, recognition in his eyes.

Swallowing, I smiled. "Yes, I got her letter."

"She's a doctor," Mason said with pride in his tone.

I grinned. "From what little Mason has told me, intelligence isn't an uncommon trait around this place."

Reid's expression softened as a smile came to his lips. "She'll be happy to see you. We just need to..."

I lifted my hand that thankfully wasn't trembling as much as my insides were. "Please, no explanations. We're invading your home." I looked around. "At too late of an hour."

"If you'll excuse me, I need to take..." He looked back at Mason. "...I never thought I'd be saying your name again."

"Do you believe me?"

"I do," Reid said. "But as you know, my part of the vote won't be the deciding factor." He started to turn. "Come with me."

"Reid," Mason said, stopping Reid Murray's movement. "Laurel. Whatever Sparrow decides about me, I need your help. She's in danger. It's a long story, too. Promise me, no matter what happens regarding my future, she's safe."

Reid looked at me. "If Lorna recognizes and remembers you..." The smile returned to his face. "...nothing will happen to you."

Mason and I simultaneously let out the breaths we'd been holding.

"Laurel, stay here," Reid said. "Mason has a command performance he better not screw up."

Mason reached for my hand. "I'll be back."

"I hope so."

"If you see her, tell Lorna..." His neck straightened, the cords and tendons pulling tight. "...tell her that I do too."

I stood motionless as the two men disappeared across the room and down a hallway. Standing in place, I spun, taking in the magnitude of the technology around me. Huge screens hung from the ceiling and yet there were weight benches and other common accessories.

"Laurel."

A smile came to my lips as Reid returned. "You're married to Lorna?"

"I am. The last time I saw Mason, he wanted to kill me for it."

"For marrying her?"

Reid's lips came together. "We weren't married yet."

"Oh, I see."

Reid touched the sensor near the door. The steel slab opened to the hallway with the elevator. "Let me show you someplace more comfortable."

With one last glance toward the direction Mason had gone, I followed.

MASON

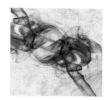

"Our men in Montana assured us that you weren't carrying when you entered the plane," Reid said as we walked.

"I'm still not."

It made sense to want that confirmed before I was to meet with Sparrow.

Reid looked my direction. "I believe you. If I didn't, I wouldn't be taking you to him."

As I followed Reid, the memories continued to bombard me. I recalled creating this maze of offices and meeting rooms. We'd left the second floor of the Sparrow outfit and made it down to the first. While this level was accessible to others within the organization, Reid had been careful to keep me to the unpopulated areas. If I were to guess, the capos out in the larger area had no idea that their king was even on the same floor.

This meant that while he'd appeared to trust me on the phone, nothing was set. I wouldn't be invited higher in his fortress without passing his test.

We came to a stop at one of the meeting rooms. In reality it was no different than the twenty others, but it was. Sterling Sparrow was on the other side of the door.

Reid's hand came to my shoulder. "Good luck."

A scoff came from my nose. I wasn't a man who believed in luck or fate or any of the shit people who haven't been to hell and back pin their future upon. Yet this meeting was for more than me, more than Sparrow, or the Sparrow outfit. This was for Laurel, to give her a place where she was safe. Even if her life's work wouldn't continue, if the Order was after her, there was no other place for her to hide.

Taking a deep breath, I straightened my shoulders, but as I reached for the doorknob, I stopped.

Before the explosion I might have dared to simply enter, especially if my presence was expected. This wasn't before.

Pulling my hand back, I rapped my knuckles against the surface and waited.

"Enter."

One word and I knew it was him. The rich fucking son of Allister Sparrow, the one with whom I'd had the misfortune of being within the same battalion in basic training. Too many things to recall had changed since that time.

With another deep breath, I turned the knob and pushed the door open.

Sitting at the end of a glossy long table was my greatest nemesis and my best fucking friend. Sitting in all his kingpin glory was the man I'd died to protect. It was an eerie reality to know without a bit of confusion that I'd do it again. That was how much I believed in not only him but in what he could do.

Without sitting, I stopped, taking him in as he was me.

He had the same dark hair and dark eyes. The years hadn't taken away from his physical stature, though I was sure he was still shorter than me. As he stood, his custom suit coat unbuttoned and tie missing, I evaluated that I was somewhere in the middle in rank. Had I been a capo or business meeting, the tie would be in place. If I were a trusted colleague, the fancy clothes would have been replaced by something more comfortable.

Sterling Sparrow wasn't certain about my identity, but he was here, meeting me halfway.

"You look different," he said, crossing his arms over his chest.

"So do you. You've aged."

Sparrow scoffed. Removing his phone from his jacket pocket, he looked down at the screen and with a brief glance my direction, he said, "I'm paraphrasing...*if I would have sat the fuck down and finished the game, your knight most certainly would have taken my rook*. Did you say that?"

"Yes."

Laying his phone on the table, he turned his dark stare my direction. "To clarify, you sent a message like that, speaking to me that way, through an underling?"

Though my pulse had kicked up a notch, I replied, "I did. And if you had sat back down, I would have won."

"Do you know who-in-the-fuck has ever had the balls to think, much less say something like that to me?"

"Besides me..." I shrugged. "I can't come up with a soul."

A smile came to his lips. "Besides you, there's one other. Maybe I'll let you meet her. Convince me of who you are. I saw you die with my own fucking eyes. I pulled you—"

My neck stiffened as I interrupted. "You pulled me from that building. I'd heard the girls screaming. I fucking heard them scream in my sleep and even when I was awake for weeks afterward. I heard you yelling. It all goes black after that."

Sparrow had returned to his chair, his dark eyes on me. "We buried you. Explain that."

I inhaled. "I don't know the particulars. I...they—"

"Who are they?"

My fingers went to the buttons of the shirt I was wearing. "The explosion took away everything from me, but I don't regret it. I don't regret that you're sitting here or that you've made Chicago your own. I'm way behind on local shit, but I believe you're the badass you always claimed." Exhaling, I did what I wasn't certain would be possible without Laurel. I opened the shirt and pulled the sleeves from my shoulders.

"Fuck." Sparrow's one word lingered in the air as he stood again. "Tell me if this..." He gestured. "...goes on below your waist. I'll take your fucking word for it."

A smile caused my cheeks to rise. "It does. The pain was...indescribable."

He leaned back against the chair. "Not one fucking message, nothing even to Lorna."

There was something in the way he said my sister's name that told me she was no longer a distraction in his eyes. Maybe Reid was responsible for that, but more likely it was her. Sighing, I resecured the shirt and nodded toward a chair. "May I sit?"

"Sit and talk."

"I saw Reid. Is Patrick still...?" I didn't want to learn of any casualties since I'd gone.

"They're both here."

Sitting, I sighed again. "Sparrow, I will be as fucking honest with you and them as I can. I didn't make the decision to break away from the outfit. Fuck, I died for the outfit." My neck straightened as Sparrow flinched. "Like I said, no regret. But the pain, the girls' screams...I couldn't take it. I fucking blocked it out. One day it stopped. I guess it was my mind, but it snapped. And then I was able to move forward, to be who I was told I was meant to be. It worked. I worked until I couldn't be a killing machine any longer, not without reprieve."

"Who are they?" he asked again.

"Through it all, I never mentioned...I didn't remember, but even if I did, I wouldn't have told anyone about you and about the Sparrow outfit."

"Are you saying you were or are part of another family? Where?"

"No. That's not what I'm saying."

"Mason, I fucking believe you, but I can't allow you to return, not here to the outfit, not upstairs to our homes. I won't unless you're completely honest with me."

I inhaled. "Is Patrick here now?"

"Yes."

"Call him and Reid down. You're the only people in the fucking world I'd trust with this, but you need to know that this knowledge is dangerous, not the same as drug dealers and pimps dangerous."

Sparrow scoffed. "Yeah, you're fucking Mason. Your bad guys are worse than ours."

"That's the thing. They aren't all bad guys."

Reaching for his phone, Sparrow sent a text. It didn't take long until there was another knock on the door. When it opened, I took them both in as my mind barely comprehended that the four of us were again together.

Reid narrowed his gaze toward me as he addressed Sparrow. "Did you call us down here to kill him?"

"No," Sparrow said, "I called you two down here because together we're going to decide if we can trust him."

"You need a fucking haircut," Patrick said, coming forward and extending his hand.

"Fuck that." I stood, and like big fucking babies, hugs and

back pats were exchanged. By the time we all sat, I began. "Telling you what I'm about to tell you could be a death sentence for all of us. If you don't want that, leave."

All three men settled around the table, their attention on me.

LAUREL

*T*he elevator door closed, leaving me on a floor that was indicated by the letter A. If I were to be completely honest, it felt a little like a hotel lobby, with sofas and chairs that appeared unused and underutilized. Besides this area, there were three doors leading to where, I didn't know. And since Reid hadn't offered me entrance to any of them, I chose to remain in the lobby-looking area.

Though I should be exhausted, I was mostly worried and alone.

On the plane, Mason had filled me in a little about his history with Sterling Sparrow, Reid Murray, and Patrick Kelly. They'd met in basic training and become friends. From our little conversation down below, I also ascertained that Reid was now married to Lorna, making him more than Mason's friend. Reid was also his brother-in-law.

The powerful and mighty Sterling Sparrow was CEO of Sparrow Enterprises, a real estate conglomerate. I didn't doubt anything Mason had said, yet I had the distinct feeling I wasn't getting the entire story.

There was the whole cloak-and-dagger feeling I'd had since we landed in Chicago. Private drivers, hand scanners, private meetings...it all had my nerves stretched beyond what had happened today, that little thing about having my life threatened.

After pacing the length and width of the lobby, I settled on one of the sofas, careful not to wrinkle the dress I had borrowed. Despite my stress, or maybe because of it, I had just about drifted to sleep when the elevator opened.

My chest grew tight as I blinked away the sleepiness and focused on the red-haired woman stepping through the open door. She wasn't alone. There was another woman with her. She was blonde and beautiful, the kind of beauty that seizes your attention and doesn't let it go. If she wasn't a model, she should be. Yet it was the redhead who had my greater attention.

Taking a deep breath, I stood.

"What are you doing here?" the blonde asked. "How did you get here?"

"I-I...Reid, Mr. Murray told me to wait here."

The redhead continued to stare my direction. "I know you. I think I do."

"Lorna?" I asked.

Lorna took a step closer. As she did, I scanned, comparing the girl I knew to the woman before me. When I'd mentioned the blonde's beauty, it was in no way a comparison. It wasn't that one detracted from the other. It was more that together they represented two different examples of attractiveness.

While the blonde was taller with an air of splendor and regality, Lorna was the epitome of loveliness, the kind that made anyone in her presence smile. Her countenance screamed contentment and self-assuredness. With the same petite athletic body she'd had as a teenager, she'd matured, in a good way, and her hair was still as fiery red as I recalled. Yet at the moment my attention zeroed in on her stunning green eyes, the same as her brother's.

"Laurel? Is this you?"

I nodded.

"What happened?" Lorna asked, her neck tensing. She reached for my hand. "Are you all right? Why would Reid bring you here?" Her green eyes widened. "Does Sparrow know you're here?"

The blonde came forward, extending her hand. "Hi, I'm Araneae."

"Araneae," I said with a grin. "I love your name. It's unique."

She shrugged. "It's different, but I'm getting used to it."

Used to her own name?

Lorna pulled me toward the sofa, sitting beside me as Araneae sat across from us. "It's so good to see you. I-I sent you a letter." She sat taller.

"I received it. Thank you."

"Is that how you found me?"

I looked from Lorna to Araneae and back. "I don't know for sure how I'm here or how long I'll be staying."

Araneae sat back, crossing her arms over her chest. "Nope. There's more to this." She looked at Lorna. "Reid and Patrick just took off after they received a text. Their only comment was for us to stay upstairs."

Lorna smiled. "Which meant one thing." They both laughed. "We had to find out why."

I feigned a smile. "I guess that reason would be me."

Lorna turned to Araneae. "I met Laurel..." She tilted her head my direction. "...at the Boys and Girls Club when we were just kids. She was always so nice. Her dad would come and help people." Her green eyes filled with moisture and she swallowed. "He helped me and...well, both of us."

They didn't know. I was sitting here with Mason's sister and she didn't know he was alive.

"I'm glad. I really am."

"How is he?" Lorna asked.

He?

My mind scrambled.

"Oh, you mean my dad..." I sighed, wishing I knew. "...he was good the last time we spoke. Things have been a bit crazy."

"Crazy is another day in paradise around here," Araneae said. "I still don't understand what's happening...but if you're here, Sterling must trust you." Her nose scrunched. "Not many people come here."

Lorna reached for my hand again. "Are you staying? Are you in trouble? Are our men helping you?"

Sucking in a breath, I shook my head. "I really don't know. Yes, I'm in trouble. It's a long story. I helped develop something—"

Lorna turned to Araneae. "Laurel was always so smart."

"Thank you," I replied, my cheeks filling with warmth.

"So what did you develop?" Araneae asked.

"Well, it wasn't done. It's a compound."

"Are you an architect?"

"No," I said with a scoff. "A pharmaceutical compound."

"A medicine?" Lorna asked.

"Yes, hopefully one day."

"Damn," Araneae said. "That's seriously impressive."

"More serious than I realized. I understood the potential of what we were doing. I didn't want to realize that not everyone sees the good."

"So you're in danger because of this medication you helped invent?" Araneae confirmed.

"Yes, and then there was a hit."

"On you?" Lorna asked, her green eyes widening.

I sighed, leaning back against the sofa. "Explaining it to myself is difficult enough."

Araneae smiled. "Oh, I get that. We all have some crazy stories. How long are you here?"

"I don't know. Mr. Murray asked me to wait here."

Araneae looked at Lorna. "I say this reunion needs wine. I can go upstairs and get some."

"No," Lorna jumped up. "Let's go in my place."

My head shook. "I can't. He said to wait here."

Araneae stood as she pursed her lips. "If you're here for a few hours or longer, the first thing to learn is that these men like to be bossy, but we've learned to work around it."

Her feisty attitude made me smile. "Oh, and how do I do that?"

"Reid said to wait *here*. Right?"

"Yes."

"Did he define *here*?" Lorna asked with a grin.

"It could be this spot," Araneae offered, "or this floor, the level of the building."

"Or this set of floors," Lorna said.

"Or this building."

"Or the city."

They both smiled.

"Okay," I said. "I'm getting the picture."

Lorna walked to the door on the far right. "We won't push too much. We'll keep you *here*, on this floor. Come on in. I'm pretty sure that's what Reid meant, here as in this floor. And since I'm his wife, my opinion matters most."

"In other words," Araneae said with a laugh, "she'll tell him what he meant if he questions it."

As we stepped through the door, I was awed by the surroundings. No longer plain and lobbyish, the apartment we'd entered was colorful, chic, eclectic, and still very welcoming. "This is beautiful."

"You should see her place," Lorna said.

I turned to Araneae. "I'm sorry. Are you married to one of them?"

"Yes," she said as her cheeks filled with a light shade of pink. "I sure am."

"Her man is Sparrow."

My eyes widened as I felt the blood drain from my limbs. "Oh shit. You're Mrs. Sparrow."

"I guess I am. I think Araneae sounds fine."

I looked down at my dress and back to her. "This is yours and...the shoes. Thank you. I didn't realize."

She stepped back and looked at me. "I didn't recognize them. They look great on you. Please keep them." Her light brown eyes opened wide. "Wait, were you on the plane?"

I nodded.

"The couple who needed to clean up and have fresh clothes?"

"Yes again."

Lorna had gone into what I assumed was the kitchen and returned with a bottle of wine in her grasp. "Couple?"

I felt the moisture again prickling the back of my eyes. "Yes."

"Who are you with?" Lorna's voice began to quake. "A man?"

"Yes."

"Who?"

As she asked again, the door to the hallway opened and in the frame was Reid. "Lorna."

Her green eyes went to her husband. Her body grew

completely still as her hand holding the wine dropped. Except for Araneae who stepped forward to wisely rescue the wine from her grasp, the rest of the room remained unmoving until Reid stepped to the side and Mason came into view.

"Lorna."

Her head began to shake as she took him in. It was as he went closer that Lorna began to fall, to crumple. Yet she wouldn't fall. Mason wouldn't allow that, pulling her to his broad solid chest.

"Did she tell you?" he asked. "Did Laurel tell you?"

"N-no, nothing."

He kissed her forehead. "Good. Then I get to say it."

She reached up to his cheek and stared into his eyes. "It's really you?"

"It is."

"Goddamn you," she said, her neck straightening as tears cascaded down her cheeks. "You left me—us."

"I'm back, and Sis...me too. I may have forgotten, but damn, me too."

With my arms wrapped around my midsection, I looked around Lorna's living room and beyond the doorway into the hallway. The large space we'd entered had shrunken with the addition of Mason, Reid, and a blond man who also had gotten the *you must be big and scary* memo. It wasn't until Mason had Lorna in his embrace that I noticed the man peering in from the hallway.

Tall with dark hair and dark eyes, in just one sighting I sensed his commanding personality. It was an aura surrounding him. There was no doubt that the man watching the scene within dominated a room, a boardroom, and I would venture to say, a city. I was also certain that this was the man who owned a plane painted like a bird.

"Araneae," he said, his voice as deep as I imagined.

"Join us for wine, Sterling," she said, lifting the bottle. "There's a celebration in here."

"Tomorrow. We're headed upstairs now."

Araneae handed me the bottle. "It's hard to redefine upstairs." She winked. "It's good to pick your battles." Smiling, she added, "It was nice to meet you, Laurel."

"You too, Mrs. Sparrow."

She leaned closer. "Please never call me that again."

My cheeks rose. "Araneae."

"I'm still a bit lost and I don't know how you did it." Her eyes went to Lorna and Mason and back to me. "But thank you. Whatever just happened is making her happy. I hope you two will stay."

Stay?

LAUREL

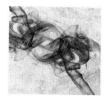

*R*eid and Lorna welcomed Mason and me into their home. It was more than Lorna's acceptance of her brother's return. I had the distinct feeling that we wouldn't be present without Sterling Sparrow's permission. It wasn't until we were settled in their guest room wearing Reid and Lorna's night-clothes that I finally had the chance to talk to Mason about his command performance.

"I guess he believed you?"

Mason reached for me, pulling me closer. The air filled with the rich cologne he'd applied on the plane as I settled against the t-shirt he wore, the one with short sleeves.

"I was as honest as possible," he said.

With my head on his shoulder and his bare arm around me, I peered up at his cleanly shaven jaw line. "I've always liked your sister. Mrs. Sparrow seems like a lot of fun too."

"I didn't get the chance to meet her. I can't believe that a woman who'd put up with him exists."

My cheeks rose. "I thought he was your friend."

"He was. He is. That doesn't mean he's not an arrogant asshole sometimes."

I sat upward and looked Mason in the eye. "Was he today?"

His expression grew solemn as his head shook. "He wasn't. I'm sure it was difficult for him to hear everything I said and see all he saw, but he did." He exhaled. "He accepted what I said or we wouldn't be here."

"Saw?"

Mason nodded. "I showed him the evidence, the reason my handprint doesn't work."

My eyes widened. "You did?"

He leaned forward, bringing his lips to mine. "I couldn't have done that if it weren't for you."

"No, Mason. You did it." Settling back down on his hard shoulder, I laid my palm over his chest. "I'm proud of you. I'm sure it wasn't easy."

All at once the world shifted as Mason rolled, landing me upon my back with his massive torso over me. "You've given me my life back." His mint-scented breath skirted over my cheeks. "I'm going to get yours back. I still don't know how, but, Laurel, these guys, they're something else. I was successful by myself. That's nothing compared to what can be done with them. I promise you, with their help, we will succeed."

I let out a long breath as I cupped his smooth cheek. "I don't even know what that means. Russ is dead, Eric, and…" I shuddered at the memory. "Dr. Oaks."

"I'm sorry for those losses. I am. But Doc, that doesn't define you. Getting your life back means that you weren't meant to live your life in a high-rise castle. Dr. Laurel Carlson, you have discoveries to refine and more to be made. You were put on this earth to help people. I know that with one hundred percent certainty because you've fucking saved me."

I sighed. "Mason, I don't know what I want any longer. Today...with Stephanie...I haven't really talked about it. Clinically, I am trying to reason with myself. Seeing Russ for only a second was awful and traumatic. Today was that moment expanded over hours. How can I ever move past that?"

"Complete your work and give yourself a daily dose."

Looking up at his green stare, I smiled. "I love that you have that much faith in me. How will that ever happen? What university or pharmaceutical manufacturer will take me on? And according to what Eric said and Oaks and even Stephanie, it was our own government who wanted to shut down our research. I don't understand."

Mason sighed as he lay back on his pillow. After a minute, he turned my way, our noses near one another. "We don't have the answers, but we'll find them. I told Sparrow, Reid, and Patrick everything, even things I swore never to say. I trust them even more than I did Jack." He sighed. "That's a shame because Jack died for me. I know that. I believe in the Sparrow men."

"Wait, are they brothers?" I smiled. "Wait, no."

"In a way. Sparrow is more than real estate."

"No shit." I tried for my most sarcastic tone.

"It's a family. I say we gather together and you fill them in. I'm not saying to share your formula. I doubt any of us would get it. Maybe Reid." Mason shrugged. "Let's brainstorm with them. My notes aren't stuck in Montana. I just need to access the secure cloud."

"What about Stephanie?"

"Fuck."

I sat up. "What?"

"Hell, I've been a little preoccupied with us. I need to learn what's happening at the ranch." Mason sat forward. "I hate to bother anyone, but I'm going to see if Reid's awake."

It was late, but I understood. "Okay. Wake me if you learn anything."

Mason stood from the bed and kissed me good night. "Will you be all right?"

"I think if Lorna and Mrs. Sparrow are here, I'm safe."

"You are."

I watched as he turned toward the door, long sleeping pants over his legs and socks on his feet, yet what amazed me were his exposed arms, their colors swirling like ribbons for anyone to see. "Mason?"

He stopped. "What?"

I tilted my head his direction. "Are you sure?"

"Yes, I am."

Tears prickled my eyes as my cheeks rose. "I love you."

"Me too."

"No, Mason. That may be good enough for Lorna. I want more."

In a stride or two he was back, his lips hovering near mine. "Laurel Carlson, I fucking love you. I will say it every damn day, twice a day to make up for the time we missed." Bringing his hands to my cheeks, he pulled my lips toward him. "I love you."

My eyes closed as his lips took mine.

When he pulled away, his green stare was still there.

"Me too," I said with a grin just before Mason stepped back into the hallway of Lorna and Reid's apartment.

MASON

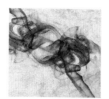

*L*ow voices coming from the kitchen drew me their direction. With only the dimmed illumination shining from some weird flame-looking lights over the counter, I stopped, watching as Reid and Lorna stood in what appeared to be a confrontation. After a few seconds of not hearing their hushed words, I stepped forward.

"Is this about us?" I asked.

They both turned.

"Mace, no," Lorna said, her green eyes wide as she stared my direction.

Suddenly, I wasn't certain exposing my arms was such a good idea. I waved her off. "I'm not trying to bother you."

My words didn't slow her progress as she came all the way over to me.

"Wow, your arms…"

"Lorna."

Without asking, she ran her small hand over my forearm. "Oh my God."

"Yeah, it's not very—"

"No," she exclaimed. "This is so you."

I looked from her to Reid, wondering what exactly she meant with her comment.

"Don't you get it?"

"No, I don't. I was just wondering..." I looked to Reid. "...if I could find out what happened on my property. I'm completely disconnected these days."

"Mason," Lorna said, pulling my attention back to her. "Do you have more tats?"

"Yes. Please drop it."

"No, it's you. It's amazing and I want to see more."

"What do you mean *it's him*?" Laurel's question came from behind me.

I turned, my gaze meeting Laurel's.

Lorna grinned and went to the sofa in the living room. Wearing a small tank top and long flowing pants, she sat on one leg and pulled her other knee to her chest. Seeing her there, I tried to remind myself that she was a grown woman, not my little sister. Fuck that, she was a grown married woman and apparently had been for over six years.

Taking a deep breath, she scanned from Reid to me to Laurel. "No one here is unaware of our shitty childhood." She waited for any response. While no one spoke, the only person to move was Reid, who moved to the couch and sat beside her.

"There's no reason to relive that," he said, his voice calmer than I'd ever heard.

"No, I'm not. It's seeing Mace's arms that I remember so many things." Her head shook. "Reid, it's not bad. It's good." She looked over at Laurel. "You probably know what I mean."

Laurel's eyes widened. "Help me."

Lorna turned my way. "Reid was telling me that for many years you couldn't remember who you were."

So that had been their conversation.

"That's true."

"Did you get the tats then or after you remembered?"

"Then, Lorna, what's your point?"

She sighed, fighting back tears. "Do you remember that awful one-room studio where we lived with Mom and Missy after Grandma died?"

My neck stiffened, knowing there were memories I didn't want to recall. "Again, your point."

She turned to Reid. "I don't know if I've mentioned it because really it wasn't much to mention. We didn't have real furniture. I recall an old table. It only had three chairs. There was an old TV that someone threw out. We got like two chan-nels. Remember?" She turned to me.

I nodded. The memory was coming back, the dinginess, the musty scent, all of it.

Laurel came forward, wrapping her arm through mine. "Are you all right?" she whispered.

Again I nodded. "Get on with it, Lorna."

"We were so young. The three of us would sleep on this dirty old mattress on the floor, but that's not the point..." She grinned. "...the one that Mace wants me to get to." She sat taller. "Near our bed, on the wall, were these pictures. Not really pictures but color-ings that Missy and I had done." She tilted her head toward my arm. "Very impressionistic as I recall. We were ahead of our time.

"Like your tats, in my young mind I saw ribbons and swirls filled with color. Each night before we went to sleep and when we woke, you told us to look at the colorings." Her head moved from side to side as tears filled her eyes. "Every night, Mace, you told us that. Look at the colors, dream in color, and tomorrow when you wake, the colors will be there."

Laurel's hand on my arm began to tremble. I reached up, covering it with mine.

"You made what was ugly beautiful," Lorna went on. "And now you did the same thing with your scars." She jumped from the sofa and came to me, again laying her hand over my arm. "Even without remembering." Her green eyes came to mine. "I'm not saying the scars are ugly. They aren't, but I know you. You thought they were. And you took what you thought was unsightly and made it colorful. Each night you gave yourself color, to dream in color and wake with color."

Her arms came around my waist and her head fell against my chest.

"I've missed you so much." She stood back and smiled at Reid. "I think that's why I love our home. It's full of color."

Looking around, I saw she was right. Her sofa was filled with colorful pillows, and on the walls, she had paintings full of color. Even the tile in her kitchen glowed with sparks of red, yellow, and orange.

"I'm glad I'm back," I said as she turned back to me with her big green eyes. "So you two weren't discussing kicking us out?"

"You've not even slept here one night," Reid said.

Before I could respond, Reid looked down at his phone.

One memory I could recall was the look, the expression he would have, when something needed attention.

"What is it?" I asked.

"Patrick wants a meeting on 2," he said, standing and going toward the door. As he opened it, he turned my way. "Why the fuck are you just standing there? Are you back or not?'

Laurel squeezed my arm. "You're home."

"I love you, Reid," Lorna said.

"I love you, too. Go to bed, ladies."

"Mason," Laurel said, "me too."

I leaned down and gave her a kiss. "Unacceptable."

"I love you," she said softly.

"I love you. Go to bed."

As the door shut, before we made it to the elevator, I heard Lorna's voice. "We told you that they're bossy."

After Reid scanned his hand by the elevator, he turned to me. "You said you had scanners at your ranch. What did you do without fingerprints or palm prints?"

"My eye."

He nodded. "Tomorrow I'll have you hooked up."

As we stepped into the elevator, for the first time in…I wasn't certain how long…I truly felt at home. "What's this meeting about?"

"I don't know. Patrick said there was a message from the Sparrows in Montana, the ones who found you."

My warm feelings disappeared. "That was why I came out, to ask if anyone had news."

"It sounds like Patrick does."

After Reid raised his hand to the scanner outside of 2 and the door slid open, we were met by two sets of eyes.

"What?" I asked.

"I," Patrick said, taking a deep breath. "I don't know how to say this other than we're fucking glad you're back here and not there."

My pulse increased as I stared him down. "This is about me? Or is it about Laurel?"

"Your ranch," Sparrow said. "Your house."

"What about it?"

"It's gone."

"What the hell do you mean? It was there when we left."

"The Sparrows. After they brought you to the plane, they went back to the ranch. I'm not apologizing, but if that woman in your office was a threat, I gave the order to eliminate her."

I sucked in a breath. "I would have liked to question her, but fuck, the end would have been the same. What happened?"

"We don't have details. The reason it took so long to find out what was happening there was that none of the Sparrows returned."

What?

"A second recon crew was sent," Sparrow went on. "Your house is a fucking smoldering lump of kindling. There was a volunteer fire unit there. They told our men that there was nothing they could do when they arrived other than contain it."

Contain? What did that mean for my other buildings?

My eyes were wide. "Your men?"

Sparrow shook his head.

"Stephanie?"

"You said your office was sealed in metal shutters?" Patrick asked.

"Yes."

"She either roasted like a chicken in an oven, sucked in smoke, or the flames made it to her," Patrick said. "There's no way the temperature in a brick and metal box didn't reach lethal levels."

I reached for a chair and spun it, straddling the back. "There was a hole blown in my commander's head before he bled out in what was supposed to be a safe place. My house is ashes." I looked up at all three men. "I wouldn't take me in if I were you."

"Good thing you aren't me," Sparrow said.

"Or me," Reid and Patrick said in unison.

"We'll know more after the Sparrows gather information," Patrick said. "Sparrow and I thought you should know."

Sparrow cleared his throat. "There's one more thing we need to discuss."

"What?" I asked.

"Laurel."

My shoulders straightened. "What about her?"

"She's Rudy Carlson's niece."

My eyes closed as I inhaled. "She's Dr. Carlson's daughter. You know he had nothing to do with what his brother did. Hell, he and his wife packed up and left town after Allister and Rudy died."

Sparrow looked to Patrick and Reid.

"Neither of her parents has ever shown any indication of being Allister supporters," Patrick said.

Sparrow nodded. "It needed to be mentioned."

"She has no idea," I said, recalling the recent conversation about her parents' sudden move to Iowa.

"Her father will," Sparrow said.

"I'll cross that bridge when it arrives. All he needs to understand is that she's safe with me—with us."

Sparrow nodded.

Patrick stepped over to one of the desks and lifted a phone. Coming my way, he handed it to me.

"Yours?" I asked.

"No, Mason, yours. Reid will probably get sick of being your secretary."

I looked down at the phone in my grasp. There were too many things to be upset about, too many things to worry about, yet despite it all, I looked up at the assholes around me and smiled. "Despite it all, thank you. It feels right to be back."

"Like colorful ribbons," Reid said with a smirk.

"Shut the fuck up."

"Seriously, Lorna and I are happy to share. However, once we stop whoever is trying to kill you or Laurel, I suggest we move you to your own place."

We looked at Sparrow.

He nodded. "You'll need to start from scratch."

My brow furrowed as I tried to decipher his meaning.

"Your furniture is gone," Reid said.

I sighed. "My apartment—here."

"Always been yours," Sparrow said. "It's time to fill it again."

LAUREL

*S*itting alone in Lorna's kitchen at the tall island, I wrapped my hands around a coffee mug and stared out of the floor-to-ceiling windows filling two of their walls. The view of Chicago was stunning from this high above the city. This was our third morning and I'd grown accustomed to waking alone.

Mason had spent most available moments working with Reid, Patrick, and Sparrow to learn more about the ranch, Stephanie, and the government involvement related to my research. I'd been told that most mornings were spent upstairs eating together.

There was a lot of togetherness. The thing was for me to go upstairs required calling Lorna or Mason. While I was happy to have a phone to reach them, there was part of me who missed the time Mason and I spent alone.

The sky beyond the windows continued to brighten as the sun continued its rise. Like Montana, the sky over the city was also filled with blue. These windows faced the wrong direction, but I knew that Lake Michigan was out there too.

And yet it wasn't Montana. The loss of Mason's ranch house seemed to hit me harder than it did him. I couldn't decide why, but I had a theory. While I now knew without a doubt that Mason Pierce didn't have dissociative identity disorder, I feared I did by proxy.

Scoffing to myself, I took another drink of coffee and pondered my self-diagnosis. Since the night Mason and I reconnected, the night of the gathering, I'd known him as two men, three if I counted Edgar; nevertheless, two very different men with glowingly similar and different personalities.

Kader attracted me like no other man. And if I were honest with myself, not even Mason. Mason and I had been too young and innocent when we fell in love. Kader was danger personified, sexy and unpredictable, stubborn and controlling. A simple change in his tone could send my body into overdrive. That wasn't to say that Mason didn't also possess those traits—he did. However, since returning to Chicago, he seemed content to leave Kader behind in a way that I wasn't.

That was why I believed he was indifferent to the loss of his ranch. The day we boarded the helicopter, Mason left Kader in Montana. His house or lack thereof no longer mattered. Kader no longer existed.

There was no doubt in my mind that I loved Mason Pierce, and I was in love with Kader. Perhaps what I wondered was if Mason loved me and brought me to safety because, like the boy who told his sisters to dream in color, he was my protector instead of the passionate lover Kader had been.

Was it too much to want both?

Was it possible to mourn a house and a personality?

A knock on the door to the hallway startled me out of my thoughts.

Who could it be?

I was certain there were only seven people living in these apartments and four lived together. Standing straight in the new soft yoga pants and t-shirt Lorna had helped me order with next-day delivery, I opened the door.

"Araneae." She'd convinced me to stop with the Mrs. Sparrow moniker.

The pretty woman before me smiled. Her blonde hair was pulled back, and she was wearing a light-blue blouse with a beautiful scarf and navy pencil skirt. Add her blue high heels and I was suddenly underdressed for coffee.

"Laurel, can we talk for a minute."

I opened the door wider. "Yes, of course." It was her husband's property. I wasn't certain that saying no was an option. "Come in."

Her brown eyes lit up as she peered toward the breakfast bar. "Is that real coffee?"

"It's not fake."

"No, silly. I mean the real thing with *caf-feine*." She elongated the word.

"Yes," I said, smiling. "It's not mine, but would you like a cup?"

"I would love one. And I'll keep Lorna's secret."

As I prepared the coffee, I turned. "What secret is that?"

"She has us all on decaf upstairs with talk about it being healthier and down here, she has the good stuff."

I couldn't help but smile. "Oh, oops."

A few minutes later we were both seated at the breakfast bar, my stocking feet and Araneae's heels perched on the metal bar below.

"May I ask," she began, "why you don't join us for breakfast?"

"I guess, I'm not sure I belong."

Araneae reached out, her hand covering mine. "I know exactly how you feel. It may not seem like it, but until you arrived, I was the new one to the group. My entrance was a little different, but nevertheless, this..." She gestured about. "...is fucking overwhelming."

My cheeks rose. "A bit."

"Oh, and don't get me started on Sterling."

I lifted my hand. "Not my place."

Araneae sat back. "It is, Laurel. As long as you want to be here and Mason wants you here, it is your place."

"Thanks," I said with a sigh. "Tomorrow, I'll give Lorna a call and come up."

Her brown eyes narrowed. "What?"

"I'll call Lorna."

"Why?"

"Because I can't access the elevator."

"Oh hell no."

Before I knew it, Araneae had her phone out and judging by her body language, sent a strongly worded text. My eyes grew wide. "Oh shit. What did you just do?"

"First, I just realized that I've grown as fucking oblivious as the men, and for that, I apologize."

"What—?"

"No one is feeling trapped in this glass castle as long as I'm queen." She picked up her coffee and hummed. "Unless there's a lockdown and then we're all in this together."

My head shook. "I have no idea what you're saying."

Araneae smiled. "You will. Let's not overdo. Laurel, I'm about to head to work. Could you tell me more about what you do?"

How did I not realize she worked outside the castle?

I wrapped my hands around the cooling mug. "What I *did*." Taking a deep breath, I pushed back against the loss of my work. "What do you do? Obviously..." I eyed her lovely attire. "...you don't stay here all day like Lorna."

"Two things. When I was in college, my best friend and I put together a proposal for a company. We wanted to specialize in women's fashions. When I was little my mom..." She hesitated. "...I would draw clothes for my Barbies and she would make patterns. I know it sounds silly compared to medications and chemicals."

"It doesn't. It sounds amazing. And so you own a company?"

"I do," she smiled. "I'm co-owner. It's called Sinful Threads."

"Oh. I have a scarf." I took a breath. "I did." I looked down at my clothes. "I don't have anything."

Araneae's lips thinned. "I have a connection. Let me know what you'd like and I'll get you hooked up."

"That's wonderful."

"It is, but that's not what I wanted to talk about."

"What did you want to talk about?" I asked.

"Please tell me about your compound. I asked Sterling and I swear that man can do a hundred things at once..." Her eyebrows danced. "...really well."

I couldn't stop my giggle, suddenly feeling like a schoolgirl.

"But he sucks at particulars that he doesn't care about."

"Oh."

Araneae shook her head. "Fuck him." Her eyes opened wide. "Sorry, that's my job."

My head shook. This woman was crazy and fun and had an innate ability to pick up on more than was being offered. "I'm not applying. He's a bit...intimidating."

"Wow, let's not compare intimidating. Sterling showed me a picture of Mason—before."

I nodded. "I know. The plastic surgeons made him look different."

"Except for his eyes."

"Yes." My cheeks rose. His eyes were the same, like his sister's.

"Laurel, we're going to call this baptism by fire, but I'm going to lay it on the line. Sinful Threads isn't my only endeavor. A while back I had the opportunity to help people. Sterling told me just enough about what you have done to pique my interest."

My neck straightened.

"From what he said, your formula and compound have the potential to help people with traumatic memories. I'm working with a foundation. It's not-for-profit. I'm not promising big money."

She had my full attention. "Please tell me more."

"This foundation is for child and adult victims of human trafficking and exploitation. The foundation is up and running. We have counseling, medical treatment, and education. We have worked to find subsidized housing and affordable day care." She let out a long breath. "It's un-fucking-believable what a decent apartment and a scholarship to a community college can do for someone." Her brown eyes glowed as she spoke about her project, even more than her company. Araneae's passion was contagious.

"Oh my goodness. That's amazing. Human trafficking. Why?"

"Can you help?"

"I don't know. What do you need?"

She smiled. "I don't know. I'm out of my league with this. I have a fantastic board. I was thinking, how about a medication to help with their traumatic memories? How about a skilled PhD in psychology? How about a million other things that I may never imagine."

Tears filled my eyes as I realized this wasn't possible. "I-I...people are still after me. I can't be me."

"Then who do you want to be?" she asked.

"I don't understand."

"Mason's brother-in-law is about the most kick-ass person I've ever met. Reid can make you appear or disappear." For the second time, she covered my hand. "Are there others?"

"Others?" My thoughts went to Russ, Eric, and Carl.

"People who miss Laurel Carlson."

I nodded. "My family. I have parents, a sister, and niece who I can't contact."

Did I have other friends?

That list was now filled with people no longer living.

Araneae took in a deep breath; after letting it out, she drank the rest of her coffee. "Damn, that was fantastic." She stood, lowering herself from the stool and straightening her skirt. "I'm sorry about your family. Please consider my proposal. I don't go to the foundation every day, but I'd be happy to take you with me the next time I go. We have thousands of unused square feet. It's just sitting there empty. Someone..." Her eyes rolled. "...thinks he knows real estate and acquired a huge space." She shrugged. "Maybe we could begin private research?"

"My research? It would cost—"

She shook her head. "We're not-for-profit, but funding isn't an issue."

"It will take a lot of money to do it right."

"Then let's do it right."

"Are you serious?" I asked.

"I am."

It was a tiny seed of hope. One small seed that she'd just planted and yet it was quickly growing within me, sprouting and sending nutrients. Like oxygen from a plant, Araneae's plan gave me the essential element I needed.

"I can't tell you what this means."

Araneae shook her head. "Come with me tomorrow. Just spend some time with these women and children. A lot of them with minimal assistance are able to move on. Others can't. It's heartbreaking." Her soft brown eyes grew glassy. "We've lost a few since this began." Her head shook. "Some have too much baggage, too many memories to get past." Her smile returned. "I would love it if we never lost another victim. Just maybe your compound could help."

Stepping down from the stool, I lifted my arms around Araneae's neck. "Thank you."

She stood back and winked. "I'll see you at breakfast tomorrow, upstairs. Then we'll head off to the foundation."

"But..." I looked down at my yoga pants.

Araneae smiled. "No one there cares what you wear, including me. But I have an idea. You fit so well in my dress. By this afternoon you better-the-fuck have access to the penthouse. Go up to my closet. Get whatever you want to wear."

"No, I can't. You and Mr. Sparrow have done too—"

She lifted her hand. "Stop. My husband is fucking nuts when it comes to a lot of things but especially me. Seriously, he is. I have more clothes than I could wear." Her brow rose. "Just leave the lingerie. Most of that he picked out himself and..."

I shook my head. "No worries. I will stay away from lingerie."

"Tomorrow morning?"

"I'm missing, though—officially, as in the FBI is looking for me," I said. "What if I'm recognized?"

"We'll talk to Reid. He has the answers to everything. Then it's settled?"

"Thank you, Araneae."

MASON

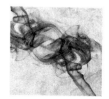

"So where did you first encounter them, the Order?" Patrick asked as he paced back and forth in the command center on 2. Days had passed and yet I felt we were no closer to resolution.

Reid was sitting at a desk with multiple keyboards, listening to our conversation and doing his best to find any presence of the Order.

I shook my head. "We've been at this for nearly a week and gotten no place. I know how fucking good you are at what you do. They can't be found."

"First encounter?" Patrick asked again.

It was my turn to stand and pace. "I don't fucking know. I woke up and I was there."

"Where's there?" Reid asked.

"In a hospital bed, my body covered in bandages. I couldn't really move—they were everywhere." My entire body tensed at the memory, my skin becoming tight and itchy. "I was a fucking mummy." My stomach twisted.

"I couldn't see much." I shook my head. "No, at first I couldn't see at all. The bandages covered my eyes. I could hear, but even that took time for the fucking ringing to end."

"Their medical staff must be amazing," Reid said as up on the screens over his head he had medical references detailing treatment for severe burns.

After one quick glance up at the screen, I turned away. "I'd rather not..."

"Fuck, sorry," Reid said as the screen turned to surveillance throughout the city. I suspected he'd moved the burn information to a smaller screen that only he could see. "But they must have some of the best. You look good, man."

"Maybe the two of you should stop worrying about me and the Order and concentrate on that." My chin rose toward the screen showing multiple places throughout the city.

"Multitasking," Patrick said. "Sparrow is at his office on Michigan. Zachary is with him. Araneae and Laurel are at the foundation. Garrett's with them. And Lorna's upstairs. Our people are well protected."

"I hate letting her leave this building. The threat concerning her is still real until I can confirm it isn't."

"No one is getting close to Araneae," Patrick said. "No one will get close to Laurel."

I sat back down, straddling the back of the chair. "Laurel doesn't understand the danger, not just about the hit and the Order, but what it means to be with the Sparrows."

"Araneae does," Patrick said matter-of-factly. "She understands that Sparrow would fucking burn this city if anything happened to her. She knows not to take unnecessary chances."

"But the foundation."

Patrick's hand came down on my shoulder. "Swarming with Sparrows. Do you think Sparrow would have it any other way?

No one is getting close to his queen. Garrett is the goon in the suit, but he's hardly the only one present."

I let out a long breath. "He always has gone overboard."

"And before pales to how he is with Araneae."

"Now that Laurel's with her, I'm glad to hear it."

"And as far as the city as a whole, the Sparrows are out there reporting to their capos. It's a fine-fucking-tuned machine and for right now it seems to be working," Patrick said.

"I want to get back out to it," I said. "I've just worked alone for so long that it's hard to trust others to do my job."

"No more. And don't worry, your woman is safe with the Sparrows," Reid chimed in.

My woman.

I didn't fucking deserve her, but damn if I didn't like the way that sounded.

"Now think about this," Patrick said. "We, the people closest to you, thought you died. Not only because Sparrow saw you go into a building and watched it blow, but also because he pulled you from the rubble and helped extinguish your clothes...helped extinguish you. According to him, the only part of you not burning was the vest."

"It burnt, but it needed to stay in contact with the accelerant to keep burning," I piped in.

"The ambulance took you," Reid said, continuing the story I didn't want to hear. "Sparrow saw you at the hospital. You were unconscious but alive. And then you were dead. They showed us your body."

"Us?" I asked.

"Lorna, as your next of kin, was asked to identify you," Reid said.

Just the thought of her doing that twisted my gut. "She could have refused."

"She could have. We told her that. They agreed to allow her to identify some of your personal effects rather than for her to see your body. It was the vest, a few other things that were charred." He shook his head. "It was more of a formality. Sparrow saw you. We believed..."

My chest ached as I shook my head. "Fucking Order. I never would have put her or any of you in that—"

"Can't turn back time," Reid said. "She made it."

"Because of you."

"I'd like to take all the credit, but it wasn't just me. It was all of us. You're her brother through blood. You're ours too. We all mourned, all of us."

I shook my head. "That's another thing that's different about the Order. There's no fucking connection. A casualty is a replaceable member. All that mattered was success, only success."

"No going back for a man?" Patrick asked.

"Nope. You got yourself out or you died." I took another breath. "Not that it mattered. Every fucking one of us was dead already."

"The body, how did they provide the hospital with a body?" Patrick asked.

I shrugged. "The Sovereign Order's resources are vast. It's a fucking government-supported division that the damn government doesn't know exists. Hell, the body might have belonged to some team member who died in the line of duty. For all I know, they could keep remains on hand for a situation like that. I can't say for sure. I was never in the position of command, but we all heard things."

"And they let you leave?" Patrick asked. "Just walk away. With all your knowledge, that seems...unlikely." He looked around. "If anyone with too much knowledge of the Sparrow outfit decided to walk away, that person wouldn't make it far."

I sighed. "I see what you're saying. And I think at the time I was willing to take that out. I was done—over it. Somehow Commander Jackson worked out the deal."

"Jack?" Reid said.

"Yes, Jack." As I closed my eyes the image of his dead body came back. "He went out on a limb for me. Whatever he negotiated gave us some freedom. I was an independent contractor." I scoffed. "Sounds like I fucking renovated kitchens or something. I sold my skills to the highest bidder on the dark web. My specialty hasn't changed since Special Forces. I kill. Now it's not only people. I also kill things. And at the same time, I answered when the Order called."

"And with Laurel...?" Reid prompted.

"That's where this gets weird." As if my whole fucking life wasn't weird. "Taking the job to kill her wasn't through the Order."

"You're sure?"

"Yeah, I'm sure. The jobs from the Sovereign Order came through Jack. He was their contact."

"You said up until right before you came here, you had no idea the Order was involved."

"They weren't at first. I was hired by Carl Oaks, the dean of the university where Laurel's research was conducted."

Reid's fingers stopped as his dark eyes came my way. "So on the dark web, you always knew who hired you?"

"No, usually never. I reported that the job was complete— Laurel was dead. That is usually all it takes unless the original request asks for proof of death or sometimes it's requested that the body be found. No two assignments are exactly the same."

"But you found out it was Oaks?" Reid asked.

"I went back to Indianapolis and yes, I believed it was Oaks. I watched as his hit man took out the dean of Laurel's department. At that point, I was confident it was him...until Stephanie."

"Stephanie Moore," Reid said, his fingers again flying. On the screen above where the city's surveillance feeds had been, there was now a ten-foot-tall picture of Stephanie. It was from the university directory: *Stephanie Moore, MS, Research Assistant.*

"That's her."

"What do you know about her?"

"I know she received her master's degree from Columbia," I began, admitting the piss-poor research I'd compiled on her. "I know she's not married and she's been Laurel's research assistant for two years." I shook my head. "I know I screwed up with her because I was too focused on Laurel. Stephanie was sleeping with Laurel's research partner and more than likely getting advanced information on their data from him.

"My goal was to learn who put out the hit on Laurel, eliminate the threat, and let her have her life back. Carl Oaks is dead, but if the Order is involved, that doesn't eradicate the threat.

"When I began to suspect that the Order was involved was while I was back in Indianapolis. Laurel was in Montana, and my highly advanced security and communication system at the ranch—everything—went off-line."

"I'd suspect not the work of an everyday hacker," Reid said.

"Fuck no. It was top-notch."

"You believe Stephanie was part of the Order?" Patrick asked.

"Nothing else makes sense. She was there at the ranch, and after I was drugged, Stephanie confirmed to Laurel that she directed Oaks to hire me. That means Stephanie had the knowledge to find me, Kader. She also admitted to killing Cartwright,

Laurel's research partner, in a plan to frame Laurel. I couldn't understand how anyone could disarm my surveillance so easily or infiltrate my system at the ranch. Only someone within the Order would have that knowledge.

"I'm certain that I never saw her before; however, my gut tells me that she knew or at least recognized Jack—and he her. No one could have killed him without more of a struggle, no one other than the Order. I can't come up with a reason why the Order would want him dead. He never would have compromised them."

"Is it common for the Order to kill their own?" Patrick asked.

"I suppose it's like you said. If the Order felt the member would compromise them, then yes, they'd eliminate that person without remorse. That wasn't Jack or me. We'd been relatively free from the Order for over four years. And yet we'd answer their call. We stayed to ourselves other than the ranch hands. We weren't a liability."

"Didn't Laurel say the other night that Oaks said the government wanted their research stopped?" Reid asked.

"Yes, Laurel said the dean of the university and Stephanie confirmed that."

"Listen, I'm not discrediting Laurel's research findings," Patrick said. "I saw where major pharmaceutical companies were interested. But why would the government give a damn about research being done at some university in Indiana?"

"I've been racking my brain with the same question." Standing, I ran my fingers through my hair and resumed pacing. "To me, it doesn't make sense. I would think the government would be interested in the research continuing. Laurel has this way of seeing only the benefits, but think about those. Her compound could be a godsend for our military." I turned to Reid and

Patrick. "We were there. We know what we did and what we saw. Think of our fellow soldiers who can't channel those memories as we do."

Patrick scoffed, "As we do—organizing an underground army to run Chicago and more."

"Hey, it works," Reid said.

"Yet according to Oaks and Stephanie," I said, thinking aloud, "the government wanted it shut down, doors closed, NDAs signed, and lights out." Just like the project Laurel had been on in grad school.

"Why would a member of the Order be pretending to be Laurel's assistant?"

"Infiltration wasn't really their thing as far as I knew. It was get in, get the job done, and get out."

"The black-market sale?" Patrick asked.

"Laurel said Stephanie confirmed it was her. Oaks thought they were in it together. The body on the driveway at my ranch confirms otherwise."

"Wait a minute," Patrick said, going to a different computer and hitting some keys. "Shit. I didn't tell you this. We got this full report late last night." He pulled something up on the screen. "After your house burnt, the new Sparrows on the scene said there were no bodies, no one on the driveway and no one in Jack's house. The house was spotless. No sign of a bleed-out, nothing. There were also no vehicles not titled to you or Jack on the property. No plane or helicopter. Even our helicopter was missing, which Sparrow isn't happy about."

My gut twisted. "Bodies. None?"

"That's what they said."

"What about the three Sparrows that are MIA? What about Stephanie?"

"*No* remains of anyone. Other than the fact that your house is now rubble, there's no evidence of anything unusual."

Gripping the back of the chair, I sucked in a breath and leaned back. "That's the only answer. It was them. The Sovereign Order cleaned up the mess. They're the only ones who could do that, the only ones to make bodies and large equipment disappear without a trace. Jack and I lived on that property. They couldn't risk any connection to them. I'm not sure what that means for me or Laurel. It was the government that wanted her research stopped. It's just not the government most people know, but the Order. If they still want it stopped, there's only one person with the knowledge standing in their way—Laurel. And as for me, they must think either I'm dead or that I'm responsible for the carnage at the ranch and am now on the run." I looked from Patrick's stare to Reid's. "In any of those scenarios they won't stop until they're sure."

LAUREL

"You get used to it," Lorna said as I helped her with our dinner dishes.

"At least I have the foundation now. Araneae has been amazing. It won't be easy getting the research back up and running without others finding out, but she doesn't seem concerned."

Lorna smiled as she put the last dish in the dishwasher. "Covert operations are what we all do best. Welcome to the hidden world of the Sparrows."

I looked around Lorna's living space. "I love what you've done here. I just wish..."

"That my brother would forget his friends and remember you?"

"No, I don't want him to forget—"

"Stop," she said. "I get it. I do. These men can be like a dog with a bone. And believe me, every time one bone is buried, there's always another bone, another *something* that keeps them working until all hours of the night and back up again before we wake. Right now, besides the normal fires, they're consumed with helping Mason—from what little I've gleaned, and that is how we learn. They don't tell us shit.

"I believe they have multiple fronts going," Lorna went on. "First, they want to figure out what happened to Mason and how he disappeared. Then there's what happened on the ranch and who is after you. From what you've said, this whole thing started because someone wanted to stop your research, and they were even willing to kill you to do it." Her expression darkened. "If I haven't told you, I'm sorry you lost so many friends and colleagues...that had to be difficult."

"I guess it is. I haven't had much time to mourn."

"Hey, I have an idea."

"If it involves wine, I'm in," I said, forcing a smile.

Lorna laughed. "You're starting to sound like Araneae."

"It helps me sleep."

"Come with me," Lorna said.

"Are we getting out of here?"

"Yes and no."

I followed as Lorna led out into the hallway, the area with the sofas and chairs. I grinned at the elevator, knowing that I now had the ability to use the scan and access the penthouse up above. It was a beautiful home, literally a castle in the sky. I couldn't make the elevator go down, but Araneae could and we never left alone. There was always one of Sparrow's men with us.

That was both disconcerting and oddly comforting. There was an air about all the men around here that would probably have made me turn away from them on a dark street—forget that, at noon on a crowded street I would have held my pepper spray, turned tail, and run.

Instead of heading toward the elevator, Lorna turned, stopping at the far door on the left.

Since I'd seen Patrick—who, by the way, was super quiet, tall with blond hair, and almost as intimidating as Sparrow—enter the door in the middle, the door where she was standing was the only one of the three I'd never seen anyone use.

"Is this...?" I asked.

"It's Mason's and I would guess that means it's your place. The men are only in a hurry when it comes to their latest emergency. I say we women take matters into our own hands. Check it out and decide what you want done."

She turned the knob and pushed the door inward. Like her apartment, there were two walls of floor-to-ceiling windows now showcasing the dark sky and lights of Chicago. In the dark apartment, the only light coming from the hallway, I walked to the tall glass and peered out. "Oh wow, I love that we can see the lake."

"Yeah, it's beautiful when it's not filled with floating ice in the dead of winter."

"I love your place, but after Mason...why didn't you move for the view?"

Lorna's head shook, loose fiery-red tendrils floating around her face. "No, this was Mace's. Sparrow had it emptied before I could tell him to stop."

My eyes widened. "Does anyone tell him to stop?"

"Once in a while. That was a different time. Sparrow was...let's just say it was very dark around here." Her smile returned. "I did manage to salvage a few things. I haven't really looked at them in years. Sparrow declared this apartment off-limits to everyone."

"The door wasn't locked."

"Didn't need to be."

Suddenly, I had a thought about Kader's home and lack of locks.

Lorna's expression lightened. "Let's look around and start making some plans." She went toward the kitchen area and hit a switch, filling the room with light that spilled beyond onto the dust-covered wood floors.

"Mason's ranch had hardwood floors. He must like those."

"Yes, ours has more tile because it's what Reid wanted. You can change whatever you want."

This apartment was very similar in size and setup to her and Reid's, only the layout was flipped.

Taking in the expensive countertops and appliances, I smiled as I imagined Mason cooking as Kader used to do. "I don't think anything needs to be done except furniture and things."

"Well, let's walk around."

As we did, we opened the various doors, stirring the dust that had settled during seven years of abandonment. Like Lorna and Reid's apartment, the space was insanely big with a large master bedroom suite, huge closets, two extra bedrooms, an office space, another full bath, and a large living room that fed into the dining area and kitchen.

"It's hard to believe there's so much space in an apartment."

"And yet, all three apartments could fit on Sparrow and Araneae's first floor." She spun around. "The possibilities are endless. What do you want?"

I opened the door and stepped into a large carpeted closet lined with empty racks, dressers, and shelves. "Furniture and clothes. I don't need much." Something caught my eye. "What's that?" It was the only thing in the entire apartment that wasn't built in.

"Oh, remember," Lorna said, "I mentioned I'd salvaged a few things? Since I wasn't certain how Sparrow would feel about it, I left them in here where no one would find them."

"So those are Mason's things?"

Lorna's smile grew. "Something in there was how I knew to contact you after he...died."

"I don't understand."

Lorna had gone to the large plastic tub and removed the lid. Reaching inside, she pulled out a stack of envelopes, bound together with an old rubber band. I didn't need to see what they said or who they were addressed to. Even from a distance, I recognized my own writing, my messy chicken scratch as I'd been told.

My eyes filled with tears. "Mason saved my letters? I stopped sending them when he was overseas."

"He saved them and brought them here with him after he returned home." She reached in with her other hand. "I found these too. They have dates." Pink came to her cheeks. "I'm sorry, I looked inside."

"What are those?" I asked, going closer.

She extended the stack toward me. "Like I said, the dates are on the inside. The letters were never postmarked."

Tears trickled down my cheeks as I took the stack. Falling to my knees on the plush carpeting, I pulled them from their binding and scattered them onto the carpet. I looked up at Lorna. "He wrote me back?"

She nodded. "Hey, I know this whole move here has been hard. I think of all three of us women, mine was the easiest. I came here with Mace and stayed with Reid. I'm not saying it hasn't been tough. Even now, lockdowns suck."

I tilted my head. "Araneae mentioned that. What does that mean?"

Lorna smiled and waved her hand. "You'll learn. Like I was saying, it's not easy getting used to all of this. And it is a lot. My brother seems a bit overwhelmed too."

"I'm trying to understand," I said, making myself a bit more comfortable on the floor, sliding my shoes off and tucking my legs to the side. "He's dealing with a lot. The memories have to be overwhelming. He wakes up multiple times a night, all agitated and twitchy. I don't want to push. When I do, he complains that I'm analyzing him."

"Are you?"

I shrugged. "Probably, it's what I do. The thing I've been struggling with is that I want to help him recognize that he didn't abandon you or..." I gestured about. "...any of this. He said he used to blame the people who saved him for taking away his memories, but now that they're back and he's back here, I believe he's blaming himself for not remembering."

"So is amnesia real?"

"Yes, it can be. It's a real phenomenon."

"He went through trauma," Lorna said. "I guess it's similar to what your medication is supposed to help."

A smile came to my face. "I would love for it to help him. Before he remembered who he is, he'd forgotten everything, including the explosion and his recovery. From what he mumbles in his dreams or nightmares, I believe those are the memories that are haunting him now." I swallowed. "I just want to help him and others like him."

"You will. Araneae is very excited to get your lab up and running."

I shook my head. "I don't think it will be as easy as she makes it seem."

"Oh, you wait and see. If she wants it, Sparrow will make it happen."

My attention went back to the letters scattered before me.

"Hey, I'll leave you alone," Lorna said. "After all, this will be your place if you want it."

"I'm beginning to wonder if he wants me here."

"What?" Lorna asked. "My brother has loved you his whole life. Read those and find out."

I flattened my lips as I swallowed. "I love him and I want any part of him I can have. Since we got here, I feel like those parts are slipping away, like he's slipping away."

"They come back," she promised. "I've been here and watched each one of them. They're big men with big hearts. It's true that they pledged their love and loyalty to Sparrow and his outfit. It's also true that they can love more than that. Reid with me and Sparrow with Araneae. It's a lot, but they manage it. It's not always the way we'd like, but that doesn't lessen their loyalty to their women and the outfit. There's nothing any one of them won't do for each other." She emphasized the next sentence. "Mason died for Sparrow."

I nodded.

"If you don't believe Sparrow knows that, you're wrong. He lived with that every day. Nothing broke his darkness, nothing until Araneae. From what I understand, Mace was caught in darkness too. He was trapped and the only person in the world who could bring him out did. He loved you before. Now the way he looks at you..." She took a deep breath. "If you want my opinion, I think maybe we should get moving on this apartment sooner rather than later. It would do you two good to have some space to yourself. And I'll be honest..." She smiled. "...you're cramping our style."

A smile came to my lips.

"Not you being there," she clarified. "I love that. It's that we can be loud."

Standing, I smoothed the slacks I'd been wearing. "I totally understand. No hard feelings."

"Nothing hard at all," she said with a wink. "Let's get his place ready so we can fix that problem."

"How can we have people here and deliveries if Sparrow doesn't allow—?"

"There are certain things that require playing by his rules. This is one. Let me talk with Reid and Patrick. They'll have people within the organization they trust. We'll do it their way but on our schedule."

I let out a breath. "I think it would help to have some privacy."

"I'll let you spend some time with those," Lorna said, nodding toward the letters. "You know, it's pretty amazing that fate brought you two back together."

"Mason doesn't believe in fate."

"Of course not. He's a man who wants to be in control. If he believed in fate, he'd have to admit that he isn't always."

"Lorna, thank you for accepting me."

She came closer and gave me a hug. "Thank you for accepting us when we were young. You didn't have to."

"I didn't. I wanted to."

"If Mace comes to our place before I go to bed, I'll tell him where you are." She shrugged. "I bet they know." She pulled her phone from her pocket. "They know everything."

"Thanks."

MASON

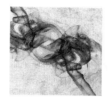

*R*iding the elevator up from 2, my mind was consumed by my decision. It was the only way I could see going forward, for Laurel and for me. The Sparrow outfit could and would protect us unless the Order was out to get me. If that were the case, my presence was endangering everyone I'd ever cared about. They'd already taken Jack; I wouldn't allow them to cause harm to the outfit and more importantly, the people in this fucking glass tower.

Everything went back to Stephanie. She encouraged Carl Oaks to hire me. Operating under the assumption that she was sent by the Order, I could concede she had the knowledge to disable my cameras at Laurel's house and my whole system in Montana. She was more than capable of killing Cartwright and leaving his body to frame Laurel. She had the knowledge to track me down to my ranch. Based on her size, she was also the one who left the small-sized boot prints and as a member of the Order would have contacts to access a plane or helicopter to search my land. And she could have been familiar with Jack, the only reason he would have welcomed her into his home.

If the Order planted Stephanie as Laurel's assistant, it was also the government entity who contacted Oaks to shut down the research.

I'd said everything went back to Stephanie. The truth was that everything went back to the Order.

The elevator door opened and I scanned the area with the sofas and chairs. My pulse kicked up as I eyed the door on the left, the one that had been mine. Before I left the control center, my phone told me that Laurel was in there, not in Lorna and Reid's place.

While entering the apartment freaked me out a bit—I wasn't ready to face more memories—getting a moment alone with Laurel superseded that concern. Turning the knob, I pushed the door inward and stepped inside.

Fucking empty.

I had never thought about it being cleaned out.

My boots tapped upon the hardwood as I made my way to the tall windows and stared out at the dark lake. When we'd first moved up here, I loved that damn view. Growing up in poverty in South Chicago, being up here felt like I was king of the damn world.

I let out a breath.

Knowing that it was Sparrow who held the title of king—of Chicago—didn't distract from my sense of achievement. No, I was part of the reason he held that title and that was more than good enough for me.

Staring at the lake, I heard something. My head turned toward the hallway as I followed the sound. Stilling within what was the master bedroom, I listened to the soft cries coming from the closet.

What the fuck?

As I came to the doorway to the closet, Laurel turned, her eyes red with dark drippings of makeup on her cheeks.

"What?" I asked, before seeing what she was holding in her hand, what she was reading. I stepped forward, pulling the paper from her grasp. "What the hell? How did you even find those?"

She stood. "You wrote them to me. They're addressed to me."

I crouched down, gathering the letters and envelopes. "I didn't mail them. That makes them mine, not yours."

"Why?" she asked.

When I turned, she was standing, her fist on her hip and her bloodshot blue eyes staring my direction. I continued to gather the loose papers. "Why what?" I asked. "These were written by someone else. It was a long fucking time ago."

"You lied? In those letters where you talk about us and a future, it was all a lie?"

"It wasn't a lie or the truth, not anymore. It was a fucking lifetime ago. Hell, it was many lifetimes ago. You know I love you now. Why the hell would these letters matter?"

"Why wouldn't they, Mason? You wrote them to me. You wrote about the roof and the stars. You wrote about things you wished you'd said."

"Fine," I said, staring at her. "I should have mailed them then. I didn't. Now none of it matters. It's over." The papers began to crumple as I wadded them together.

"Don't you dare destroy those letters," Laurel shouted as she came toward me.

"I'll do whatever I want. What I want is to throw them away."

Pulling the papers from my grasp, she was like a viper, her words as sharp as her nails. "Like hell you are. You can't just keep throwing away parts of your life." Retrieving a few, she looked up at me as she shook the paper. "In these letters you remembered who you were when we met."

"I was fucking no one."

"That's not true," she said. "You were never no one, not to me..." She pointed the direction of Lorna's apartment. "...not to Lorna or Missy and not to these people. Not to Jack. No matter who you were, you have never been a no one."

Dropping the letters, I took a step toward her. "I moved on because I could. I moved on because I am fucking good at things that kid never imagined. Even when it was all taken from me, I moved forward. I moved forward as no one. That's who I was. That's what I do. Those..." I pointed to the crumpled pages on the floor. "...aren't moving forward. They're moving back."

Her chin came up. "So you'll throw them away? Just like you threw away your childhood. Like you threw away Jack. Like you're throwing away Kader and Edgar, and like you want to throw me away."

I took a step back. "What the hell? I have never wanted nor would I want to throw you away."

"No, Mason, you're already doing it. I feel it. Each day you're stepping farther and farther away. You haven't mourned Jack or your house or even the ranch. What is happening there? What about the livestock? Do you even care, or have you thrown it away because now you're back and Mason's back and that's what you do, throw away what you no longer need?"

Moving forward, I didn't stop until Laurel was trapped, her body between me and part of the built-in closet. I lifted my hands to the edge of the dresser, caging her between. With each breath her boobs pushed against my chest and her warm breath skirted over my cheeks, yet through it all, her blue-eyed stare never left mine.

"Talk to me, Mason. You haven't talked to me since it all happened, since we got here."

"I've fucking talked to you every damn day. I sleep beside you, eat with you, we talk."

"That's not talking. I need more."

Like the flicker of a spark, her plea ignited a fire, an all-consuming blaze that I'd ignored since I'd awoken drugged at the ranch. "I fucking want more, Laurel." I tugged at the silk blouse, freeing it from the waist of her slacks. My hand snaked over her soft skin as my fingers splayed and I pulled her closer.

"That's not talking."

"I don't want to talk. I want to fuck you."

"Tell me why?"

I stopped, my fingers ready to release the clasp on her bra. "Tell you why I want to fuck you?"

"I need to know. Is this it? Is this a goodbye fuck?"

I took another step back. "Goodbye? Are you leaving?"

"I don't want to."

I spun, my muscles tight, my body tight. "Don't."

"What has been going on?"

"I failed, Laurel. I fucking failed."

Her blue eyes searched. "Failed at what?"

"Fucking everything. I failed Missy. I failed Sparrow. I failed you."

She came to me, reaching her petite hands to my chest. "You're wrong. I'm alive because of you."

"No, you're alive because of him." I pointed upstairs. "If I'm right, Stephanie killed Jack and drugged me. She was going to kill you. He saved you. The Sparrows saved you, not me. I'm back here and part of me is so fucking happy. It feels right, but the other part of me knows that the only reason I'm here and you're here is because I couldn't do it on my own."

"Who cares?"

"What?" I asked.

"Who fucking cares?"

I wasn't sure, but I believed it was the first time I'd heard her use that word and damn, it was hot. "I care."

"Did you fail when you were in the military? When you were with these men?"

"No."

"Why? Did you succeed all on your own?" When I didn't respond, she continued, "Was my research a failure because Russ helped? Is success only success when it's accomplished alone?"

I shook my head. "There's so much in my mind. So many thoughts that I can't decipher which is which."

"Then talk to me or Sparrow or someone else. Just don't shut me out."

I reached for her waist, splaying my fingers again under her blouse. "It's not a goodbye fuck. How about an I'm back fuck?"

LAUREL

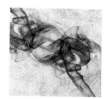

"**W**ho is back," I asked, staring up at his strikingly handsome face with his clenched jaw, high cheekbones, and taut expression.

Narrowing his gaze, Mason released me and stepped back.

The clock ticked as his stare darkened, growing hotter. The semblance of flames flickered, bringing life back to the golden flakes. Such as the flowing of lava over a dry ground, his molten green gaze heated my skin. It was more than that and yet each change was barely perceptible. I wasn't the only one who felt it. Even the air around us crackled with electricity as number three returned.

With the power of thunder warning of an impending storm, his deep timbre rumbled through me. "Me. *I'm* back, Laurel. You promised me a striptease when I returned from Indianapolis. What happened in the truck doesn't count. It's time to pay up."

With the simple change in his tone, my nipples drew taut and core twisted. "I-I—"

His finger came to my lips. "No talking. We're done talking. Only me."

Oh hell yes.

I reached for the hem of the blouse and began to lift.

"No, not yet. Me first. My dick is fucking hard." He pointed to the floor. "On your knees and take me out."

My breasts heaved against my blouse as I did as he said, my knees colliding with the soft carpet. Looking up at the man before me, he appeared bigger and larger, his legs longer and chest wider. I reached up to the button of his jeans. From where I was kneeling, his growing erection was before me, straining against the denim.

I twisted the material, freeing the button, but it wasn't until the zipper was lowered that his length sprang free. Heavy with need, his cock bobbed, the velvety surface stretched and lined with veins as I lifted myself higher.

Salty and tart, I licked the tip, grasping the length between my two hands.

"Fuck..." he groaned. "Suck me."

My thighs squeezed together as I opened my mouth, taking him bit by bit, each time deeper than the last. His taste on my tongue, his length teased my throat. It wasn't only the way his thighs strained under my touch or the sound of his groans echoed off the closet walls that fueled my desire. It was the sense of empowerment I felt as this hulk of a man could come undone from my ministrations.

I was doing this.

Me.

Beneath my fingers his balls tightened and cock grew harder.

It wasn't until he pulled away that the closet filled with the loud pop. Through veiled lashes, my gaze went back to his.

"Stand up. I have a show to watch."

With his hard cock before me, Mason offered me his hand.

Taking it, I stood. Reaching for the hem of the blouse, I pulled it over my head. Next were the slacks, revealing the black lace panties I'd recently ordered.

"Fuck me," Mason said. "Where's my sweet, naïve white-panties good girl."

When I started to answer, to tell him she too had changed, his finger again came to my lips. "No talking. Show me."

Flicking the clasp, I unbuttoned my bra, lowering it until it too was on the floor. The sway of my body came naturally as my hands skimmed over my exposed skin, moving upward until the weight of my breasts was pushed upward. A soft whimper escaped my lips as palming my breasts, I kneaded one and then the other, rolling the tight nipples between the tips of my fingers.

After freeing my hair and fanning it over my back, I came toward him, pushing him backward until he collided with another wall within the closet. Without a word, I bent down, lowering my panties as I took one last long suck of his cock and his legs stiffened.

Standing, I lifted the hem of his shirt, revealing his colorful masterpiece beneath. Throwing it to the floor, I skirted my palms over his inked skin, reached for his shoulders, and lifted myself up as I wrapped my legs around his torso.

Rising higher, I positioned myself over him as our eyes met.

This was his show.

I was his dancer, yet he was the choreographer.

Mason wanted control and I wanted him to have it.

My whimper filled the air. My lips parted and my back arched as he pulled me down, sheathing his cock and filling me to the brink. His hold of my hips tightened as he moved me up and down. Thrust after thrust, my body came to life. My nerves sparked synapses connecting as what was happening at my core radiated to my extremities, curling my toes. My thighs squeezed his torso tighter as his neck stretched, his fingers digging into my skin.

Without releasing me, Mason fell to his knees and laid me down on the soft carpet. His arms came to the side of my face as he hovered over me, all the while our union unbroken.

As his green stare dominated my view, Mason continued, taking me to the edge, watching as my back arched and nails dug into his shoulders and clawed at the carpet. With the expertise that only he'd shown, he lifted me higher and higher until we were as high as this castle in the sky.

The echo of my scream faded as his roar took over. His body shuddered inside me while mine quaked around his.

It was as our breathing slowed and our hearts found their normal beat that he spoke. "You asked me why I wanted to fuck you. I fucked you because I can. You're mine, Laurel Carlson. You have been and you are. Don't ever think I want to throw you away. You were meant to be right where you are."

I lifted my hands to his cheeks. "I'm where I want to be."

"Then it's settled. If we have to sleep on the damn carpet, we're moving in here."

I shrugged. "Lorna and I have plans for furniture."

"Unless you're having it delivered in ten minutes, tonight it's the carpet." He pushed himself upward and stared down at my body, exposed for him. A smile came to his lips as he eased in and out. "I'm not fucking done with you."

"It's a good thing we're not going to the foundation tomorrow," I said with a smile. "I may need a nap."

Holding my hips, Mason rolled until he was the one on the carpet and I was above. "Ride me." His lips came to my breasts. "While I leave my marks on these gorgeous tits."

I didn't respond as I leaned forward, placing my weight on his colorful broad shoulders, providing him unimpeded access to my breasts while I moved up and down, finding the perfect friction until once again my body trembled and I collapsed onto his bare chest.

This time I rolled to his side. When our eyes met, I asked, "Are we really sleeping here?"

"From now on. I'm grateful for everything Reid and Lorna have done. And you were right: success doesn't have to come alone. That doesn't mean I don't want you to myself when I can."

I nodded. "I like having you to myself too."

"Do you really want to keep those old letters?" he asked.

"I do."

"Just because I'm not that kid anymore doesn't mean I don't still love you." He teased a strand of my hair away from my face. "It's different."

"We're both different," I said. "I'm different from the woman you approached at the gathering. People grow and change. I just want to keep doing it with you."

Mason nodded. "I'm not going to lie. I've been racking my brain about everything that happened. I don't want us living in hiding. I think I've figured out a way to lay this on the line. I'm planning to meet with someone tomorrow. I'm hoping it will put an end to all of this mess."

My heart skipped a beat. "Who? Could it be dangerous?"

He leaned forward and kissed my nose. "Nothing and no one will keep me away from you."

"Please tell me you aren't going alone."

"Don't you have faith in my ability? I worked alone for a long time."

"No, Mason, that's not it. I do have faith. But these people lost you once. They aren't ready to do it again. Let them help."

"Go to sleep." He pulled me against his side, as I slid my head onto his hard shoulder.

"At least in the truck we had pillows and a blanket."

"Don't worry. I plan to keep you warm all night long."

MASON

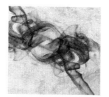

$\mathcal{T}$he conversation around me was lost as I came to terms with my decision. My mind was filled with the possibilities for my plan. This situation couldn't be settled until I did the same thing with the Order as I'd done with the Sparrows, being as honest as possible. The difference would be that I couldn't and wouldn't disclose too much on the Sparrows. What the government knew officially or what the subversive unit of the government knew about the underground of Chicago wasn't going to come from me.

I'd pledged my loyalty to both the Sparrow outfit and the Sovereign Order. One was voluntary, the other was obligatory, my life saved for my service.

My decision wouldn't matter until I made contact with the Order.

It wasn't like I could make a phone call and meet with Top. I couldn't even make a call and meet with a commander from the Order. That wasn't how it worked. Then again, Stephanie must have been reporting to someone as was Jack.

Therefore, my plan was simplistic—the way of life and death since the beginning of time.

Man survived because as a species we were superior—opposable thumbs and cognitive thinking. One could argue the cognitive superiority, but not the thumbs. That gave us the ability to construct tools and weapons, to no longer forage off the land but till it and plant what we needed to survive. Most importantly it afforded us the ability to hunt, creating weapons that gave us, the weaker species, an advantage over more ferocious larger beasts.

Laurel's hand settled over mine on the slate-topped table in Sparrow's kitchen. While he'd already left for his office on Michigan Avenue and Patrick had gone to settle a disturbance between two factions in the Fulton River District down by the warehouses, the remaining five members of this strange family were present, eating breakfast and discussing furniture as if there weren't emergencies and threats around every corner.

"Will you tell me what's wrong?" she whispered.

Forcing a smile, I shook my head. "A lot on my mind."

"That meeting?"

"Oh," Araneae said to Laurel, "I didn't get any input in this place. It was fully decorated when I arrived." She shrugged as she stood. "I like it, but I'd love to help you decorate your apartment if you want any help." She lifted her hand. "But if you don't want my input, I completely understand."

Laurel shook her head. "Honestly, I am pretty simple. My house..." She sighed. "...it was old and my furnishings were minimalistic. Ka-Mason's house was beautiful quality and also simple. I'm guessing that's what we want."

"But there has to be color," Lorna chimed in.

Laurel looked from the two women to me.

I lifted my hands. "Doc, a bed, preferably California king,

and I'm set. I'd like more than a mattress, but right now, I'd take a mattress on the floor. The rest is up to you." I stood and looked to Reid. "I'm headed downstairs."

"Will you two be around for lunch," Lorna asked as Reid stood.

"I..." I took a deep breath. "...have someplace I need to go. Don't plan on me for dinner either."

Lorna shook her head. "Someplace." She smiled at Laurel. "Just so you know, we rarely get more detail."

Laurel stood and came toward me. "Mason, can we talk?"

"We talked, Laurel."

As her eyes filled with moisture, I tugged her hand until we were in one of Sparrow's sitting rooms. This one was large and open with the giant windows that looked out onto the lake. "Don't worry," I said, tracing my finger over her cheek. "I'll come home."

"This isn't my home, not without you."

"Then work with Lorna and Araneae and make it a home. It's complicated, but soon I'll be able to access my investments —Edgar's. Don't worry about cost. Whatever you want is exactly what I want. Make that apartment your home, mine, ours."

"I don't like you leaving."

"It's going to happen. It will be me doing what Patrick's doing this morning. I'll be with Sparrow if he needs or asks. To do that, I need to be sure I'm not the prey but the hunter. I also need to be sure you're not being hunted."

"But we're safe here. I can feel it."

"You need to be safe at the foundation, on the street, anywhere. I'm going to be sure of that."

"Just tell me," she pleaded, her blue eyes widening, "who you're meeting and that you'll be safe."

My lips came to her forehead. "I love you. I promised you your life, not being captive in a glass castle above Chicago."

"Mason, come back to me."

Leaving Laurel near the large windows, I stepped away toward the elevator. As I reached the hallway, the pocket door was already open and Reid was waiting near the sensor. His dark eyes narrowed before he activated the elevator. Neither of us spoke until the door closed.

"You didn't mention a meeting."

"I need one of the cars."

He nodded. "You know, Sparrow trusts us for a reason, me and Patrick. He knows we'll make the best decision based on the outfit, not based on our feelings."

The door opened.

Leaning down near the sensor to the command center, the one on the stark cement-block wall, the light scanned my eye and the metal door opened.

"That right there," Reid said, gesturing to the opening door, "means he still trusts you. Then why didn't you mention a meeting?"

I stood taller, straightening my neck. "This *is* for the outfit. I can't be of any help to Sparrow if I'm a hunted man."

"We're all hunted, even him. You don't think there aren't people on the street today who would love to be the one to take down Sterling Sparrow."

"My bad guys are more dangerous than yours. It's plain and simple."

"You can't kill them all."

I scoffed, looking up at the large screen showing a rotation of different areas of the city. "You know this remembering shit can be like déjà vu. Do you remember telling me the same thing the night Allister died?"

"I do."

"I'm going back to Montana. There's a flight leaving O'Hare in three hours. I can't call the Order, but Jack could. I'd suspect his computer equipment has been scrubbed, but Jack was resourceful. He had a safe room. Even if the Order accessed it, I believe I can configure the database to send them a message. If they didn't clean the mess, they need to know it happened. If they did, they need to know I'm alive."

"Why, Mason?" Reid asked. "So they can fucking kill you? I won't let you do that to Lorna again."

"I need a car to get to the airport. I have alternative IDs. I came down here during the night and created them."

"You don't fucking think I know that?"

I turned to leave. "I'll take a damn taxi."

"Let me call Sparrow. If he's not using the plane, which he isn't scheduled to do, we can avoid all the airport bullshit."

"No way am I going back to Montana in a giant bird. I won't connect the Order to the Sparrows and there is no *we*."

Reid took a step toward me until we were nearly chest to chest. "There's a fucking *we*. Get used to it. Fine, you don't want to fly in a giant bird, I'll get us something less conspicuous. Either way, there's a we because I'm not going to tell your sister again that her brother died and that once again, I didn't do a fucking thing to stop it."

MASON

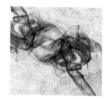

*R*eid took a set of keys from a cabinet in control central and stepped toward the steel door. "Come on."

"This isn't what I want."

He pointed at his own chin, his dark stare focused on me as we both stood tall. "Does it fucking look like I give a shit what you want?'

My eyes closed as I took a deep breath. "You don't understand what I'm up against. If I don't come back, I don't want to take you with me. You need to be here for Lorna. You need to be here for Laurel and Sparrow and Patrick. Listen, I see what you've done with Chicago. I know you're all capable of running this city and beyond without me. You've done it for seven years. Why would you risk any of that?"

He lifted his hand to the sensor, causing the door to open to the hallway with the elevator. "You better come or it's going to be me on this damn ranch calling out to an entity I shouldn't know exists. How do you think that will go?"

We didn't say another word to one another as we sat in the front seat of a black SUV and Reid drove through the tunnel and out onto the street.

I watched as familiar landmarks passed by, as well as new changes to the city since I'd last lived here. The weather was warming and the sidewalks were bustling with people.

"Do you ever think about how they don't have a fucking clue?" I asked.

"Every day. That's the way Sparrow wants it. The city is thriving, revenue is pouring in. That means happy people, happy business owners, and even happy subversive businesses. It's a balance that has been better maintained of late."

I sighed as the scenery changed. Onto 94, our speed increased. "Wait, we're not headed toward O'Hare."

"Because we're not boarding some fucking plane with a hundred and fifty other people, and..." Reid turned toward me. "...we're not flying in a giant bird."

"You know what I like about working alone?"

"No one disagrees with your plan. I get that your philosophy has kept you alive, but I'm here to tell you, this plan of yours sucks."

"You don't know—"

"I do, not as much as you, but I do. For nearly the last week since you came back, Patrick and I have been scouring the web for anything. I've found shit in places that others either don't know to look or haven't figured out. This Order is fucking hiding in plain sight. They're funded by our government, the people we elect. You know how?"

"No."

"You know how bills get passed, ones with thousands of pages and a shit ton of amendments...well, that's where their funding comes from. Patrick picked up on this first. He's done some legwork while I've continued to dig. It's a few hundred thousand here, a few billion there. We started researching the sources of the amendments."

"The people or person who added the amendment?" I asked, a rush of excitement washing through me.

"Right. It's really the same fucking plan we've used for other discoveries. It's following the money. The amendments say different things; they name obscure companies and foundations as the recipients. It's not like they specify the Sovereign Order. It would take longer than we have to track down all the funding. After all, this has been going on for decades."

"I did know that."

"So here's the thing, there's no party affiliation."

"I knew that too," I said, grateful I'd accumulated some knowledge. "The Order doesn't care what party thinks they're in charge."

"Because they think they're in charge," Reid said.

"It sure as shit seems like they are." I turned and looked at my friend, my colleague, my brother. "I'm fucking impressed." I leaned back on the seat as Reid turned the SUV onto an exit ramp. "I am."

Why had I never done what they'd done?

Maybe being a part of the Order held its own mystery, one that Reid didn't see. He wasn't a part of it.

Silence returned as we drove out of the city.

The private airport wasn't the one where Sparrow housed his large plane. This one was rural with only a few hangars. The plane Reid led me to was bigger than mine back at the ranch but smaller and less obtrusive than Sparrow's giant bird. I followed as he led me up the small stairway. With the cockpit to the left, my attention went to the plush seating area. There were only four seats, one on each side of the small aisle, two facing the tail and two the cockpit. The perfect configuration for four people to create a strategy. Based on the two sets of eyes coming from the large men staring at us, that was the plan.

"What the fuck?" I said as Sparrow and Patrick stared our direction.

"You're late," Sparrow said.

"You're not supposed to be here at all."

He looked up at Reid. "Marianne is in the cockpit. Tell her that everyone's here and we're ready."

"No," I protested.

"Mason, sit the fuck down," Sparrow said. "Listen, I want to trust you. I do. I know why you ended up where you did. I know it was because if it hadn't been you in that explosion, it would have been me. And there's no guarantee that I would have survived. I'm not sure if the Order would have deemed me worthy of saving. You were always better at being a soldier. It meant more to you. I did it. I did what I needed to do to bide my time and get back here. What if I had been the one who died? Where would we be now? Where would Chicago be?"

I crossed my arms over my chest.

"As I was saying," he went on, "sit the fuck down."

Shaking my head, I did as he said and took the only available seat, the one facing him. If we could all stand and play just one round of musical chairs, I'd choose another. Apparently, that wasn't in the cards. So now I was seated knee to knee with the man who had the last word in all things Sparrow. No, the last word in all things.

Looking around, I said, "This isn't right. All four of us shouldn't travel together. And what about the women?"

Sterling looked to Reid.

"They're safe," Reid said. "They're home."

"But Araneae was on her way to Sinful Threads," I said. "And what if Lorna decides to go out? If this shit connects to Sparrow, they could be targets."

"Not to worry," Sparrow said. "The three floors are on lockdown. No one enters and no one exits. By the way, this always pisses off my wife, and since it wasn't planned, I didn't have the chance to inform her in person. Just so you know, you owe me."

My first thought was that having Mrs. Sparrow upset seemed like a small price to pay for their collective safety.

"Mason," Patrick began, "we're not headed to Montana. That's a fucking death sentence and you know it."

My gaze went to Reid. I hoped it conveyed my anger that what we'd discussed in private was now a general conversation.

"Listen," Sparrow said, "did Reid fill you in on the Order's funding?"

"Yes."

"We all have our strengths." He tilted his head toward Patrick. "What the two of them looked through was a lot of economic shit. Patrick caught it right away."

"It has to do with what's hot when the bills are authored," Patrick said. "The entities listed to receive funding were untraceable and yet relevant at the time. In the sixties they were related to military funding. Then in the seventies it was energy. On the surface it all was very PC, nothing to set off alarms, all easily approved by whoever read the bill down to that much detail."

"Okay, but why aren't we headed to Montana?"

"Because," Sparrow said, "we're headed to Washington."

"State or DC?" I asked.

"DC," he replied. "I have connections—"

"No." The plane was now airborne. "Tell the pilot to turn around. My plan was to do this without connecting Sparrow."

"It's not possible," Patrick replied. "They knew of your connection when they took you from that hospital. No matter where they took you, you were in Chicago at the time of your injuries. Your records indicated you were working for Sparrow Enterprises. They killed and disposed of three of our men and a helicopter. It's true that what we do is under the radar, but just like the Order, it's also sanctioned mostly by neglect. We do what we do and that helps what they do. Quid pro quo. What they do is because we allow it. If you ask me, that sounds very similar to the Order."

"Chicago needs us," Sparrow said. "The strongest, most efficient parts of underground have had the support at all levels of law enforcement, politics, and the judiciary system since before my father and McFadden ran the city and vice versa. Patrick and Reid's discoveries connected recent funding of the Order to the office of a senator from Pennsylvania. During the last administration, the amendments were authored by a representative from South Carolina."

"How is that connected?" I asked.

"It's not the senators," Patrick said. "They probably have no clue. It just so happens that both representatives employed the same senior legislative aide, one who's worked for various legislators for nearly thirty years."

My eyes opened wide. "An aide?"

All three men nodded. "Yes, we're going to pay this aide a visit."

"More accurately, he's paying us one," Sparrow said.

"You think this aide is connected to the Order?"

Again, they nodded.

"And what do you think you can do?" I asked. "If we threaten them with the knowledge of what you've learned or what I've told you, I'm still dead and now you are too."

Sparrow looked down at the cuffs of his expensive shirt sticking out from his silk suit coat and flicked an imaginary piece of dust from a gold cufflink. "We aren't going to *threaten*, Mason. That would work for some two-bit meth dealer who made the bad decision to infringe on someone else's territory. Threatening is not how we deal with the *bigger bad guys*."

"What you're doing is making them your bad guys too."

"No, we're not. We are simply engaging in negotiations for your freedom and that of Laurel's research."

Fuck.

The Order didn't negotiate.

I turned, letting out a long breath and looked out the window, trying to temper the concern bubbling within my chest. As the clouds passed below, I wondered if this was how Laurel felt when I took her to Montana. Yes, I boarded this damn plane, but it was definitely against my better judgment, and now I was being kidnapped to DC.

MASON

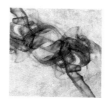

The Kimpton George Hotel was just north of Lower Senate Park and walking distance from the Capitol building. The suite we had booked had been thoroughly examined by Sparrows who had been rallied from other destinations for the job.

Sparrow wouldn't take the chance that anything could be recorded or leveraged against his outfit in the future. Likewise, he made sure it was safe, no explosives, nothing to cause harm.

Edison Walters, a man in his sixties, was on his way, agreeing to a meeting that would garner support for his senator's recent proposal for renewable energy. Walters had a long record of service in and around Washington DC, yet never had he worked to obtain higher positions, seemingly content to serve his country while maintaining anonymity.

Reid and Patrick were in the large living room area of the suite while Sparrow and I waited in the attached master suite. Reid had set up a closed-loop camera for us to see what was happening in the other room.

Though my nerves were stretched, that was a sense of calm compared to the moment Mr. Walters entered the suite and I saw his face.

"Fuck," I said, immediately recognizing the man on the screen.

"Talk to me," Sparrow said.

"He's not with the Order. He *is* the Order. That's fucking Top."

"Top?"

"That's what we call the head commander. Think five-star general." I turned to Sparrow. "Fuck. Think higher." I lifted my hands toward him. "Don't do this. Let me talk to him. If your negotiations don't go well, one call from him and Chicago could burn."

Sparrow stood taller. "No one fucks with my city." He walked to the window and back as Patrick's and Reid's voices could be heard discussing wind and solar energy. "Will he know you?"

"Yes, not everyone meets him, but I did. He's the one who gave Jack and me the final authorization for us to break free, becoming a team of two."

"And you want to talk to him?"

"I do."

I saw the conflict on Sparrow's face.

"Sparrow," I said, calming my tone. "This isn't like the last time."

Since my return, Sparrow confirmed that traffickers had been the ones who planned the explosion, the one that resulted in my death. They were unhappy with Sparrow for shutting down their sales channels and figured his death would give the entire operation to McFadden.

"I'm not walking into an ambush," I continued. "We know

the suite is clean. We have Sparrows in here and outside. This time we're doing the ambushing."

With a quick nod, Sparrow sent a text. A few moments later, Reid and Patrick entered the bedroom.

"We won't take our eyes off the fucking screen," Sparrow said, explaining to Reid and Patrick the change in plans. "This guy is bigger than we realized. Mason knows him. He's going to negotiate."

Standing under the gaze of all three men, I nodded. Turning and taking a deep breath, I opened the door. Walters's eyes widened as he realized who was standing before him. As that realization became clearer, the mild-mannered legislative aide disappeared before my eyes. Top's neck straightened, his shoulders broadened, and he stood.

"Pierce."

"Top."

"I was saddened by the loss of Commander Jackson. It was unusual for him to go days without communicating. Imagine the surprise when our team arrived."

"Yes, sir. I too was saddened. Jack was my commander and my friend."

"I am also disappointed," he said. "We thought things had been working with the two of you. Your betrayal of the Order was unexpected."

"That didn't happen, sir. I'm here to tell you that."

He tilted his head toward the bedroom door. "Those men?"

"I trust them with my life. I did and I do again."

His gaze narrowed. "You did?"

"Yes, sir, before the Order."

"You remember before?" he asked.

"Yes, sir. I remember everything. I also didn't cause the carnage at my ranch. I do believe Jack—Commander Jackson—

was killed by a member of the Order. I find it impossible for anyone else to have lulled him into a false sense of security."

Top sat again on the sofa. "Tell me about your side jobs."

"Sir, I answered whenever the Order called."

"You're the only knowledgeable member who can explain what occurred on your ranch. That is either a position of power or one that's very precarious."

I took in a deep breath. "Stephanie Moore, I don't believe that's her real name, was positioned at a university in Indiana. She is responsible for Jack's death as well as the deaths of multiple civilians."

"Tell me, Pierce, how many deaths are you responsible for?"

"I don't know that, sir. I do know that I never took out a fellow team member and certainly not a commander."

"Come back to the unit," he said. "We'll follow protocol. The board can decide your fate."

"No."

"Excuse me, Pierce. That wasn't a suggestion. It was an order."

"No, sir," I said. "I'm done. The Order took seven years of my life. It took one of my best friends. I've repaid you with my service. Now repay me with my freedom."

"I believe we had this conversation before. How many people walk away from the Order?"

"I only care about one."

"I want to know more about the return of your memories. We have medical staff that needs to know."

My head shook. "I was told that the memories could come back and they did."

"It was a lie. No one's has returned."

"What do you mean *no one*?"

He stood again. "Let our doctors learn what happened and you'll have your freedom."

The door to the bedroom opened and Sterling Sparrow entered the main suite. There truly was something about him. It was probably conceit, but it worked for him, an aura of importance. "Mr. Walters."

Top's eyes narrowed. "Do I know you?"

"I don't care. I know you. This man is now free from his obligation with you and yours. It is time to allow Mason Pierce to go on with his life."

Top's chin rose. "Mason Pierce is dead."

"Not anymore," Sparrow said.

"Why, sir, should I even entertain this conversation?"

"Because it could be mutually beneficial."

"And what," Top asked, "can you possibly offer me?"

"Today, the offer is that you'll leave here alive. The future holds endless possibilities."

Top's brow furrowed. "I do know you." He scanned Sparrow from the top of his head to his shoes. "I don't make it a habit to deal with criminals."

"Bullshit," I said. "That's what you turned every fucking one of us into. We were criminals for the greater good."

"Son, for the greater good is bigger than all of us." Top turned to Sparrow. "You'd go into my debt, into my organization's debt for this man?"

"I'm in debt to no one. I'm available to few. You are being offered an opportunity for an audience for a limited time. Choose wisely."

Top turned to me. "Tell me about Morehead."

"Morehead?"

"Otherwise known as Stephanie Moore."

"She was one of..." I almost said *us*. "...a team member?"

"She was. There had been a transgression brought to my attention. We planned on apprehending her as she left the country. Instead, her body was discovered by our team."

"She had the research and development data for a compound up for sale on the black market. She'd worked with others to get the data and sell it. Her partners are now dead by her hand. From what I could deduce, she planned to keep the money for herself."

"That research was supposed to be stopped. Once she reported the progress that had been made, we sent the order."

I shifted from foot to foot, wondering if the order included killing Laurel. "The order for the *research* to be stopped?"

"Yes, Pierce. You've been on information-killing missions. I'm aware that everyone involved with the research is either dead or missing. That wasn't the order. It seems as though Morehead wanted to obtain the highest price for her sale by eliminating the possibility of any further research."

"And why stop the research in the first place?" Sparrow asked.

Walters turned to him. "How would the government feel about a civilian team recreating one of its top biochemical agents? What if it was reinvented and fell into the wrong hands or was used for the wrong purposes? What if our enemies acquired it?"

"So you're saying the government already has it?" I asked.

"Pierce, you should be proud."

Of Laurel? What did he mean?

"Sir?"

"You were one of the first successful recipients. That is why our doctors need to assess your memory retrieval."

My knees weakened as I fell back into a chair situated near

the sofa. "You're saying that it wasn't my mind's defense. You're saying my memories were erased."

"You wouldn't have been of any use to us the way you were. Your success has proved useful with other members."

"How many other members have had their lives erased?" I asked.

"What does it matter?" Top asked. "You're all dead anyway."

That was one of their favorite reminders. We were no one. We were officially dead. Complete the mission. If you don't, you simply disappear. You can't die twice.

"Mr. Walters," Sparrow said, "it is clear that your organization creates an insurmountable imbalance, anchoring your members to servitude. I will restate that this man's debt is paid in full." Sparrow's chin rose. "Do not call on him. You may contact me; however, after what I just heard, I cannot make any guarantees. I will do what is in the best interests of my city."

"Isn't that what we're all after on some level?"

Sparrow's tone lowered as his cadence slowed. "Confirm Mr. Pierce's freedom."

Top came closer to me and extended his hand. Standing, I accepted and shook.

"Thank you, Pierce, for your service. While I can't give you back those seven years, I can agree to the future as long as you maintain your silence regarding our existence. If we have any reason to doubt..."

"The existence of what exactly?" Sparrow asked.

Top nodded to Sparrow.

As our handshake ended, I said, "Commander Jackson deserved better."

"Goodbye, Pierce."

Once the door shut and Walters was gone, Reid and Patrick

entered the room. "We'll keep him under surveillance for a while," Patrick said.

I paced the length of the room and back. "They fucking drugged me."

Instead of responding, Reid said, "It's up to you, Mason, but we can get you your identity back. We have to come up with a story on where you've been because no one will believe the truth."

"Figure it out. It's time to go home," Sparrow said.

LAUREL

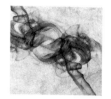

*I*n a silk camisole and boy shorts ready for sleep, I sat against the headboard, hugging my knees to my chest. The bed I was in was from Lorna and Reid's apartment. Since the three of us ladies were stuck between this floor and the penthouse all day, I decided to clean the apartment, ridding it of its seven years of dust. Lorna and Araneae joined me, and then together we moved the bedroom suite from Lorna's guest room to our bedroom. A few supplies pilfered from various bathrooms throughout the three floors and Mason and I had enough necessities to at least sleep and stay in what was going to be our new home.

"So you did it?" I called through the bathroom door. "I'm safe and free." The declaration was hollow as I thought of Russ's and Eric's deaths and even that of Carl Oaks. Russell had been right when he'd said that Oaks had been greedy; nevertheless, his sentence carried out by Stephanie seemed extreme.

"Yes and no," Mason said as he entered the bedroom and crawled onto the bed, the mattress dipping with his weight.

The movement of the bed didn't have my attention. My attention was focused on the man beside me. After he'd showered, he hadn't covered himself in socks, long pants, and a long-sleeved shirt as he normally did. Instead, he was wearing only a pair of black basketball shorts, the waist riding precariously low, showcasing the V of his hips. Sitting beside me, his wide chest, arms, legs, and even feet revealed his beautiful bright ink.

Thinking of Lorna's story, I smiled. "I'm going to dream in color."

His cheeks rose. "Every night, Doc."

Trying to regain focus of our conversation as the scent of bodywash settled around us and Mason's wet hair dripped onto his broad shoulders, I asked, "What do you mean by yes and no?"

"First, yes, you're safe," he said. "There's no contract out on you. That was all Stephanie going rogue. She was the greedy one. Her fate was sealed. No one goes against the Or-organization."

"Mason, be honest with me about the organization."

Closing his eyes, he leaned against the headboard. Taking a deep breath, he began, "After the explosion, I was brought back —nursed back to health and retrained—by a group of people who wanted my skills."

"Killing people?" I asked.

"Yes, amongst other things. The point was that this group led me to believe I owed them my services for their resurrection of my body and skills. I did it, but it never felt right. I can't say it felt wrong. You see, there was nothing else. No other memories. Jack and I met in that group. He negotiated our recent situation. I could do what I did, be Kader on the dark web, and my obligation was to answer when the organization called."

I hugged my knees tighter. "I know I asked, but when you talk about the nothingness, it makes me sad."

Mason reached over to one of my knees and squeezed. "Don't be. I could have not experienced any of that and I'd be where I am right now. If it had happened that way, you wouldn't be here. Someone else would have taken the contract on you." He lifted my hand to his lips and lowered kisses to my knuckles. Peering upward, his green eyes shone. "Laurel, I'd do every damn minute—every damn thing, all of it—again to have you here with me."

Sighing, I leaned closer. "Does this mean I can be me?" I shrugged. "Maybe contact Sinclair or another company?"

"Speaking of your formula, I learned something today about my memory loss."

"What?"

"It wasn't due to the trauma. The government wanted to shut down your research because they already have the drug."

"No." My head shook as I sat taller. "How can they have it? We were still in early clinical trials."

"I didn't *lose* my memories. They were taken from me. In that hot, stuffy, awful place they took them from me."

I jumped up, standing by the bed, my heart racing as I stared down at Mason. "What did you just say?"

"That group, part of the government, *took* my memories."

"No, Mason. The description."

His broad shoulder shrugged. "It's been coming back. When I woke after the explosion, I didn't know where I was. I still don't. I remember that it felt like the desert. I was bandaged and my skin...well, it was fucking gone. The debridement was excruciating. The bandages essential, but..."

"Stop." Tears prickled my eyes as I thought of him in pain. I crawled back on the bed and sat on my knees. "I don't believe this."

"What?"

"I was there. I saw you. That study I told you about, the one that just stopped. It was someplace...hot and stuffy. They wouldn't tell us where we were either. The air conditioning would blow, but nothing could cut through the heat. One day I got lost, wandering where I wasn't supposed to go. The area was restricted, yet for some reason I was able to keep going." I shook my head at the memories, my long hair skirting over my back. "I think it scared me so much, I blocked it out of my mind." Our gazes met and I smiled. "I am not by nature much of a rule breaker or adrenaline junkie."

Mason grinned.

That's right, you've changed me.

I went on with my story. "I hadn't thought about it for years. And then after I saw you at the gathering, I dreamt about that incident. I swore it wasn't real, but it was. Oh, it was you in a locked room." I ran my hand over his chest, the unevenness of his scars under my fingertips. "You were all covered in bandages."

"Maybe it wasn't me," he said. "Maybe it was someone else."

Closing my eyes, the scene came back as clear as if it had been today. *Looking through the window, the participant's gaze came my direction, peering at me from small openings in the white bandages. Though hidden, the intensity of the stare caused me to stumble backward —the green-eyed stare.*

"Oh, Mason, I didn't realize it at the time, but it was you. I know in my heart." Again I ran my hands over his chest and his arms, taking in his colors and the texture beneath. "I can't believe we were in the same place."

"Didn't you tell me that you researched that study, looked for information, and couldn't find any?"

"Yes, I wanted to reference what I recalled. It was so strange. There was nothing."

"When did you do that?" Mason asked.

Pursing my lips, I thought back. "I'm not sure. It was after we started making some progress. I wanted to compare data. I think it was about two years ago, maybe more."

"Maybe before Stephanie was hired?"

I sat straighter. "Yes. What does that mean?"

"I believe that it means your online search probably drew the attention of someone who didn't want your research to reproduce what they already had, and they sent Stephanie to infiltrate your lab. They just never suspected she'd try to personally profit."

"But it isn't the same as the drug they used on you," I said. "Russ and I were working to avoid what happened to you. We were so close to isolating the traumatic memories without taking away all."

"The government is going to fight the manufacturing of any similar medication, and they don't fight fair. I would suspect that no matter how much money Sinclair or any other pharmaceutical company throws at this, they won't get a patent."

I sighed. "What about the foundation?"

Mason's cheeks rose. "Araneae wants you to carry on. It won't be government or publicly funded. We need Reid and Patrick to explore the legalities and limitations, but for now, Doc, I'd say that what Araneae Sparrow wants, she probably gets."

A smile came to my face. "You should have seen her. She was not happy about her sudden change of plans today." I recalled her return to the kitchen shortly after she'd left for Sinful Threads. "That woman is beautiful, but boy...she has a temper and cusses enough to make a sailor blush."

Mason scoffed. "I bet she and Sparrow are a match for one another."

I shifted, bringing my lips to Mason's. "They can have their match. I found mine."

Suddenly the world turned, leaving me on my back, pinned by the handsomest man I'd ever seen, the one who made my circulation rush and my core twist with need.

"I believe it was me who found you," he said, his voice lowering and rumbling like thunder.

"All that matters is that we're together."

Mason's lips captured mine, demanding and possessive, similar to our first kiss in that old basement. His chest pressed against my breasts as his kiss took unapologetically, his tongue seeking entrance as the room filled with my approving moans.

Then all at once, he was gone, his weight no longer pinning me to the mattress.

"What?" I asked, looking around.

Mason wasn't on the bed, but beside it with his tats completely exposed, minus those hidden by his dark shorts, and his hair unrestrained, its length near his chin. Yet my gaze focused on his sexy, possessive stare as my brain made sense of what was happening. This tragically beautiful man was kneeling before me.

Oh my God.

"Mason?"

"Some may think this is fast, but damn it, two decades isn't fast. Laurel, I want to ask you a question."

The lump forming in my throat moved higher as I scooted to the side of the bed and turned; keeping my knees together, I placed my toes on the floor. "What question?"

"You know what? Not yet. I think I should ask someone else first."

Dazed, I shook my head. "Who? Sparrow?"

Mason's grin grew as his green eyes shone. "No. He may

think he's the ruler of all, but that's not who I want to ask for your hand. It's not his to give."

Tears filled my eyes as I leaned forward and cupped his cheeks. "You want to ask my dad?"

"Isn't that the way it's supposed to be done?"

If these were normal circumstances, I'd remind the man hinting at proposing that I wasn't a child. I was a strong, independent woman who made her own decisions. There was nothing normal about being with Mason Pierce.

"My dad? My parents? They can learn I'm safe?"

"Don't you think they should?"

I nodded. "Oh yes."

"Then tomorrow we'll head to Iowa."

I couldn't temper my smile if I wanted to.

As Mason came back to bed, he laid his head on his pillow and pulled me close. "Reid is certain you're safe with your real name. It's the research at the foundation that needs to stay under wraps."

"I'll agree to whatever it takes to stay safe and continue my work."

"He also thinks that I can fight the premature news of my death," Mason said. "We need to work out the particulars, but if your dad says yes..." He rolled toward me, our noses nearly touching. "...I hope you will too. I don't care if you keep Carlson for your professional name, but if I'm honest, I've always dreamt that one day you'd be Mrs. Pierce."

My grin grew even larger as I thought back to the gangly boy on the basketball court, the one who caught my eye over two decades ago, the one whose name I doodled in my notebook, and the one I was bound to, even then. "I used to have the same dream. Let's hope my dad says yes."

EPILOGUE

Mason

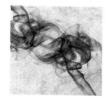

Four months later

I stared across the chessboard at Sparrow. His elbows were on his outspread knees, and his brow was furrowed in concentration.

"You've left the fucking board sitting here for seven years and you haven't figured out your next move?" I asked with a grin as I leaned back and crossed my ankle over my knee.

Sparrow's dark eyes looked up. "Shut up, I'm concentrating."

"Again, Sparrow, seven fucking years. You don't have a next move because I'm going to win and you know that. We're flying to Montana in the morning. Do you think you might be able to admit defeat by then?"

Just the other day I'd finally received the documents nullifying my death certificate. It was like a new birthday, acknowledging that I was truly alive. That didn't mean I didn't still exist in the shadows. I did in Chicago as one of the top men in the Sparrow outfit.

There had been a time when I'd given up on ever having a life that included other people. Laurel brought it all back and in two days she was going to be my wife.

Sparrow sat back without making a move. "I've thought this out with every fucking possibility. You haven't won. I'm not sure that you can make the next two moves to actually do it."

I grinned. "Try me."

I may not have played chess in the last seven years, but ever since I saw this board and realized it was still our game, I'd been racking my brain with possible moves and scenarios. Sparrow's hand came down, and pinching the top of his rook, he lifted it.

It was one of those fucking moments that if it were in a movie, it would be in slow motion.

Slowly, he set it back down in its same spot. Then he moved his queen, capturing my bishop.

"Interesting sacrifice," he said with a cocky smirk, "leaving your bishop vulnerable."

"Indeed." After taking his rook, I reassessed the board. "That's check."

"Not checkmate, though."

I looked up and grinned. "Not yet." There was no doubt that I was up against a worthy opponent. Perhaps what I'd wanted seven years ago, I no longer needed to prove. I'd wanted Sparrow to see that I too was a worthy opponent and an even worthier ally.

It wasn't two moves, it was three. We both saw it coming. "Checkmate, Sparrow. I won."

He leaned back with a grin and reached for his glass of whiskey.

"Seriously, you're not going to get upset so I can revel in this win?"

"No, I'm too busy reveling in the fact that you're back, legally alive, and in two days you're getting married. Who would have ever thought there'd be a woman out there who could put up with you?"

"Laurel's always been that woman. But I have to say, I thought the same thing when I heard you were married."

"There's never been another woman for me either. I guess that's how we know we have the right ones." He lifted his glass toward me.

Picking mine up, we brought them together.

"Cheers. Congratulations, Mason. Enjoy the win. It won't happen again."

I took a drink of the whiskey. "That doesn't matter as long as there is an again."

As the sun shone in the endless blue sky overhead, I stood alone on the front porch of the new home I'd had built on my ranch. The house, the property, all of it was mine, Mason Pierce's. After recovering the money I'd sent to Stephanie's Cayman accounts, we'd used a shell company to purchase the land from the estate of Edgar Price. Theoretically, it was Edgar's money we'd used.

Don't try to follow the trail.

It's long and twisted and unnavigable.

I'm good alone; however, with Reid and Patrick, we're fucking amazing.

Now that Mason was declared alive, I'd purchased the land again from the shell company. Each time I'd given myself a great deal.

While I'd considered giving the property up, I couldn't. The land held too many memories. Over the last few months, I'd learned that those were too precious to lose, the good and the bad.

The construction of the house happened extremely fast. Thankfully it was summer in Montana and the ground wasn't covered in feet of snow. I also had a shit-ton of money and the combination worked to our advantage.

As soon as the shell company received possession, I hired a full-time ranch manager and allowed him to staff the ranch with ranch hands year around. Though Edgar had never met him, the new manager was a man who'd worked for Jack. His name was Seth.

Even before Edgar was declared deceased, Seth received an anonymous call explaining that Jack had to leave unexpectedly and asked if he'd come and take care of the livestock.

He did.

A man with that kind of commitment to my land and animals was the kind of man I needed.

For the record, Reid and I did a thorough and extensive background check on Seth. My new manager was not part of the Order. He was simply a good man who knew his stuff. He was now a man who was very well paid for his knowledge, work, and dedication. It was good to see Jack's home filled with Seth, his wife, and two young children. Family was never an option in the Order.

Jack told me once that before his death and rebirth into the Order there'd been someone. Seeing his home now filled with a family, I believed would make Jack smile.

It did me.

I no longer wanted the ranch for its seclusion.

That wasn't completely true.

Our living arrangements in Chicago worked well, and Laurel and the other women had done a great job of decorating and furnishing our space. However, this house overlooking the ravine was our special place where we could go to be alone. It was where I'd brought Laurel to save her from danger. Little had I realized, it was also where she'd save me from isolation, returning both my memories and my life.

As a favor to my soon-to-be wife and to honor my word, we'd also worked to assure that Eric Olsen's wife received his promised retirement. She wasn't a wealthy woman, but she was safe and had a solid financial standing.

"Mason, man, it's time," Reid said, his grin in place as he stepped onto the porch. "Are you ready?"

I scanned my brother-in-law from head to toe. The custom tuxedos may have seemed out of place with my choice of footwear, but the cowboy boots were what I wanted.

"I think I've been ready for this since I was eleven years old."

"Then you're late," Sparrow said, the screen door slamming behind him. "By the way, your bride is beautiful."

"Yeah, she is."

"I can't believe she's really going to marry your ass," Patrick said, joining the three of us. "I thought she was supposed to be smart."

"Right?" Reid chimed in. "If she were smart, she would have run when she saw you."

For only a moment I recalled seeing these guys for the first time on a bus as we were transported to basic training.

Memories like that would come and go, the way they were supposed to do.

"You know, you guys are a real pain in the ass."

Sparrow's arm came around my neck. "Get used to us. We're not going anywhere."

A few minutes later, we were all standing on a balcony—a new addition to the new house—that protruded over the ravine.

I stood in the soft breeze with my heart pounding, staring into the house. The officiant was on one side of me with Sparrow, Reid, and Patrick at my other side.

Around us, the railing was lined with draped linens and upon the material and draped above was garland made of wildflowers of all colors. Facing us were two chairs, only one occupied. Our guests were few and that was the way Laurel wanted it. She said she always dreamed of a wedding that wasn't large but intimate with only the people she loved most.

If that was what my bride wanted, it was what she would have.

Holding my hands in front of me, I smiled at Dr. Carlson, Laurel's mother, our one seated guest. I doubt she dreamt of her daughter marrying a kid from South Chicago or someone connected to the Sparrows, but none of that mattered as we pulled up to their home and she and her husband got their daughter back. Of course, we couldn't share all the details. Nevertheless, Eric Olsen was dead and Carl Oaks and Russell Cartwright were forever missing. Having Laurel back was more than they ever dreamt.

When she explained that she was alive because of me, I don't think her parents cared any longer about where I was from or who I associated with. I was the man who saved their child, even if she was no longer a child but a beautiful, accomplished woman.

My back straightened as music began to play.

The first one down the aisle was cute and short with brown hair like her mom and her aunt. She smiled a big front-toothless grin as she came forward in her white dress and bouquet of multicolored wildflowers. The next was her mother and my soon-to-be sister-in-law, Ally, wearing green and also carrying the multicolored flowers.

With each bridesmaid my anticipation grew.

Araneae.

Lorna.

The music changed as Laurel's mother stood.

Taking a deep breath, I stared as they appeared in the doorway.

With her hand on her father's arm, Laurel was the most beautiful bride I'd ever seen. I recognized her beauty the night I saw her at the gathering. The difference with now was that as I scanned her beautiful curves covered in flowing white, I didn't have to use my imagination as to what was beneath. As I took in her long, slender neck, her gorgeous face, and even the way her hair was so beautifully styled beneath a tiara of wildflowers, I saw more.

As she came closer, I saw the young girl at the recreation center, the one with dreams big enough for both of us. I saw the way she smiled when she talked about the foundation and the way she cried when she was reunited with her family. I saw her hair mussed when she woke or splayed over a pillow as her blue gaze stared up at me. I saw her neck strained and back arched as she willingly accepted our union, and the way she shuddered as she came apart. I saw the colorful small butterfly she'd had tattooed upon her round ass, the one for my eyes only.

They say that there are times in your life when you see your life pass before your eyes. Those are memories and I had those of this beautiful woman.

"Who gives this woman to be married?" the officiant asked.

Dr. Carlson looked up at me with blue eyes that I also recalled; they were the same color as his daughter's. Those eyes had calmed and soothed me when I was an eleven-year-old boy and felt helpless. Now those same eyes were shining with pride.

"With love and adoration, her mother and I." He lifted her

hand and placed it in mine. "We couldn't be happier." He smiled. "We love you both."

Laurel looked up at me.

"I love you," I whispered. "Let's make new memories."

She nodded. "Forever."

THE END

If you haven't read WEB OF SIN (Sterling and Araneae's story) I hope now that you've had a peek, you will. The books must be read in order: SECRETS (turn the page for a sneak peek at SECRETS), LIES, and PROMISES.

∾

Please watch, because what has been created, cannot be uncreated. The webs continue to be spun!

WEB OF DESIRE, Patrick's story, will begin with SPARK, January 14, 2020.

∾

"From a little spark may burst a flame." ~ Dante Alighieri
A simple ember to dried kindling can ignite a raging fire.
I've made my mark and proven my loyalty to a man, a city, and a way of life. That loyalty has provided me with all the spoils of success. Until now that hasn't included a woman at my side.
What is it about this unobtainable beauty that brings my untapped desire to life?
Cracking open the stone and striking the flint is my doing.
What follows is hers.

With something so intense will this spark lead to a blazing inferno? Will we make it out of the ashes before everything I hold dear is ravaged?
From New York Times bestselling author Aleatha Romig comes a brand-new dark romance, *Spark*, set in the same dangerous world as *Secrets and Twisted*. You do not need to read the *Web of Sin* or *Tangled Web* trilogy to get caught up in this new and intriguing saga, *Web of Desire*.
SPRARK is book one of the *WEB OF DESIRE* trilogy that continues in *FLAME* and concludes in *ASHES*.

Have you been Aleatha'd?

A PEEK AT SECRETS, BOOK #1 WEB OF SIN

Araneae

PROLOGUE

*M*y mother's fingers blanched as she gripped the steering wheel tighter with each turn. The traffic on the interstate seemed to barely move, yet we continued to swerve in, out, and around other cars. From my angle I couldn't read the speedometer, though I knew we were bordering on reckless driving. I jumped, holding my breath as we pulled in front of the monstrous semi, the blare of a truck's horn filling our ears. Tons of metal and sixteen wheels screeched as brakes locked behind us, yet my mother's erratic driving continued.

"Listen very carefully," she said, her words muffled by the quagmire of whatever she was about to say, the weight pulling them down as she fluttered her gaze between the road ahead and the rearview mirror.

"Mom, you're scaring me."

I reached for the handle of the car door and held on as if the seat belt couldn't keep me safe while she continued to weave from lane to lane.

"Your father," she began, "made mistakes, deadly mistakes."

My head shook side to side. "No, Dad was a good man. Why would you say that?"

My father, the man I called Dad for as long as I could remember, was the epitome of everything good: honest and hardworking, a faithful husband, and an omnipresent father.

He *was*.

He died less than a week ago.

"Listen, child. Don't interrupt me." She reached into her purse with one hand while the other gripped tighter to the wheel. Removing an envelope from the depths of the bag, she handed it my direction. "Take this. Inside are your plane tickets. God knows if I could afford to send you away farther than Colorado, I would."

My fingers began to tremble as I looked down at the envelope in my grasp. "You're sending me away?" The words were barely audible as my throat tightened and heaviness weighed down upon my chest. "Mom—"

Her chin lifted in the way it did when her mind was set. I had a million visions of the times I'd seen her stand up for what she believed. At only five feet three, she was a pit bull in a toy poodle body. That didn't mean her bark was worse than her bite. No, my mother always followed through. In all things she was a great example of survival and fortitude.

"When I say your father," she went on, "I don't mean my husband—may the Lord rest his soul. Byron was a good man who gave his...everything...for you, for *us*. He and I have always been honest with you. We wanted you to know that we loved you as our own. God knows that I wanted to give birth. I tried to get pregnant for years. When you were presented to us, we knew you were a gift from heaven." Her bloodshot eyes—those from crying through the past week since the death of my dad—briefly turned my direction and then back to the highway. "Renee, never doubt that you're our angel. However, the reality is somewhere darker. The devil has been searching for you. And my greatest fear has always been that he'd find you."

The devil?

My skin peppered with goose bumps as I imagined the biblical creature: male-like with red skin, pointed teeth, and a pitchfork. Surely that wasn't what she meant?

Her next words brought me back to reality.

"I used to wake in a cold sweat, fearing the day had arrived. It's no longer a nightmare. You've been found."

"Found? I don't understand."

"Your biological father made a deal against the devil. He thought if he did what was right, he could... well, he could *survive*. The woman who gave birth to you was my best friend—a long time ago. We hadn't been in contact for years. She hoped that would secure your safety and keep you hidden. That deal...it didn't work the way he hoped. Saving themselves was a long shot. Their hope was to save you. That's how you became our child."

It was more information than I'd ever been told. I have always known I was adopted but nothing more. There was a promise of *one day*. I used to hope for that time to come. With the lead weight in the pit of my stomach, I knew that now that *one day* had arrived, and I wasn't ready. I wanted more time.

The only woman I knew as my mother shook her head just before wiping a tear from her cheek. "I prayed you'd be older before we had this talk, that you would be able to comprehend the gravity of this information. But as I said, things have changed."

The writing on the envelope blurred as tears filled my sixteen-year-old eyes. The man I knew as my dad was gone, and now the woman who had raised me was sending me away. "Where are you sending me?"

"Colorado. There's a boarding school in the mountains, St. Mary of the Forest. It's private and elite. They'll protect you."

I couldn't comprehend. "For how long? What about you? What about my friends? When will I be able to come home?"

"You'll stay until you're eighteen and graduated. And then it will be up to you. There's no coming back here...ever. This city isn't home, not anymore. I'm leaving Chicago, too, as soon as I get you out." Her neck stiffened as she swallowed her tears. "We both have to be brave. I thought at first Byron's accident was just that—an accident. But then this morning...I knew. Our time is up. They'll kill me if they find me, just as they did Byron. And Renee..." She looked my way, her gray eyes swirling with emotion. While I'd expect sadness, it was fear that dominated. "...my fate would be easy compared to yours."

She cleared her throat, pretending that tears weren't cascading down her pale cheeks.

"Honey, these people are dangerous. They don't mess around, and they don't play fair. We don't know how, but they found you, and your dad paid the price. I will forever believe that he died to protect you. That's why we have this small window of time. I want you to know that if necessary, I'll do the same. The thing is, my death won't stop them. And no matter what, I won't hand you over."

"Hand me over?"

We swerved again, barreling down an exit until Mom slammed on her brakes, leaving us in bumper-to-bumper traffic. Her gaze again went to the rearview mirror.

"Are we being followed?" I asked.

Instead of answering, she continued her instructions. "In that envelope is information for your new identity, a trust fund, and where you'll be living. Your dad and I had this backup plan waiting. We hoped we'd never have to use it, but he insisted on being prepared." Her gaze went upward. "Thank you, Byron. You're still watching over us from heaven."

Slowly, I peeled back the envelope's flap and pulled out two Colorado driver's licenses. They both contained my picture—that was the only recognizable part. The name, address, and even birth dates were different. "Kennedy Hawkins," I said, the fictitious name thick on my tongue.

"Why are there two?"

"Look at the dates. Use the one that makes you eighteen years old for this flight. It's to ensure the airline will allow you to fly unaccompanied. Once you're in Colorado, destroy the one with the added two years. The school needs your real age for your grade in school."

I stared down at one and then the other. The name was the same. I repeated it again, "Kennedy Hawkins."

"Learn it. Live it. Become Kennedy."

A never-before-thought-of question came to my mind. "Did I have a different name before I came to you?"

My mother's eyes widened as her pallid complexion changed from white to gray. "It's better if you don't know."

I sat taller in the seat, mimicking the strength she'd shown me all of my life. "You're sending me away. You're saying we may never see one another again. This is my only chance. I think I deserve to be told everything."

"Not everything." She blinked rapidly. "About your name, your dad and I decided to alter your birth name, not change it completely. You were very young, and we hoped having a derivation of what you'd heard would help make the transition easier. Of course, we gave you our last name."

"My real name isn't Renee? What is it?"

"Araneae."

The syllables played on repeat in my head, bringing back memories I couldn't catch. "I've heard that before, but not as a name."

She nodded. "I always thought it was ironic how you loved insects. Your name means spider. Your birth mother thought it gave you strength, a hard outer shell, and the ability to spin silk, beautiful and strong."

"Araneae," I repeated aloud.

Her stern stare turned my way. "Forget that name. Forget Araneae and Renee. We were wrong to allow you any connection. Embrace Kennedy."

My heart beat rapidly in my chest as I examined all of the paperwork. My parents, the ones I knew, were thorough in their plan B. I had a birth certificate, a Social Security card, a passport matching the more accurate age, and the driver's license that I'd seen earlier, all with my most recent school picture. According to the documentation, my parents' names were Phillip and Debbie Hawkins. The perfect boring family. Boring or exciting, family was something I would never have again.

"And what happened to Phillip and Debbie?" I asked as if any of this made sense.

"They died in an automobile accident. Their life insurance funded your trust fund. You are an only child."

The car crept forward in the line of traffic near the departure terminal of O'Hare Airport. A million questions swirled through my head, and yet I struggled to voice even one. I reached out to my mother's arm. "I don't want to leave you."

"I'll always be with you, always."

"How will we talk?"

She lifted her fist to her chest. "In here. Listen to your heart."

Pulling to the curb and placing the car in park, she leaned my direction and wrapped me in her arms. The familiar scent of lotions and perfumes comforted me as much as her hug. "Know you're loved. Never forget that, Kennedy."

I swallowed back the tears brought on by her calling me by the unfamiliar name.

She reached for her wrist and unclasped the bracelet she always wore. "I want you to have this."

I shook my head. "Mom, I never remember seeing you without it."

"It's very important. I've protected it as I have you. Now, I'm giving it to you." She forced a smile. "Maybe it will remind you of me."

"Mom, I'd never forget you." I looked down to the gold bracelet in the palm of my hand as my mom picked it up, the small charms dangling as she secured it around my wrist.

"Now, it's time for you to go."

"I don't know what to do."

"You do. Go to the counter for the airlines. Hand them your ticket and the correct identification. Stay strong."

"What about those people?" I asked. "Who are they? Will you be safe?"

"I'll worry about me once I'm sure that you're safe."

"I don't even know who they are."

Her gaze moved from me to the world beyond the windshield. For what seemed like hours, she stared as the slight glint of sunshine reflected on the frost-covered January ground. Snow spit through the air, blowing in waves. Finally, she spoke, "Never repeat the name."

"What name?"

"Swear it," she said, her voice trembling with emotion.

It was almost too much. I nodded.

"No. I need to hear you promise me. This name can never be spoken aloud."

"I swear," I said.

"Sparrow, Allister Sparrow. He's currently in charge, but one day it will be his son, Sterling."

I wished for a pen to write the names down; however, from the way they sent a chill down my spine, I was most certain that I'd never forget.

❧

WEB OF SIN is completely available: *SECRETS*, *LIES*, and *PROMISES*.

WHAT TO DO NOW

LEND IT: Did you enjoy BOUND? Do you have a friend who'd enjoy BOUND? BOUND may be lent one time. Sharing is caring!

RECOMMEND IT: Do you have multiple friends who'd enjoy my dark romance with twists and turns and an all new sexy and infuriating anti-hero? Tell them about it! Call, text, post, tweet...your recommendation is the nicest gift you can give to an author!

REVIEW IT: Tell the world. Please go to the retailer where you purchased this book, as well as Goodreads, and write a review. Please share your thoughts about BOUND on:

*Amazon, BOUND Customer Reviews

*Barnes & Noble, BOUND, Customer Reviews

*iBooks, BOUND Customer Reviews

* BookBub, BOUND Customer Reviews

*Goodreads.com/Aleatha Romig

MORE FROM ALEATHA:

If you enjoyed SECRETS and want more from Aleatha, check out her backlist encompassing many of your favorite genres.

WEB OF SIN TRILOGY (Dark romance trilogy)
SECRETS
LIES
PROMISES

THE CONSEQUENCES SERIES: (bestselling dark romance)
(First in the series FREE)
CONSEQUENCES
TRUTH
CONVICTED
REVEALED
BEYOND THE CONSEQUENCES
BEHIND HIS EYES CONSEQUENCES

BEHIND HIS EYES TRUTH
RIPPLES (A Consequences stand-alone novel)

STAND ALONE MAFIA THRILLER:

PRICE OF HONOR
Available Now

THE INFIDELITY SERIES: (acclaimed romantic saga)
(First in the series FREE)
BETRAYAL
CUNNING
DECEPTION
ENTRAPMENT
FIDELITY

INSIDIOUS (stand-alone smart, sexy thriller):

THE LIGHT DUET: (romantic thriller duet)
INTO THE LIGHT
AWAY FROM THE DARK

THE UN-NOVELLAS: (short, erotic reads exploring hidden
fantasies)
UNCONVENTIONAL
UNEXPECTED

ALEATHA'S LIGHTER ONES (stand-alone light, fun, and
sexy romances guaranteed to leave you with a smile and maybe a
tear)
PLUS ONE

A SECRET ONE
ANOTHER ONE (free novella)
ONE NIGHT

ABOUT THE AUTHOR

Aleatha Romig is a New York Times, Wall Street Journal, and USA Today bestselling author who lives in Indiana, USA. She has raised three children with her high school sweetheart and husband of over thirty years. Before she became a full-time author, she worked days as a dental hygienist and spent her nights writing. Now, when she's not imagining mind-blowing twists and turns, she likes to spend her time with her family and friends. Her other pastimes include reading and creating heroes/anti-heroes who haunt your dreams!

Aleatha impresses with her versatility in writing. She released her first novel, CONSEQUENCES, in August of 2011. CONSEQUENCES, a dark romance, became a bestselling series with five novels and two companions released from 2011 through 2015. The compelling and epic story of Anthony and Claire Rawlings has graced more than half a million e-readers. Her first stand-alone smart, sexy thriller INSIDIOUS was next. Then Aleatha released the five-novel INFIDELITY series, a romantic suspense saga, that took the reading world by storm, the final book landing on three of the top bestseller lists. She ventured into traditional publishing with Thomas and Mercer. Her books INTO THE LIGHT and AWAY FROM THE DARK were published through this mystery/thriller publisher in 2016. In the spring of 2017, Aleatha again ventured into a different genre with her first fun and sexy stand-alone romantic comedy with the USA Today bestseller PLUS ONE. She continued with ONE NIGHT and ANOTHER ONE. If you like fun, sexy, novellas that make your heart pound, try her UNCONVENTIONAL and UNEXPECTED. In 2018 Aleatha returned to her dark romance roots with WEB OF SIN.

Aleatha is a "Published Author's Network" member of the Romance Writers of America and PEN America. She is represented by Kevan Lyon of Marsal Lyon Literary Agency.

facebook.com/aleatharomig

twitter.com/aleatharomig

instagram.com/aleatharomig

58949949R00236

Made in the USA
Middletown, DE
09 August 2019